HAMMERHEAD

Time to nail a brutal killer...

Ex-copper Sam 'Mad' Carew is bored, so when a beautiful woman asks for his help he can't help but be intrigued. It seems Sam once helped to put away her father, Kevin Kilpatrick, for murder. Kilpatrick confessed to two violent murders, but his daughter Alison adamantly refuses to believe in his guilt and uses every womanly wile to get Sam to investigate. He doesn't bargain on getting mixed up with one of the most ruthless and sadistic crime families in the country. As the body count racks up, Sam realises he'll have to face up to the killer – the elusive and aptly named 'Hammerhead'.

Dedication

To my lovely daughter Jane,
of whom I'm so proud.

HAMMERHEAD

by

Ken McCoy

Magna Large Print Books
Long Preston, North Yorkshire,
BD23 4ND, England.

British Library Cataloguing in Publication Data.

McCoy, Ken
    Hammerhead.

    A catalogue record of this book is
    available from the British Library

    ISBN   978-0-7505-2754-5

First published in Great Britain in 2007 by Allison & Busby Ltd.

Published in Large Print 2007 by arrangement with
Allison & Busby Ltd.

Magna Large Print is an imprint of Library Magna Books Ltd.

Printed and bound in Great Britain by
T.J. (International) Ltd., Cornwall, PL28 8RW

Acknowledgements

To Ian Harrison – ex-copper, ex-squaddie – for his insight into the way coppers really do behave.

To Stephen Oldroyd of Zermansky's solicitors for his legal knowledge.

To Bill Mutch for his expert knowledge of life insurance fiddles.

To my darling wife, Valerie, for pointing out all my mistakes – a task she selflessly began long before I began writing.

He had loved her all along, with a passion of the
* strong.*
The fact that she loved him was plain to all.
She was nearly twenty-one and arrangements
* had begun*
To celebrate her birthday with a ball.

J MILTON HAYES
The Green Eye of the Little Yellow God

CHAPTER ONE

Unsworth. West Yorkshire.

Kevin Kilpatrick didn't know what the job was to be, other than it was some bookie they were turning over. He'd driven them there in the Jaguar, as normally as possible under the circumstances; legally and sedately, through the April rain; Radio 2 drifting through the speakers; internal temperature set at 68 degrees Fahrenheit; wipers reacting to the rain sensor; everyone wearing Looney Tunes masks; and they were all agreed that they couldn't have picked better weather, because bad weather is good weather for such work. Witnesses don't notice much in bad weather – eyes to the ground usually.

They bundled Harry Henshawe into the back of the Jag. Through the eyeholes in his Tweety Pie mask Kev viewed the bookie in the rear view mirror and Harry didn't look a well man, which was hardly surprising. He was made to sit beside Daffy Duck whilst Bugs Bunny, in the front passenger seat, sang along to the radio – Johnny Cash's *Folsom Prison Blues*. Kev thought it might have been a better idea simply to put a blindfold

11

on Harry if they didn't want to be recognised, but it wasn't up to him to tell them their job. If it was, he'd have told them that a mask doesn't disguise a Scouse accent.

'Today we're Bugs, Daffy an' Foghorn – an' you're Tweety,' was what Kev had been told. 'Them's the names we use. For obvious reasons we do not want our man knowing our names.'

'Fair enough.'

It seemed to Kev that this was pretty much the full extent of their planning. He was a bit taken aback when he saw it was Harry Henshawe. Kev had invested quite a few quid with Harry over the years and he hoped the psychos wouldn't hurt the old man. He'd always got on with Harry but relieving a wealthy bookie of a few quid didn't go against Kev's principles – so long as they didn't hurt him. Shit! How could he trust them not to hurt him? One job and no more, that's what he'd been told. He could well do without this. He was fifty years old and had been going straight for eleven years – well, as near to straight as made no difference. Eleven years as an odd-job man, delivery driver and part-time used-car dealer, shifting the odd moody motor, but that's all part of the game. He'd been pulled a couple of times by the benefit people – whom he'd neglected to inform about his side-lines – but he was now back on full dole, including housing and incapacity benefit due to his arthritic spine, which went into spasm in accordance with necessity, mainly when the DHSS doctor came round to check on his condition. Kev would put pebbles in his shoes to make walking a genuine pain that he didn't have to act out. He wasn't much of an actor but you try walking with pebbles in your shoes; no doctor with an ounce of humanity will declare a man fit who walks in such obvious agony.

Life had been sweet until the Psycho Family Robinson had come knocking on his door; calling in a favour was what they called it. He knew what they were talking about, but they'd never done him a favour in his life, nor were they ever likely to.

The youngest of them, hidden behind a Foghorn Leghorn mask, had been left behind at Harry's 5-bedroomed detached out in Fairburn to keep a threatening eye on Mrs Henshawe while her husband was taken to get the cash from the shop safe. Harry's hands were shaking so much that the safe keys jangled when he took them from his pocket. His face was putty grey when he opened Wannabet's shop door and was prodded inside by the short barrel of a Glock 9mm. Back in the car, Kev didn't know Bugs Bunny had a gun. Kev still had nightmares about guns – or one particular gun. It could have, and should have, ruined his life. It still might if this job went wrong.

Funny how things come back to haunt you.

Kev's job was transport coordinator; i.e. nick a fast motor, do the driving, and dispose of the vehicle afterwards, for which he was due twenty per cent of takings. His share would most likely be no less than five grand, according to Bugs Bunny, could be as much as ten. Kev could use ten grand but he'd much rather have said 'no' to the offer. But they weren't the sort of people any sane man would want to antagonise. And Harry Henshawe was nothing if not a sane man.

'You know I won't breathe a word of this to anyone, you know that, don't you boys?'

'We know that, Harry-boy,' Daffy Duck assured him.

'Like I said lads, I don't keep much money in the shop, no bookies do. If I've got a big payout I give 'em a cheque or they have to come back the next day.'

'Don't give us that crap, Harry,' said Bugs, who was the larger of the two by a long way. 'Busy fuckin' shop like this. Everybody knows yer've got at least fifty grand stacked away.'

'Not in here, lads. I've got seven grand in here, as God is my judge.'

'God might be your judge, Harry, but we are the jury, and it is our unanimous verdict that you are giving us a load of old bollocks.'

Harry led them between a row of blank televisions on one side and notice boards on

14

which were pinned newspaper racing pages, displaying that day's runners and riders. The safe was sunk into the concrete floor behind the counter. His trembling fingers made it hard for him to get the key in the lock. Bugs Bunny held out a hand.

'Harry, yer shivering like a shiting dog. Give me the keys before yer drop 'em!'

Bugs took the keys, opened the safe and took out seven wrapped-up bundles of notes and a handful of loose ones. 'Just over seven grand here,' he told Daffy, then to Harry, 'So, where's the rest?'

'Honest lads. I wouldn't lie to you. There isn't any more – not in the shop.'

Bugs pressed the gun to Harry's head and handed a mobile phone to Daffy Duck. 'Tell Foghorn ter put the old bag's lights out, good an' proper.' He could have been ordering a cheese sandwich.

Harry screamed at them.

'NO, no, no ... please lads!'

His anguish and fear sent acid surging from his stomach. His throat contracted. Speech was now difficult. His words came out in a series of croaks.

'I've just ... remembered, there's some in the back office – in the fridge. Not much, just ... just a couple of grand. Honest lads, that's all there is.'

Bugs and Daffy went through to the office which was dingy and scruffy and smelled of

15

stale booze and cigar smoke. Paint flaked off the walls behind expensively framed photos of Mill Reef, Brigadier Gerard and Best Mate. There was a small table, a couple of chairs, a small gas cooker and a small fridge. To one side was a door on which someone had written in felt tip, *It's here*. Correctly assuming that was the lavatory Daffy went through to relieve himself as Bugs opened the fridge.

From behind a six pack of Fosters Bugs Bunny took out another two bundles of notes. He turned to Harry, who was standing behind him, and exploded into a violent rage, sending out a spray of spit through the mouth hole in his mask.

'Nine grand! We go to all this trouble and yer give us nine grand. We've laid out good money for funny fuckin' masks and a getaway driver an' all we get's nine grand!'

Then the anger went from his voice as quickly as it had come and was replaced by a friendly menace. 'Yer see, this just isn't good enough, Harry boy – just not good enough at all.'

Harry had preferred the anger. You know where you are with anger. Daffy came into the room, zipping up his trousers, grumbling. 'Harry your fucking facilities are absolutely disgusting! If the Health and Safety came in here they'd be down on you like a ton o' bricks.' He looked at the money in

Bug's hand, then at the hapless bookie.

'Nine grand,' Bugs told him. 'I'd have been better off stoppin' at home watchin' *Emmerdale*. They find out who's been poisonin' them sheep ternight. I wanted ter watch that.'

'It'll be repeated,' Daffy assured him before casually taking Harry by the scruff of his neck. 'Harry, do we look stupid? Do we look like twopence ha'penny fuckin' scallies?'

'No, you don't look like that at all, lads. I can get you a lot more when the banks open tomorrow.'

'Harry Henshawe – yer a proper fuckin' liar!'

'I'm not lying lads. I've got over sixty grand in me business account that I can draw out in cash. There's no need for this. My wife's bad with the angina. She's on medication. She'll probably need some right now. D'you think your friend'll let her have some? Could you ask him, please lads?'

'Friend – yer mean our good friend Foghorn Leghorn?'

'What?' said Harry. 'Oh, I see, yes.'

'In that case, I shall ring our good friend Foghorn Leghorn up.'

'Thanks, lads.' Harry was weeping with gratitude. 'That's really good of you. Tell him to tell her I'm sorting things out and everything will be OK. Tell her – tell her she's got nothing to worry about.'

Bugs Bunny stabbed two of the numbers

on his mobile. 'Hey up, Foghorn, count ter twenty, if yer can count that far... Hey! *And* you, yer cheeky little bastard! Then, if I don't tell yer no different, belt the old bag over the head with yer hammer.' He held the phone away from him and spoke to Harry. 'I once saw her kill a racehorse with one blow, just because it came in second. She walked straight into the stables, bold as bloody brass, into the fuckin' stall and dropped the bastard wi' one crack right between the eyes – one fuckin' blow, Harry! I were right behind her. Yer've got to admire a kid who can do that. Best thing was, nobody saw her do it, except me. I wouldn't care, I told her ter back the bastard each way.'

Harry dropped to his knees and grabbed Bugs Bunny's legs. 'Please, don't hurt my wife.' Tears streamed down his face. 'Please, I beg you, lads. I can get you the money. Look, take my car – it's in the garage – brand new Merc. It's worth forty grand. It's yours. The wife'll get you the keys and documents. Please don't do this, lads.'

Bugs Bunny held the mobile to Harry's ear so that he could hear the voice on the other end counting out loud: 'Sixteen, seventeen, eighteen, nineteen, twenty...'

Harry's howl of anguish drowned the thud as the heavy, ball pein hammer ended his wife's life. Bugs Bunny held the phone back to his own ear.

'All done Foghorn? ... I see, I'll tell him. It'll be a comfort to him...'

Bugs smiled at the wretched bookie. 'Hey, what's it like ter be a widower, Harry? Actually it's not really Foghorn Leghorn, it's our Tanya, me little sister. She says ter tell yer that yer wife knew nothing about it – she went out like a light, halfway through a nice cup o' tea an' a Jaffa cake. I told yer she were magic. I bet yer didn't believe me.'

He handed the gun to Daffy, then he lifted the weeping bookie's chin up with a finger and gave him a look of admonishment, like a teacher of infants talking to an errant pupil. 'Now look, Harry, this story o' yours about givin' us yer car. It's all a load o' fanny ter buy a bit o' time. Did yer think yer'd got us fooled? Do yer honestly think we're that fuckin' stupid?'

Harry had gone rigid with grief. He didn't care about anything any more. Bugs stepped away as Daffy took aim with the handgun. 'Well, Harry,' Daffy said, 'we'll have ter love yer and leave yer. We're going for a ride on us new pushbikes. Do yer cycle much, Harry?'

Harry remained mute. Bugs nodded at Daffy, who fired at the bookie's head from a range of six inches. The bullet went straight through and embedded itself in the floor, taking with it some of Harry's brain.

Daffy Duck looked down at the bookie's body, wondering whether it might require another bullet to make sure, but the man seemed dead enough. 'We live in violent times, Harry, boy,' he said, apologetically. 'I blame the gover'ment.'

'I agree,' said Bugs Bunny, who had picked up the shop phone and was calling the police. Daffy Duck took a can of paraffin from a holdall he'd brought with him and splashed the contents all around the shop.

Kev was wondering whether or not he might sell the motor on. He'd picked it up in Alwoodley in Leeds where many of the houses had at least one nice motor parked in the drive because they already had two cars in the garage. He'd walked up to the front door of a small mansion on Wigton Lane carrying a holdall full of cheap brushes and cleaning equipment that he'd bought in Leeds market. If anyone answered his light knock he was ready with the false smile of a Kleeneze salesman, all set to accept a polite refusal, but quite prepared to flog a cheap brush or artificial shammy leather for twice its value. Luckily, no one answered his knock and he ascertained that the occupants were in the back garden, attending to the spring weeds or whatever people do to gardens in April – Kev lived in a council flat so he wouldn't know. Then he quietly opened the door, picked up a set of car keys that had been helpfully left on the hall table and had driven off in a brand new Jaguar XJ6. Given half a chance he could shift it tomorrow morning for four grand in his pocket. His buyer would alter the VIN, fix it up with false plates and documents, have it on a cross-channel ferry within a day and flog it on the continent for twelve grand minimum. It was the best way for a car to disappear – the easiest way as well, now that the hard work was done. Trouble was, he knew he'd have to clear this with the Looney Tunes. If they found out they'd be annoyed and he didn't want to annoy them. In any case they were a bit ahead of him in this as they'd made him hand over his house keys as a form of security until the job was done, which included satisfactory car disposal. He wasn't sure how his house keys constituted any form of security but you didn't argue with these people. He heard a shot from inside the bookie's.

'Aw shit! What's goin' on?'

The noiseless engine was already switched on in readiness for a seamless and swift departure. He flicked on the wipers and cleared the rain from the windscreen; he looked all around him to see if anyone else had heard the shot. There were a few people in the distance but the steady drizzle in the air was keeping their eyes to the ground, hunched forward, mooching along like Lowry figures. Around here the bang could have been anything from a firework going off out of season to a garage door being slammed. Kev knew different.

Bugs Bunny walked quickly out of the shop to the car. He opened the back door and threw a plastic carrier bag on to the seat.

'Nine grand,' he said. 'Less than we thought. Your share's eighteen hundred.' He took the Glock from his pocket using a gloved hand and, holding it by the barrel, handed it to Kev through the driver's open window. 'Stick that outa sight afore the silly sod shoots us all.'

Kev took it and turned it over in his hands. It was still warm. 'What's happened?'

'Silly sod thought he'd try an' scare the daft owd bugger. The fuckin' shooter went off – took half his head away.'

'Jesus! You never told me you were carrying.'

'Didn't know meself 'til he pulled it out. Wait here a couple o' minutes, we've gorra bit o' cleanin' up ter do.' His manner was just a bit too nonchalant for Kev.

'Jesus! Shouldn't we be on our way? I mean, someone might've heard the shot and we're hanging around in these stupid masks. We could get picked up any minute.'

Bugs Bunny put his head through the car window. His voice now laden with chilled menace. 'Listen, Tweety fuckin' Pie, so we understand each other – just do as yer told. If this thing goes on top an' yer get nicked, keep yer trap shut about us.'

''Course I will,' Kev assured him.

'I mean,' Bugs pushed his head further into the car until Kev could smell last night's beer on his breath, 'yer wouldn't like nowt to happen to that beautiful daughter o' yours, would yer? – Alison isn't it? Like havin' nitric acid thrown in her mush. Yer know we'll do that, Tweety boy. Yer know we don't make empty threats.'

Kev confirmed that he wouldn't like this to happen to his daughter and Bugs turned and ran back in the shop leaving Kev wondering what the hell this was all about. His stomach began to churn like a clapped-out washing machine and his mind raced with very unpleasant thoughts. This was bad, none of it stacked up. There was something very wrong here, only he couldn't figure it out. On the seat beside him was nine grand – they hadn't even bothered to deduct their share. Surely they wouldn't leave the money with him if they thought it might go on top. These were seriously weird bastards. Had it been anyone other than them he'd be driving away now. But letting them down on a job would be a very unhealthy move, especially for his daughter. He cursed because the air was suddenly filled with the howling of a police siren.

'Shit, shit, shit!'

He judged it to be coming from in front –

or was it behind? Still cursing, he put gear-stick into Drive, did a U turn and sped off, tyres screeching. An unmarked police car pulled out from a side road and blocked his path. Before Kev could slam into reverse a marked car pulled up behind. PC Sam Carew leapt out from the passenger side just as Kev was jumping out of the Jag and hurling himself over a six foot high wall. Neither of them saw the shop go up in flames.

Bugs and Daffy had swapped their masks for regulation cycle helmets and had left by the back door. They were pedalling away in different directions as Kev, still wearing his mask, was pounding down an alleyway with Sam in hot pursuit. Sirens screamed as police drivers tried to anticipate the direction of Kev's flight and tried to cut him off. A bell was ringing in the fire station and Red Watch was springing into action.

Kev knew the backstreets well. With surprising speed for his age he was outrunning Sam. He emerged onto a road and ran straight into a passing cyclist, knocking him off. He mounted the bike and was wobbling away when Sam arrived and made a desperate dive for the back wheel. He screamed in agony as his fingers became jammed between the spokes and the fork. Kev fell into the road and was getting to his feet as Sam was extricating his injured hand. The irate cyclist, who would win a bravery award for this, set about Kev with fist and boot and Kev was too out of breath from the chase to put up much of a defence. He went down just as a police car arrived. The drizzle had picked up to a downpour as Sam sat on the ground nursing a handful of blood and broken fingers. At the time he'd no idea what crime had been committed. He just hoped it was something worth all this pain.

There were many things Kev hated about that day, one of which was being captured whilst wearing a Tweety Pie mask. It's the sort of thing that tends to lumber you with a label you really don't need, especially when you're banged up with a twenty-two-year tariff and the other lags are just waiting for someone they can take the piss out of.

HM Prison Durham. Three months previously.

Annie studied her husband's approaching face as he weaved an unsteady path between the tables. He sat down in front of her, breathing heavily and saying nothing, as if he didn't want to speak until he was spoken to. He wore a yellow plastic sash and belt to identify his prisoner status – or lack of it. It was the only colourful thing about him. His erstwhile blue eyes were mud grey, his lips bloodless, his cheeks pallid and hollow. She knew he'd not been well, but she put that down to the bout of flu he'd mentioned when they last spoke on the telephone. That was three weeks ago. It was four and a half months since she'd actually visited him. It was a frequency that suited both parties.

'George, I have ter say, yer look like shit!'

Twenty years living in Yorkshire hadn't diluted her Scouse accent. George Robinson's mouth opened far enough to display his bottom teeth, which were sporadic and nicotine stained.

'Yer should join the Samaritans, Annie.'

'Have yer seen the doctor?'

'Nice ter see you as well, Annie. Kids all right? Has Lewis turned up yet?'

'No.'

'Never thought he had it in him ter do a runner. Been gone a while. Good fer him. How long's it been now – four years?'

'Yer should see a doctor.'

'As a matter of fact I never thought Lewis were mine. I know Lloyd definitely wasn't.'

'Antibiotics is what yer need.'

He stared at her for a long time, wondering what he'd ever seen in her. He knew that at least one of their kids wasn't his, maybe two. He thought he might as well tell her of his suspicions now rather than never. Never's a long time for her to think he's a thick bastard. Tanya was his, definitely – he could see

26

himself in Tan. She was a bit weird, but he recognised himself in her. Nathan had arrived a few years before he came on the scene – a teenage accident. Whoever Nathan's father was he hadn't been of local origin. Judging by the colour of his skin he, or his ancestors, came from somewhere a damned sight warmer than Unsworth. George hadn't bothered asking. Around the time Lloyd was conceived he'd been doing 3 months in Armley for receiving. It told him that Annie had been doing some receiving of her own. Dirty cow. She had given him some fanny about the dates, but he wasn't that stupid. He wasn't sure about Lewis. Annie had put it about when they were first married, mind you he'd done the same, so what the hell? It was screwing around that landed him a life stretch in here, and Annie knew it. Never said anything, though. She knew she'd no room to talk. She'd started out as a looker, but she had one of those faces that dropped to bits early on in life. In the space of twenty-seven years it had shrivelled up like a Christmas Eve balloon on Boxing Day. It had been like marrying Miss Brahms from *Are You Being Served* and ending up with Pauline Fowler from *East-Enders*. Wouldn't be putting it about much now, not with a mush like that. A thought forced a smile to his face.

'Hey, we're not exactly the bleedin' Waltons are we, Annie?' His smile developed into a rattling laugh, which disintegrated into a fit of coughing.

'George, have yer seen a doctor?'

'Doctors? I'm sick o' seein' doctors.'

She took out a packet of Marlboro. 'Here, have one o' these ter settle yer down. What's the matter with yer, like?'

Her husband took the cigarette. His fingers shook so much he struggled to make contact with the lighted match she held out for him.

'Put it this way, Annie, yer can't give me any bad news.'

'What d'yer mean, George?'

He frowned, as if trying to get his act together. 'I got some test results back, that's why I sent yer a VO. Thought I'd best tell yer meself – it's only right and proper.'

Annie felt herself taking his shaking hand and holding it steady. Such demonstrations of affections were very much contrary to her nature, especially in a large visits room such as this. She hadn't kissed George since before he got locked up. His eyes misted over. She thought making a joke of it might make her worries go away.

'Test results? How d'yer mean, test results. Yer haven't failed yer City an' Guilds again have yer?'

'I've got the big C, Annie. I'm riddled with the bastard.'

'The big...?' She shook her head, not wanting to put an interpretation on his words.

'Cancer,' he said, 'terminal bleedin' cancer. If I'd been on the outside they might have caught it sooner. I just thought it were prisonitis. Yer don't expect ter feel well when yer locked up in a shit'ole.'

It was the first time she'd felt a morsel of compassion for a human being since she'd killed her son, Lewis, in a fit of homophobic rage. His funeral had been private – very private indeed. George didn't know. He thought the soft lad had left home and wasn't expected back.

'George, this is a proper bastard an' no mistake ... are yer sure?'

'How d'yer mean am I sure? – 'course I'm sure. I wouldn't come out with summat like this if I weren't sure. Jesus, Annie! What yer take me for?'

He drew, deeply, on his cigarette. His illness manifested itself in sunken eyes, his deathly pale skin, his lank hair, his shaking fingers and his croaking voice. There was an unhealthy emptiness between his shirt and his body, whereas not too long ago she'd called him a fat bastard and advised that he get himself down to the gym to work it off. He cleared his throat and Annie winced at the rattle that seemed to travel up from his belly. The life was being sucked out of him from within.

'They reckon I might have six months – if

29

I look after meself. An' before yer say it, no I'm not givin' up smokin' – it's a bit late fer that.'

'I wasn't gonna say it. What about chemo? They can do wonders now. I were readi–'

He stopped her with a wave of his hand. She bit her lip. Losing him to the prison system was one thing, losing him forever was something she wasn't ready for. She'd be a widow, a woman without a man, and she'd be fifty this year.

'I'm beyond all that, lass,' he said. 'They've offered ter treat me, but it'll only prolong what's definitely gonna happen. All I know is I feel like shit and this is as good as I'll ever feel.'

She gripped his hand, tightly. 'Is there owt I can do, George? The business is going well – anything that money can buy, I'll sort it.'

He summoned up a thin smile. 'I allus thought that when I got out, I'd leave runnin' the business ter you. Yer ten times better than I ever was.'

'I had a good teacher, George. You laid the foundations – all I did was to build on it.'

'Annie, yer talkin' crap.'

They stared at each other in silence, searching for something to say. George's face suddenly crumpled, like a small boy wanting his mother to make everything better. He had once been a strong man, both physically and mentally, but there was only a shell left.

'I don't want ter die in here, Annie, lass. Can yer get me out, please? Me tariff runs out in a year. I've asked if I can get early release on compassionate, but it's not lookin' good.'

'I'll fix it, George. I'll buy you out of this shit'ole if it takes every penny we've got.'

He wiped his eyes with his sleeve, suddenly ashamed of his self-pitying tears. 'Yer a good owd lass, Annie. I know me an' you were never hearts an' flowers, but we were a good team. Give us a kiss, lass.'

She leaned forward. Their lips touched for the first time in ten years, and the last time ever.

Annie Robinson found that money could buy many things. It could buy men, muscle, bent coppers, fake passports, false alibis, even judges, but it couldn't buy George out of prison; at least not before he died ten weeks later – just two weeks before the Henshawe murders.

The timing of these two events was no coincidence.

CHAPTER TWO

Pear Tree Inn, Unsworth.
Nine years later.

Such was the noise they were making, and although he wasn't interested, Sam had a fair idea why the six young Leeds men were celebrating. It was something to do with end-of-year figures being up, and bonuses, and an all expenses paid trip to St Lucia on the firm. Outside London, neighbouring Leeds was the most vibrant centre of commerce and finance in the country and these lads evidently had something to do with the money markets. Sam preferred men who made a living by earning an honest crust, not simply shifting other people's money around. They were drinking champagne, disturbing the normally quiet, early evening ambience of the place. The more they drank, the louder they became. Still, it was a pub, and he could hardly complain about people enjoying themselves. If only they weren't so damned noisy. He could hardly read his paper.

'All right, Sam?'

Sam looked up. 'Hello, Bernard.'

Bernard, the glass collector, was euphemistically classed as having learning difficulties, which is a much kinder way than he'd have been described not too many years ago. The gaffer employed him on minimum wage and Bernard earned every penny of it – although he did create a lot of the work himself. He stuck out a hand for Sam to shake.

'How's it going, Sam? Long time, no see, eh?'

'It's going OK, Bernard – you?'

'Same as ever, Sam. Been ter college today. Domestic Science today. Made another omelette today. Brought it home. Had it for me tea. Very nice, thank you very much.'

Bernard had been enthusiastically studying first year domestic science for four years and had neither the ambition nor the aptitude to move up to the second year.

Sam looked towards the door, wishing that Owen would be on time for once. The Welsh DC had summoned Sam here on a matter of great urgency – but obviously not so urgent that he needed to be here on time himself. Sam smiled at Bernard. 'I wish I could cook, Bernard. Pierce and ping man myself.'

'I don't know what that is, Sam.'

'Microwave meals, Bernard. Pierce the plastic wrapping and bung it in the microwave until you hear the ping.'

Bernard nodded, sagely as he formed his reply. 'We're not allowed microwaves. Not

33

proper cooking that. Can't yer cook properly, then?'

'Boiled eggs and cornflakes, that's about my limit,' Sam said. 'Sometimes I get mixed up and boil the cornflakes.'

It was enough to bring a howl of laughter from Bernard, who looked of indeterminate age, but he was in his late twenties. He touched his nose with a knowing finger.

'Very much alike, me and you, Sam. Very much alike indeed.'

'What, you mean we're both handsome devils? I'd have to agree with you there, Bernard.'

Another howl of laughter. 'No, it's what they call us.'

'Call us?'

'You're Mad Sam Carew and I'm Barmy Bernard.'

'They're only jealous of us, Bernard. I take no notice. Best way all round.'

'Take no notice – I'll do that, Sam. Take no notice, best way all round.'

The noise from the Leeds lads seemed to crank up a notch. One of them made a coarse remark about the young woman behind the bar. Sam looked up in time to see the woman give as good as she got. He'd never seen her before, but then again he wasn't a Pear Tree regular, this was more Owen's haunt. If he'd been a regular he'd certainly have noticed her before now. She was a real looker.

There was a crash of glass as Bernard accidentally knocked over a couple of champagne flutes, splashing some of the young men. One of them sprang to his feet and held out his arms to indicate the extent of his soaking. Sam noticed, with some satisfaction, that it was considerable.

'Are you some sort of fucking idiot?' He had a sunlamp tan and gel on his fashionably spiky hair. 'Look at my suit. Cost me eight hundred quid this suit! Are you gonna pay for its cleaning, you useless prat?'

Bernard froze, not knowing what to do next. Apologies were beyond his scope of social interplay. He clamped a hand over his mouth and tried not to look at the man. The barmaid appeared at the table with a cloth.

'It's OK, Bernard, love,' she said, 'could you empty all the ashtrays?'

Bernard moved off, grateful to be back in a world where he could cope, but still confused by events. The barmaid smiled at the men. 'No harm done, boys,' she said. 'We'll replace your drinks.'

'You want to replace your fucking staff. Is this a pub or some sort of nuthouse? We're spending real money in here and we expect real service!'

Sam looked on to see if the gaffer might intervene. Apart from the young men, the place was almost empty and it seemed the

35

barmaid was having to cope single-handed. The swearing continued, unabated. He sighed and folded his paper, then got to his feet and walked across the room. Maybe if the barmaid had had a face like a bag of spanners he might not have got involved. It was a question he'd ask himself later, but he'd have no answer.

'Excuse me, lads. I didn't come in here to listen to your foul language.' He kept a smile plastered to his face as he spoke to them. It was a false smile but it was the best he could manage. 'So I'd appreciate it if you'd just cool it.'

'Fuck off!' said the man with the sunlamp tan. He squared up to Sam.

'Don't be silly, lad.'

Sam took a step back and held up two calming hands to indicate he didn't want trouble. The young man pushed him with both hands, Sam took another step backwards. The young man followed, and walked straight into an armlock. The barmaid looked on, impressed. Sam whispered into the man's ear. 'Look, this is very silly. I'm going to let you go, but if I have to do this again I'll break your arm, do you fully understand?' He applied pressure until the man screamed.

'All right, all right, I understand!'

Sam let him go. He ran a finger and thumb down the man's lapel, then stepped back and cast an appraising eye over the suit. 'There's an alteration tailor three doors down, you could get this made to fit properly for twenty quid.'

The young man returned, sullenly, to his seat, as did Sam, but experience should have told him this wasn't over by a long way. Pride had been dented, the lads were all drunk and common sense had been thrown out of the window. These lads thought they were the cock o' the walk but they'd had drink spilled over them and one of them had been made to look foolish by a scruffy-looking workman who probably earned in a year what they took home in a month.

Bernard, who, among other things, had bladder problems, especially when upset, went to the Gents. Sam didn't notice him go, but Sunlamp did. He and one of the others followed suit. The barmaid watched them. She also watched the four remaining men sniggering to themselves. Too many minutes ticked by with no sign of anyone returning. She went over to Sam's table and spoke to him in a low voice.

'Excuse me – Bernard went to the toilet and two of them,' she inclined her head in the direction of the four sniggering men, 'followed him in. They haven't come out yet. I'm a bit worried.'

Sam put down his paper again. He glanced at the door to see if Owen might put in a timely appearance. No such luck. Owen never put in timely appearances. 'Right,' he sighed, 'I'll see what I can do.'

Bernard was in one of the cubicles. The two men were laughing and holding him by his legs. His head was down the wc pan and he was sobbing with fear, not knowing why this was happening to him. One of the men was flushing the toilet just as Sam opened the cubicle door. Sunlamp let go of Bernard and made to step out of the cubicle. Sam took him by his lapels and dragged his coat half-way down his arms, thus immobilising them. Then, with a short, powerful jab he punched the man clean on the end of his nose, causing blood to stream out, and down his presumably expensive shirt. Sunlamp screamed in agony.

'Hurts, doesn't it?' sympathised Sam.

With Sunlamp still trapped in the improvised strait-jacket, Sam took him into the next cubicle, forced his head right down the wc bowl, flushed it and held him there until the flush was finished. In the meantime the second man had run past him, straight into the path of the barmaid who kicked him between the legs, sending him, gasping, to the floor. She helped the weeping Bernard to his feet and looked at Sam. 'You'll be the one they call Mad Carew.'

'Sam,' said Sam, yanking Sunlamp out of the toilet bowl, and propelling him out of the cubicle with the sole of his boot, 'my friends call me Sam, and I'm not mad, I'm quite friendly really.' He looked down at the man on the floor who was crippled with agony. 'Wow! Did you do that to him?'

'He ran into my foot.'

Sam winced. 'He's a very clumsy boy – is Bernard OK?'

'I think so,' She shook Sam's offered hand. 'Alison,' she said. 'Actually, I know who you are because you once arrested my dad for murder.'

'I did?'

'Yeah, nine years ago.'

Sunlamp moaned as he clutched his nose with one hand whilst struggling to get his jacket back on. 'You a copper? You don't look like a copper.'

'Would you like me to arrest you for assault?' Sam said. 'It might run to attempted murder. He could have drowned, you know – well, obviously you know now. Useful lesson learned, eh?'

The other one had got to his knees and, between gasps of pain, was cursing at Alison. 'I'm going to ... to the ... fucking police about this.'

'Aw, don't be so ... so stupid,' said Sunlamp, between moans. 'He *is* a copper. C'mon, let's go somewhere else – this place is a dump.'

The two of them staggered off, leaving Sam and Alison comforting a distressed Bernard.

Their faces touched, briefly, and the nearness of her sent Sam's hormones into orbit. It was a pleasurable feeling because he thought his hormones had gone into hibernation long ago.

'Sorry about your dad,' was all he could think to say to her.

'So you should be. He didn't murder anyone.'

'Didn't he?'

'I'm Alison Kilpatrick, my dad's Kevin Kilpatrick. My dad didn't kill anyone.'

Sam found it hard to think straight. There was something incredibly sensual about her – albeit diluted by the fact that she was having a right go at him.

'Kevin Kilpatrick ... yeah, I remember him.' He tried to cast his mind back. 'I er, hmm ... Kev Kilpatrick, yeah, I must admit I did wonder about it at the time, but I was only a plod back then. Actually, it wasn't me who arrested him. I had too many problems of my own, to do that.'

'No, but you chased him and caught him.'

'I did,' conceded Sam. 'I remember he pleaded guilty – which I thought was a bit odd.'

'He did it to protect me.'

'Right ... er, how do you know?'

Alison glanced at Bernard, who was now beginning to take an interest in their conversation. He had an odd ability to repeat

40

conversations, verbatim and parrot fashion, at the most inopportune moments.

'I'll tell you later,' she said. 'I don't think the Gents toilet's the ideal place for this.'

'How come you're never around when you're needed?'

Owen ignored Sam's grumble and took a huge gulp of his pint. Not for the first time Sam thought it was like pouring beer down a sink.

'I'm having problems with my digestion,' Owen told him, sadly. 'It's giving me some gyp. I'll have to have to myself looked at. One of them endoscopy things where they stick a camera down your throat into the belly. It'll be like something out of a Hammer horror film when they get down there.'

'You could ask them to stick a camera up the other end as well,' Sam suggested. 'It's called an upyerendoscopy. They meet in the middle and compare notes.'

'Well, that's just typical bloody Carew *schadenfreude*, isn't it?'

'I suppose that's Welsh, is it,' said Sam, 'like eisteddfod and Saucepan Vach?'

'It's German and it means taking pleasure out of the misfortunes of others. Nobody knows how much I suffer.'

'Well,' said Sam, 'you can't blame yourself for that, you do your best to tell us all.'

'Carew, you are a callous bugger. You have

no fellow feeling whatsoever. It's your Yorkshire genes, they should be removed at birth and buried in a lead-lined coffin. We Welsh are a gentle race of poets and singers, you Yorkshiremen all are bloody hooligans. I don't know how Sally puts up with you.'

'Sally?' said Alison, who was standing just at the other side of the bar, listening to the exchange with some amusement. 'Is she your wife?'

'No,' Sam said, hurriedly. 'I once had one of them – she's er, she's my assistant.'

'A bit more than your assistant, boyo,' Owen commented, finishing off his pint, and placed the empty glass on the bar. 'Two more please, Alison.'

Alison took out a couple of clean pint pots and held one under a pump. She looked from Sam to Owen. 'Do you work together?'

'Not officially,' Sam said, inclining his head towards Owen. 'He's a copper, I'm either a private detective or a bricklayer. Our paths sometimes cross.'

'I know all about you, Sam Carew. Ex-copper – kicked out for trying to electrocute a superintendent.'

'Ah – he was actually an inspector – now a DCI – and it was just a prank gone wrong.'

'Hence your nick-name.'

'Mad Carew,' said Bernard, sticking his grinning face between them. 'Mad Carew reckons we're both handsome devils. I'd have to agree with you there, Sam.'

'Bernard, get on with your work!' scolded Alison. As they both watched the grinning glass collector move away, she leaned towards Sam. 'Do you think my dad did those murders?'

'A jury did, that's all that counts, I'm afraid.'

'No, it's not. *You* need to know as well. You were never sure, were you? I've read things about you.'

'Really? What have you read?'

'I've read an article on you. It said you hate injustice of any kind – which is a weakness in a copper. Coppers just capture people, dispensing justice is someone else's job. But you like justice, which is your Achilles heel.'

'And you reckon your dad didn't get justice?'

'I know he didn't – still, what's done's done and can't be undone.'

She turned away to serve another customer. Sam took his drink to a table, followed by Owen, who asked him, 'Do you think she's making it up, just to make you feel guilty about arresting her dad?'

Sam shrugged. 'Actually I remember the case quite vividly. I remember feeling baffled that he'd held his hands up to it straight away. It was before you came to Unsworth. The bookie he's supposed to have murdered

43

must have squirted blood all over the place. He was shot from close range, so whoever did it would have had quite a lot of blood on him. Kev Kilpatrick didn't have a speck on him, yet he pleaded guilty in the car on the way to the station. Pleaded guilty in his statement, but he wouldn't say a word after that. Not a single word. It was obvious that he didn't do the wife as well. In fact it was obvious he didn't *know* about the wife until we mentioned it to him. Yet he held his hands up to it as soon as he knew.'

'Wife?'

'Yeah, the bookie's wife was murdered as well – her at home, him in the shop. Two different weapons. He was shot, she was bludgeoned – we only found the gun.'

'He could have thrown the first weapon away,' Owen suggested. 'Maybe he didn't want to use the gun on Mrs Henshawe because of the noise in a residential area.'

Sam thought about that then shook his head. 'No, that doesn't quite explain it. At the time CID reckoned it had the hallmarks of a hostage crime, but it couldn't be if Kev did both murders.'

'I don't follow.'

Sam explained. 'If Kev killed the wife, the bookie must have been there to see it happen, so where was the incentive for him to help Kev get the money? The man would have been a mess, a complete liability.

Incentive is the whole point of hostage taking. On top of which, forensics found no evidence to put Kev in either the house or the bookie's shop. Not a fingerprint, not a footprint, not a hair ... nothing.'

'There must have been some evidence to put him away.'

'Well, he was at the scene. I know because I collared him – eventually. The gun that killed the bookie was in his car, covered in his fingerprints and no one else's. He also had the stolen money on him, and he was wearing a mask.'

'A mask?'

'A Tweety Pie mask,' Sam said, 'and he also pleaded guilty.'

'I'd say he didn't leave himself a leg to stand on, boyo.'

Sam looked across at Alison, whilst nodding at Owen. 'Douglas Bader had more legs to stand on than Kev. Would you say the man was fitted up, DC Price?'

'I'd say there was every chance, ex-DS Carew – but why, and what can we do about it?'

'Not a lot, in fact I wish she hadn't told me now – with me being the one who captured him. I hate it when things come back to haunt you.'

'You could take it on professionally.'

'I doubt if there's much money in it. Barmaids aren't renowned for their wealth.

Besides, she hasn't asked me to do anything about it.'

'You could do it for love,' Owen suggested, glancing at Alison. 'I imagine the rewards would be considerable.'

'You're a dirty old man, Owen. You know that, don't you?'

'I'm not all that old. Anyway, I didn't ask you to meet me here just to talk about women.'

'Don't tell me,' Sam said. 'Bowman.'

'How do you know it's Bowman?'

'It's always Bowman, unless it's a woman. It beats me what they see in you.'

'I'll tell you what they see in me, boyo. When I was a boy my fairy godmother appeared by my bed and tapped me on the shoulder with her wand. She said I could have one of two things – a very long memory or a very long willy.'

His voice carried across to Alison, who had been listening, intently.

'Which one did you choose?' she called out.

Owen shook his head. 'I'm blessed if I can remember.'

CHAPTER THREE

'Sam, don't get me wrong, I don't mind doing the Carew and Son side of things, but how long is it since you did any private detective work?'

Sam looked up in surprise at Sally's sudden question. He was sitting at a desk directly opposite her. They were in his office and he'd been poring over a plan of a housing scheme, wondering if it was too big for them to tackle.

'I thought you'd know to the day.'

'Eleven months, two weeks. Since then we've turned down umpteen jobs, some of them quite lucrative. Aren't you missing it?'

Sam shrugged. 'Nothing of any interest's come up. It's not like the States where they give you guns and licences to do all sorts of crime work. All we're ever offered are insurance jobs and extra-marital naughtiness. I'd sooner be laying bricks.'

'So, this is nothing to do with you feeling guilty about what happened to me, is it?'

Sam thought back to the day when Sally had been shot during his last job. Maybe she was right. She'd nearly died that day and, if she had, Sam would've been bereft. It probably would have destroyed him after all that'd gone before. But he was a copper at heart and he definitely missed the buzz.

'Nothing to do with you,' he lied. He returned his attention to the drawing, but she'd broken his concentration. 'Something did crop up the other day,' he mentioned, 'but there'd be no money in it.'

Sally rattled a pencil between her teeth. 'The building firm's doing OK – you don't actually need the money.'

She missed the buzz as well, despite having spent most of the past year in a wheelchair, only now was she graduating to crutches. She'd enjoyed the fuss Sam had made of her but his attentiveness hadn't run to a sincere proposal. Still, she did have some pride and she wouldn't want him to marry her out of pity – at least that's what she kept telling herself.

'Aren't you due at physio today?' Sam asked her.

'I've cancelled it. I reckon I can do the exercises on my own now. Besides, I've been told that I'm at the sexy stage of recovery – alluring and vulnerable.'

'Who told you that? Don't tell me, let me guess ... long, miserable, Welsh, always eating sweets, has a loyalty card at *Help The Aged*. Am I close?'

'He's also an expert on the alluring woman,' said Sally. 'Let's face it, he's had plenty of them.'

'I've never seen him with anyone I'd call alluring.'

'What's this job?'

'It's only a job when there's actual money in it. This is a...'

'Freebie?'

'It's actually nothing, because even if I was being paid I doubt if I could do much, apart from sniff around and annoy a few people.'

'That's what you're best at – what is it?'

Sam took out his cigarettes and offered her one. She declined. Sam lit up.

'Nine years ago I caught a man who was subsequently arrested for murder and sent down for life. I bumped into his daughter the other day – she tells me he didn't do it.'

'Ah, nothing new there then.'

'Except...' he drummed his fingers on the desk, 'except that she might have a point.'

'I see – nine years ago?' Sally said, now interested – when Sam sniffed, there was usually a bad smell. 'He'll be due out any-time now, then.'

'No, – he got two consecutive life sentences. They would have been concurrent had he blown the whistle on his accomplices.'

'What, he's gone down for two murders?'

Sam nodded. 'A bookie and his wife. Different locations. One a shooting, one a blunt instrument job. It was obvious he wasn't working on his own but he held his hands up to both of them. Such is the British legal sys-

49

tem that the court had to accept his confession. The judge didn't see the funny side.'

'I'm with the judge – was there a funny side?'

'I reckon the real killers might have found it amusing.'

'Real killers? Ah, so you do believe he's innocent?'

Sam examined his fingers which had healed up quite well, considering the damage he'd done to them that day. He'd been given a commendation for his efforts, as it was considered that the killer might well have escaped without detection had it not been for his determination and courage. At the time his colleagues thought it was more to do with lunacy than courage. Sam now wished he hadn't caught up with Kev.

'Do you know, I've never given it a thought all these years, but right now I think it's highly possible – in fact, highly probable.'

'Oh.'

'Which means I was instrumental in getting a bloke banged up for twenty-odd years for two murders he didn't commit – and I didn't give it a second thought. Had it not been for me he might have got away with it.' He looked at her. 'And what happened to you was down to me. What's it all about, Sal? What's my life all about?'

She watched him looking at his fingers, stretching them, remembering. She knew he wasn't just thinking about her and Kevin Kilpatrick. He was thinking about Kathy as well. The one who had died saving his life. The love of his life.

'Was he the one where you damaged your hand?' She'd heard most of the Mad Carew stories.

He nodded. 'I had eleven fractures altogether – eleven fractures and thirty-four stitches.' He held up his hand for her to admire. 'You wouldn't think so, would you?'

She watched him put his head in his hands. A few minutes later, when he looked up at her, she thought his eyes were wet.

'I think I need to do this one,' he said.

'I think you do,' she said. 'Where do we start?'

'God knows.'

'Owen might help.'

Sam thought back to last night's conversation with his old pal. 'Owen's having problems with Bowman again. He's been given a job that's baffling everyone – building site theft. Bowman's brother-in-law's the site foreman and apparently Bowman's wife's giving him some earache, so Bowman's passing the same on to Owen.'

'You realise,' said Sally, 'that while Owen has anything to do with you, DCI Bowman will have it in for him. Owen's a better pal to you than you realise.'

'Sal, I didn't go down on my bended knee

to ask Owen to be my pal. He's my pal because I'm a very likeable person.'

'You should do something about this inferiority complex of yours.'

'On top of which,' Sam went on, 'I solve a lot of his cases for him. Bowman's a bitter man, bears a grudge. I send a few measly volts of electricity shooting through him and he hates me forever.'

'It was a stupid thing to do.'

'Sal, it was a prank and it was years ago.'

'It was revenge,' remembered Sally.

'It was me getting my own back for him being a prat to me. Anyway, I had to leave because of it. You'd have thought that might satisfy him.'

'He's maybe bitter because you keep sticking your nose in where it's not wanted.'

'And making him look a plonker, you mean? I've just picked up on the odd police cock-up and put it right. You'd think Bowman might be grateful.'

'He might be more grateful if you didn't keep directing all the credit Owen's way.'

Sam leaned back in his chair and stretched. 'All I've done for the past year is building work. Maybe you're right, maybe it's time I stuck my nose into police business again.' He thought about it for a few minutes, then decided, 'Maybe I'll give Owen a hand with his site theft case.'

'And then take on the case that you really

want to solve,' Sally said. 'The one that's niggling at your conscience.'

'I've a feeling that one might turn out to be out of my league.'

She shook her head and got on with her work, murmuring under her breath. 'That'll be the day.'

Somewhere at the back of his mind Sam had made a connection between the Kev Kilpatrick killings and something more recent. It was one of those thoughts that struck him at the time, then disappeared as soon at it had come, as good thoughts often do. What the hell was it?

'I'm going out on site to have a word with Alec,' he said. 'He'll have to arrange a replacement brickie for a while. He'll moan about it because he knows he won't get one as good as me.'

'Or one as modest.'

Owen was sitting with his feet on Sam's oak desk, eating a Jammie Dodger when Sam got back.

'Oy! Get them coffin lids off my desk!'

'I told you he wouldn't be pleased,' said Sally to the Welshman, without looking up from her work. Owen, unapologetic, swung his feet down and wiped away a few crumbs from his mouth with the back of his hand. 'There's been another robbery,' he said, mournfully.

Sam spotted an empty biscuit packet on the desk and addressed his grumble to Sally. 'Sal, have you let him eat all my Jammie Dodgers? Those were my personal biscuits, for my consumption only.'

Sally held her hands up, as if to say, *leave me out of this.* Owen ignored him. 'Same MO as last time,' he said, 'which means there was no sign of a break in, and removing the stuff was a physical impossibility. I've been thinking of asking David Copperfield where he was on the night of the robbery.'

'Where does Charles Dickens fit into this?' asked Sam.

'I'm talking about the American magician chap, look you. Do you not watch your television? He makes railway engines and elephants disappear at the snap of his fingers. A shed full of building materials should be child's play to him.'

'Not struck on magicians,' Sam said. 'I liked Tommy Cooper, but that's about it. Do you think I could sit in my own chair?' He pointed to two old dining chairs. 'Those are the visitors' chairs.'

Owen grudgingly got up and asked, 'Are you going to come out and look at the scene of my robbery with me?'

'I suppose I could.' Sam looked across at Sally. 'Is that OK by you – or do you need me for anything?'

'Why would an able-bodied woman like

me need you?'

With that she heaved herself to her feet and lurched three paces across to a filing cabinet, her last lurch was more of a fall; had it been another yard away she would have ended up flat on her face. She held on to the cabinet and caught her breath, then she slid a drawer open. Sam looked on with admiration; Owen with concern.

'She won't be told,' Sam said.

Sally riffled through a file, then nodded her head as she arrived at what she was looking for.

'Just before you go. The final account on the Hasting's Developments contract should have been paid a week ago. Shall I chase it up?'

'How much do they owe us?'

'Including retention money, most of which is due, just short of sixty-two thousand. Do you think they've got problems?'

'Haven't heard anything. Tell them we're a bit strapped. Ask them very nicely if we can we have fifty today and the rest next month.'

She gave him a look of disapproval. 'Why give them the opportunity to pay us short?'

'Because no one wants it to get around that they've got problems,' explained Sam. 'Bad for business. Take whatever they offer and get Alec to call round for it. I'm sure they're sound but my dad always taught me to get what you can and worry about the rest later.'

'It's a great pity your dad's not still around.'

She saw the look on his face. 'Sorry, Sam. It was tactless. You didn't need telling that.'

He shrugged. 'I wish he was around all the time, Sal. There isn't a day goes by that I don't miss the curmudgeonly old sod. Will you do me a favour?'

'What's that?'

'Stay in your wheelchair when you're in on your own. I don't want to come back and find you lying flat out on the floor.'

She threw him one of her Benny Hill salutes. 'Yes, sir.'

'And keep your mobile phone on you at all times.'

'What about speaking to strange men and taking sweets from strangers?'

'I mean it, Sal.'

Rohan Construction was building an exclusive development of twenty-five luxury homes on the north east boundary of Unsworth. Up until now there had never been a truly posh end of Unsworth and it was the developer's ambition to change all that. The whole six acre site was fenced off to keep out sightseers, kids, intruders, thieves and riff-raff. Within the site was a secure compound in which bricks, sand, gravel, timber, roof tiles, drainage pipes, dumpers, a JCB and other site equipment were kept. Also within the compound was a large storage hut, thirty feet long by fifteen wide in which was kept more valuable materials and equipment: plastic windows and doors, central heating equipment, kitchen units, cement, copper, lead and power tools. The hut was kept very securely locked and alarmed and was periodically checked throughout every night by a security firm. To steal anything from it should have been very difficult indeed. To practically clear it out overnight, twice in three weeks, should be impossible.

Sam stood inside the double doors and surveyed the almost empty, windowless, building. For the second time in three weeks over forty thousand pounds worth of goods had been stolen; all that was left was half a ton of cement, four rolls of polythene and the largest of the windows. He stamped his feet on the wooden floor and was rewarded with a cloud of cement dust. Desmond Broughton, the site foreman, who was also DCI Bowman's brother-in-law, looked on, sniffily.

'If the real coppers can't figure it out I don't give you much chance, Carew.' He knew all about Sam.

'Oh,' said Sam, 'why not? Would you prefer me not to bother?'

'I'm not fussed whether yer bother or not. I'm just sayin' that's all. It's all insured.'

'What about all the aggravation and lost time?' asked Sam. 'Is that insured?'

Broughton shrugged. Sam turned to Owen. 'I assume SOCO's been round.'

'Not yet, boyo. In the list of their priorities, building site theft comes just below a missing cat.'

'Have you disturbed the scene?' enquired Sam of the foreman. As he spoke he concentrated his attention on the crime scene, not sparing Desmond a glance.

'How do you mean?'

'I mean have you been walking all over it, disturbing the thieves' footprints?'

'I stepped inside, but there were no need ter walk all over it ter see stuff had gone. It were all here last night. If yer don't believe me ask our night watchman.'

'Might be an idea, DC Price.' Sam said it mainly to annoy the foreman, who looked suitably aggrieved. 'And the doors were properly locked up last night?'

'I locked 'em meself.' There was a hint of petulance in Desmond's voice. 'The security men'll have checked the locks half a dozen times during the night.'

Sam looked at the list of stolen goods and shook his head, baffled. 'It'd take a couple of men and a wagon a full day to shift this lot out of the doors, never mind spirit it away without anyone seeing.'

'Well,' said Desmond, defensively, 'there's a dozen fellers on this site who'll tell yer the place were full o' gear last night, includin' the building inspector. He came round last thing ter check on the gauge of the polythene we were using under the oversite.'

'Sounds like Atkinson,' commented Sam.

'It is Atkinson,' Desmond confirmed. 'Dun't know his arse from his elbow but he's a world expert on the thickness of polythene. I think he must have studied it at building college. I think he's trying to work his way up to being a speed bumps inspector.'

Sam lit a cigarette as he tried to figure out what the hell had happened to all the stuff. Then he examined the dusty floor through narrowed, searching eyes. It was littered with footprints and he knew it would be virtually impossible to eliminate the legitimate ones and he doubted if forensics would waste much time on it.

'Would you two not come with me, please?'

He walked, very slowly, in a straight line down the centre of the building, disturbing as few prints as possible, examining the floor on either side of him.

'What're you looking for?' called out Owen.

Sam spoke without taking his eyes off the floor. 'If they took the stuff out through a trapdoor in the floor they'd have somehow had to close it behind them from underneath, without being able to cover their tracks. This would at least have left the trapdoor's outline visible in the dust.' He walked to the end, then retraced his steps, pulling a disappointed face.

'There's nothing obvious. I suppose after forensics have finished we could sweep the floor and see if there's a trapdoor or some loose boards or something.'

'If yer really insist on being bloody stupid I'll have it polished so yer could eat yer dinner off it,' said the foreman, 'but I think it's worth pointing out that there's barely enough room under the hut fer a ferret ter squeeze through.'

'Maybe there's a sewer running underneath?' suggested Owen. 'One big enough for a man to walk through.'

Desmond laughed. 'Yer've been watchin' too much telly. We're out in the sticks here. Big sewers are in the middle of big towns.' Then he grinned. 'Mind you, they could have dug a tunnel like they did in the Great Escape.'

'Anything's possible,' said Sam, sourly, as he got back to the door.

Desmond shook his head as if he couldn't believe such stupidity. 'Come off it,' he said. 'It'd take a gang of men a month ter dig a big enough tunnel. This place were robbed four days after we erected the hut – and if there was a tunnel I think even Taffy here would have spotted the other end of it by now, and according to my brother-in-law Taffy couldn't find his arse with both hands.'

Owen reddened. 'There's no need for that

60

sort of talk,' he snapped. 'We're here to help.'

'Well get bloody helpin'!' retorted the fore-man. 'This is the second time I've had ter stop the job because of thieves that you can't bloody catch! My job's on the line here.'

'I thought you said you weren't bothered,' Sam reminded him.

'I said I weren't bothered about havin' you nosin' round. I very much doubt if you nosin' round'll save me me job.'

'Surely they can't sack you for something that's not your fault,' said Owen.

Desmond shook his head, despairingly. 'This is the building trade, Taffy, and I'm the foreman. Everything that goes wrong on this site's my fault. If everyone gets struck down with bubonic bloody plague it's my fault for not getting 'em all vaccinated. Time's money in this business.'

'Time's money in every business,' said Sam, coolly. 'And I wasn't serious about a tunnel. I do know a bit about building my-self.'

'I sack them as only knows a bit about building,' sneered Desmond. He transferred his scorn back to Owen. 'I shall have to have a word with me brother-in-law about you. I'll ask him why they're bringin' in builders ter do copper's work. Are you coppers too useless ter do the job yersens? It's like me settin' a butcher on ter do me plumbin'.'

'He's a former detective sergeant with

61

building expertise,' said Owen, through gritted teeth. 'I thought you might be glad we were making such an effort on your behalf.'

'Effort, what effort? I haven't seen no signs of an effort.'

Owen was tempted to say that it was only because the foreman happened to be Bowman's wife's brother that the police were bothering at all. He'd met the miserable woman and was of the opinion that she and Bowman thoroughly deserved each other. Sam was walking round the outside now, examining the walls and roof, looking for easily removable bolted-on panels, but he didn't expect to find any – any more than he expected to find a trapdoor in the floor. This theft would have taken many hours. A security light covered the compound and any such coming and goings would have been spotted not only by the security firm but by any curious passer-by. A thief wouldn't risk that. Despite the objectionable foreman this crime was beginning to fascinate Sam. It was an impossible theft but he knew there was something he was missing – hopefully something simple. The trouble was, it didn't have to be obvious to be simple. After Desmond had left he turned to his Welsh pal.

'It's bit of a poser is this, Owen.'

'A pain in the arse is what I'd call it.'

Sam rubbed his chin, deep in thought. 'Could you find out the name of the insurance company?'

'Won't they have their own people?'

'Usually. But if I'm helping you anyway, no harm in doing a deal with the insurers on a payment-by-results basis.'

'Do I detect a glimmer of an idea, boyo? Do we have something to go on?'

'No, but I need more incentive than just keeping Bowman out of your hair. If the cash keeps ticking over, so does my brain.'

'I thought the incentive was me helping you put right your wrongful arrest of nine years ago.'

'I don't remember asking you for help – in fact I don't remember mentioning that I was going to do anything about it.'

'There are things you don't have to mention, Carew – I know you only too well.'

'So long as we know where we stand,' said Sam, satisfied that he now didn't have to spend time persuading Owen to help with the Kevin Kilpatrick case. 'This is either very clever and complicated stuff or it's something very simple.'

'Give me simple every time, boyo. I've never been a great fan of clever and complicated. Very bad combination in a woman – clever and complicated. One's bad enough, but the two together leads to disaster every time. Simplicity is the key to a happy life.'

'Talking of a happy life,' said Sam, 'you know that murder you were telling me

63

about last month, the one where the bloke got hit over the head?'

'You mean the one Bowman wouldn't let me touch with a bargepole?'

'Did they find the weapon?'

Owen took an interest in all murder cases, despite rarely being involved in one. 'No, but it was thought to be a hammer.'

'What sort of head – round or square?' Sam knew Owen would know.

'Round, but bigger than the average claw hammer.'

'And the killer first placed a towel over the victim's head?'

'Yes – probably to prevent him being splashed with blood.'

'Or *her*,' said Sam. 'The victim was male and naked and there were no signs of a struggle – the killer could be a woman.'

'Do you mind telling me why you're so interested?'

'It's just a hunch, that's all,' Sam said. 'You know how I get hunches.'

'And?'

'One of the killings that Kevin Kilpatrick got sent down for sounds very similar. Single blow over the head with a blunt instrument, some sort of heavy hammer with a round head – probably a ball pein. It's an engineer's hammer, you can get them in graphite up to two pounds in weight.'

'And was the victim naked?'

'No, the victim was a woman in her sixties. She was found sitting in a chair with a blood-soaked towel over her head.'

'But that was donkey's years ago.'

'Bad habits have a habit of resurfacing many years later,' said Sam. 'Has anyone else made this connection?'

'Not that I know of.'

'How far have they got with the investigation?'

'Not very – Bowman's having one of his brainstorm briefings on Wednesday morning. I think the Super's sitting in on it.'

'Will you be there?'

'I won't be at the top of the guest list but I'm supposed to go.'

'Good,' said Sam. 'Wait until they've gone round in circles for a while and got nowhere, then, when Bowman asks if anyone else has any bright ideas you casually ask if any of the investigating officers ever checked out the similarities between this murder and the one of Mrs Henshawe that took place not a mile away about nine years ago.'

'You mean the murder that Kevin Kilpatrick's already doing life for?' said Owen. 'They think I'm a buffoon as it is. I might as well give them something to work with.'

'Listen,' said Sam, 'there wasn't a copper on that case who thought Kevin did both murders – even the judge called him a liar. If I was on the investigation team and someone

65

asked that question I'd be just a bit embarrassed. If anyone tries to be sarcastic just ask them how many other hammer/ towel murder combinations they've come across in their careers.'

'There was one last year in Unsworth Hospital,' Owen reminded him.

'Ah, but they got the man who did that,' countered Sam, 'and he used a lump hammer. This killer's much more precise – clinical, even. The hammer went in just at the junction of the frontal bone and the sphenoid bones. It went straight through and killed the brain dead.'

'And how the hell would you know a thing like that?'

'I have many friends – including the police pathologist. It's very handy being popular, you should try it some time.'

'You're confusing popularity with morbid curiosity, boyo.'

'Knowing the Super,' said Sam, 'he'll wonder why one of the more experienced investigators hasn't already checked out the Henshawe connection.'

'And how will this help you?' Owen asked.

'No idea, but it's a connection that links the victims. Connected victims can lead to killers. On top of which I should get the cream of Unsworth CID working for me.'

'If they thought they were helping you, boyo, they'd all volunteer for traffic duty.'

CHAPTER FOUR

Warren Kilpatrick clattered, dangerously, down a flight of concrete steps that led from Bailey Towers to Ascot Heights. His pals cheered when he fell off his skateboard. Ten floors up a woman winced, then her face relaxed into head-shaking relief when Warren rubbed his backside and got to his feet with a broad grin on his face. He was eight years old. Patsy Kilpatrick opened a window and shouted down.

'Warren! Don't do that again, yer've got school in the morning!'

Her grandson pretended he hadn't heard. Patsy shook her head and muttered, 'Like father like bloody son – God I hope not!' Then she lit a cigarette and looked around the family flat. Two bedrooms, every window saturated with condensation; the heating more often broken than not; a constant smell of cannabis on the graffiti-stained communal landing and staircase and an even more constant smell of urine in the lift – which also was more often broken than not. Because she was type 2 diabetic and having to share a bedroom with her daughter they'd been classed as priority on the housing list for three years, but each time they put in for a house they were beaten by someone on priority extra – usually immigrants. There were three immigrant families living in her block; as it happened they were no trouble. On the sixth floor was 68-year-old Mrs Irene Peiterson who bought and sold bent gear right under the noses of the local constabulary, who had better things to worry about than arresting pensioners. There was no kudos in arresting pensioners. Patsy wasn't above buying fags and the odd item of decent clobber from Mrs Peiterson. Most of Warren's clothes came from shoplifters via the aging fence, who supplied knock-off goods at knock-down prices to virtually the whole block.

Two floors below Mrs Peiterson was a small-time drug dealer who called himself Flicky. Patsy had known him as Francis Herbertson when he was at school with her daughter. She bought weed off him now and again, which she shared with Alison. Neither of them was into anything heavier. Heavy stuff cost heavy money and the only way to get that was horizontally. It was the one thing neither mother nor daughter had sunk to.

Most of the street trouble came from the local scallies for whom an ASBO was the only qualification they'd ever get. Warren was heading that way and there seemed little that Patsy or Alison could do about it. Patsy returned her attention to the telly where they were showing an omnibus of *Coronation Street*. She took a deep drag on her Marlboro – £2 for twenty, courtesy of Mrs Peiterson – and allowed her gaze to settle on the quaint, cobbled street with its graffiti-free, satellite-dish-free, brick houses, all occupied by interesting characters with jobs and neighbours worth having and a basic decency and a local pub free of drug dealers and prostitutes and foul language, where there was no danger of a broken bottle being jabbed in your face for no apparent reason. Then she looked through the window at the twin hell of nearby Ascot Heights and she doubted if even Les Battersby could bring himself to live in a shithole such as this.

In a couple of hours Alison would be home from her job in the pub and Patsy would be leaving to work the switchboard at Jack Lane Cabs. They paid her in cash, which was handy as it didn't affect her Giro. For the past month Alison had been working four nights a week behind the bar at the Pear Tree. Her employment rarely lasted long, there was always some lecherous prat trying it on. By and large they got by – they'd get by a lot better if Patsy didn't spend half her Giro on drink. She was aware of that, but she couldn't get through the day without drink.

She justified this by comparing herself favourably to the man on the floor above. He was an alcoholic whose habit would challenge a whole regiment of AA volunteers. He'd recently knocked on Patsy's door to ask if she had any Brasso she could spare – apparently his current tipple was Brasso and Carlsberg Special Brew. She'd offered him half a bottle of Windolene.

'What's it taste like?'

'Crap, but it leaves your eyes nice and clear.'

He was too far gone to appreciate humour. Her own addiction meant they'd never have enough money to get away from this dump. She dragged herself away from the TV and went into the kitchen where a pile of laundry awaited her. Sam knocked on the door. Patsy froze for a moment. She didn't like daytime knocks. It could be anyone. Police, benefit fraud investigator, bailiff.

She waited for a second knock and wished she had the means to know who was at the door. On the other hand it could be someone she actually wanted to see – like the man from the National Lottery, come to give her a cheque for ten million quid. But she'd spent too much on scratch cards that week to have any left over for a lottery ticket. Sam figured out the problem. He shouted through the letter box.

'Mrs Kilpatrick, my name's Sam Carew. I think Alison might have mentioned me. I told her I'd call round and see you about Kevin. I'd have rung, but I don't have a number.'

He was still half bending down when Patsy opened the door and saw, for the first time, the man who was responsible for her husband being locked up for the last nine years. He looked decent enough. Younger than she'd imagined.

'Yer must have been very young when yer collared my Kev,' she said, after scrutinising him for several seconds.

'I was nine years younger.'

'And so yer've come round her ter put right a wrong, have yer?'

'I've come round to try and get to the truth. Once I'd arrested Kevin it was out of my hands. When I bumped into Alison the other night it got me thinking.'

'Yer'd best come in.'

'Thank you.'

'I've just got ter put some washin' in. If I don't do it now it'll never get done.'

'That's no problem, Mrs Kilpatrick.'

Patsy went in to a small kitchen where she began to load the washer. She picked up one garment and stuffed it into the machine with some distaste as Sam looked on, patiently.

'Our Warren's undercrackers. D'yer have any kids?'

'Two boys, both fourteen – fifteen shortly, twins.'

She shook her head. 'I bet they're the same. Lads are all the bloody same. Our Warren leaves more skidmarks than Michael bloody Schumacher.'

'Warren's your son, is he?'

'Grandson – he's our Alison's lad.'

'Oh – I didn't know she had a son.'

'Well, she has. Are yer still married?'

'Not any longer.'

'Divorced, eh?'

She looked up at him with interest. Sam hoped this interest was on behalf of her daughter and not self-interest. Not even Owen would be interested in Patsy Kilpatrick. He moved the conversation along.

'Mrs Kilpatrick, bearing in mind that I'm not a copper, do you have any idea who fitted Kevin up?'

She returned her attention to the washing machine. He watched as she filled the soap powder container and poured in fabric conditioner. Then she switched the machine on and looked at him.

'Only Kev knows fer sure. There's no way he'll ever tell me and I don't want ter play guessin' games. Guessin' wrong could get our Alison into as much trouble as guessin' right.'

'I reckon Alison wants me to do something about it.'

'Is that what yer reckon? I reckon yer must be barkin' up the wrong tree.'

'Do you know why he was fitted up?'

Patsy gave a shallow laugh. 'Now that really is the $64,000 question. He'd been going straight for years before that happened. God knows how he got mixed up in it.'

'Maybe he had no option.'

'Oh, I think he definitely had no option. What I don't know is, why did they pick on him? They've had him banged up under a threat of something happening to our Alison for last nine years with another thirteen ter go. What the hell have they got against him? Kev knows, but he's not saying.'

'It's no way for any of you to live,' Sam said. 'That threat could be hanging over your daughter well after Kev gets out. Don't you think it needs sorting?'

Patsy shrugged. 'We've racked our brains over the years but we've come up with nowt. The only thing we do know is that it's no use going to the police. The case is closed as far as they're concerned, and maybe that's the way it should stay. In any case, Kev reckons they've got one of the coppers in their pocket.'

Bowman immediately sprang to Sam's thoughts, then he cast the thought aside as wishful thinking. Bowman was a completely disingenuous prat but, as far as Sam knew, he wasn't bent.

'Really? Did he say who?'

'Nah – then again it might be just Kev givin' us a load o' flannel ter make us leave well alone.'

'And also leave him stewing in jail?'

She gave a helpless shrug. 'Yer obviously a

good man, Sam. It's just a pity yer were such a good copper. Most coppers'd never have caught my Kev. It were just his luck ter get you on his heels. Did yer know he were a junior champion at five thousand metres when he were a lad? I've got some trophies somewhere. He used ter say his legs had got him outa years o' porridge – none o' your lot could catch him.'

'Wasn't he claiming some sort of disability benefit?' Sam asked.

'He used ter claim a lot o' things. He used ter claim that he were too good fer this place.' She shook her head. 'If he'd been as quick between his ears as he was on his feet mebbe he'd have got us out of here.'

'I'd like to speak to Kev. Do you think you could organise me a VO?'

'Yer might be better off talkin' to our Alison before yer go jumpin' in. She's gorra mobile, do yer want her number? Maybe yer can fix something up.'

There was a look in her eye that told Sam she might be match-making – or maybe it was just wishful thinking on Sam's part.

74

CHAPTER FIVE

Tanya Robinson turned and smiled at the man in the passenger seat beside her. Now in her mid-twenties she was quite passable in the looks department and she had a great body. A fit body that she honed down at the gym four times a week. She was wearing a very expensive blonde wig and tinted designer spectacles, despite having perfect vision.

Her passenger was called Mick. Last night Mick had bumped into her in a club in Manchester. He took a ride home in her taxi and she gave him such exquisite oral sex that he was sure she must be a pro. But she didn't ask for money. She even paid for the taxi. Did he want to see her tomorrow? Wow! You bet your life, darling. Can you take the day off? For you I'll take the week off.

Today she was taking him for a spin in her car, which was a seven series Beamer, would you believe. No wonder she didn't ask for money last night, she probably had more dosh than him.

'I fancy somewhere deserted and quiet where we can get naked without being seen,' she said. 'I know this great game we used to play when I was in the sixth form at Dunhill Grange Grammar. We called it, You-Catch-Me-You-Fuck-Me. You can't beat a grammar school education.'

Mick laughed out loud. He'd never met anyone quite like Tanya. 'Well, it doesn't get much more deserted than these moors,' he said, 'unless you're self-conscious about stripping off in front of sheep.'

'Would your wife do this? Get naked out here?'

'You're joking. I haven't seen that cow naked for months. After we got married we went at it like rabbits until we had our two kids. When she fell on with the second that was pretty much it. Job done, no need for her to bother any more. Nowadays it's like sleeping with a fridge. I'm telling you, when my missis opens her legs a light comes on.'

'So that's why you started playing around is it?'

He shrugged. 'Not at first. I relieved the tension the DIY way, then I started visiting naughty ladies who give massages with a happy ending, but that got a bit expensive, what with having two extra mouths to feed, so I started playing away. It's cheaper and more fun – especially with someone like you.'

'Does she know?'

He shrugged. 'To be honest, I don't care.'

'Marriage made in heaven, eh?'

'Marriage is for mugs.'

Ten minutes later they had stripped off and she was running away from him. Teasing him with her surprising speed and agility. He was younger but he couldn't catch her and all this nakedness and teasing was giving him an additional handicap. She screamed with laughter when she saw his erection.

'You should be able to catch me – you've got one more leg then me!'

Eventually she let him catch her and pin her down on the mossy ground behind a large rock where they had energetic, delirious sex, with Tanya thrusting upwards with even more vigour then he was thrusting down. The climax was frantic, mutual, burning and ecstatic with Mick collapsing on top of her. Tanya lay beneath him, very tempted to do it again after he'd recovered, but she knew that would be unprofessional.

They lay on the ground, looking up at passing clouds and sharing a joint. It had taken Mick a while to get his breath back.

'Wow! That was, er,' he searched for a description, '...quite knackering.'

'Wait here,' she said, 'I've got something in the car that'll give you a real bang.'

'What?'

'Wait and see.'

As he lay there he felt his juices flowing again. So soon after. His wife could never do that to him.

Tanya came back, still naked, carrying her

shoulder bag. As she appeared around the rock Mick sat up and frowned, suspiciously. 'If it's Viagra I don't need any, thanks.'

She looked down at the hard evidence. 'I can see that. No, it's not Viagra.'

'Coke?'

Tanya smiled at him with her head to one side. She liked him, so there was no need to scare him. 'It's not coke. You only get three guesses, then you're out.'

'If it's crack, I don't do crack – sends me bonkers.'

'Wrong again.'

'OK – what is it?'

She knelt down in front of him, allowing her breasts to brush against his face as she kissed him, sensuously, on his lips. Then she took a towel from her shoulder bag and placed it over his head and face.

'What?'

'Mick, don't move or you'll spoil the moment.'

She reached into her bag and brought out a two pound, ball pein hammer, the heaviest available – the same one that had ended Mrs Henshawe's life. Applying power that seemed out of all proportion to her build, she struck him where the towel was covering the crown of his head. She felt and heard bone disintegrate beneath the force of the blow. It would make a circular depression in his skull almost an inch deep. Mick slumped backwards. The towel was already soaked with fine blood that had sprayed from the wound, and thicker blood that had been forced out of his ears. The towel had served its purpose. It had hidden her intention from Mick's eyes and it had protected her from splattering blood. Without lifting the towel she checked his pulse and didn't find one. She didn't expect to.

From her bag she took a packet of wet-wipes and took great care to wipe away all traces of herself from Mick's genitalia and surrounding areas. Then she lifted up the towel just enough to wipe his face and his mouth. She then gathered her clothes and dressed, quickly. After which she picked up the hammer and his clothes and took them with her, back to her car, leaving Mick's naked corpse hidden behind a rock.

An hour later she was on the Yorkshire side of the Pennines. The stolen BMW would be found by the police in an NCP car park in Bradford and returned to its grateful owner who would never know it had been used in a murder.

After a nervous two weeks, waiting for Mick's body to be found, his grieving wife was delighted with the excellent service she'd received and had paid up the balance of the £30,000 fee without a quibble. Small price to pay for a half a million pound insurance payout on a lousy husband.

The Robinsons lived in a spacious old house in the countryside between Leeds and Unsworth – Wickham Farm. Annie had bought it ten years previously and had converted part of it into three separate apartments to accommodate her three surviving children. The main part of the house, where she lived, still had four bedrooms, three spacious reception rooms, an oak-panelled study and a huge kitchen where Annie spent a lot of her spare time. Cooking, she reckoned, was her only vice; that and her membership of the Unsworth Women's Institute. There were those who might give her an argument – had they the guts. The house was set in eight acres of walled grounds and approached through an electronically controlled gate and then along a two-hundred yard drive with security cameras at each end. Household staff came and went on a daily basis and the grounds were tended by a local firm of gardeners. All in all it was a vast improvement on the three-bedroomed Wimpey semi on the outskirts of Unsworth, in which they'd lived when George went to jail.

Annie had taken over the family businesses and had run them with brutal efficiency and flair, quadrupling the profits in the first year. From then on the businesses had gone from strength to strength. Had George ever come out of jail he'd have been hard pressed to step into his wife's shoes. Tanya's new contract business looked like being a useful addition to the family firm, with her picking up sixty grand on just two jobs. Annie had estimated that Tanya should pick up at least ten hits a year, although she wasn't pleased that Tanya insisted on taking her marks out with a hammer. It was so unprofessional.

'I've a good mind not ter put any more fuckin' jobs your way if yer keep disobeying me.' Her accent was Liverpudlian, where she'd lived up until her marriage to George back in 1969.

'Ma, you know I'm no good with guns. I always look away when I pull the trigger. I can't help it.'

'Tanya, yer must learn to help it. An iron is the tool of your trade. As far as I'm concerned this is downright bad behaviour. Yer leaving trademarks, Tan – that's fer sick-minded serial killers. Yer a professional now, remember that. Yer brothers'll never make real pros – too uncarin', both of 'em. You care about yer job. It's a carin' profession is this. People say it's not, but it is.'

'I sent him out with a smile on his face, Ma – and isn't it better for the bizzies to be looking for a serial killer rather than a contract killer.'

Annie narrowed her eyes, trying to figure out her daughter's reasoning. Tanya explained:

'Contract killers have clients, Ma – and clients are a weak link in a very short chain. Serial killers are just nutters, social inadequates – they don't have clients, so the bizzies won't go looking for one. They'll be looking for patterns, might even bring in a forensic profiler to look into my mind.'

'And what d'yer think they'll be looking for?'

'For a start they won't be certain that the killer's a woman. The sex angle points in that direction but the method of killing points to a man. If I start picking up jobs all over the country it'll drive 'em mad. They like their serial killers to operate locally.'

Annie shook her head, unconvinced. 'Yer'll be givin' yerself a name next – the Unsworth Assassin.'

'No names, Ma – just a nice hammer and a low profile.'

CHAPTER SIX

Alison Kilpatrick was twenty-nine and one of the sexiest women Sam had ever seen in the flesh – and there was plenty of that on display as she answered his knock. She used the door to shield herself from prying eyes as she invited him in, out of the rain.

'Sorry about this. I was in the bath. Hang your coat on that hook.'

Sam looked at his watch. It was 7 p.m. – the time he was expected. So, if he was expected, why was she only wearing a bath towel? He wasn't usually this lucky.

'Have I got the time wrong?'

'No, no, no, it's me – come through. I always slop around when I'm in on my own. Our Warren's staying the night at a friend's house and Mum's on nights.'

He followed her through to the living room where she sat down on a settee, curled her feet beneath her and arranged the towel in such a way as to cover as much of her as it could. Sam sat opposite her. The room was tidier than it had been when he'd called to see her mother. Somehow her presence made the place a lot more agreeable.

She examined her fingernails for a full minute as if trying to get her words in order. Sam couldn't help but notice that her fingernails were as exquisite as she was. What the hell she was doing working behind the bar in the Pear Tree?

'Do you want to know how I know my dad didn't do it?' she said, eventually.

'Yes.'

'It's actually a very painful subject...' She paused again.

Just to keep the conversation moving, Sam said, 'I can well imagi–'

'I've been bottling it up for years, but,' she looked at him, 'with you turning up out of the blue I...'

She paused again, which gave Sam the chance to reflect that he actually wasn't sure that he *did* want to know. It was hard for a daughter to believe her father was a murderer. But this wasn't just any old murderer's daughter. Alison was a cracker. How come Owen hadn't mentioned her before now?

'You were saying?' he asked her, gently.

'Well,' she said, 'when you were in the papers last year it sort of struck me that if anyone could sort this mess out it would be you. I've never approached you because I can't afford to hire you. Maybe I thought with you being the one who arrested him you might take the job on out of...' She paused, searching for a suitable word.

'Guilt?' he suggested.

She shrugged, but didn't dismiss his suggestion. She fixed her gaze on him and said, in a low voice, 'The day after my dad got sent down someone broke into our flat...' Her voice tailed off, re-living that time. 'It was gone midnight and I was in on my own. Mum was working a late shift; she hadn't worked much during the trial and she just wanted to be busy. Me, I was dog-tired, what with everything that had gone on. I was in bed, fast asleep. I hadn't slept much during the trial and I was completely knackered.

'Then I heard something, or sensed something. The light went on and I opened my eyes and there was a man standing over me. Big feller, with a mask on – a Bugs Bunny mask. God knows how he got in, I'd locked the door. Jesus! I was terrified. He told me to sit up, but I couldn't move, so he grabbed my arm and yanked me up, then he pulled all the bedclothes off me.' She held Sam in her gaze. 'I sleep with no clothes on, so … you know…' She shrugged as if it was sufficient explanation, then she frowned away a tear as she summoned up the strength to continue. Sam sat back, saying nothing, allowing her as much time as she needed. Alison went on with her story:

'He took a small bottle of what turned out to be acid from his pocket and unscrewed the lid, then he poured some on the carpet. It started to burn a hole in it. Then he laughed behind his mask. I can hear that laugh today, it gives me nightmares.'

'Did you say anything to him?'

'Yes … I asked him if he was going to rape me because if he was I wouldn't struggle, so long as he didn't hurt me. Then he laughed again and said I wasn't going to get away with it that easy. I started crying and he laughed even louder and punched me in the face. He said he was going to rape me, then he was going to burn my face off so no one would ever want me, ever again. He said I'd always have the memory of him being the very last man to ... to touch me. Only he didn't put it quite so politely as that.

'He pushed me back on the bed and poured a bit on to the pillow at the side of my head. I could hear it sizzling and burning. It smelled foul. I remember wetting myself and he went mad and told me not be such a dirty cow. He called me all the names under the sun and kept slapping me. Then he pulled me off the bed and threw me on the floor and then he ... you know...'

'I know.'

'He kept hitting me as he did it but I couldn't feel it because all I could think of was being burned with the acid. Being raped and punched didn't mean anything.'

'Were you screaming?'

'Not then. I tried, but nothing came out. I couldn't make a sound. I could scarcely move a muscle, I was so scared.'

'Fear does that to you. Did he take his mask off?'

She shook her head. 'No, and that was one of the scary things. All this stuff was being done to me and it was Bugs Bunny who was doing it. Bugs Bunny? When he comes on the telly now I have to switch it off. I hate Bugs Bunny.'

'So, what happened then?'

'Well, when he finished with me he rolled off and just lay there for a bit. Like I said, I couldn't move I was so scared. I just watched him out of the corner of my eye. He straddled me with his knees on my arms, then he took the bottle out of his held it over my face. That's when I screamed. I pleaded with him not to do it to me and he just kept laughing that same awful laugh. Then he emptied the whole bottle on me. I felt it hit my face and I must have passed out with the shock. The next thing I knew I opened my eyes and he'd gone. I knew I was disfigured for life but I couldn't understand why I couldn't feel any pain. I touched my face and it felt OK, so I got to my feet and looked in a mirror. I was OK.'

'He'd switched bottles,' guessed Sam.

Alison nodded. 'It was water.'

'Did you call the police?'

She shook her head. 'I went into Mum's bedroom and curled up in her bed. Sam, I was in bits. I couldn't do anything.'

'I'm not surprised after the trauma you'd been through.'

'Mum came home early, in bit of a state herself. I heard her go into my room, shouting my name. I got up and ran to her. He'd rung her, the bastard. He'd rung her and told her what he'd done – and why.'

'Why?'

'She was told to pass a message on to dad that the next time I'd get burned for real if he didn't keep his mouth shut.'

'I er ... I assume no one was caught for it?'

'I didn't report it.'

'No ... I can understand that. What about now? Would you like to see him caught now?'

'I'm still scared, but it's a very bad way to live. Trouble is I've never had anyone to turn to,' she looked Sam, 'up to now.'

Sam avoided her eyes. She was looking for a guardian angel and right now his feelings were far removed from those of any angel. She had beautiful teeth and dark, damp hair that clung to the silky skin of her shoulders. Alison was a woman who obviously spent a lot of her time and what money she could spare on looking good. Sam couldn't help but look from her to the view from the window and ask himself what was a woman like her doing in this dump? *The best she could*, was the answer, and her best was a damned sight better than anyone else's around here.

'What did your dad say when you told him about it?'

'Well, Mum had already rung him. I saw him about a fortnight later. He just started crying and saying he was sorry. He said he'd make sure no one ever hurt me again.'

'And has anyone?'

'No – but I know my dad's protecting me by staying in prison when he could shop the real killers and maybe get out. Even the street scallies stay away from me. I don't get hassle from anyone – pimps, dealers – no one.'

'Did you ever ask him about the murders?'

'Loads of times. All he ever says is, "Well, I pleaded guilty, didn't I?"'

Sam was running her story through his head, trying to figure out some way of helping. It wasn't going to be easy. She dropped another bombshell:

'Then I found out he'd made me pregnant.'

'Oh,' he said, somewhat inadequately.

'Mum took me down for a termination straight away, but I couldn't go through with it. I think I must be one of those Pro-Lifers.'

'I suspect a lot of woman are, when it comes down to it,' Sam said. 'The lad'll be no worse for it, if his mother loves him, which I'm sure she does.'

Her demeanor changed. She brightened considerably and smiled at him. 'Do you know, that's a really helpful thing to say. Mum just couldn't understand it, and no one else knew the circumstances. I never really knew if I'd done the right thing.'

'Surely, every time you look at your son it should give you the answer to that.'

'I know – and you're right. I love him to bits.' She smiled and held Sam in her gaze. 'You probably won't believe this, Sam, but since then I've never actually been with a man. The very thought has always scared me,' she raised her eyebrows, suggestively, '...until now, of course.'

Sam tried to ignore the hint. It seemed it wasn't a guardian angel she was looking for, after all. 'You, er, you obviously look after yourself,' he said. 'Whatever it is you're doing makes you very attractive to men. So, if the thought of men scares you, why do you do that? Why not go around as a plain Jane?'

'Because having men attracted to me gives me power over them – even if I don't let them near me. I guess it's a game I play to make me feel good about myself.'

'It sounds like a dangerous game.'

'I don't claim to be any more sensible than you – Mr Mad Carew.'

Sam smiled, 'Touché.'

So that was the reason for the towel – she was playing her game with him. What the hell? Such games are for kids who know no better. He'd been tempted before and not taken the bait. He took out his cigarettes and offered them to her. The towel slipped slightly as she took one, she didn't adjust it but leaned forward to take the light he offered. His pulse rate went from seventy to a hundred. The housewives who had tried it on in the past, offering themselves in lieu of payment, had been easily resistible. He had never fallen for it. This was so very different. Alison Kilpatrick was a Premier League temptress. How Kevin and Patsy had managed to produce a daughter like her was anyone's guess. Her voice was deep for a woman, and effortlessly seductive. She drew in a lungful of smoke. Her breasts heaved, the towel slipped down below her left nipple. Sam didn't look directly at it but his periphery vision told him it was on show. He felt beads of sweat on the back of his neck.

'Alison, are you playing your game with me?'

Her bath had evidently failed to remove the make-up from around her eyes, which were smoky brown and incredibly alluring and fixed on him. He returned her gaze, steadily, despite his eyes being magnetically tempted towards her naked breast.

'Tell me about Sally,' she said. 'Do you fancy Sally as much as you fancy me, Sam?'

'What?' He was wondering how the hell Sally had crept into the conversation. 'I think we'd better keep Sally out of this game.'

'Maybe it's not a game, maybe I'm doing this because I fancy the pants off you, Sam Carew. The truth is I'm tired of playing games. Nine years is a long time.'

'That's all very flattering but I came here to try and minimise the danger you'd be in if... Oh, shit!'

She swung her feet on to the floor, stood up and let the towel fall away completely, leaving Sam with no option but to take in the glorious sight of what was probably the most magnificent body in Unsworth, and he knew he'd lost the game. She stubbed the cigarette out in an ashtray and took his hands.

'Why don't you tell me how much danger I'm in as you make love to me, Sam?'

Sam was persuaded to his feet. Her body was so beautiful and warm and compliant that he felt it would be rude to refuse.

CHAPTER SEVEN

Heavy rain drummed against the window of Sam's flat, waking him up. Alone. It had been a while since he'd woken up beside Sally, but only a few hours since he'd lain beside Alison. The thought sent a twinge of guilt through him. Sally's paralysis had confined her to her own bed in her own house since the shooting and Sam had promised that no one else would be sharing his bed during her convalescence. Of course he hadn't actually broken his promise; it was Alison's bed he'd been sharing during their six hours of lovemaking. There was one thing he knew for certain – he'd never have been unfaithful to Kathy. Had she not died saving his life in the fire he'd have been with her now. Probably married. Sally knew that. Would it always be a barrier between him and Sal? He carried this thought through to his dreams as he fell asleep again. The phone rang. He peered at the clock through half-closed eyelids – 6.30. It had to be Owen. He sounded annoyingly chirpy.

'With reference to Bowman's brainstorm briefing. I asked if anyone had noticed the amazing similarity between Mrs Henshawe's murder and the latest victim...' Owen paused as if awaiting Sam's congratulations.

'Uuh?'

'And everybody went quiet, including Bowman. I mentioned that even the judge thought Kevin Kilpatrick had made a false confession...'

'Uuh?'

'And the Super's asked the team to work on the basis that they're linked. There's flooding on the Leathley Road. Must have had an inch of rain overnight.'

'Owen, it's half past six.'

'Leathley Road leads to the Rohan Construction site.'

Sam was trying to tie these facts together. He and Alison had lubricated their love-making with a bottle of Chivas Regal (£10, from Mrs Peiterson). Christ! He'd driven home. She and the drink had driven him well and truly out of his mind. He never did that. Too much to lose. His head was thudding now. Mrs Henshawe, flooding, Leathley Road, Rohan Construction. It was all a bit much for that time on a morning, especially after the night he'd just had.

'Ring me back in a couple of hours, Owen. I'm not a well man.'

He pulled the duvet over his head and stuffed the phone under the pillow. No sooner had he closed his eyes than it rang again. Its close proximity to his ear caused him to jump, violently. Owen again.

'Bloody hell, Owen! I told you to ring me back in a couple of hours.'

'That was two hours ago, boyo.'

Sam looked at the clock. 8.30. His head was still bad. He was thinking of asking for another two hour extension.

'The flooding's worse. If you're thinking of going down there I'd leave it, if I were you.'

'Right, I'll leave it.' Sam was wishing he'd arranged to leave it the last time Owen rang. He would still be fast asleep. 'Owen, have I arranged to meet you or something?'

'Not that I know of. You could return the favour if you like.'

'What favour?'

'Me getting CID to link the two murders.'

'Owen, that's a mutual favour – at least it will be if you get your finger out.'

'Clog and Shovel, noon.'

He was the only person Sam knew who called it noon. On site it was known as dinner time.

'Er, what's this favour I'm doing you?'

'You're discussing the thefts from Rohan Construction with me. You can bring me up to date with your latest theory.'

'Right, I'll do that,' said Sam, who had no latest theory. He pulled open a bedside drawer, took out a packet of paracetamol and pondered whether to take two or three. The pounding in his head told him three. Never again. Malt whisky was designed to be sipped, not drunk out of a bottle during sex with a woman who was making up for nine celibate years.

Wearing just his boxers he walked, with careful step, across to his kitchen to turn on the kettle. A cup of strong coffee would help clear his head. Sally, whose health regime had been curtailed by a bullet in her back, had left some decaf in his cupboard. It had been there, unopened, for many months – and would remain so until she made it up his steps, alone, unaided and unafraid. In Sam's world, decaf was of the same ilk as skimmed milk, margarine and non-alcoholic beer. It was the Elvis impersonator of the coffee world.

With a cup of strong, black, fully caffeinated Kenco in his hand, he sat at his dining table and gave the day ahead some thought. The lousy weather had conveniently cancelled one option. You can't lay bricks in the rain – washes all the cement out of the compo. And going into the office might be a bad move. Sally had an uncanny ability to read his mind in times of physical frailty, and this was such a day.

He sipped his coffee as the pounding in his head eased, and he looked out of his window to admire the view. Once again the same old thought crossed his mind. If God were to give the world an enema, He'd stick the tube in Unsworth. A mishmash of Victorian terraces, oblong council flats like piles of cheap dominoes, a church spire rising from what was now Olleranshawe's Carpet Clearance Warehouse, a quintet of disused factory chimneys pointing at the grey sky like dirty fingers, and a general air of squalor. Over the years there had been a tree-planting scheme to bring the country to the streets; the trees had grown with all the vigour and enthusiasm of weeds growing through cracks in the pavement and had been treated with as much love and care.

He was on the second floor and could see right across to the town centre, which was dominated by the Town Hall and half a dozen grey office blocks. Rain or shine it was a view made remarkable by its total absence of beauty. Today it was early July but the rain-dark sky and steady drizzle made it look like late November out there, which wasn't unusual. There had never been much of a call for sunglasses in Unsworth. If you went out in dark glasses some well-meaning Unsworthian would stop and help you across the road, perhaps wondering where you'd left your white stick. It was a peculiarity about Unsworthians. They were very kindly to each other, as are all comrades in adversity.

The clock on the top of the Town Hall said 8.55, which meant it was a quarter to nine and Sally's taxi to take her to work would arrive in five minutes. He wanted to hear her voice. She picked the phone up on the first ring, so she must be have been in her hallway, waiting.

'Hello, it's me.'

'Hello you,' she said.

Just those two words, spoken with Sally's warmth, made him feel absolutely bloody rotten, although not rotten enough for him to admit his infidelity and throw himself at her mercy. In Sam's experience, admitting infidelity might be good for the conscience but it's always very bad for the earhole. No one ever cemented a relationship by admitting infidelity if they could get away with it.

'I'm not feeling so good. Won't be in this morning.'

'Sam, you said that as though you were a nine-to-five man. I only ever expect you when I see you. What's the problem?'

'Headache – it could be flu.'

She tried her own diagnosis. 'Could be a hangover. Did you have a session last night?'

'A bit of one.'

'Thought so. I rang a couple of times but

you weren't in – and your mobile was switched off.'

Guilt again.

'Did you want me for anything special?' he asked her.

'Only to me. I walked from the bedroom to the kitchen without any sticks. I just felt like celebrating – getting legless – now that I'm getting the use of them back.'

Normally he'd have made some crude quip involving the word legover but his guilt wouldn't allow him to joke about that. Not today. The trouble was that his session with Alison had been so spectacular that he couldn't admit to being sorry he'd done it with her. Sorry means you wish you'd never done something. Where sex is concerned, guilt and sorrow are on opposite ends of the emotional spectrum. Nor could he swear to himself that he wouldn't go back for more. It was a question of just how much guilt he could bear.

'I'll come round for a session tonight,' he said, 'if it's OK by you.'

'By a session I hope you haven't got anything too physical in mind, Mr Carew. I still can't stand jerky movements.'

'I can wait for the jerky movement bit.'

'I can't,' she said. 'It's driving me mad, if you must know. I don't suppose it's any fun for you. Tell you what, you come round tonight and we'll improvise. My taxi's here,

98

I'll have to go or my boss'll go mad. He's a real tyrant.'

'Wouldn't surprise me if he rang in sick.'

CHAPTER EIGHT

Annie Robinson put the phone down and went into the dining room where Tanya was just finishing her breakfast. 'A private dick called Carew's been pokin' his nose in where it's not wanted.'

Tanya looked up from the *Yorkshire Post*, which was propped up against a jar of strawberry jam. She knew the name. 'You mean that ex-copper? I heard Nathan and Lloyd talking about him. Word from Unsworth is that he was round at Kev's wife's place the other day.'

'He were round again last night, visiting the daughter.'

'Do you know him, Ma?'

'I know *of* him. After sortin' Kev out we never did much dodgy business around Unsworth – never shit on yer own doorstep an' all that – but I've made it my business ter know about Carew.'

'And what of him?'

'For a start he's done nothing but build houses fer the last year, but if he's takin' an

99

interest in Kev Kilpatrick I might find it a bit unsettlin'. Apparently when he gets his teeth into something he breaks rules and causes bloody mayhem – and I don't like mayhem unless it's us who is causin' it. From what I've heard of Carew he's more danger to us than any bleedin' bizzies.'

Tanya returned her attention to the newspaper and spoke without looking up. 'So, what do you want? Do you want me to take him out?' She said it casually, through a mouthful of toast, as though all she needed was the go ahead and the job was as good as done.

Her mother pondered before answering. 'It might be the only way in the long run. If we go for the girl again it'll leave Kev with no reason ter keep his trap shut – nothing to lose – which could be awkward.'

'Ma, who's gonna believe him after all these years?'

Annie went quiet for a while, as if she was wondering whether or not to reveal a secret. 'The bizzies might believe him,' she said, eventually.

Her mother's long silence gave Tanya time to realise what her mother just said. She looked up from the paper again.

'Ma, when you said "go for the girl again", what did you mean?'

Annie got to her feet and lit a cigarette. Tanya remained in her chair and watched her mother pace around the room. This was fascinating. She had never seen her mother at such a loss. Annie Robinson's reputation spread way beyond the boundaries of Yorkshire. There might be some woman down in the Smoke with a more fearsome reputation, but if there was, Tanya had never heard of her.

'The day after Kev was sentenced,' said Annie, 'our Nathan paid the girl a visit. I sent him, but it was just ter put the frighteners on her – make her and her dad realise how easy it would be ter punish her for any slip of his tongue.' She took a deep drag on her cigarette and paced up and down the room.

'And...?' said Tanya, impatiently.

'And the stupid fucker went too far – and when I say fucker, I mean it literally.'

'What, you mean he raped her?'

Annie nodded. 'He's a most uncivilised bastard at times.'

Tanya's lips curled in disgust. 'He's a dirty bastard. Do the coppers know?'

Her mother shook her head. 'As far as I know she didn't report it.'

'So, there's no way they can prove it was Nathan who raped her – no DNA or anything like that.'

Annie continued to pace up and down. Tanya watched for a while, then got to her feet and stood in front of her mother.

'There is something, isn't there, Ma?'

'Someone else, Tan, someone else.' She held her daughter in her gaze until realisation sunk in.

'Aw, Jesus, Ma, that's really bad!'

'He's called Warren. My grandson – Nathan's son – your bastard nephew, in the true sense of the word bastard.'

'How do you know the lad's Nathan's?'

'Because the dates tally and because I asked him if he had used a condom.'

'And he hadn't,' guessed Tanya, '...still could be someone else's.'

'I've seen the lad recently,' said Annie. 'He's got Nathan's hooter, and his colouring – he's a Robinson all right. I reckon I've allus known. I put the word out with a couple of people I know around there that the lad and his ma – and his other grandma, should be left alone. I don't know – maybe I should have lerrem all swim in the same shit as everyone else round there. Maybe I've given 'em the strength ter try an' stand up ter me.'

'Do they know who they're up against?'

'Not unless Nathan introduced himself, which I wouldn't put past the brainless bastard!' Then she shook her head, dismissing the possibility. 'No, I don't think they know who we are – but Kev does, and he's got another thirteen years to go, unless he decides to blab to have his sentence reviewed.'

Tanya sat down again. 'This is bad, Ma. This could blow up in our faces if we don't play it right.'

'A right can o' worms is what it is, Tanya – an' I'm not sure what's the best way ter keep the lid on it.'

'Strikes me the best way is to take Carew out. A move like that should scare the absolute shit out of 'em. Let me take Carew out, Ma.'

'If I give you the go ahead, girl, you take him out with a shooter. Keep the hammer for the serial killer dodge – which is a very good dodge, by the way.'

'Just let me know when yer want it done, Ma.'

CHAPTER NINE

Sam stopped his Mondeo just short of the flooded road and changed into his wellingtons for the rest of the journey. The chances were that not too many men would be on site on a day like today, which made it a good day to investigate the place. No one to distract him as he gave the problem some thought; hopefully he would have something to cheer Owen up with at dinner-time. With any luck dear Desmond, the site foreman, will have rained himself off.

Sam sloshed through the water which, at

its deepest point, came nearly up to the top of his boots. A council van was parked at the other end of the flooded area. As he walked past he nodded at the driver, who wound his window down.

'What is it?' asked Sam, conversationally, 'a blocked gulley?'

'Prob'ly – never had any problems here before. It'll be all the crap from them site wagons. They should make that lot pay for unblockin' it.' He jabbed a thumb in the direction of the Rohan Construction sign. 'I've been comin' up and down this road all me life. First time it's been flooded. If it were me I'd make the buggers pay. It'd teach 'em ter run a cleaner site.' Sam exchanged a few more pleasantries and walked on. The site was fenced off but the entrance gate was open. The unyielding rain was soaking the site and the only sign of life came from a joiner who was laying the ground-floor joists on one of the plots. He looked up as Sam strolled past and called out, 'Hey up, Sam.'

Sam squinted at him through the rain. 'Andy? Hellfire, I thought you were out in Iraq.'

'I was up to a few weeks ago – left in a rush.'

'Some woman?'

'No. One minute I'm hangin' a fire door, next thing I know there's a bloody great bang – bloody suicide bomber. Young lad drove a car on site and flicked the bloody switch. BANG! They found his head a good quarter of a mile away – nice lookin' lad by all accounts.'

'How come you're OK?'

'Well, as luck would have it the door acted as a shield – saved my life as sure as I'm stood standing here. A local feller labourin' on me got blown ter bits. I wouldn't care we were workin' on a mosque. Yer'd think we'd be safe in a mosque. Trouble is we were workin' on a Shi-ite mosque and the bomber were a Sunni. It's like Rangers an' Celtic, they hate each other. I don't know how we were supposed ter tell 'em apart. They ought ter wear team shirts or summat. He were only sixteen were this kid. It's allus the young uns that fall fer all that crap.'

'Anybody else hurt?'

'Three killed altogether – two locals and an Aussie electrician. I came out of it wi' cuts and bruises. Our firm closed the site down, paid us off, and here I am, back in sunny Unsworth.'

'Working in the rain.'

'I love it,' said Andy. 'I used ter dream about workin' in the rain when I was out there.' He downed tools and looked around. 'The last time I was here I was playin' cricket. It was all sports fields from Leathley Road down to Priory Beck. How come they got permission to build on it? I thought it

105

was green belt.'

Sam shrugged. 'I don't think there's any such thing as green belt any more.' He smiled as he recalled those times. 'Blimey, it must be twenty-odd years since I played here. Whereabouts is Priory Beck? I've lost my bearings.'

Andy pointed. 'Over there I think. Best place in Unsworth fer tadpoles.' He looked at Sam. 'I gather yer left the police, then?'

'I did.'

'Sorry to hear about yer dad. He was a good bloke. Wish I'd had the chance to work for him.'

Sam nodded his appreciation. 'You can maybe do some work for us one day – I split my time between running the firm and running a detective agency. What do you think of the gaffer on this site?'

'Dezzy? – seems OK. I only came on site last week. Same as any other foreman. Mind you, he keeps goin' on about all this thievin' they'd been havin' – ter be honest he's ger-rin' up my bloody nose. Told me they were having to keep a close eye on all the sub-contractors – cheeky sod. I told him he could have Sherlock bloody Holmes followin' me around, he'd not catch me nickin' nowt.'

'I think he might be worried about his job,' Sam said. 'I know if we had a foreman who kept having gear pinched from under his nose I'd think twice about keeping him on.'

'Are you involved in the investigation?' Andy asked.

'Unofficially at the moment – just helping a friend out.'

Andy grinned.

'What?' asked Sam.

'Mad Carew.'

'Oh, that.'

'Me mam used ter ring me every week with all the news from home. Yer've been in the news quite a bit.'

'Not for a while,' Sam said. He got out his cigarettes and they talked for half an hour before Andy said he'd better get on with his work. The rain had now almost stopped and Sam had a walk round the storage hut, not sure what he was looking for. Nothing jumped out at him.

He wandered down to Priory Beck for no other reason than to see if it was as he remembered it. In weather like this there used to be a second, underground, stream that fired out water, almost horizontally, through a metal grill set in one of the banks. He paddled through a shallow part and wandered up and down the far bank looking for it. As he remembered it, it was quite spectacular and kids used to dare each other to run through it; he'd gone home soaked to the skin many a time. Apart from the trees being more mature the place hadn't changed all that much. The beck was swollen but he remembered walking along this very bank as a lad. Clambering over the same stones, wading through the high ferns, carving his name on one of the trees that lined the stream. He tried to find it but couldn't. He found the grill through which the water used to shoot out. It was bent and rusting, with just a disappointing trickle. Good job really. He might have been tempted to run through it. As kids, when they first discovered it, they thought it was an underground spring with probably the purest water in Unsworth. Sam had drunk some of it and it had tasted OK to him. That evening he threw up and had to miss playing football for the school juniors the next day. He remembered telling his dad, who told him exactly where the water came from and why he should never drink it again. That was the difference between his mam and dad. Had his mam still been living at home she'd have clipped him around the ear for being so stupid. But by that time she'd run off with her fancy man.

He checked the time and realised he'd be late for his appointment with Owen if he didn't get a move on. His time here hadn't produced a theory about the thefts but he'd had a pleasant hour.

On his way back to his car he passed a sludge gulper parked in the flooded road with its hose disappearing into the water, and presumably into a blocked gulley. The operator was pulling the hose out and shaking his head at the man from the council.

'It's not this gulley. Yer gonna have ter rod t' drain out.'

It was at times like this that Sam was thankful he was more private eye than construction worker. It could be a mucky job at times. Far better for a man to use his brains on a day like this.

As he got into his car, he somehow knew the method the thieves had used was now staring him in the face. It was an odd feeling he'd had many times before. All the clues were there, it was just a question of piecing them together. He was pulling into the Clog and Shovel car park when the key piece of the jigsaw dropped into place. It produced a wide beam on his face which was still there when he said 'Hello' to Owen.

There was a pint of Bootham's waiting on the bar for him. The lugubrious Welshman had almost finished his. 'Tell me you have a theory, boyo. Bowman's making my life a misery over this. I'm seriously considering going back into uniform.'

'Which is Bowman's plan,' said Sam. 'He knows you're hooked up with me and you've made him look an idiot a couple of times.'

'It's not me who's made him look an idiot,' grumbled Owen. 'It's you. He hates you.'

Sam picked up his pint, 'Cheers, by the way – oh, and cheers to my dad as well.'

'Your dad?'

'I think he might have solved your case for you. In fact he solved it when I was a kid. You see, he explained to me why I shouldn't drink the water and I never forgot it.'

'That's it, is it – your full explanation?'

'It'll do for now, trust me. Did you get the name of their insurance company?'

'Northern Alliance.'

'Good – I've done some stuff for them before.'

'Look,' said Owen. 'If I'm going to tell Bowman I've cracked the case I'll need more than you've given me.' He hated the way Sam sometimes talked in riddles. 'By the sound of it, Bowman's wife's giving him very serious earache, which he's passing on to me. From what I hear she's a bit of a nutter.'

'I once met her,' remembered Sam, 'she is a bit strange. Mind you, she can't have all her chairs at home to be married to Bowman.'

'The last thing he said to me,' grumbled Owen, 'was if his brother-in-law gets the sack he'll make sure I get the same. There's bloody charming for you!'

'There's something you and I have to check on first,' Sam said. 'Have you heard a weather forecast?'

'I think the rain clears up today, then it's fine for the rest of the week.'

'Good, tomorrow then. Wear some scruffy old clothes.' He eyed Owen's jacket, which had seen better days. 'What you've got on should do.'

'You irritate the hell out of me at times, you know that, don't you, Carew?'

Sam put his arm around his pal. 'Owen, we're a unique team. What Bowman hates about you is your success rate. CID are allowed outside help. All the others have to pay for it but you and I work on a quid pro quo basis. I save the force money.'

'Be that as it may, you're not very popular down at the nick, Sam – er, excuse me one moment.'

Out of the corner of his eye Owen had seen a youth looking at the choices on the jukebox. He walked, quickly, across to him and flashed his warrant card. 'Don't put money in this, sir. It's evidence, see. I'm waiting for forensic right now. There's a child molester operating in the area and we know he's got a thing about jukeboxes. We're checking the fingerprints and DNA on all the jukeboxes in this town against our records. We may have to take yours to eliminate you from our enquiries. Do no harm to tell your friends – and tell them to tell their friends. They won't want to get labelled as nonces. Hard label to shake off, that one.'

The youth backed away from him in horror, then turned and walked over to his pals. Owen rejoined Sam who was impressed by this inspired misuse of a warrant card. 'You really hate jukeboxes, don't you?'

'Nearly as much as I hate Bowman. I knew there was something I was meaning to ask – how did you get on with Alison last night? I gather you were going to pay her a visit.'

'It was a productive meeting.'

'And are you going to help her?'

'I'm not sure. We sort of got off the subject towards the end of our meeting. You know how some meetings go.'

'Presumably you'll be reporting the minutes of the meeting to Sally.'

'I'll be seeing Sally this evening, she's cooking me a meal at her place.'

'Good cook, that Sally. Good woman in many ways. A man would be foolish to let such a woman slip through his fingers.'

'Owen, I take your point, you don't have to lay it on with a trowel.'

Sam sat back in his chair and gazed, admiringly, at Sally. 'All these fancy cooking programmes you get on the telly nowadays: Nigella Lawson, Antony Wotsizname Thompson and – you know, him who swears a lot.'

'Gordon Ramsay.'

'That's the one. I bet none of them can cook up a nice stew like you.'

'Nice stew?' protested Sally. 'It wasn't a nice stew, it was a lamb casserole – and it took me ages. You spend too much time in Tomato Dip caffs to appreciate good food.'

Sam took a deep drink of wine and regarded her, seriously, wishing to hell he hadn't allowed Alison to seduce him. Every time he thought of her he got stirrings, very guilty stirrings, which only added to the excitement, and then piled on more guilt. It would all fade away with time, he knew that much – provided he didn't go anywhere near the tempting Miss Kilpatrick. Perhaps if he and Sally had not been forced into months of abstinence he might not have strayed. Sally returned his gaze, with twinkling eyes.

'You're planning on seducing me, aren't you, Carew?'

He feigned innocence. 'You naughty lady, the thought never crossed my mind – but now you come to mention it.'

'I've made a pudding, but it can wait.'

'It seems the pudding has more self-control than we have. Would you like me to carry you through to the bedroom, Miss Grover?'

'I'd like that very much indeed, Mr Carew. You might also have to disrobe me.'

'It's all part of the service. Would madam like the slow, sensuous disrobing or a bit of lustful ripping and panting?'

'Slow and sensuous with a bit of lustful ripping and panting please.'

'Ah, madam wants the full five-course menu. I might have to alert the little chef.'

'I was hoping the little chef was already alert.'

113

'He's on standby, madam, as he has been these many months.'

Their lovemaking began in warm, easy comfort. The usual teasing and joking progressed via fond exchanges, deep kisses, mounting passion, into complete and noisy abandon, especially for Sally. Sam, nervous of doing her damage, but not wishing to be a disappointing lover, went along with her every step of the way until they arrived at an electrifying mutual climax with all worries about Sally's condition forgotten. Alison, in the meantime, made her way to the back of his mind before departing through the back door, leaving Sally in sole custody of his affections. For the time being.

CHAPTER TEN

Two miles away, as Sam was carrying Sally through to the bedroom, the whole Robinson family was in the study at Wickham Farm.

Annie was sipping a glass of whisky and smoking a small cigar. She'd had her hair done and Tanya reckoned she'd been at the Immac again. The fuzz above her upper lip was gone. This meant trouble. Annie always presented herself well when delivering a bollocking. She addressed herself to Lloyd.

'What's the current situation with the girls?'

'All the girls are off the streets, Ma. All in premises now. Twenty-eight in the massage parlours and thirty-one in the flats.'

'Which is the best take?'

'Now that there's 24-hour licensing, the massage parlours. We've got punters coming in at all hours. The flats are getting to be more trouble than they're worth.'

'What sort of trouble?'

'Neighbours complaining to the bizzies.'

'I don't suppose it's much fun living next door to a brothel,' commented Tanya, who wasn't too keen on this side of the business. Her mother ignored her.

'Are the Leeds bizzies sweet about it?'

'So far,' said Lloyd, 'our friendly sergeant's getting a bit greedy and it's costing more and more in sweeteners. To be honest it's getting to be uneconomical.'

'Do we have compromising snapshots of all our Leeds bizzies in action?'

'Photos and videos, Ma. Sound and vision.'

She nodded her approval then took a drag on her cigar before asking, 'What's last month's net take?'

'After the laundry bill, a hundred and thirty-three grand and some change. The accountant's transferred it to Dominica.'

'Receipt,' said Annie, holding out a hand.

Lloyd took a slip of paper from his pocket and handed it to her. She glanced at it and placed it in a drawer. Annie knew this would be the correct figure. Lloyd knew better than to try and cream anything off the top. Her expression hardened as she turned her attention to Nathan, who looked after the drugs side of the business. Tanya tried not to appear smug; she knew what was coming.

Among other things the family owned a builders' merchants, which had been raided the previous day by police looking for drugs. Nothing had been found. Annie had made an official complaint about unwarranted police harassment. She kept her business discussion with Nathan quite brief.

'Last month's take.'

'I did a great deal wi–'

'Just the fuckin' take, Nathan.'

'A hundred and sixty-three grand and some change.' He took a receipt from his pocket and handed it to her. She placed it in the drawer without taking her eyes off him.

'You are really beginning to piss me off, Nathan. We were very lucky yesterday ter get word of a police bust. If we hadn't been very lucky the bizzies would have landed themselves a right fuckin' catch. Twenty kilos o' coke plus me and Tanya banged up fer god knows how long. The bizzies knew the gear were comin' dressed up as filler. Fortunately we had word that they were coming and rearranged things to suit. As it happens they confiscated a load o' Polyfilla and I've registered a very strong complaint about police harassment.'

'The point is,' Tanya took up the story, 'there'll be no more drug deliveries at the yard. You and Lloyd are never there, which puts me and Ma in the frame when things go pear-shaped. From now on, it's completely legit. It's supposed to be a front, and fronts are supposed to be clean.'

'Oh yeah, since when did you run the fuckin' show?' sneered Lloyd.

Annie chipped in. 'Since I said so. From now on she runs the merchant's business and does the contracts when they come. I'm makin' it a limited company with me and Tan equal shareholders. We'll run it at a loss if we have to, but it stays clean. The money comes from Tan's contracts, the gear and the girls.'

'Yer mean we do most of the work, apart from her cappin' a shag-happy mark now and then,' complained Nathan.

'Running the merchant's is a job requirin' brains and knowhow,' said Annie, tapping her temple with a finger. 'Tan has her degree in business studies. We all work as hard, and the money is split four ways.'

'Four ways? She's always been on wages. Since when did Tan become an equal fuckin' partner?'

'Since today,' Annie told Nathan, forcefully, 'not only that but if, for any reason,

I'm not around, she's in charge of the whole shooting match – kapish? This organisation needs someone who can think clearly and not go off on one when things don't suit him.' Nathan didn't answer.

'Ka-fuckin'-pish?'

'OK, Ma,' he grumbled, 'we're not deaf.'

He turned away as Annie caught his eye. His pupils were just pinpoints and his speech nasal. Without taking her eyes off him she rose from her chair and walked around the desk. She was a strongly built woman with fists like a Liverpool docker. Taking his cheeks between her hands she forced him to look directly at her.

'Yer brainless pillock! Yer've been puffin' on that filthy crack pipe again.'

'No, ma,' Nathan lied. 'Not after the last time – I told yer, never again.'

'Never again my arse! Yer never stopped. I can see it in yer eyes, lad. It's makin' yer fuckin' anxious an' careless.'

She turned her attention to Lloyd and stared deep into his eyes. He returned her gaze with confidence.

'Not me, Ma. Just a bit o' weed fer relaxation, same as everyone else. It's not even illegal now.' He took a fat joint from his pocket, lit up, and sniggered at his own humour. 'Vote New Labour. Tough on crime, tough on the causes of crime. Tony Blair, my fuckin' hero.'

118

'What I want to know is how come we were grassed up to the bizzies?' Annie's eyes returned to Nathan, demanding an answer. 'So, who knew about the Polyfilla?'

Nathan shifted in his seat, uncomfortably.

'I'm talkin' ter you, Nathan!'

'Ma, I know who yer fuckin' talkin' ter.'

Without warning she punched him hard in the mouth, knocking him clean out of his chair.

'Don't you give me any of your lip, lad. There's a snitch on your team.'

'Well if there is, it's news ter me,' he muttered, fingering a cut lip and checking his teeth. 'My lads wouldn't dare.'

Annie dragged him to his feet and thrust her face into his. 'Maybe one of your lads has got a big gob. Maybe one of your tinted lads has mentioned something to his baby brother whose jaw yer broke last year when he gave yer some back-chat.'

'What? Yer mean Yousuf's brother – their Shoib?' Nathan gave her suggestion some consideration, then dismissed it with a shake of his head. 'No – he's too shit-scared ter grass me up.'

'Not according to my information, which is extremely fuckin' reliable,' his mother said, returning to her chair. 'Shoib's been working as a snitch fer months. The little shit's not shit-scared of you at all – and that troubles me, Nathan, boy. This lack o' fuckin' respect gets handed down the line – and that troubles me no end.'

'Your boy in Unsworth nick wasn't much use when we needed tellin' about the drugs bust,' Nathan pointed out.

'I'm told what's available fer tellin'. No one knows everythin'.'

'If you can't handle the snitch, Nathan, I'll do it for you,' Tanya taunted.

He scowled. 'I can handle Shoib fuckin' Nazir – and his brother fer that matter.'

'I'll go with him,' said Lloyd.

'That's good,' said Annie, 'because it might give you two boys a bit o' practice to handle Neville Latimer.'

'Neville who?'

'Latimer,' said Tanya. 'He's a Manchester lad who thinks he can walk into Leeds and muscle in on our girls.'

'I've heard of him,' said Lloyd. 'Big feller, black as the ace o' spades.'

Annie shook her head scornfully. 'How come neither of yer know what's happening under yer fuckin' noses? Now can yer see why I've made Tan me second in command? It were Tan what sussed out Latimer.'

'I got wind of him when I was in Manchester,' Tanya explained. 'Things had got very warm for him. He'd got a bit rough with one of his girls and she turned up dead. The Manchester bizzies pulled him in and gave him a hard time. You know what these pimps are like – they don't like a hard time.' She addressed that remark to Lloyd, who ran the girls. 'So he's moved over the hills and far away and landed in our back yard.'

'Maybe yer can persuade him that there's better business in Bradford,' Annie suggested to her younger son. 'Either way, I don't want no Manchester pimp moving in on us.' She got up to go, then paused and said, over her shoulder, 'And boys, do it neatly. I want people to be impressed by yer. I want it done neat an' clean and ever so fuckin' nasty. Let's bring some respect back into our firm.'

Nathan stretched his arms and gave a yawn. He didn't like to give the impression that his mother had so much control over him. 'Is that it, then?' he asked.

'No, it's not fuckin' *it* now yer come ter mention it,' snapped his mother. 'I want this feller Carew keepin' an eye on – and I want you ter do it.'

'What, yer want me ter tail him full time?'

'Either you or one of yer team. You, whenever yer can spare yerself. I want ter know everythin' about him – and I don't want him ter know anythin' about you. Just remember he's an ex-bizzie and he'll know better than most when someone's tailin' him.'

CHAPTER ELEVEN

Rain had given way to warm sunshine, which was drawing steam out of the sodden ground. Over the years the metal grill set in the bank beside Priory Beck had rusted away to a state where it was easily pulled away by Sam. Owen was wearing a boiler suit, and a balaclava that he'd apparently owned for many years. He was the only law-abiding balaclava owner of Sam's acquaintance and he was looking more dismal than usual. Sam chose to ignore this. He had enough to think about without listening to Owen's tales of woe, and no one he knew had more woe than Owen. But, after several minutes of silent digging his curiosity got the better of him. He looked up at the Welshman.

'Is it Bowman or a woman?'

'What?'

'It's usually one or the other – it's a woman, isn't it?'

'I'll have you know that things between me and Eileen are very hunky-dory.'

'Wedding bells in the offing?'

'Not that hunky-dory. I have enough commitments as it is.'

'You mean Child Support Agency commitments?'

'I'm no longer in CSA clutches, look you.'

'You are the world's most unlikely Lothario, Owen. So, what's the problem if it's not women?'

Owen took his balaclava off and scratched his head. 'I had what I thought was a very solid tip-off a couple of days ago about a major drug deal going down at a builders' merchants. I told Bowman and he said he wouldn't act unless I gave him the name of my source.'

'Which you shouldn't have to do,' said Sam, still digging. 'Unwritten rule, that.'

'Not as far as Bowman's concerned. Anyway I gave him the name and we set up a bust with half a dozen of our troops and an armed response unit.'

'And?'

'And we ended up with two dozen boxes of Polyfilla.'

'Polyfilla?'

'I was told that cocaine was being delivered disguised as Polyfilla. It was very well disguised. There's people plastering over cracks with it as we speak.'

'And how much did you pay for this info?'

'Fifty pounds.'

'Owen, there are some very nasty men involved in drugs. No one's going to blow the whistle on them for fifty quid. Did that not strike you as odd?'

'Not really. I've known the lad for a few years, see – arrested him a couple of times for misdemeanors, but apart from that he's a decent enough sort. I gather he had a bit of a grudge to settle against a man who had knocked him around a bit.'

'Did he give you the man's name?'

'No, he wasn't very forthcoming about names. But the builders' merchants was Robinsons in Unsworth.'

'Cowboys,' commented Sam, 'we never use them.' He grinned. 'I guess Bowman wasn't pleased.'

'He pretended to go ballistic.'

'Pretended?'

'It wasn't proper ballistic. I'm a world expert on Bowman going ballistic. I should be – he practises on me most of the time.'

Sam stopped working. 'Owen, are you telling me that Bowman warned the drug dealers?'

'Either that or my informer was taking the piss – and I can't see why he'd do that, not for fifty quid. He came to me with the information and he seemed very genuine.'

'Maybe your man just got his wires crossed,' Sam suggested.

'Maybe he did,' said Owen, but he didn't sound convinced. Sam got back to work.

Using a small shovel, known in the trade as a grafting tool, which he'd brought for the purpose, Sam dug away around the edges of the hole that the removed grill had revealed. He shovelled away a pile of debris then poked his head into what looked an ancient, damp tunnel. It was roughly five feet wide and four feet high with stone walls, roof and floor. Water was running along the floor at a depth of about an inch and trickling out into the beck. Sam shone a powerful torch along the tunnel, Owen peered over his shoulder as the beam disappeared into distant blackness. It was the sort of tunnel down which small boys would always shout in order to hear their echo.

'Hellooo!' shouted Owen. The tunnel returned his shout with interest. It drew a toothy grin from him. 'What the bloody hell's this, boyo? Some sort of mediaeval sallyport?'

'It's a culvert,' said Sam. 'The only reason I know about it is because my dad once mentioned it.'

'Ah, a culvert,' said Owen, knowledgably, as if this explained everything. 'Remind me, what's a culvert?'

'It's a tunnel for carrying a stream underground,' Sam explained. 'There used to be a stream running across where they're building. It was culverted when the field was made into playing fields, about eighty-odd years ago. Leathley road was not much more than a dirt track back then and when it was made into a proper road back in the Fifties the culvert was in the way, so they had to divert the stream and leave the culvert abandoned. It'll be filled in under where the road is, but the rest of it will probably be intact. The odds are that it won't show up on any up-to-date Ordnance Survey maps, which is what the site plans are based on.'

'So, how on earth do you know about it?'

'It was the flooding that gave me a clue. You see, when they put the surface water sewer in the road, way back in the late Fifties, they ran a storm overflow pipe from one of the man-holes into the culvert, which is why the road shouldn't have flooded. The reason I know is because my dad worked on the drainage. I remember him telling me about it.'

'And you think this is how the thieves stole the building materials?'

'I'd say it's a hot favourite,' said Sam. 'Come on, let's have a look.'

Virtually on hands and knees they made their way along the dripping tunnel, with Owen grumbling every inch of the way.

'By god, I hope you're right about this, boyo. My knees aren't built for damp, and I'm claustrophobic.'

'Claustrophobic? You never told me you were claustrophobic.'

'How could I? I've only just found out.'

The air grew staler and the culvert twisted and turned, following the path of the original stream, for about a hundred yards before Sam's torch reflected off two tiny eyes that could only be a rat's. He didn't mention it to Owen who wasn't keen on rats. Around the next bend the light illuminated something that was neither rat nor stone wall.

'Hello, 'ello, 'ello.'

Sam's voice echoed off the damp walls as he imitated the archetypal copper. 'What 'ave we 'ere?' As he approached he called back to Owen, identifying the objects blocking the tunnel. 'Plastic windows, shower units, rolls of lead, copper tubing, two condoms, a dead rat...' He crawled right up to the pile of windows and shone his torch over the top of them. 'Bloody hell! There's stuff crammed in as far as I can see.' Then he shone the torch upwards to reveal an opening in the roof and what must be the floor joists supporting the site store. In the middle of the floor was an obvious trap door.

Sam was delighted that all this trouble had been worth it. 'This is great.' He shone the torch on Owen, whose face was pale and bilious. He was not sharing his pal's enthusiasm. 'OK this is all we need to see,' Sam added, 'unless you want to look round a bit mor–?'

Owen's reply came before Sam's question had ended. 'No, no, I've seen enough, boyo.'

Back in the warm daylight Sam lit a cigarette and ran events through his mind. He and Owen were caked in mud from head to toe. 'What they've been doing is bringing the stuff out through a trapdoor in the floor and storing it in the culvert so they can take it away at their leisure. This rain will have cocked their plans up a bit. All the stowed gear will have slowed down the flow of water from the storm overflow and made the water back up into the road – hence the flooding. Some of the gear will also be well knackered because of all the water.'

As Owen sliced a fingernail through the silver wrapping on a KitKat bar a thought struck him. 'Are you sure this is where they bring the stuff out? This entrance looks as if it hasn't been disturbed for years.'

Sam blew smoke into the morning air. 'That's because they haven't been bringing stuff out this end.' He watched as four fingers of chocolate disappeared, one after the other, into Owen's mouth. 'It's no wonder you have trouble with your digestion, the amount of stuff you stick in your cake-hole.'

Owen ignored him and asked. 'How do you know they haven't been bringing it out this end?'

'Owen, just look around. What are they going to do with it once it's out, float it down the stream?'

'There's no need for sarcasm, boyo.'

'I wish you wouldn't call me boyo. Anyway, they need a handy road where they can load the stuff straight onto a vehicle. There has to be another exit between where the stuff is stored and Leathley Ro–'

Owen chipped in, to prove he'd been paying attention earlier. 'Because the culvert will be filled in under the road.'

'Exactly,' said Sam.

It took them less than half an hour to find the other end of the culvert. It was about twenty yards off the road, next to an area the council used for storing road grit. The hole was covered by two steel plates which had partly been disguised by someone who had thrown a few shovelfuls of sand on them.

'Right,' said Sam, 'it's all over, bar the waiting, which is your job. I doubt if they'll want to leave it down there too long.'

Owen's demeanor had lightened considerably. 'I'll see if we can get an obbo set up. Bowman's off for a couple of days so at least I don't have to get him to clear it.'

'Give me a bell when it kicks off, I've got an insurance man to see.'

CHAPTER TWELVE

Nathan Robinson was parked on Leathley Road about two hundred yards behind Sam's car. He hadn't followed him on to the nearby building site because he didn't see much point – Carew was probably about his usual business, which was what Nathan should be about. He took out his mobile, forced an unaccustomed smile on to his face and tapped in a number.

'Yousuf, how're yer doing?'

'Oh, hiya Nathan.'

Yousuf sounded guarded when he recognised Nathan's voice, but Nathan put him at his ease. Yousuf knew about the raid and he knew where the police had got their information.

'Right as rain, our kid.'

'I hear yer had a spot of bother the other night.'

'What? Oh, that – load o' bollocks, nowt we couldn't handle. Look, I've got a job fer yer – well it's a two-hander actually and I haven't got a second man available. Is your kid still up for a bit of work or is he still moanin' because I had ter give him a slap that time?'

'No, he's right.'

'It's worth a grand apiece but I need yer to nick a motor with a big boot – big enough ter transport a passenger, if yer get me drift.'

'Oh, right.'

'There'll be some diggin' involved. Yer haven't gorra bad back or owt, have yer?'

'Our Shoib's pretty handy with a shovel. He works on the buildin' sites.'

'Good, tell him I'll provide the shovel. All you have ter do is drive and let him do the diggin'. The hardest part's nickin' the car.

Money fer jam, really. I'll meet yer in the car park behind your old cricket ground in Leeds. D'yer still play, Yousuf?'

'Nah, they dropped me into the B team so I told 'em ter piss off – fuckin' racists. What time?'

'Eleven o'clock ternight. Don't let me down, Yousuf, boy.'

'I won't, I promise.'

Yousuf and Shoib had been waiting ten minutes when Nathan turned up in an Audi. The area was deserted, as Nathan knew it would be. Lloyd was supposed to have come with him, but bollocks to that. He'd show his cow of a mother that he was more than up to the job. Things had never been the same since Lewis. There were days when Nathan felt guilty about that. It was he who had told Ma about Lewis being queer. He could have broken the news more gently. She hadn't believed him, and maybe he should have left it at that. But he had to go and prove it to her; take her to a house where Lewis was in bed with a rent boy. And now it was as if Ma had blamed him for all that happened that night. He should have known that Ma would lose control big time. She had a psychotic loathing of all things homosexual.

It had been like watching someone possessed by an evil demon. The way she beat

Lewis unconscious with her bare fists was awesome and terrifying. She wouldn't stop – she *couldn't* stop. She was landing random blows all over his body. Kicking, slapping, headbutting. It was a vicious punch to his throat that did the most telling damage, crushing his windpipe and causing him to choke, violently.

'Lewis, you fu–!'

As if being snapped out of a trance, her senses returned. She had a bloodied fist in the air and a frozen curse on her lips as she realised what she'd done. She howled with anguish and guilt and rage that it had come to this and it wasn't her fault. It was the fault of Lewis for being so disgusting.

'LEWIS!'

She now attempted to shake some life into him as he desperately tried to draw in some air, but the passage between mouth and lungs was far too damaged. He drowned in his own blood in his mother's arms.

Nathan might have tried to stop her but he was holding on to the male prostitute. It wasn't until he realised that Ma had killed Lewis that he knew he'd have to do the same to the rent boy. He'd strangled the life out of him as he watched his Ma retching with grief over the son she'd just murdered.

The brothers were leaning against the bonnet of a big Volvo saloon. Nathan got out of his car and gave the stolen vehicle a nod of approval.

'Well, this is just the dog's bollocks, boys.'

'What is it we're buryin', Nathan?'

'A stiff, boys – a stiff who needs a final resting place.'

'Oh, right.'

It was what they thought, but at a grand apiece they weren't going to grumble. Nathan took a large spade from the boot of his car. 'Can yer open the boot fer me, boys? I just need ter check it fer size.'

Yousuf leaned inside the Volvo and pulled the boot release catch. The three of them walked around the back. Nathan swung the spade against Shoib's shins. The younger brother howled in agony and fell against the open boot.

'That's fer grassin' us up, yer little twat!' snarled Nathan. He swung the spade again and shattered Shoib's left shoulder, then he heaved the younger brother into the boot of the Volvo.

'No, leave him!' screamed Yousuf. He backed away as Nathan threatened him with the spade.

'You keep yer trap shut or yer'll get some o' the fuckin' same. It's you openin' yer trap that got the boy into this. So keep it shut – OK?'

'OK,' wept Yousuf.

'Good boy. The good news is that you get

your kid's share of the money – two grand, all fer you. Not a bad night's work, eh?'

'Please don't kill him,' pleaded Yousuf.

Shoib was screeching in agony. Nathan swung the spade at him and knocked him unconscious. 'Noisy bastard!' Then he returned his attention to Yousuf.

'Course I've got ter kill him. We can't let someone get away wi' grassin' us up. How would that fuckin' look?'

He delivered a series of violent blows that ended Shoib's life, then he handed the spade to Yousuf.

'Now, Yousuf boy, if you don't want to end up the same, yer dispose of the body as per our agreement. Two grand, cash money, lesson learned – I fuckin' hope. Dispose of it deep where no one'll find it.'

Yousuf was on his knees, weeping profusely. 'Please, Nathan, yer can't make me do that. I can't do that. Oh Shoib, I'm sorry, Shoib...'

Nathan cursed, viciously. 'Fuckin' hell, Yousuf! If I'd known yer were gonna mis-behave like this I wouldn't have bothered askin' yer to nick a motor. This is a total waste o' my time an' yours, this is! I'm doin' you a favour here, teachin' you a valuable lesson and yer not appreciatin' me, Yousuf. Well I'm not doin' any diggin' – not wi' my back.' His voice rose to a scream. 'Fuckin' listen ter me when I'm talking ter yer!'

He swung the spade at Yousuf's head,

almost decapitating him. Yousuf fell over, sideways, blood shooting out of his neck. Nathan, still cursing, strode back to his car. He flung the spade in the boot and took a can of paraffin out. Then he splashed some on Yousuf and laid a trail to the Volvo, where he emptied the can, first on Shoib's body, and then all over the car. He then took out a box of matches, lit three at once and threw them on Yousuf's body. It caught fire immediately.

Nathan sat in his car watching the flames hurry towards the Volvo then, satisfied that his work was done, he drove away.

CHAPTER THIRTEEN

It was 5.30 p.m. the next day, Friday, when Sam's mobile told him that Owen was ringing. The site had closed down for the night and a three-ton van had arrived and parked in the council road-grit dump.

'According to the boys on the obbo there's four of them gone down the hole,' reported Owen. 'I've just arrived. Oh, I've just rung Bowman at home to tell him what was happening. He didn't sound so pleased but he's on his way.'

'So am I,' said Sam.

He parked in a lay-by behind Bowman's

car and tapped on the DCI's window. Bowman had his mobile phone in his hand. He made no attempt to conceal his irritation as he wound the window down.

'Carew. I gather from DC Price that you're involved. It's a pity he can't work on his own. Let's hope this isn't a major cock-up, like his last effort.'

'Come off it,' retorted Sam. 'You only put Owen on this because you thought it was too tricky for him to solve. As it happens he did a lot of useful legwork. Very resourceful detective is Owen.'

A voice on Bowman's radio was telling everyone to be on the alert as someone had appeared from the culvert. Then the voice became urgent as it shouted, 'Go, go, go!'

Sam strolled on. Bowman got out and followed him. 'Don't get involved, Carew,' he warned. 'This is a police matter.'

'It's also an insurance company matter,' Sam pointed out. 'I'm looking after my client's interests.'

They turned into the area where the truck was parked. Sam's face broke into a beam when he saw Owen handcuffing Desmond Broughton. A uniformed sergeant and three PCs were holding two more men.

'Your missis is gonna be well pleased with you, Mr Bowman – arresting her brother,' said Sam.

Bowman had an odd expression on his

136

face – more exasperation than embarrassment. Sam sidled up to him.

'I assume this really is a great shock to you, Mr Bowman – or did you think it might be him who was behind it, all along? Is that why you gave it to Owen – because you thought he was the one least likely to solve it?'

'Don't talk so damn stupid.'

'You're right, I must be talking stupid,' conceded Sam. 'Had you known it was Desmond you'd have warned him we were on to him – probably at great risk to your career, but that's what families do.' He snapped his fingers as if just thought of something. 'But you couldn't warn him, could you? Owen only told you at the last minute.'

Desmond was giving Owen a hard time, struggling and cursing as the Welshman tried to put him in the back of a police car. A mobile phone dropped out of the foreman's pocket, Sam stepped forward and picked it up, helpfully. He waited as Owen continued with his struggle, then he looked down at the phone. It was registering one missed call. As Owen slammed the door on Desmond, Sam looked across at Bowman who was standing several yards away. He pressed the key that would call the missed number.

'Someone tried to call him as he was down in the culvert,' Sam called out to Bowman, 'probably tried to warn him but got no signal down there. I'm ringing back.'

137

The mobile in Bowman's pocket began to ring. The DCI looked on, dry-lipped, as Sam put Desmond's phone to his ear. The police were all too preoccupied to notice.

'Aren't you going to answer your phone, Detective Chief Inspector?' enquired Sam, innocently. Bowman remained frozen. Sam pressed the "off" key on the foreman's phone. Bowman's phone stopped ringing.

Sam looked at the screen which recorded the last caller's number plus the time and date when he'd rung. He stepped right up to the DCI and spoke into his ear.

'I'm guessing that if I gave Desmond's phone to the Superintendent you'd end up with quite a bit of explaining to do. But you're gonna have enough troubles at home without having to face a disciplinary, so I'll hang on to it for the time being. Just think – if you hadn't put Owen on this job both you and your crooked brother-in-law might well have got away with it.'

Sam was considering going for broke and tackling Bowman about the failed drugs bust. The DCI was vulnerable right now and vulnerable people give away more that they should. Almost as if he could read Sam's thoughts, Owen led him away.

'Sam, if you're thinking what I think you're thinking I wish you wouldn't. I'm perfectly capable of knackering up my own career.'

'You're right on all counts, Owen.'

Someone was saying that there must be one person left in the culvert. Discussions were taking place as to who should go down there and flush him out. There were no volunteers so the job was handed to a nervous probationer on the grounds that it would be good experience.

Sam left Owen and strolled down through the building site, heading for Priory Beck. It was a pleasant evening, his work was done and there had even been an unexpected bonus – Bowman owed him a favour. A familiar figure was approaching from the direction of the stream. Sam moved behind the store hut to avoid being seen.

'Been catching tadpoles, Andy?'

Andy spun in his tracks. He was caked in mud, just like Sam and Owen the day before. Sam stepped into his path.

'Dezzy and the other two are on their way to the nick. I'm guessing you're the fourth man they're after. Came out of the other end, did you?'

Andy shrugged. It was daft to deny it. 'I should have known you'd twig how it was being done.'

'I didn't twig you'd be involved in something so stupid,' Sam said. 'Andy, you're a bloody good tradesman, you don't need to be a thief.'

Andy winced at Sam's reproach. 'I had nowt to do with the first robbery,' he said.

'Dezzy asked me, this morning, if I fancied earning a few quid on the side. He just said they needed a bit of extra muscle for two or three hours and there was a couple of hundred in it for me. I should have known it was moody money.'

'I assume it was Dezzy who organised it all.'

'Dezzy – yeah. He organised it and had all the stuff fenced out to some dodgy builders' merchant; everyone else were just on wages. It'd have been the last job. He reckoned his bosses wouldn't stand another one.'

'Do you know who the merchants are?'

'Never asked.'

Sam narrowed his eyes. 'Andy, I know you. You're a nosey sod. You'd have asked him for chapter and verse how it was done.'

'I'm bein' straight with yer, Sam. I never asked who the merchant was.'

'Did he position the store hut there on purpose?'

Andy gave a dismal nod. 'Before the job started they sent him out to dig a few trial holes. That's how he found the culvert. With it not being in the way of anything he said nowt and stuck the hut on top of it. It's not on any survey drawings. He thought he was the only person in the world who knew about it.'

'I knew about it.'

'So I gather,' said Andy, gloomily. 'Dezzy were convinced he'd get clean away with it.

Let's face it, the coppers would never have worked it out.' He looked at Sam, with questioning eyes. 'Have I got away with it, Sam?'

'It's not Carew you should be asking.'

They both turned to see Bowman leaning against the store hut.

'Who's he?' asked Andy.

'Detective Inspector Bowman,' said Sam. 'Dezzy's brother-in-law.'

'And you're the man they're looking for,' said Bowman to Andy. 'One of the thieves.'

Andy's shoulders slumped in dejection. He looked to Sam for help. Sam shook his head and said, 'Well, it's a good job I hung on to Dezzy's phone.'

'The man's a thief, Carew. He'll go down for this.'

'I know what he is, Bowman – and I know what you are. Do we have a deal?'

'Just give me that bloody phone!'

'Deal?'

Bowman nodded, grudgingly.

Sam turned to Andy. 'Andy, go home.'

'What?'

'You're in the clear. Just go home ... NOW!'

'Right.' Andy was relieved and mystified. He nodded towards Bowman, whose face was expressionless. 'What about him?'

'DCI Bowman and I have a deal.'

CHAPTER FOURTEEN

Nathan had left one of his men to tail Sam. The man had hung around until the police turned up and had driven away just as the arrests were being made. He rang Nathan and reported that Sam had been working on something that had nothing to do with them. Nathan was just pulling up outside Neville Latimer's house. He listened to what the man had to say, grunted his acknowledgement and clicked off the phone. He was about to get out of the car, but Lloyd stopped him.

'You wait here, I'll handle this on me own.'

Nathan shrugged. 'Is that because I topped Yousuf and Shoib without your help? There's no need, yer know. Yousuf an' Shoib were a pair o' pussy cats compared ter this feller.'

Lloyd took out his mobile. 'Ring me up.' Nathan obliged. When it rang Lloyd pressed the answer button and slipped the phone into the top pocket of his jacket. 'Just keep listening. If it sounds as if I'm in trouble come in mob-handed. If not, leave it ter me.'

Nathan glanced into the rear-view mirror at the two men sitting in the back. 'Are yer both tooled up?' He got nods from both of

142

them. 'Right, grand each bonus, if we have ter go into action.'

'Yer won't need to pay,' said Lloyd.

'Let's hope not, our kid. I'll put the phone on hands-free, so we can all hear. Just shout "Go Go GO", like they do on *The Bill* and we'll GO GO GO like shit off a shovel, won't we, boys?' Two more nods.

Lloyd knocked, politely, on the door of the house where Latimer had taken up residence. In the first half of the twentieth century it had been a high class area of Leeds, but not now. Now it was a bleak area of violence, squalor and prostitution. Mostly the prostitutes were white girls from troubled homes and mostly the pimps were black, with the exception of Lloyd Robinson – and he wasn't going to give way to Neville Latimer; he was far more scared of Annie Robinson than he was of any Manchester black lad.

A completely bald black man came to the door. Lloyd looked up from under his baseball cap. It was an area where CCTV abounded and looking up should be kept to a minimum. Lloyd took out a wad of cash.

'I've got a grand here fer Mr Neville Latimer.'

'Who the fuck are you?'

Lloyd fanned out the twenty-pound notes to prove he wasn't kidding. 'I'm the feller who's been sent ter give Mr Neville Latimer a grand – does he fuckin' want it or not?'

143

The man held out his hand for the money. Lloyd snatched it away. He had a description of Latimer and this man didn't fit.

'I was told to give it ter Mr Latimer an' no one else. D'yer want ter get me into trouble?'

The bald man stood there, undecided. 'Wait there,' he said at length. He walked away down the hall and turned into the back room. Lloyd followed him. Latimer was sitting on a long, leather settee. Beside him was a naked white girl whom Lloyd recognised as one of his, although it was the first time he'd ever seen her naked, which annoyed him somewhat.

'There's a guy at the door–' the bald man began, then he saw Latimer looking past him at Lloyd. The bald man turned and raised his hands to shove Lloyd back but, by now, Lloyd had a gun in his hand.

'I'd like the three of you standing against that wall, please. That includes you, Paula.'

'Honest Lloyd, I'm not doing business behind your back, I–'

'Please don't give me that shit, Paula. I know what I know. I've come here ter talk ter Mr Neville Latimer – that's you, I take it?'

Latimer nodded. He was a very big man; former bouncer, former pro boxer, former Mr Great Britain finalist and former inmate of HM prison system where he had served four years of a seven-year sentence for robbery with violence. He wasn't used to having men try to scare him, usually it was the other way round and he'd made up his mind to reverse this insolent intruder's fortunes as quickly as he could.

'I heard yer tryin' ter move into my area,' Lloyd told him, 'and the presence of this girl proves it.'

Lloyd was actually an insignificant looking man. Unlike Nathan, who was well over six feet tall and built like a tank, Lloyd was maybe five-feet-seven and, apart from a couple of incongruous eyebrow rings, he looked more like a bank clerk than a villain. Despite the gun, Latimer was finding difficulty taking this little creep seriously. He wasn't even sure if the gun was genuine or a replica. He took a step towards Lloyd and sneered, 'Are you sure that's a real gun?'

'I'm not sure,' said Lloyd, 'let's see, shall we?' He swung his arm around and shot the bald, black man between the eyes. Then he swung the gun back to cover Latimer. 'Seems real enough ter me, do yer want me ter give it another try on you?'

Latimer thrust his hands in the air, even though he hadn't been asked. 'OK, OK, ya made ya point, man.'

Paula was screaming so Lloyd reversed the weapon and clubbed her unconscious as Latimer stared, in jaw-dropping horror, at his dead henchman.

'Is there anyone else in the house?' Lloyd

asked him, moving so his back was against a wall. 'An' don't lie ter me, Mr Latimer else I'll fuckin' shoot yer – as a matter of fact I might do that anyway.'

Latimer's face was drawn and glistening with sweat. 'Take it easy man, – no one else is in right now. Look, there's no need for this, man. I'm only here on a flyin' visit.'

'As it happens, that's a good answer,' said Lloyd. 'Well, if I let yer go, yer'll have ter tidy this mess up.' He pointed with the gun at the dead man.

'It's no problem, man,' Latimer promised, fervently. 'I get rid of him an' ya don' see me no more, man.'

Lloyd nodded, apparently satisfied. 'And yer'll have ter be gone by ternight, because if yer don't go I'll have ter set me brother on yer and he's not easy goin' like me, he's a fuckin' psycho – hang on a sec.' He could hear Nathan shouting at him down the phone. He took it out of his pocket and spoke into it without taking his eyes, or the gun, off Latimer.

'What...? I've had ter put one down but there's two ter go, including the Manchester pimp an' one o' my girls... Paula... Well, if that's what yer want – but it'll mean you lot helpin' me ter tidy up. If I have ter cap 'em both I'm fucked if I'm tidyin' up on me own. An' he's a big bugger, we'll have ter chop him up. Tell yer what, I could leave

Paula, she'll never dare say owt, an' she is pretty good at her job... Yes, I know what you'd do, yer psycho bastard, but the way I see it, if I leave it as it is he'll have ter sort out his own stiff before he goes – job done, we can be home in time fer *Coronation Street*... Come on, he's hardly gonna blab, is he? Manchester pimp with a warrant out on him with a stiff in his house, blamin' it on someone else. Who the fuck's gonna believe him? Anyway, I'll leave it up ter you.'

He listened and nodded as Nathan seemed to ramble on, then he became exasperated and shouted down the phone. 'So, do I shoot the bastard or not...? Right – that's all I wanted ter know.'

Latimer felt his legs buckling beneath him. He knew that the verdict had gone against him and that he'd be dead within five seconds. Lloyd's eyes hardened and his finger tightened on the trigger. He took steady aim with the gun. Latimer lost bowel and bladder control simultaneously. Lloyd looked down at the spreading stain in the black man's crotch and wrinkled his nose as the stench reached him. He laughed out loud and spoke into the phone.

'Hey, guess what, our kid, he's just pissed and shit hisself! He's got some mess ter clean up now!'

Latimer was on his knees with his hands clasped together, beseeching Lloyd to spare him his life. Lloyd held the phone out so that Nathan could hear. Laughter came from the car as Lloyd took a step forwards and kicked Latimer in the face, sending him sprawling over Paula, who was now coming round. Lloyd bent down and spoke to the weeping man.

'Are yer listening, bastard?'

Latimer nodded through his tears as he listened to Lloyd's instructions: 'Get rid of the stiff and fuck off outa this city, in fact, fuck off outa Yorkshire. If we ever hear that yer in Yorkshire, Mr Latimer, we'll be very angry with yer. D'yer hear me, Mr Latimer?' Latimer nodded, Lloyd continued: 'Our Nathan'll cut off all yer favourite bits: fingers, toes, tongue, ears, nose, eyes, dick, bollocks – an' please don't think I'm kiddin', Mr Latimer, because he's a bugger with a Stanley knife is Nathan. He'll stuff what's left of yer in a wheelie bin, where it'll take you up to a day ter die. Now I want yer to imagine all this happening ter you, Mr Latimer, because it's not the most dignified way ter depart this mortal coil – I'm told it stings a bit as well.'

Then to Paula he said. 'Yer work fer six months on half pay. An' if you open yer mouth about what happened here yer'll be as dead as baldy over there. Do I make meself clear, Paula?'

'Yes, you do, Lloyd.'

There was blood dripping all down the

side of her head, but Lloyd's attention was fixed on her breasts. 'Have yer never thought of havin' a tit job? Yer know – build 'em up a bit.'

'I will if you want.'

'Fair enough. I'll put the money up, but yer pay me back, mind.'

'Yes, Lloyd, thanks Lloyd.'

'Right, wash that blood off and get some clothes on. Let's get out of here before the dirty bastard gasses us.'

CHAPTER FIFTEEN

The phone interrupted Sam's sleep and, when he looked at the clock, he knew it would be Owen.

'Owen, it's half past bloody five. This had better be really good.'

'Did you hear about the double murder in Leeds the other day?'

'What?' Sam sat up and tried to clear his head. 'What double murder?'

'In Leeds, two Asian brothers.'

'What? Oh, yeah. What about it?'

'One of them was my informer. It's bothering me, Sam, that it might have had something to do with me. If Bowman warned the drug dealers off he might have given them the lad's name.'

Sam was wide awake now. 'Bloody Hell, Owen! Bowman's a prat but he'd hardly get mixed up in a murder.'

'Maybe he got himself in too deep with these people.'

'Owen, you're making it up as you go along. It's more likely to do with the lifestyle these lads lead.'

Sam was telling him this simply to ease Owen's feelings of guilt. Sam knew all about such feelings. But he wasn't convincing himself.

'Do you really think so, boyo?'

'I really think so, Owen. Anyway, this sort of thing goes with the territory.'

'If it does, I'm not sure I like this territory, Sam. The lad was only nineteen.'

CHAPTER SIXTEEN

Alec wasn't usually given to dramatics, so when he rang Sam to tell him they'd unearthed a murdered man, Sam took him seriously – until he got to the site and found the murder to be only circumstantial and in any case it had happened many years ago – close on a thousand, as he would find out later.

The skeleton was eight feet under the

ground in a trench they were digging for a sewer connection. The ground was solid clay, undisturbed, certainly in recent centuries. The bones must have been there for quite a while. Sam knelt down and took a good look from the top of the trench. It was still poking out from under the clay, completely intact, apart from the skull which lay a couple of feet away

'When I saw the skull I got Mick and Curly to hand dig around the rest of it without disturbing it too much,' Alec explained.

'Why didn't you tell me it was an ancient stiff?' Sam asked.

'Because I wanted you here, pronto. And now you're here I want you to take it seriously. He was killed by an arrow. You can see it inside his ribs.'

'Seriously? It's bit late to get serious. He could have been killed by Robin Hood, for all I know.'

'We're supposed to report this to the police,' Alec said, 'who'll report it to the council who'll report it to some archaeological organisation who'll deem the whole site an ARCHI.'

'What's an ARCHI?'

'A site of archaeological and historical interests.'

'My God, you know some stuff you do, Alec. Where d'you get that from?'

'It once happened to me in York. York's a

dodgy place to go digging. Most York builders who find bones throw 'em to the nearest dog. Otherwise these ARCHI people'll close the site until they've dug everything up.'

'Right.'

Sam climbed down into the trench and examined the skeleton more closely. There was an arrow lying between its ribs. All the clothing had rotted away, apart from a belt buckle.

'We can't throw this to a dog, Alec.'

'We can't stop the job for God knows how long, either.'

'Surely they won't do that.'

'They might, Sam.'

Sam looked at the skeleton once again. 'I don't know if it's man or a woman.'

'I reckon it's a man.'

'He's not very tall.'

'They weren't in them days.'

'What days?' asked Sam.

'That's what the archaeologists'll want to find out – and they'll want to know if there's any more bodies lying around. They be looking for artifacts and coins and stuff. The job won't be worth a bean to us.'

Sam looked up at his partner. 'What are you saying, Alec? We can't just pretend we haven't found it.'

'Why not?'

'Because you told me about it, that's why not. If you thought it was OK to pretend you hadn't found it you wouldn't have bothered telling me. Who else has seen it apart from Mick and Curly?'

'No one. I've told them to keep it to themselves until I spoke to you.'

Sam looked over to where the two Irish groundworkers were shovelling concrete. 'We could relocate it,' he said.

'Relocate?'

'Shift it,' said Sam, 'to somewhere where it doesn't get in our way.' He looked down at the skeleton. 'I don't suppose Archie'll mind.' He called the two Irishmen across. 'This is Archie,' he said to them, 'and I want to move him without disturbing him.'

'He looks fairly undisturbable ter me,' commented Curly. 'A good feed o' cabbage and bacon might liven him up.'

'I tink he might be dead,' said Mick. 'A man with his head dat far away from his body would struggle to swallow his food.'

Sam ignored them. 'And I want it doing without anyone knowing,' he said. 'Do you think that's remotely possible? I want him transplanting to the far side of the site where any future archaeologists can dig away to their hearts' content. If anyone finds out we've shifted him, the job stops.'

'And your jobs with it,' added Alec, ominously.

'Dat's no problem, boss,' Mick assured them.

'Well, I don't suppose a few more years underground'll make much difference to yer man,' commented Curly. 'He's prob'ly lost all track of time, anyways.'

'Could be a woman,' said Mick. He looked a bit more closely. 'I definitely tink dat's a woman. If she had more teeth she'd have a nice smile on her. Tell ye what, if she's a woman she's better lookin' than the wife.'

A trench of a similar depth was dug at the far side of the site, well away from all the building work. Sam chose its location with a purpose in mind that he didn't reveal to Alec because he thought Alec would pick holes in his idea. Many of Sam's ideas didn't stand up to close scrutiny.

The skeleton was moved after the rest of the men had gone home. Mick and Curly dug out beneath it with far more care and expertise than any amateur diggers would be capable, a door was slid under it and Archie was lovingly transferred to his new resting place and buried with reverence. Mick and Curly said a couple of Catholic prayers over him – or her – before they filled in the new grave.

Sam waited until everyone had gone, then walked around the site – a group of industrial units they were building for a large development company. Because of his firm it was growing from an area of waste ground into a living, almost breathing, place. A real place where people would work and do business and talk and argue and laugh and earn money. Not for the first time he wondered why he kept turning his back on such a useful and rewarding job in favour of the dangerous and often seedy world of the Sam Carew Investigations Bureau. Like everyone else in this world he'd end up like Archie, a pile of bones that, in a thousand years, someone might find inconvenient. You only get one life, why make it so difficult? Christ! He wasn't even a cop anymore. It'd do no harm, he thought, to go back on the tools for a while, if only to clear his mind.

The sun had been shining for five consecutive days, which was a record for Unsworth. Owen was moaning about global warming and had even appeared in the Clog and Shovel in shirt sleeves. Sam thought it was the first time he'd ever seen the Welshman's arms, and weren't they hairy? CID had made no progress on the hammer murders and Bowman had decided there was no connection between the two – mainly because of who suggested it – and had instructed the team to ignore the Henshawe case as it was already solved.

This left Sam struggling to raise any enthusiasm for the case and he knew, deep down, it was because he didn't trust himself to see Alison again. If that got out it wouldn't be long before Sally got out – out of his life. Owen knew something had gone on between Sam and Alison but he didn't ask about it. There were enough skeletons in his own cupboard without him rattling someone else's. In the meantime Sam had gone back on the tools and was happily laying bricks.

He had his shirt off and the sun was on his back, things were going well and, once again, he was wondering why the hell he bothered with this private eye stuff. He wasn't sure if he'd done more harm than good in the time he'd been at it; he'd certainly done Sally more harm than good. Alec, who had been his business partner almost from the time the firm had been left to Sam by his dad, was happy having Sam back on the team. Radio 2 was blaring out of a portable radio sitting on a pile of bricks and the gang were doing the backing vocals to *Any Dream Will Do*. Then the news came on and they switched off their attention as effectively as someone switching off a hearing aid. An item pierced Sam's consciousness and he took a step towards the radio to listen better:

'The walker, who found the body, told our reporter how the man was just lying there with a blood-soaked towel over his head. He asked the man if he was all right and when the man didn't respond the walker lifted up the towel and found the top of the man's head looked to have been "smashed in", to use the walker's own words.

156

The police who are treating the death as suspicious...'

One of the labourers laughed. 'Head smashed in and they're treating it as suspicious – not much gets past them lads.'

Sam perked up like the disillusioned golfer who's on the verge of dumping his clubs in a nearby lake when he hits a screaming drive straight down the middle of the fairway. His problems are forgotten and his enthusiasm for the game is back. He put down his trowel and stabbed Owen's number into his mobile.

'Owen, I assume you've heard about the bloke in Manchester who's had his head smashed in...? No? Well, it's just been on the news ... found by a walker who says the man was lying with his head covered by a blood-soaked towel. Look, you must have the Super's ear on this, after the Mrs Henshawe thing.'

'Bowman's given the connection theory the elbow.'

'That doesn't make it any less credible. Have a casual word with the Super before anyone else gets in. Just mention that it wouldn't surprise you if the Manchester MO didn't match the other two, right down to the type of hammer used... Owen, sod the proper channels, and sod Bowman! I need you to be put on this case in some capacity and I'm sure you wouldn't object to it yourself.'

They met three days later in the Clog and Shovel. Sam didn't want to endure the obvious distraction behind the bar in the Pear Tree. Owen opened the conversation with: 'Alison's been asking after you. She say she has further information for you if you'd like to get in touch with her.'

'Did you ask what sort of information?'

'I did. She said it was of a very confidential nature – I wouldn't mind her taking me into her confidence, boyo.'

'She can always ring the office,' said Sam.

'That's what I told her but she said she enjoyed the personal approach you took last time.'

'Did she?'

'Those were her very words, boyo. I'm sure if she passed that same message on to you via Sally it might convey the wrong impression.'

'Owen, what have you got for me?'

Owen gave one of his toothy grins. 'Janet Seager's been made up to DI. She's been given the Unsworth murder and I'm doing the legwork for her.'

'So, you mentioned the Manchester killing to the Super?'

'I did, and there's a definite connection to the Unsworth killing.'

'Aha.'

'So, we're liaising with Greater Manchester.'

'And would they have connected the two killings so quickly if you hadn't mentioned the similarity?' asked Sam, who didn't like his invaluable help to go unappreciated.

'It's doubtful, but I didn't give you any credit for giving me the idea.'

'Good man, and as a reward the Super suggested that you be put on the murder team?'

'It was never actually said, but I imagine it had something to do with it.'

Sam beamed. 'Me, you and Janet, eh? Owen, we could crack this between the three of us. What have you got so far?'

Owen sipped at his pint. 'Nothing you don't already know. Both victims were male, mid-thirties and naked. Neither were robbed or sexually assaulted or put up a fight and both were struck by a single blow delivered to the top of the head with a heavy hammer – according to you, a ball pein hammer. In each case the blow smashed through the skull right into the brain. Death will have been instantaneous.'

'Mrs Henshawe certainly wasn't naked. Wrong sex, wrong age, fully clothed, same town, same weapon, same injury.'

'Which all adds up to–'

'Same killer, different motive. There's no serial killer pattern.'

'There's the beginnings of a pattern as far as the police are concerned,' Owen said. 'They're looking at two out of two, you're looking at three out of three.' He finished his drink with a flourish and placed it where Sam could see it. Sam took the hint and signalled to Dave the landlord to bring them two more pints across.

'It's not waiter service,' called out Dave.

'No, but I've got this great joke if you bring them over,' said Sam, cheerfully.

'There's something else the forensics people found out,' Owen said. 'Both the recent victims had sex not long before they were killed.'

'Bloody hell!' said Sam. 'How the hell could they know that?'

'It was quite rough sex, apparently,' Owen explained. 'There was some genital bruising, and burst blood vessels in the organ.'

'Went out happy, then.'

'The strange thing is,' said Owen, 'that there's no sign of any residue left by the sexual partner. Whoever the partner was took great care to wipe away all traces of themselves. Bowman thinks it could be the early work of a serial killer.'

'Surprise, surprise – has a profiler had a look at it?'

Owen nodded. 'With both victims being heterosexual the profiler thinks the killer is either a woman or a woman working with a man.'

'Really?' said Sam. 'My money's on Torvill and Dean – always thought there was

160

something very sinister about them.'

Owen ignored him. 'The woman will be physically attractive, probably white, mid-twenties to mid-thirties.'

'I think I could have worked that out without a profiler,' said Sam. 'What about social group, personality, size, shape, hair colour, nationality, introvert, extrovert, lunatic, maniac, psychopath, sociopath, neuropath, garden path...?'

'Their analysis is still in its early stages,' said Owen.

'What do *you* think?' asked Sam.

Owen felt guilty at not being able to come up with a bright idea. He eventually shook his head.

'Serial killers,' said Sam, 'usually go for certain, vulnerable types – old people, prostitutes, children, gays. I mean it *could* be a serial killer, but if we bring Mrs Henshawe into the equation it kind of knocks that theory on the head. She was killed as part of a robbery – a very strange robbery I grant you, but her and her husband's killings weren't the work of a serial killer. They were killed by professionals, the same as these latest victims. What we have here, my leek-eating friend, is a contract killer who's found a cheap and efficient way to bump people off. Maybe she has an aversion to guns.'

'So,' said Owen, 'all we have to do is find a woman with a hammer in her handbag and we have our killer.'

'Could be,' said Sam, 'or it could be that she decides the old hammer method has run it's course – especially if the papers make a meal of it. Time for a change of MO.'

'You keep saying "she",' said Owen.

Dave arrived with the drinks. Sam paid him and was about to resume his conversation with Owen when he noticed Dave hadn't moved.

'One great joke, please,' Dave said.

'Ah,' said Sam. 'What's orange and sounds like a parrot?'

Disappointment was already showing on Dave's face.

'A carrot,' said Sam.

Dave picked up the two pints, did an about turn and took them back to the bar. Owen smiled, but not at Sam's joke. Sam went to the bar to retrieve the drinks. 'That was only the beginning of the joke,' he said to Dave. 'You'll never get to hear the end now. It's the best joke of all time.'

Dave shrugged. 'I'll just have to wait till it comes out on video.'

Sam took the drinks back to the table. 'Miserable sod!' he muttered.

'I heard that!' Dave shouted.

'You kept saying "she",' repeated Owen.

'What? Oh, right.'

Sam held his pint up to the light to check for cloudiness. Dave saw him and knew Sam was trying to wind him up. He pulled the best pint in Unsworth.

'Stop trying to antagonise the landlord,' grumbled Owen, 'and tell me why you're so sure the killer is a woman.'

'Well,' said Sam, 'both victims are heterosexual and neither was sexually assaulted. Both were naked, which makes it odds on that whatever sex they had would have been with a woman. All forensic traces the woman would have left had been wiped away. Is that a job you'd like to do, Owen? Give a dead man's wedding tackle a good old wash and brush up? Most men would shy away from such a job – I'm not sure a feller would even think of it. Believe me, it was a woman on her own who did that. She was responsible for the man being naked, she provided the sex to make him drop his guard – and his pants, covered his head with a towel on some pretext or other – probably sexual – and delivered the death blow. Then she wiped away any evidence she might have left on the body. She would neither have wanted or needed a male accomplice. Contract killers almost always work alone – especially a woman with this MO.'

'She wasn't working alone when she killed Mrs Henshawe,' Owen pointed out.

'She was when she committed the actual murder,' said Sam, 'and that was nine years ago. My guess is that the killer's still a young

163

woman – attractive enough to pull these two victims – so, when she did Mrs Henshawe she must have been nine years younger. I think when she killed Mrs Henshawe she was working with a gang. Whoever it was, trusted her to do the job – most likely a family firm.'

'Hellfire, boyo! You make it sound like the Cosa Nostra.'

'She's definitely got connections from nine years ago,' mused Sam, rubbing his finger around the perimeter of his glass. 'Has she gone solo or is she still linked up to a gang?'

Owen stared at him, awaiting the answer. Sam took a drink of his pint then did a double take of his friend.

'What?'

'You were about to tell me if this woman has gone solo or is she still with a gang?'

'Owen, this is a pint pot, not a crystal ball. How the hell am I supposed to know the answer to that?'

'I thought you were on a roll, boyo.'

'I was just making sense of the facts. We have no facts regarding associates.'

'Nor do we have any facts regarding motive,' said Owen, wanting to make a contribution.

'Of course we do – the motive is profit,' said Sam. 'What we need to find out is who profits from these two deaths? Were they married?'

'One of them was – the Manchester man

whose body was found the other day. I believe the widow has been interviewed and is suitably distressed.'

'Had she got him well-backed?'

'I believe his company had him insured for a considerable sum, but there's nothing out of the ordinary in that. The first victim was divorced, living on his own – not a wealthy man by all accounts.'

'Someone definitely profits from these deaths,' said Sam. 'The first victim is in your patch, I should check all beneficiaries of his death – even potential beneficiaries.'

'Potential beneficiaries?'

'It's a beneficiary who hasn't benefited yet. Maybe he, or she, was second in line, up to our boy being popped off. Now they're first in line, waiting for rich Uncle Rupert to fall off his perch.'

'Maybe when we track down rich Uncle Rupert we should keep an eye on him,' said Owen.

'Maybe – or maybe it's something completely different. But the first place to look is into his background. Assume he wasn't a random victim; assume he was selected to die for a reason – which isn't forced to be financial. We find that reason and we should find the beneficiary of his death – once again not necessarily a financial beneficiary. Could be a scorned woman, a vengeful man, our victim could have been a person whose very existence was an embarrassment – or even a danger to someone.'

'Such as?' Owen posed his question as a challenge to which he didn't think Sam would be able to rise.

'Well,' mused Sam, 'he could be the lover of a married woman, threatening to reveal himself as the father of her child, or he could be a bishop's son, only he's not because he's just discovered his real dad's the chief rabbi, or–'

Owen stopped him before he got into full flow. 'OK, I get the picture.'

'Finding the beneficiary of our victim's death,' Sam went on, 'is our best chance of finding the killer. Dig deep, Owen, and share this new found insight with Janet Seager. Oh, and could you find out who the Manchester victim's insurers are? I need a legitimate reason to interview the grieving widow.'

'At some point DI Seager's going to know you're working on the case from the outside,' Owen said. 'What shall I tell her?'

'By that time I'll probably be working for a reputable firm of loss adjusters, quite legitimately, on a no result, no fee basis. You can tell Eager Seager that I'm still battling with my frustration that she and I aren't sexually compatible.'

'By all accounts she's got a new girlfriend,' said Owen. 'So I wouldn't tease her if I were you.'

CHAPTER SEVENTEEN

Sam wore his second best suit over a plain white shirt and a tie from George at Asda. It was an outfit befitting an insurance representative. It crossed his mind that had he worn a hat he could have removed it with a flourish when Mick's wife came to the door and thereby display a measure of good manners which would instantly disarm her. But this only worked with trilbys, homburgs and bowlers, which they didn't sell in Asda. He made do with a friendly smile. She wasn't expecting him.

'Mrs Crowther?'

'Yes?'

'My name's Carew, Mrs Crowther. I've been sent here by Hepworth and Heaton who are acting as loss adjusters for the Manchester Victoria Insurance Company. There's just a couple of questions I need to ask you before the matter is resolved.'

'Oh, right, yes. Won't you come in?'

He followed her through to her living room which was full of condolence cards. 'Thank you, Mrs Crowther. Oh, and may I offer my condolences. I know it's a sad time, but the quicker we can get things in order the quicker we can get out of your hair – unless you'd like me to leave it until you feel up to answering a few simple questions.'

This last remark was designed to throw her off her guard – giving her the impression that whatever he had to ask her wasn't so important that it couldn't wait. In fact she was the one who didn't want to wait.

'Will it take long?'

'I'll be as brief as I can, Mrs Crowther.'

'If you would, my baby needs feeding and I have to pick up my son from nursery in an hour.'

Sam heard the squeak of a sleeping infant coming from a cot in the corner of the room. He stole a peek and smiled at the child.

'I assume it's a little girl.'

Mrs Crowther nodded. 'Her name's Rosie. Mick loved her to bits.'

'I bet he did, Mrs Crowther,' Sam's voice held genuine sympathy. At the moment it was only his suspicious mind that told him this woman was party to her husband's murder. And Sam had been wrong before.

'Look, I know you've been asked all sorts of questions by the police about Mick's friends, acquaintances, enemies etcetera.'

'I have,' she confirmed, 'and to be honest I'm sick of answering questions Mr Carew.'

'It's just that his death was so...' he purposely hesitated because he wanted to get the maximum reaction, 'so premeditated.'

'What?'

He saw a hint of guilt flash across her face. Had she been innocent it would have been a hint of annoyance – more than a hint – but her annoyance, when it came, was too late for it to be genuine.

'What are you suggesting, Mr Carew?'

He held up his hands. 'I'm not suggesting anything, Mrs Crowther. I'm just hoping to go back to my employers with answers to some of their questions. Do you mind if I sit down?'

'Please do.'

She sat down as well, on the chair opposite. He frowned, trying to frame his next question delicately. 'Look, er, I can't think of a tactful way to say this, but...'

She finished it for him. 'My husband had sex just before he died.'

'That was sort of it – yes.'

'I know that, Mr Carew – and it doesn't make his death any easier to take. Obviously I don't know the circumstances but I tell myself that the sex must have been forced upon him by the killer. Mick would never be unfaithful to me.'

'No, Mrs Crowther, I'm not suggesting he was. I was wondering, do you have a photograph of him? The reason I ask is that I've no idea what he looks like and I always feel that I ought to at least have some acquaintance of the person I'm enquiring about. It's probably me being silly but–'

'I'll see if I can find you one.'

She got up from her chair and went into another room where Sam could hear her opening and closing drawers. Eventually she came back with a photograph that had three young men on it.

'Mick's the one on the right,' she told him.

Sam looked at it with studied interest, then he gave it back to her. 'He was a fine looking man.'

'Is there anything else I can help you with, Mr Carew?'

He got to his feet and held out his hand for her to shake. 'No thank you. Like I said, my coming here is just a formality. From here on in things will run their natural course.'

'I don't suppose you know how long it'll take for my er, my money to come through?'

She was trying to make it sound as though a payout of half a million pounds was very much secondary to her grief, but Sam detected the masked greed in her voice.

'It's actually got nothing to do with me,' he told her. 'But once I send my final report in it shouldn't take long.'

'Right,' she said, uncertainly.

Within a minute of Sam leaving she picked up a pay-as-you-go mobile and dialled a number that connected her, almost immediately, on to an answering machine that gave no identification but asked for any message to be left after the beep. She took a deep breath as spoke as calmly as she could.

'This is Mrs C. You asked me to notify you if there was any come-back. A man from the loss adjusters came round. I'm not sure he believes me. His name is Carew. I do hope my money comes through. The thirty thousand I gave you was all borrowed on credit cards.'

She clicked off the phone, sat down, and for the first time since Mick's death she cried, but the tears weren't for her husband.

Sally looked up as Sam came into the office. 'A chap from the loss adjusters has been on – he wants you to ring him back. You haven't been harassing that woman, have you?'

'Harassing? I was unbelievably charming. Can you get him for me? What's his name?'

'Mr Heaton, he gave me his direct number.'

She dialled the number. 'Mr Heaton? I've got Mr Carew for you?'

Sam took the phone and said, in a business-like fashion that raised one of Sally's eyebrows, 'Carew'.

Heaton sounded tetchy. 'Mr Carew, we've had Mrs Crowther on the line. She's accusing you of being very insensitive. If nothing else you could have advised her that you were coming and not just turn up out of the blue. She's suffering a great loss.'

'Mr Heaton, if I'd given her warning she'd

171

have had photographs of her dear departed all over the house, with maybe a burning candle or two thrown in. As it was she didn't have a single photo of him on display and when I asked to see one she had to go rooting through drawers to find one.'

There was a pause before Heaton responded. 'Not everyone bothers to display photographs.'

'Mrs Crowther does. I saw photos of her kids, her relatives, herself, even one of George Clooney, but not one of her husband. I found that a bit odd, Mr Heaton.'

'Well, maybe they weren't happily married, it's no reason to suspect fraud.'

'The only way she can have committed fraud, Mr Heaton, is if she had her husband murdered, and I think her husband was killed by a contract killer. The fact that she rang you up and accused me of being insensitive tells me she's a frightened woman – I wasn't insensitive in the least.'

Sally's eyebrow went up again. There was a long silence from Heaton, eventually broken when he said, 'Are there any further investigations you can carry out?'

'It's really a police matter from here, Mr Heaton. I'll send you my full report for you to pass on to the insurers. I would advise that the money isn't paid until the police make further enquiries. Personally I think if the police bring her in for questioning she'll crack. She was very dithery when I spoke to her, and I wasn't accusing her of anything.'

Tanya listened to the message from Mrs Crowther being played to her by her mother.

'This Carew's beginning to really piss me off.'

Tanya shrugged as if the solution was obvious. 'And...?'

'OK, take him out, but you don't do this one alone.'

Sam had barely put the phone down on Mr Heaton when his phone rang. Tanya spoke to him in the strong Scouse of her child-hood. She had smoothed off all the rough edges since then, but she could switch it back on when needed.

'I know who Mick Crowther was with the night before he got shot.'

'Who is this?' asked Sam.

Tanya used the name Mick to establish her familiarity with the dead man. 'Me name's norrimportant. I know who the tart was, though – is it worth anythin'?'

'How did you know to ring me?'

'Diane Crowther's a mate o' mine. She told me yer'd been ter see her. Hey, don't tell her I've rung yer.'

'How can I? I don't know who you are.'

Tanya giggled. 'That's right, yer don't, do yer? I reckon the name's worth a monkey. It might not be worth nuthin', but it might be worth a lot more than a monkey.'

Sam pondered for a while, wondering if the loss adjusters might underwrite the extra five hundred on the off-chance of saving their clients half a million.

'Where shall we meet?'

Tanya was ringing him from less than a mile away but she suggested the car park of a closed down, country pub, in the back of beyond about ten miles east of Burnley – a forty mile journey for both of them.

'When?'

'Midnight ternight.'

She rang off before he could argue against such an unearthly hour. He dialled 1471 on the off-chance that he'd get her number and wasn't surprised to hear that the caller had withheld it.

He put the phone down and exhaled a lungful of breath. Many implications were hitting him at once, not the least of which was that he might just have been talking to the killer. Or it might have been genuine, or it might have been a crank caller, or–

'Who was it?' Sally interrupted his thoughts.

'What? – er, it was a woman who says she knows who Mick Crowther was with the night before he was murdered. She wants five hundred for the name.'

'Why not just tell the police?'

Sam nodded. This was probably a most sensible idea. 'She might not give the police the name without the five hundred.'

'I thought the police had a fund for that sort of thing?'

'They'd be reluctant, in case she's needed as a witness. Paid informers don't make credible witnesses.'

'Ah, rules and regulations, eh?'

'She wants to meet me in a fairly deserted place in Lancashire. I'm not sure she's telling the truth.'

'What did she sound like?'

'Scouse.'

'You can't tar them all with the same brush. My dad came from Liverpool.'

Sam didn't share his fear with Sally that the caller could be the killer. He picked up the phone to ring Heaton, then had second thoughts. For some reason he felt that this was a meeting he needed to go to without anyone knowing – except Sally. If it turned out that the five hundred was well spent he'd screw an extra couple of grand out of the insurers.

CHAPTER EIGHTEEN

'Take Lloyd with yer.' Tanya opened her mouth to protest, but Annie silenced her with a warning hand. Tanya took the warning. 'Sort out between yer who does what. I don't wanna take no risks wi' this Carew feller.'

'OK, Ma, but I want you to make it plain to Lloyd that he does as I tell him.'

'I'll make it plain. Just don't fart around with Carew. Do whatever yer have ter do, but do it quick and do it smart.'

'Ma, give me some credit – I know the job.'

'Yer don't know Carew.'

'Neither do you, Ma.'

'I've made it me business ter know. He'll be the smartest mark yer'll ever have.'

The car park was paved but overgrown. Weeds grew through the tarmac and the stone boundary wall had been partially stripped by passers-by wanting nice stone for a fireplace or a rockery. The derelict pub had been cannibalised by passing DIY enthusiasts. Many of the roof slates were missing plus some of the roof timbers and all of the lead. The windows had been too tempting not to throw stones at; not one was intact.

Tanya and Lloyd arrived an hour early. She wanted to be definitely there first, even if Sam was of like mind. Lloyd tried the pub door. It was locked. He poked his head through one of the broken windows and sniffed the foul air inside. It seemed to be the home to some sort of animal. Being a city dweller he didn't know what but the smell was strong enough to keep him out.

'Smells like the Gents in the Dog and Gun.'

Tanya took a quick sniff and wrinkled her nose. 'Foxes,' she said. 'They're not all as cute as Basil Brush.'

'We might as well wait in the car till we see his lights,' said Lloyd.

'*I'll* wait in the car,' said Tanya, 'you wait over there in the shadows.'

'What's the fuckin' point?'

'The point is that he's unpredictable. He's going to be suspicious. He might even come in the back way on foot, or on a push bike – he might even drop in by parachute.'

Lloyd looked up at the night sky. Tanya shook her head. 'I was kidding about the parachute. I just want this to go right.'

'OK,' said Lloyd. 'How do we do it?'

'We do it by expecting the worst case scenario. It's what *he'll* be expecting. He won't even switch his car engine off until he thinks it's safe to do so.'

'I could do with him right in the middle of the car park,' Lloyd said, 'so I can get a clear shot at him.'

'Shots,' corrected Tanya, emphasising the plural. 'I want you to empty the gun into him, the last two from close range into his head – but you don't start shooting till I say so. I mean that, Lloyd.'

'OK, you're the boss – for tonight.'

She told him how she planned on getting Sam out of the car. The plan seemed to amuse Lloyd. He took a Crombie overcoat from the back seat and disappeared into the shadows. Tanya waited in the car.

Sam had bought himself a sat-nav box which one of his sons had installed in his Mondeo. Without it, he had to admit to himself that he could have been driving around all night before finding the remains of the Pendle Arms on Tollerton Hill. As it was, he arrived at five past midnight, having underestimated the time it would take him to get there.

He was kicking himself, as he'd planned on arriving first, then getting out of his car and taking some form of cover from where to watch her arrival. Some plan. A silver Toyota Camry was already there. Sam parked, facing the exit, about twenty yards away from the Toyota. He wound his window down but kept his engine running and made no move to get out. There were clouds about but plenty of clear sky in between, and the three quarter moon was bright enough to illuminate the car park. For a while there was no movement from the Toyota and Sam didn't want to make the first move. An owl glided across the moon, momentarily taking Sam's eyes with it. A voice called out to him from the Toyota.

'Mr Carew?'

'Yes.'

As far as he could tell there was only one person in the car, but he could be wrong.

'Do yer want ter come to me or shall I come ter you?' Her accent was Liverpudlian.

'I'm sorry to be so untrusting,' Sam called back. 'But for all I know you could be the person who killed Mick.'

'Could I – oh, right, I suppose I could.'

'I need to know that you're not armed and that there's no one with you.'

'Jesus, if I'd known I'd have ter go to all this trouble I'd have asked fer a bleedin' grand.'

Sam moved his car so that his headlights shone broadside on the Toyota.

'Would you get out and leave the front and back doors open.'

Tanya stepped out of the car and moved to one side so that he could see there was no one with her. She was wearing her tinted glasses, a blonde wig and an ankle-length sable coat. It did occur to Sam that there might be someone waiting in the derelict building or in the shadows. He was fairly sure that this killer worked alone – but you never know for certain.

'I need to know you haven't got a weapon on you.'

'What, yer mean like a hammer?'

'I mean like anything.'

'How do I know *you're* not armed?'

'I'm Sam Carew, not Wyatt Earp.'

Tanya shaded her eyes with a hand and smiled into his headlights. 'Actually, I'm way ahead of yer, Mr Carew. Mick's wife told me yer were a tasty feller so I thought yer might be up fer a bit o' fun after we've done the deal, like.'

She shrugged out of her coat and stood there, naked. It took Sam aback. She had a magnificent body, pretty much on par with Alison Kilpatrick, who had also offered herself to him on a plate. Had he become irresistible upon the advent of middle age? No way was she going to seduce him, but it did mean he wasn't quite as alert as he might have been; the possibility of an accomplice went right out of his mind. Tanya was banking on that. She walked, slowly, towards him and turned to fully display her body and to prove she was carrying no weapons. Sam killed the engine, switched off the lights and got out of his car. He definitely had no intention of taking her up on her offer. All he wanted was a name, a description and as much information as she could supply. Tanya now turned and walked back to the Toyota.

'Not the car,' called out Sam, who didn't want her anywhere where she might conceal a weapon.

'Yer a suspicious man, Mr Carew. I just don' fancy rollin' aroun' on the ground that's all. We can do it in your car if yer like.' She was still walking as she talked.

'I don't want to roll around anywhere,' Sam said. He was now standing by her coat. She was about ten feet away. He picked it up and checked it for a weapon. Satisfied, he handed it to her. 'You can put your coat on, now.'

'Oh dear.' She had shed her scouse accent as easily as she had shed her coat. 'I was hoping to get your juices flowing, Mr Carew. Nudity, and mortal danger.'

His heart gave a nervous judder. 'Mortal danger?'

'To your left, Mr Carew. Small man with big gun pointed at your head. He's going to kill you in a few seconds and I thought it only fair to give you a last thrill before you died.'

Her mother would have been very displeased at this. The order should have already been given and Sam should now be dead. She shouldn't be chatting to him. Tanya knew that, but she felt an odd desire to enjoy this man's company for a few seconds before he died. He wasn't the normal, run-of-the-mill mark. This man was special. On top of which he didn't look terrified, so she wasn't being cruel to him by delaying the inevitable. She didn't regard herself as a cruel person. Unfeeling, ruthless, merciless – but never cruel.

Sam looked to his left as Lloyd stepped out of the shadows, holding a handgun with both hands, legs spread, pointing the gun at him. Tanya still hadn't put the coat on. 'Do you have an erection, Mr Carew?' Her eyes glanced downwards to check.

Adrenaline was hurtling through Sam's body. This was a very bad situation. What the hell did he do now? Talking to her might give him time to think. Talking to her was the only thing he could think of. He got the impression that the man would pull the trigger only on her instruction. He fixed his eyes on her. She smiled and he noticed a slight gap between her two front teeth. Odd the irrelevant things you notice in dire circumstances. Other than that she was quite pretty.

'I assume it was you who murdered Mrs Henshawe.'

'She was old, it was more like euthanasia.'

'I'm waitin',' called out Lloyd, impatiently.

Tanya thrust out an arm in Lloyd's direction; one finger raised, telling him to hold his fire for just one moment.

'You're trying to keep me talking, Sam. It's what I would do in your plac–'

Sam let out an ear-splitting scream that took both Tanya and Lloyd aback. It was a variation on a theme he'd used over the years. Act deranged. No one knows how to handle deranged. It troubles even the most psychotic of opponents. *It was the real reason he was called Mad Carew.*

As he screamed he sprang towards her. By the time Lloyd had recovered from the initial jolt to his concentration Sam was behind Tanya, with his arms around her, lifting her off her feet and pushing her towards her brother who was trying to get a clear shot in. Tanya was screaming, 'Shoot the bastard!' as Sam was heaving her forward. Lloyd moved to one side and took aim. Sam turned with him, keeping the struggling Tanya between them. The adrenaline feeding Sam's muscles increased his strength by a hundred per cent. There was a shot. Tanya screamed and went limp. Sam dropped her and flung himself at Lloyd. They were now fighting at close quarters, which gave Sam an advantage. He grabbed Lloyd's wrist, the one holding the gun, and forced it back into Lloyd's face. All Sam wanted was for this to end with him still alive. No holds barred now. With his other hand, he squeezed his thumb into the trigger guard, behind Lloyd's finger. The gun fired, the bullet went upwards, through Lloyd's chin and out through the top of his skull, leaving an exit wound the size of a fifty pence piece, through which shot blood and brains. Lloyd froze for a second, a dreadful gurgling sound came from somewhere within his destroyed head, then he collapsed, like a marionette no longer supported by its strings. Sam staggered backwards and sat on the ground, covered in a liberal smattering of Lloyd.

Tanya had reached her car, blood was pouring down her left arm from where a bullet had creased her shoulder. It was painful, and her arm was rendered useless so she couldn't do much to improve the situation. Lloyd's situation looked way beyond improvement.

Sam was remembering his part in pulling the trigger. It was he who had made the gun go off. To all intents and purposes he had killed this man, whoever he was. It had been a necessary killing – a him or me situation – but it was Sam who had pulled the trigger. It was all he could think of.

From behind he heard a car starting up. The Toyota sped out of the car park leaving Sam looking at the corpse and wondering what the hell to do now. After a while he got to his knees and muttered a prayer that he'd remember from his Catholic childhood.

'Eternal rest, grant unto him, Oh Lord, and let perpetual shine upon him. May his soul and the souls of all the faithful departed, through the mercy of God, rest in peace.'

The agnostic in him told him he was a fraud but, once a Catholic always a Catholic, that's what they say. He then began to cry because, no matter what the circumstances, it was another person who had died because of him. The man wasn't a good person and Sam didn't even know his name. But the man was dead because of Sam, and Sam hated him for that, so he ended his prayer with, 'Amen – you bastard!'

It eventually occurred to him that if anyone were to come across them at that moment he would be in trouble – trouble he might struggle to talk himself out of. It was his duty to report what had happened to the police, but if he did would they believe his explanation? Possible, but it wasn't a certainty, especially if Bowman's advice was sought. Owen's theory about Bowman being bent crossed Sam's mind. This time he didn't dismiss it so readily.

What was his story? He played devil's advocate with himself: a mystery woman had arranged over the phone for him to meet her there to give him information that might lead to Mick Crowther's killer. So, why hadn't he simply told the police about the meeting – let them pick her up and deal with it? If the police didn't like that bit of his story what about the rest? The naked woman who had set him up. For what reason, Mr Carew? Hmm, best not mention she was naked. The gunman who was about to kill him. For what reason, Mr Carew? How come you managed to take the gun off him and shoot him through the head? If there were two of them how did you manage to do all that? He realised it was possible that they might not believe a word of his story. His poor reputation with the police was a hindrance in many ways.

The moon disappeared behind a heavy cloud, as if drawing the final curtain over the drama. Then it began to rain. Sam got up and went back to his car. By the time he got inside the rain was heavy, as it often was in the foothills west of the Pennines. His mind began to clear. If he'd left evidence of himself at the scene the rain would wash it away. He tried to think of any evidence he might have left behind. Had he dropped anything? He felt inside his pockets. His wallet was still there despite the fight. Had anything dropped out of it? 'Sod it!' He didn't know for sure. He took a torch from the glove compartment and went back to where Lloyd lay. Nothing. No evidence of any kind. Rain was bouncing off the old tarmac. A puddle was beginning to form underneath the body. He retraced all the steps he'd taken earlier and found nothing. No evidence of him or the woman. SOCO and forensics wouldn't waste too much time out here. The rain would wash away any tyre tracks, any footprints, all evidence of anyone else ever having been there. Right now it was washing all traces of Lloyd off Sam. It might well be thought that the man had killed himself. It occurred to him to search through the man's pockets to find out who he was. After what he'd just been through he really didn't fancy the idea, but he knew he had to.

A shot rang out just as he was leaning down over the body. A split second earlier and it would have hit him in the head. Sam flung himself to the ground, but not before a second shot caught him in his side, spinning him over and placing Lloyd between him and the gunman – or gunwoman. It could only be the woman. He had the flashlight in his hand, identifying his position. He hurled it away as far as he could, then rolled further into the looming darkness. As the torch hit the tarmac it went out. Sam was thankful, it meant she might not be able to use it. The pain in his side was excruciating. Another shot ended in a thud as it hit Lloyd. Sam rolled over a couple more times, then waited for the pain to subside. It didn't. He allowed himself a low moan. The rain was heavy, drowning any noise he was making. Just behind him was a wall, part of which had been reduced almost to the foundations by stone scavengers. He crawled over the rubble and along to a part of the wall that was still intact. Giving him a place to hide, to give him cover. Through the rain there was just enough light to distinguish the odd shape, the odd movement. It meant he must now keep still, movement was what she'd be looking for. He caught sight of her walking away from him, into a field. About three yards away the wall abutted the back wall of the pub, maybe if he could get in there, out of the rain if nothing else. She obviously thought he'd run off into the night. He crawled, painfully, through the drenching rain, looking for somewhere dry and safe where he could gather his thoughts and try to save his life. There were three shots in quick succession. He saw the flash of the muzzle about fifty yards away.

'Oh, shit! Why don't you leave me alone, you bloody woman!'

His protest was heartfelt but, muttered under the wind and rain, unheard by his assailant. Two bullets zinged off the pub wall; a third thudded into something that squealed in pain then dropped from a window and lay still. She was running towards him now; he could do nothing but lay there and hope for the best. He had no strength to fight. If it came, please let it be quick. At least this pain would go. But it was a poor place to die – and bloody awful weather as well. It had never occurred to him that he would die in bad weather. She ran within two yards of him, stopped outside the window, kicked at the prone fox and then glared around into the looming darkness. Sam lay as still as a stone, his pale face away from her, blessing the wonderful cover the night and the rain gave him. She looked inside the pub window and decided that an unarmed Sam Carew would have more sense than to corner himself inside an enclosed building against an armed adversary. Normally she would have been right.

She wandered around, indecisively at first, then went back to the car park. Sam just wanted to be out of the rain. He had his mobile on him and was hoping he'd get a signal in this god-forsaken place. He got to his feet and, using the wall for support, managed to get to the window that had framed the unfortunate fox in Tanya's sights. There were shards of glass sticking out of the frame. He managed to ease them out of the disintegrating putty so there was nothing there to add to his wound. The pain, and maybe the situation, made him vomit. There was nothing he hated more than being sick; it even took his mind off his wound for a few seconds. He wiped his mouth with his sleeve and he pulled himself over the window sill. The pain of his landing on the hard floor sent him instantly unconscious. He lay there for several minutes before coming round. The pain was there but the rain wasn't – at least not where he was lying. He spotted two pairs of eyes, looking at him from the far side of whatever room he was in. They were wondering how long it would be before their mother came back. Sam looked back at the eyes. He summoned up a smile and said, 'Hello and goodbye.' He might as well be friendly to the last living creatures ever to see him on this Earth. Pity he couldn't see what the eyes belonged to. Just four frightened eyes, large and round, dilated pupils framed in green. There was a stench of what he thought might be cat pee, only these weren't cat's eyes. He studied the eyes just as they studied him, and he ran through all the animals they could possibly be, before coming to the conclusion that they were young foxes. Foxes stank to high heaven. Mystery solved. He didn't want to die wondering what they were.

What a way to go. Dead of night, soaked to the skin, miles from anywhere, in a broken down pub, hastened on his way by the stink of fox pee. He'd have swapped his death for Nelson's any day of the week.

Where was *she?* Has she gone? Had she not realised how badly she had wounded him? How *could* she know? For all she knew he could be miles away by now. The thought gave him comfort. But he needed more than comfort, he needed an ambulance, he needed a blood transfusion, he needed a bloody miracle. Don't just lie here and die, you idiot, give yourself a chance. He reached in his pocket and took out his mobile.

Owen was number 4 on his speed dial,

which was handy because he couldn't have summoned up the energy or the memory or the concentration to have dialled the whole number. The time on the illuminated screen said 00.28. It rang eight times before Owen answered.

'Owen, it's me.' Sam's voice was little more than a croak. It aroused enough concern to stop Owen complaining about the hour.

'Sam?'

'Owen, I've been shot. The odds are that I've had it. A woman shot me.'

'Where are you, Sam?'

'I'm in ... in Lancashire...' He felt his strength fading. 'Sally knows ... aaagh!'

He let out a squeal of pain as something fell on him, landing on his wounded side. He passed out.

'Sam, are you OK ... SAM?'

All Owen could hear on his landline was the frightened barking and wailing of the fox cubs as the mortally wounded vixen returned to her young only to drop down dead on top of them. The Welshman kept the phone to his ear as he dialled Sally's number on his mobile.

CHAPTER NINETEEN

Tanya was sitting in her car. The bleeding had stopped, but she was as mad as hell. This was all Lloyd's fault. He should have popped Carew the second he screamed like a madman. Fancy allowing himself to be shot with his own gun. What a wanker! It occurred to her to ring her mother but, right at that moment, she couldn't stand the aggro. One thing at a time.

She knew that if she left Lloyd here it would only be a question of time before he was identified. She knew Carew hadn't got around to doing that – she'd stopped him just in time. When Lloyd was identified and tied in with Mick's killing the next obvious step would be to look for the female accomplice. And they wouldn't have to look far. Pity Lloyd hadn't done a job on Carew. He couldn't have been so badly hit or he wouldn't have had it on his toes so fast. Christ! Her mother will be spitting chips when she finds out.

No point worrying about that. She needed to get Lloyd away from here. Take him home where he could be disposed of at leisure. In secret, but with dignity – the same as Lewis. Maybe they could put him on top of Lewis. Bloody hell! Doing this with one arm's going to be tricky. Good job she had brought Lloyd and not Nathan.

Tanya reversed the Toyota up to her brother's body and flicked open the boot. She hooked her good arm beneath Lloyd's armpit and heaved him upwards, cursing with the effort and the pain. Nathan used to joke that Lloyd only weighed ten stone wet through. Well, he was wet through now and he weighed a bloody ton.

It took her several very painful minutes to heave him into the boot. She slammed it shut and looked across at Sam's car, then through the pounding rain into the surrounding darkness. For all she knew he could be watching her; waiting to follow her. She patted her blonde wig that had remained in place throughout – that would throw him if he ever tried to describe her. He'd have memorised the registration number, which didn't matter – the car wasn't traceable to her. She went over to the Mondeo and found the keys in the ignition. It was something. She took them out. He couldn't follow her and he didn't know who she was or where she came from, and he'd struggle to recognise her even if they came face to face. It had left the way clear for her to have another attempt. Next time there'd be no mistake. She congratulated herself that at least her professionalism had paid off. Shame about Lloyd.

It was doubtful if her mother would be offering any congratulations. Miserable old cow.

Annie didn't shed a tear over the death of Lloyd. The only tears she'd ever shed in her life were over the accidental murder of her son Lewis, and over the death of her pitbull terrier, Spike; destroyed after the police raided a dog fight in which Annie's dog had fatally maimed its opponent, winning Annie £500 and 28 days in prison.

Lloyd was dead and that was part of the game they were in. Tanya had taken none of the blame herself. She never blamed herself for anything. Instead she had blamed it all on Lloyd for missing Sam with his first shot and hitting her. Annie had believed her.

'Yer can't afford ter make a mistake with a feller like Carew. I've had word that he's in Burnley hospital, still in intensive care. Could be that yer've done the job. We'll have ter wait an' see.'

'What about Lloyd, Ma? He's still in the boot of the car.'

'We need to bury Lloyd privately and get rid of the car,' mused Annie. She paced up and down, with Tanya's eyes watching all the way. She was relieved her mother had taken Lloyd's death so well, she had anticipated violent repercussions. In her mind she hadn't lied to her ma over the killing. As she'd driven home she'd merely rescripted the incident and allowed herself to be convinced that this was how it actually happened. It was a faculty she'd developed over the years as a substitute for a conscience. A conscience was a luxury in this business.

Annie seemed to have come to a decision. 'We'll give the lad a decent send-off. It'll have ter be private, naturally. Just the family an' mebbe our Graham. I'll say a few words. I know as much o' that bible bollocks as any o' them bleedin' vicars.'

'If it's bollocks, why bother with it, Ma?'

'Because yer never know, girl, yer never know. He wasn't a bad son – a bit of a pillock at times but at least he was front door merchant and that's no bad thing. Never stuck his key in the back door like our Lewis. Can yer remember how deep we planted Lewis?'

'Fairly deep. Lloyd went a bit mad with that mini-digger we hired, if you remember.'

Annie laughed. 'Bugger me, I do, silly sod. If he'd gone any deeper he'd have struck oil. I wonder if he'd have been so bloody eager if he'd known he was diggin' his own grave.'

'What? You think we should plant Lloyd on top of Lewis?'

'Why not? We'll not need a digger this time, the earth'll be fairly soft. Our Nathan can do the donkey work. Do him no harm ter work up a sweat.'

'Does he know about Lloyd?'

'Not yet. I don't think there was too much love lost between them two.'

It occurred to Tanya that there wasn't much love lost between any of them. The only Robinson who had generated any sort of affection from the family was her dad. He had left behind a legacy that seemed to be causing more trouble than it was worth. Had it been left up to Tanya, she would have honoured his wishes even after his death. Not so the rest of the family. They seemed to think his death gave then carte-blanche to go for revenge. Dad had felt no need for revenge so why did the rest of them?

CHAPTER TWENTY

Sam woke up that evening. It wasn't the first time he'd woken up in a hospital ward so he didn't wonder where he was. Someone would no doubt fill him in on the details. They usually did.

A young nurse was busying herself with a drip, and Sally was sitting in a chair reading a newspaper. He watched them both through half-closed eyes and he felt himself smiling. He couldn't help but smile, because he was alive. He closed his eyes again and tried to remember what had happened to him. Piece by piece he put it all into place, even down to the eyes in the dark. The fox cubs. The last thing he remembered was speaking to Owen, and struggling to stay conscious. Then there was this thud, and then...? He remembered a brief moment, just before oblivion, when he thought this was it. Goodbye cruel world. But here he was. He opened his eyes again. Ready for them. He opened his mouth to make a wise-crack. Nothing came out.

'I think he's awake.'

The voice was Owen's, although Sam couldn't see him. The nurse filled his field of vision, leaning over him. Sam tried to talk again. The nurse gave a shake of the head.

'Don't try and talk too much, Sam.'

Talk too much? To be able to say the odd word would be nice. He could see Sally now, propped up on her elbow crutches, her face was a mask of concern. Owen was hovering over her shoulder, munching what sounded like a Hob Nob.

'You've had a long operation,' said the nurse, 'but you've come through it all right.'

Sam managed to mouth two words. 'Which hospital?'

'Burnley General. It's half past six in the evening. You were picked up in the very early hours of this morning.'

Owen's toothy smile loomed into view. 'The police will want to talk to you, boyo, as soon as you're fit enough to talk.'

Sam swivelled his eyes around and said, 'OK.' His voice was audible now. Then he turned his gaze to Sally and said, 'Thanks.'

'It's Owen you should be thanking, not me. He's the one who called the ambulance.'

'Without you, the ambulance wouldn't have known where to go,' Owen pointed out.

A thought came to Sam, 'You haven't told the boys have you?'

Owen and Sally looked at each other.

'You have,' guessed Sam.

'I had to tell Sue,' Owen said. 'She brought them – which was only right and proper considering...'

'Considering what?'

'Considering we didn't know how serious you were,' chipped in Sally. 'You took a bullet in your side. It went straight through your body, smashing a couple of ribs but missing every vital organ. You were incredibly lucky.'

'I thought I was incredibly dead for while.'

'She left as soon as she knew you were out of danger,' Sally went on, 'but not before she did her nut – putting the boys through this again.'

'Gone? Where's she gone?'

'Gone back to her husband. I don't suppose he's too pleased with you, either.'

'No, I don't s'pose so.'

'Sue's obviously still got a thing for you, that's why you're unpopular with him. Tom and Jake will never accept him while you're around. Jonathan seems a good enough bloke, but you're just too much competition for any new husband.'

Through his pain Sam preened. 'Am I really?'

'Please don't take it as a compliment, Sam. It's just a piece of friendly advice. Anyway, Sue's of the same mind as me. It's time you got out of the private dick business.'

'Oh, really? And who was it who persuaded me to go back into the private dick business?'

Sally took his hand. 'If it was me, I was wrong. I'd forgotten just how much trouble you get yourself into. Seriously, I think you should pack this one in, Sam. Let the police sort it out from here.'

It seemed a convenient time for Sam to go back to sleep. Owen went back to Unsworth. Sally stayed. Sam knew she would.

She was there when two uniforms from the Lancashire Constabulary came to take his statement. As he'd been found at the scene he saw no advantage in lying to them, although telling the whole truth to the police did go against the grain a bit. A constable had taken down his statement but a sergeant was doing all the talking.

'So, what you're saying, Mr Carew, is that one man is definitely dead as a result of a fight you had with him, and the woman who'd arranged the meeting is probably wounded – but not so badly wounded that she managed to take a few pot shots at you?'

'I want it noted,' said Sam, 'that the man shot himself with his own gun. I didn't pull the trigger. It went off during the fight.'

There was no point telling them he had deliberately forced Lloyd's finger on the trigger. Sometimes, as they say, the devil is in the detail. Dealing with the guilt of that was punishment enough; it would stay with him for a long time.

'Could you make a note of that, Constable?' said the Sergeant.

The Constable duly made the note. The Sergeant sat in a bedside chair and nodded across at Sally who was sitting at the other side. She returned his nod and added a smile.

'We actually have a bit of a problem with all this, Mr Carew.'

'What problem's that?'

'The absence of a corpse. And with the rain we had last night any evidence of one ever having been there isn't going to be easy to find.'

Sam nodded. 'She'll have taken it with her.'

'Very resourceful lady, this, heaving a dead body into a car after she's been shot. Why would she do that, Mr Carew?'

Sam did his best not to sound scornful, even though the answer was obvious. 'I, er – I think the body might have been a clue to her own identity.'

The Sergeant stared at him for a while, wishing he hadn't asked such a stupid question. He hadn't taken to this Carew bloke, not one bit. Pain in the arse, these civilian meddlers. Even if he was ex-job.

'There's no tyre tracks,' the Sergeant said, 'and the only body we've found is that of a fox what was lying dead not far from where we found you.'

'Sergeant, I had this man's blood all over me. I assume this is being looked into by your forensic people – or is forensic science a bit too advanced for you Lancastrians?'

Sally cringed. The Sergeant tried to think of a smart response, but couldn't, not quickly enough. Sam asked him, 'Had it been shot?'

'Had what been shot?'

'The fox.'

'We believe so.'

Sam remembered. 'She shot the fox thinking it was me.'

'She mistook the fox for you?' The Sergeant turned, to the Constable. 'Perhaps my memory's playing tricks. Do you remember it being a very big fox, Constable?'

'No sarge – very much an average size fox, maybe even a bit undernourished.'

'Not an easy mistake to make, then,' commented the Sergeant, who was beginning to see why this Bowman bloke in Unsworth disliked Carew so much.

'Mistakes are easy to make in the heat of the moment,' said Sam. 'Are the cubs all right?'

'Cubs, Mr Carew?'

Sally smiled and shook her head. He wasn't playing games. He was genuinely concerned about the cubs. Typical bloody Carew, this.

'It doesn't matter,' said Sam.

'So, apart from an undernourished dead fox, with human characteristics and a bullet hole in it, we haven't got much to work on, Mr Carew.'

'Well, it's really lucky I've got a bullet hole in me, or you'd think I was making the whole thing up,' retorted Sam.

'It's quite possible you might be making *something* up, Mr Carew.'

Sam patted his breast, *mea culpa* fashion. 'Yeah, it was my fault entirely. I probably just caught her at a bad time, poor woman. If you see her, you will apologise on my behalf, won't you, Sergeant?'

'I think you're being facetious, Mr Carew.'

'And I think you're talking out of your arse, Sergeant. Either that or you've been talking to DCI Bowman in Unsworth, which pretty much amounts to the same thing.'

'DCI was good enough to try and help. He put us in the picture about you.'

'How the hell did he find out?' Sam answered his own question. *Bloody Owen. Why can't you keep things to yourself?* 'Well,' he said, 'my statement is the truth as I remember it, Sergeant. I'll give you full descriptions of both the man and the woman and I suggest you get hold of the Greater Manchester Police and get them to interview Diane Crowther – this time a bit more forcefully. All this sprang from me interviewing her on behalf of her late husband's insurers.'

'Can you prove this, or is it conjecture?'

The Sergeant really didn't like being told his job by this bloody man.

'It's called stating the obvious, Sergeant.'

It annoyed Sam that Bowman's influence could travel so far. Maybe he should have shopped him over the building site thefts, and maybe Owen should have mentioned his suspicions about Bowman and the drugs bust to the Super. The DCI certainly wouldn't have done Sam any favours.

'We may need to speak to you again, Mr Carew.'

'I'll try and be in.'

The policemen wandered off and Sam turned to Sally. 'Have I got a dishonest face or something? The buggers don't believe me.'

'I think they've been told to take what you say with a pinch of salt,' she said.

'What they're saying is, it's open season on Carew. Someone takes pot shots at me, nearly kills me, and the coppers spring into action like coiled sponges. They're only interested in me when they've got a chance of nicking me.'

'Sam, that's why it's all so pointless. Why put yourself through all this when there's no payoff at the end of it?'

He thought about this for a long time as Sally hobbled outside for a smoke. When she returned he had an answer, of sorts.

'I'm doing it, Sal, because it needs doing. There's a bloke in jail for two murders he didn't commit and I'm partly responsible for him being there. On top of which, there's a contract killer out there who the cops think is a serial killer and if I can prove she's a contract killer I might get some cash out of the insurers. And I'm doing it because it's going on under everyone's noses and only I seem to know about it.'

'Maybe the police just don't want you to be right again,' she suggested. 'You've made them look idiots a couple of times in the last two years.'

'You mean they'd rather these killings go on than have my theory proved right and their theory wrong? Bowman thinks it's a serial killer and he'll have everyone else believing the same – by the way, Owen thinks Bowman's bent, and I'm inclined to agree with him.' He hadn't meant to tell her until he was certain, but he saw no reason why she shouldn't know.

'Bent in what way?'

'He thinks he warned a gang of drug dealers about a raid. If it's true he could also be partly responsible for two murders.'

'That's ridiculous, Sam.'

'I know,' conceded Sam. 'He's a prat but I doubt if he's bent. I do know one thing, Bowman's serial killer theory is wrong. I know I'm right about this.' He looked at her, searching her face. 'Do *you* believe me, Sal?'

'I believe *in* you, Sam. I don't believe every word you say.'

'Come on, I never lie to you, Sal.'

'Sam, you just have.'

It made him smile. She often did.

Diane Crowther was interviewed but she had simply acted dumb – as per the instruction passed along the chain from Tanya. Sam figured a bit of clever and forceful interviewing would have forced the truth out of her, but he also knew that his reputation wouldn't encourage the Manchester police to do anything that might show him up in a favourable light. He blamed Bowman for that.

He talked Burnley General into transferring him to Unsworth General, where he would spend a week before being allowed home to convalesce. From his bed he sent the loss adjusters a letter saying he hadn't finalised his report and that, despite what the police might say, there was a definite connection between Diane Crowther and the attack on him and that until he finalised his investigation he advised that no money be released to her.

CHAPTER TWENTY-ONE

Annie hated funerals more than most. The last had been her husband's. She'd been made to feel grateful that his body had been released from jail in order that she could bury him. He'd been a good husband when he was at home. He was the father to just one of her four children but he only knew about Nathan, who was born before he and Annie met. Tanya was his, but Lewis and Lloyd had different fathers. If George suspected, he never mentioned it. He had treated all his children with great affection. She'd never told him the truth about Lewis's death and had sworn the kids to secrecy. She didn't know what he would have hated most, the fact that his son was queer or the fact that she'd killed him. George Robinson had died thinking his second eldest son had done a runner and that was OK by him. His wasn't a model family.

He'd admired Lewis for striking out on his own although he didn't tell Annie that. Of all his kids, Lewis was the one who didn't take after Annie, thank God. He'd married her because of that weird chemistry that sometimes envelopes people who would otherwise hate each other.

Nathan had gone into the TV room to watch *Coronation Street* with his uncle Graham, Annie's brother. Annie stood in the doorway and swilled the Scotch down in one go as she realised just how little she mourned Lloyd; and how much she despised her sole surviving son, and how much she missed George – and Lewis. Jesus! She missed Lewis, but not Lloyd. Her gaze strayed to the screen as her mind strayed over her bad fortune.

The theme music played and an overhead camera zoomed in just as a tram clattered over the viaduct at the end of *Coronation Street*, which was situated – according to the camera shot – among dozens of similar streets.

'I think I'll have a drive over there one o' these days,' said Nathan, who was glued to the screen. 'I wouldn't mind walkin' down them streets – most famous streets in the world, them are.'

'It's only one street,' said Graham, 'the rest is computer graphics. No tram, nothing. It's very clever the way they do it.'

'Bollocks,' said Nathan.

'I'm tellin' yer, I've been there – workin' as an extra. I spent many a day there, walkin' up and down that very street – I thought I'd told yer.'

'I wish yer fuckin' had,' Nathan said. 'I'd have come with yer. What's it like?'

'Small – it's actually built to about three quarter scale. The inside o' the *Rovers* is about as big as your kitchen. Yer couldn't gerra snooker table in there, much less a pub with all the living quarters. All the interiors are shot in the studio next door.'

'Nah, that's got ter be bollocks,' said Nathan.

'I'm tellin' yer lad – look, take the door to the pub toilets, where does that door lead to? Straight into Ken Barlow's kitchen, that's where it leads to. Am I right or am I wrong? Funny how people never figure that one out. How come he never complains about people havin' a piss in his kitchen sink? It's all illusion, yer see.'

Nathan laughed. The screen went blank. Both men turned to see Annie holding the remote. 'I wish this were a fuckin' illusion,' she rasped. 'My son's dead and all yer can do at his wake is watch bleedin' telly an talk about Corofuckination Street.'

'I meant no disrespect, Annie,' said Graham, quickly. 'The telly was already on, I was talking ter Nathan, that's all.'

'What? Tellin' him all about yer great show business career? Earl fuckin' Gray. Third rate club comic an' TV extra.'

Graham stiffened, and anger blazed. She was his younger sister and a real hard case, but he was the only person in the house who wasn't scared of her.

'I make an honest living, Annie. I don't hurt anyone, never have. I stuck up for you against our dad. Took quite a few slaps that you should have taken, for stuff that you'd done – so don't you dare look down on me and my job.'

Annie backed down beneath his anger. She wasn't scared of him but she wanted his respect. The respect she got from other people wasn't proper respect, it was fear. Graham was the only person in the world who had ever shown her proper respect. The respect of a brother for a sister who had survived the same violent upbringing. Outside the immediate family he was the only one present at Lloyd's wake. He had been instructed not to breathe a word of this to anyone. He was trusted to do this and he knew better than to ask questions. Lloyd had been shot in circumstances that might incriminate Tanya and that was enough for him. Annie managed to turn her scowl into a smile.

'Sorry, Gray, I'm norrat me best terday, like.'

'I understand, Annie. For a mother to

209

bury her son isn't how things should be. Especially with you already having lost one lad, so to speak.'

Annie looked at her brother, wondering what the hell he meant by that. As far as she knew, Graham thought the soft son had had it on his toes.

'What do you mean, *so to speak?*'

'I mean he's disappeared from your life. I don't suppose you ever heard from him?' he asked, guilelessly.

'No.'

'Must be ten years now.'

'Eleven.'

Annie really didn't want to talk about it. The rent boy had been disposed of in an incinerator she had access to. Lewis was buried beneath Lloyd. It was a done deal, she couldn't change it. She had a life to get on with and moping about dead sons wasn't going to help. There was a warped core within her that allowed her to cope where a normal mother would be consumed with guilt.

Tanya was sitting on her own in the drawing room, staring out of the window in the direction of a piece of disturbed ground in the distance, under which her two brothers lay. They would never be declared missing or dead, just gone away. Who would bother to ask for details? She couldn't think of anyone who might summon up sufficient interest. She looked up when her mother came into the room.

'Tan, I've had word of a contract that might interest you. It's down in the Midlands and I've quoted forty grand.'

Tanya raised an eyebrow at the amount. There were people in Unsworth who would kill a man for a grand – and end up getting sent down for life, along with their client. The difference was that she offered complete efficiency and reliability.

'It's nice to be appreciated. I don't suppose we know any details.'

'None at all, neither mark nor client. Doubt if we'll get to know the client.'

'That's how I prefer it, Ma.'

She cursed when she realised Jeremy Bostock was gay. This information had not been passed down the line, which, to Tanya, was criminal negligence. She sipped on a vodka and tonic as she rang Annie from inside the gay club in Wolverhampton. Her contracts came via two intermediaries, the second of whom was her own mother, who would always have a solid alibi on the day of the hit. The other intermediary was a man who called himself Mr Small. Tanya had met him but his real identity was known only to Annie.

'He's as bent as a nine bob note, Ma. How

come I wasn't told?'

'Queer? Are yer sure?'

'Well, I'm in club called Tasty Dicks and he's got his tongue down a young lad's throat. I look upon that as a clue.'

'Jesus! I wasn't told that,' said Annie, disgusted. 'I'll make an enquiry.'

'Ma, with him being an uphill gardener my tried and tested modus operandi is completely unsuitable.'

Annie went quiet as she translated what Tanya had just said. 'Does this mean yer don't want ter do it?'

Her daughter thought for a moment. 'Ma, I believe people should pay for their mistakes. Tell Mr Small I want an extra ten grand – and that's a personal bonus. If they don't want to pay up they can look for another contractor.'

'That's fair enough, girl. Do nothing until I make the call and get it cleared.'

'You should also make a strong complaint. In future I need full information on a mark. I don't need surprises like this.'

At 9.45 a.m. three days later, Jeremy Bostock parked his Mercedes-Benz SLR McLaren in the private parking area of an office complex car park in the centre of Wolverhampton, clicked it locked from the remote fob and made his way to the exit stairs. He spurned the use of the lift as the entrance to his office was just one floor below.

Jeremy's first glimpse of Tanya was the top of her blonde wig as she came up the steps towards him. She stood to one side on the landing and fumbled in a plastic carrier bag, allowing him past.

His mind was already in his office – on the phone call he needed to make to Nigeria regarding an oil deal he was having problems with. He was doing his best to break all his ties with the Nigerians, who operated way beyond the laws of any civilised society. At first he'd seen the advantage in this but now, even in the safety of an office in the English Midlands, he was beginning to feel twitchy. He certainly wouldn't be taking any more trips to Kano. Since they adopted Sharia Law his business interests in that part of the country had taken a right kicking.

He had descended just one step when Tanya struck him on top of his skull with as fierce a blow as she had ever delivered. He collapsed and died, instantly and silently, spraying blood and sprawling downwards on the concrete stairway. Tanya stepped quickly past him and hurried down the ground floor, passing no one on the way. She didn't expect to. She knew from her observations that the stairway was rarely used at that time. In the club she'd over-heard him say he didn't like the hustle and bustle of rush hour. Well, there wasn't much hustling and bustling where he was now, so she'd done him something of a favour.

By the time she had reached the ground floor she was wearing a black, hooded coat she'd been carrying in her carrier bag. The coat covered any blood splashes, hid her face, and disguised her gender from prying cameras. She strode along Victoria Street with hands stuffed deep into pockets, head down, with the shoulder-thrusting action of a street-smart hoodie.

She had checked the positions of the ubiquitous CCTV cameras. In the street, in shops, stores, office blocks, pubs, cafés, shopping malls, all linked up to one another by the various security firms who had great fun passing on shots of local scallies from one to the other, with security guards gleefully lying in wait as their earphones told them a known shop-lifter had entered their store. She couldn't even hop on a passing bus without being videoed. This was no place for a girl in her line of work, she needed complete privacy. Previously, her marks had *insisted* on such privacy, thus helping her to snuff them out with friendly efficiency. Out here, in front of all these cameras, it was like being on the six o'clock news.

No one would actually be looking for her yet, but she knew that the progress of a hitherto unknown hoodie might well be noted and passed on.

She strolled down a back street which she knew contained no cameras and, more importantly, it contained the street entrance to an NCP car park where she'd parked her van. She had already ascertained that there was no camera between the door and her van. Outside she heard a police siren and correctly guessed that Jeremy's body had been discovered. Once inside the back of the van she took off the coat, changed her blood splattered shirt and jeans and wiped any blood specks from her face with a wet tissue. She then donned a pair of Raybans, left her blonde wig on, and five minutes later she was out of the car park heading east, looking for a sign that would take her to the M6. In the unlikely event of the van being picked up on camera she had the comfort of knowing it was untraceable to her. Such attention to detail meant she could look forward to a long, untroubled career.

For his part, Jeremy had crossed the people in his nefarious business dealings and, just for a while, those people had become Tanya's employers, despite her not knowing them, nor they her. It was the best way.

CHAPTER TWENTY-TWO

DCI Bowman stared at the email attachment he'd just received from Wolverhampton. It was a photograph of the body of Jeremy Bostock, a middle-aged businessman. The cause of death of the victim was identical to the ones in Unsworth and Manchester, the only differences being that there was no towel over his head and he was fully clothed and was known to be homosexual. Bowman picked up the phone and spoke to a DCI from the West Midlands police, then called in DI Janet Seager. By the time she arrived he'd printed off the photograph. He handed it to her.

'What's this, sir?'

'I think it's victim number three. Our serial killer might have moved down to the Midlands – Wolverhampton.'

'*Might have*, sir?'

Bowman shrugged. 'The MO's slightly different. Could be a coincidence, but I doubt it. The weapon and the injury are identical to the other two. One theory is he could be a truck driver or some sort of travelling salesman.'

'Or sales*woman*,' said Janet, with Sam's

recent experience in mind.

'It's a theory. For the time being we'll call him *he*. We'll give *him* a sex change once we've got him.'

'If *he's* operating all over the country,' said Janet, 'won't we have to hand it over to the National Crime Squad?'

'As I said, we're not absolutely sure if it's the same killer – however...'

'What, sir?'

'This latest victim was er, gay.' Normally he might have used a stronger word but with Janet being a lesbian he stopped himself in time. 'Which means it might not have been too easy to get him naked.'

'Which strengthens the theory that it's the same killer, and it's probably a woman.'

'I think the word is *possibly*,' corrected Bowman, 'but until the NCS take over – that's if they do take over – with the first crime being committed on our patch, it's still our case. We take the lead and the other two police authorities will work with us.'

Janet hesitated before saying, 'It could be that this killer has more connections with Unsworth than with Manchester or Wolver-hampton.'

Bowman gave a slight nod, without looking at her. 'I assume you mean the bookie's wife?'

'The Super said not to discount it, sir. Mrs Henshawe had the identical hammer wound *and* the towel.'

Bowman gave the idea a full minute's consideration as he inwardly cursed DC Price's unwelcome contribution to his brainstorming meeting. 'It might be worth another look,' he said, reluctantly, 'but that's all. I can't afford to have a full team looking around Unsworth for a killer who was last heard of in Wolverhampton, and Manchester before that. I want you and Price to start digging. If you come up with anything we'll put a bigger team in, if not we'll hand it over to the NCS.'

'And will you tell the NCS about the bookie's wife, sir?'

It would be tantamount to an admission that there might have been a miscarriage of justice, but now that Janet had mentioned it he knew he had no option. 'Of course I will,' he said, irritably.

She turned to go and was stopped by a parting remark from Bowman. 'Just one thing ... and I shouldn't need to be saying this.'

'What's that, sir?'

'Do *not* involve Carew.'

'I don't think he's in any fit state to become involved, sir. He's still in hospital.'

Bowman became agitated. 'No fit state? Rubbish! He's like bloody Lazarus is Carew. He's taken one bullet, big deal! If he'd been standing outside Hiroshima town hall when they dropped the bomb he'd have come out of it with a bit of earache. I mean it, Janet. DC Price stays on the case only because he's the Super's blue-eyed boy, but if either of you involve that pillock Carew, you're both on school crossing duty. Have I made myself clear, DI Seager?'

'I think so, sir.'

Sam was out of bed, in deep, animated discussion with his fifteen-year-old twin sons, Tom and Jake, who had been to see the latest *King Kong* film. Sam always found their enthusiasm very persuasive and was wondering if he could manage to sit through it without too much pain. Jake had a suggestion.

'I know someone who can get me a pretty good pirate copy.' Owen arrived just as Jake was speaking. Sam feigned shock.

'Jake Carew! I'm a law-abiding citizen – besides it wouldn't look the same on my 21" Samsung. Anyway, we'll speak later. Owen and I need to talk. Take this fiver and don't spend it on cigarettes.'

The boys grinned and got up to go. They exchanged pleasantries with Owen, whom they'd known for what seemed like forever, and wandered off to find a porter they had befriended and persuaded him to invest the fiver on their behalf, on the second favourite in the 2.30 at Kempton Park.

Owen sat down and opened the wrapper

on a Mars Bar. Sam took a box of Quality Street, that the boys had brought him, from his bedside cabinet and put it in his drawer.

'There was no need for that,' said Owen.

'It's called removing temptation. Last time you came you polished off a whole packet of Midget Gems that Sal brought me. So, what's the score with the murders?'

'Bit of good news,' said Owen. 'Bowman's agreed to let us tie in the Henshawe murders. Janet suggested it and he could hardly refuse with it being the same MO.'

Sam grinned and rubbed his hands. 'I bet that went against the grain,' he looked at Owen, expectantly. '...and?'

'And what?'

'And what progress have you made?'

'Uuuuh?'

Owen spoke with a mouthful of Mars Bar, which Sam always found irritating. He waited until the Welshman swallowed.

'Progress, have you made any?'

'Not yet, boyo. This isn't a Sherlock Holmes story. DI Seager's got bogged down with a really nasty armed robbery.'

'Yeah, I heard about that.'

'In the meantime she's asked me to do a bit of legwork. You know yourself these things take time.'

'Sometimes, Owen, you've got to give time a kick up the arse. This bloke who was murdered in Unsworth, what do you know about him?'

'What do I know? I know I'm under very strict instructions not to involve you.'

'You're not involving me. You're here as a friend. Anyway, I have an interest in the Unsworth murder because it's linked with the Manchester murder, which I'm investigating on behalf of an insurance company. Did you check on who profited from his death?'

Owen took another bite of his Mars Bar, which meant he didn't have an immediate answer and needed time to think. Sam breathed, deeply, to control his patience, which had been in short supply during his convalescence. He spoke as his friend chewed.

'Owen, I want you to keep in mind that you are, without doubt, dealing with a contract killer. Not a serial killer, a contract killer – big difference in detection methods. If it's the same person who did this to me – and I'm thinking it is – it's a young woman, about five eight, early twenties, nice body. She had blonde hair when I saw her, but it might have been a wig.'

'Would you recognise her from a mugshot?' Owen enquired.

'Doubt it. It was fairly dark and she was wearing dark glasses – might have been part of a disguise.'

'Why would she need a disguise if she was

certain of killing you?'

'Good question. I don't know; force of habit; belt and braces. I'd recognise her voice again, though. She disguised that at first, then spoke with her own voice right at the end. It was almost as if she wanted to end things on a friendly note. Quite weird, really.'

'The man who was murdered in Unsworth, his name was Corbally – Austin Corbally.'

'Owen, I do know that. It was in the papers. What we need to know is everything about him. His family, his work, his friends, his enemies. Did he have a gambling problem? Was he a womaniser? Was he involved in drugs? User or dealer? Does he have any rich relatives about to die, stuff like that. And find out who benefits from his death.'

Owen nodded along with Sam's list, then asked, 'And how would I go about finding all that out?'

Sam shook his head in exasperation. 'By being a detective. Owen you don't seem to have fully grasped the principle of crime detection.'

'It was your idea that I should go into CID, boyo. Had you not made the sun shine out of my reluctant rectum I wouldn't have got the job. I'd have been where nature intended me to be – in a smart uniform, walking around under a big helmet, maintaining law and order.'

This desire of Owen's to get back into

uniform was most inconvenient to Sam. He needed Owen to have freedom of movement, if only until he resolved this case. Luckily, Owen always responded to flattery, or so Sam thought.

'Owen, you have an innate talent for CID work – if only you knew it. Have confidence in yourself.'

'Carew, you are the world's biggest bullshitter. I have confidence in myself. What I suffer from is a lack of confidence in you. You make me nervous.'

'You're exaggerating, Owen.'

'Exaggerating? You ring me up in the middle of the night and all but tell me you're dying and you accuse me of exaggerating.'

'I *was* dying – you saved my life, you Welsh oaf. If you don't believe me, ask the doctors.'

'I *know* you were dying, you Yorkshire pillock, that's what makes me nervous!'

Sam lay back on his bed, puzzled. 'So, what the hell are we arguing about? God, I'd hate to have you for a wife, you're worse than Sue for picking fights out of nothing.'

Owen sat down, his eyes were flooded with annoyance and emotion. 'Sam, you're my best mate and you give me more grief than my worst enemy. I was scared when you rang, really bloody scared. So was Sal when I rang her.'

'Who's that then?'

'Who's what?'

'Your worst enemy?'

'I don't bloody know – but he gives me less grief than you.'

Sam held out a hand for Owen to take. 'I'm just a bit unconventional, that's all – as are you in your own way, especially with the ladies. So you can hardly blame me for being like you. Anyway, give Sal a ring. Ask her for a few ideas about how to check out Austin Corbally's background. She can be inspirational when she puts her mind to it.'

Annie Robinson was reading the front page of *The Sun,* which carried the story of Britain's latest serial killer. She wasn't impressed.

'Yer've got people thinkin' yer a nutter, lass. This ain't right. Yer a professional, not a nutter. I don't like this one bit.'

Tanya stuck to her guns. 'Come off it, Ma. This'll have the coppers running round in circles. They can't think laterally.'

Annie continued to read. 'It says here that the police are not yet ready to confirm that all three killings were carried out by the same person ... and it says here that there might be a connection with a murder that took place back in 1997, but it doesn't say what.'

'Good,' said Tanya. 'It'll all add to the confusion.'

'If they believe there is a connection it might have them pinpointing where you live, with the first two killings being in

Unsworth,' argued Annie.

'They won't push the Henshawe theory too hard, Ma. It'd mean they cocked up when they banged Kilpatrick up – and the bizzies don't like admitting to cock-ups. Anyway, I don't live in Unsworth, I live in Leeds, near enough. Ma, the beauty of all this is that the bizzies don't know where to look next, any more than I do. There's no connection between the marks, other than the connection I manufacture.'

'The clients know it's not a serial killer,' Annie argued. 'They'll be able to keep tabs on all the jobs you do. Not sure I like that.'

'Ma, what's not to like? If anyone's guaranteed to keep shtum, it's our clients.'

Owen had read through the Austin Corbally file and made notes to take to Sam. It was a thin file and contained more forensic notes than CID reports. He had been found naked and dead in a field two miles south of Unsworth, in almost identical circumstances to Mick Crowther. He had no immediate family apart from a son. Parents both dead, wife killed in a car accident, which had been Corbally's fault, with him being over the drink drive limit. He'd served five months of a nine-month sentence and had initially lost his licence for five years. This had been subsequently reduced to three and a half as it affected his job as delivery driver and was therefore having an adverse effect on his son.

'Where's the boy now?' Sam asked him, after reading the notes. It was his first day back at home and he was being looked after, to the best of her ability, by Sally, who was now getting around on a single, elbow crutch.

'The De La Salle Children's Home,' said Owen. 'Sounds a lot posher than it is. I checked with Corbally's former employers, with his neighbours and some of his former friends, but there's nothing at all remarkable about him – other than he'd become depressed as buggery, which is also unremarkable under the circumstances.'

'So,' summed up Sam, 'he was just an ordinary bloke doing an ordinary job who'd had a bit too much to drink one night, crashed his car and ruined his life. Then someone comes along and puts him out of his misery. What does Janet think?'

'DI Seager thinks the whole thing's a dead end. Corbally's a most unlikely target for a contract killer.'

'And is that what you think?' asked Sam.

Owen looked at his old pal. He knew that Sam didn't think along the same lines as normal people, which was probably something Sam had in common with the killer.

'It doesn't matter what I think, boyo. The investigation's been handed over to the

National Crime Squad.'

'But you'll be working with them,' assumed Sam, 'using your local knowledge?'

'In between my other duties, yes.'

Sam beamed. 'Owen, that's all we need, a man with a warrant card and the backing of the Met.'

Owen looked worried. Sally gave him a sympathetic pat on the back. 'I'll make us all a nice cup of tea,' she said. Then to Sam she added, 'Oh, by the way, the boys called by just before you got here, they left you a welcome home present.'

She handed Sam a small parcel, which he opened to reveal a hands-free car phone. It was far nearer the cutting edge of technology than his own mobile, which he'd had for five years.

'Look at this,' he said, amazed. 'It even takes photos. Must have cost a fortune. Where did they get the money from for this?

'I asked them the same thing myself,' mentioned Sally, 'when they told me what they'd bought you.'

'And what did they say?'

'Something about shrewd investments.'

'I'd like to know more about these investments. There's one thing for sure, Sue wouldn't have given them the money to buy me a present like this.' He looked at Owen. 'Would Bowman object to you interviewing Kevin Kilpatrick?'

Owen never failed to be amazed at Sam's ability to effortlessly change the subject. 'Who...? Oh, well, I doubt if he'll agree to it under the circumstances.'

'The circumstances being that it's been handed over to the NCS?'

Owen nodded. 'It's probably just as well,' Sam said, then added, 'I might go myself, on behalf of his wife and daughter. I'll see if his wife can get me a visiting order.'

'Why not ask his daughter?' suggested Owen, mischievously.

Sam held him in an expressionless gaze. Sally had been listening to their conversation as she waited for the kettle to boil.

'Either or,' Sam said. 'You know his daughter better than I do, maybe you can ask her.' His eyes were challenging Owen, telling him that if he took this conversation any further he might regret it.

'I only know her from her working at the Pear Tree,' Owen said, deliberately not taking the hint. 'She seems a nice young woman, look you. Didn't you interview her once?'

'Yeah, her and her mother both,' Sam said, casually. Then to close the conversation down he took a photograph of Owen and laughed at the result. 'Hey, we could sell this to York Minster works department as a model for a gargoyle.'

The kettle boiled, Sally went into the kitchen to make the tea and Sam held a threatening fist up to Owen, who feigned innocence.

'What?' he said.

CHAPTER TWENTY-THREE

The vice-captain of South Shore Golf Club, Skegness, was found lying in the middle of the sixth green. He was naked and had a towel over his head. He had been struck a single blow with a blunt instrument, probably a ball pein hammer, which had smashed his skull right through to his brain. Death would have been instantaneous.

Two months earlier he had scored a hole in one at the sixth and had often joked with his mates about going back there at night for another hole in one. He was a single man who often frequented the clubs in town and had been seen with a good-looking redhead the night before his body was found.

The NCS investigators contacted the forensic profiler who had worked on the other cases. The profiler was now convinced that the killer was a woman working alone. Young, attractive, personable, with reason to hold a grudge against men. Maybe a lesbian who had lost her lover to a man; or a prostitute who had suffered at a man's hands.

She was a woman who used her sex appeal as a weapon to lure men to their deaths.

The papers loved it. *The Sun* gave her the inevitable soubriquet – Hammerhead. Sick jokes proliferated throughout the country. She was the talk of every pub and club – especially golf clubs. Bowman had gloried in being interviewed on television. He had spoken with great gravitas about the difficulty of finding a serial killer who operated in such a massive area, but the NCS was the most effective group of investigative officers in the world and evidence was being gathered to corner the killer. He assured viewers that an arrest was imminent.

He was later told, by the NCS team leader, not to talk such crap in future.

Sam was enjoying being nursed by Sally but he hated his current state of impotence. Things needed to be done and the police were no bloody help. He got a taxi to his office, where Sally scolded him for coming in. She was working during the day and looking after Sam at night. Necessity was speeding her own recovery.

'All right,' he said, 'consider me told off. I need to pick your brains.'

'You could have picked them over the phone.'

'Sal, it doesn't work over the phone. I'm thinking about the Corbally killing. It was a contract killing, like the others. How the hell do I find out who ordered the hit?'

'The person who benefited from his death?'

'Jesus, Sal! I know that. But I can't think straight. Being shot like I was has sent my mind all over the place. There's a simple way. You know all the simple ways.'

Sally fixed him with an innocent stare. 'I also know many simple people.' She poked a biro in her ear as she thought. 'Stick an ad in the *Observer*.'

'What?'

'The *Unsworth Observer*, stick an ad in it.'

'An advert? Come on, it can't be that simple.' He thought about it as Sally got on with her work, typing up a tender for Sam's building partner, Alec. 'Is it that simple?'

'Why not?' said Sally, without looking up. 'You've still got a copper's mentality. You sometimes make easy things hard. It'll need a bit of thinking about. Your brain isn't completely frazzled is it?'

Later that day Sam placed a cryptic ad in the personal column of the Unsworth Observer:

Do you know anyone who benefits in any way from the death of Austin Corbally?

All replies will be treated with confidence. If the informant wishes to remain anonymous, this will be respected.

The notice was only allowed by the *Observer* with it being given credence and respectability by the name of a local firm of solicitors who'd accept all replies, either by phone, post or email. One of the partners owed Sam a big favour, as did many people. Sam was very good at calling in favours. He was at home with Sally when the solicitor rang him, three days after the notice first appeared.

'A woman left a message on my voicemail. She didn't give her name but she said that Austin Corbally was the beneficiary of a will.'

'Whose will?'

'A man who died of cancer two days after Corbally. He was unconscious on a morphine drip the night Corbally was killed. She reckons Corbally was due for over a million and she finds it odd that his son has been dumped in De La Salle kids' home and is not living like a young prince.'

'Did she say who the money went to?'

'I asked – she didn't know. She gave me the name of the dead benefactor and his solicitor – she seemed to know a certain amount about it, so I'm guessing she might even have been a witness to the signing of the will. If you were still a copper you could get a court order for it and find out who got the money.'

'This is very good stuff. Can you give me all these details.'

Sam made a few notes then thanked the

man and put the phone down. He looked across at Sally who had correctly figured what the call was about. He explained.

'We had a reply to the ad – there's a will that'll tell us who the beneficiary of Corbally's death is. He was due over a million but missed the gravy train by two days.'

'This is where you hand it over to Owen.'

'Who'll give it to Janet, who'll give it to Bowman.'

'Sam, you can't do this on your own. It's not your problem.'

He shook his head. Corbally had been killed before the serial killer idea had been born. How come it had taken a simple ad to get this information out of the woodwork? One thing was for certain, he wasn't going to give this to Bowman on a plate. And there was another matter he'd have to deal with first.

'Sal, I can't. You just have to let me deal with this my way.'

CHAPTER TWENTY-FOUR

He didn't tell Sally he was driving to Manchester that evening, she'd have given him too much grief. Someone had tried to kill him and the police weren't helping, so he'd have to help himself. The pain from the injury had more or less gone, but the aftermath of seriously believing he only had seconds to live was now kicking in and he needed to do something about it or he'd go potty.

He'd been in tricky situations before, but this one had really got to him. Waking up in the night, shouting, sweating, sometimes weeping. He'd never done this before. Maybe he was getting too old – thirty-seven next year – past the age of retirement for most active sportsmen. As he drove along the M62, past Scammonden Dam, he tried to think of any active sportsmen who were older than him – none apart from golfers, which isn't actually an active sport. Maybe the odd goalie or wicketkeeper – Alec Stewart kept going until he was forty. That gave Sam some comfort.

He drove across the Yorkshire border, past a sign telling him he was now in Greater Manchester and, not for the first time, he wondered why it didn't say Lancashire. What were they trying to hide? Lancashire's OK if you're not fussy and you don't mind people trying to kill you. There was an anger building up inside him that he tried to curb. Anger never helped anyone. Wild, controlled madness – as in Mad Carew – yes, but anger was bad. Sir Steve Redgrave, he was forty-two when he won his fifth gold medal. Who else? Sir Stanley Matthews, still playing first division football at fifty.

If Mick Crowther had been murdered then the woman he was going to see was ultimately responsible. Not only responsible for her husband's death, but also responsible for the constant ache in Sam's gut, the scar on his back, and the even bigger scar on his stomach. And she was walking around free. The police had gone to see her, simply as a matter of course, but they hadn't accused her of anything. They hadn't accused her because they'd been influenced by that bastard Bowman.

But he mustn't let his anger get the better of him. She didn't know he was on his way but she'd speak to him because he held a trump card. The Manchester Victoria Insurance Company wouldn't release a penny until they had his report. He held the purse strings. He'd made it clear to the loss adjusters on the day after the shooting that he had an interesting and possibly adverse report to give them – and no responsible insurance company will part with half a million pounds if there's an adverse report pending. But he had to be calm and professional. For all he knew she might not be in, but he couldn't afford to ring her and check; that would give her time to prepare her answers. He hated prepared answers. It was why he thought *Prime Minister's Questions* was a fake show. Whether they're murderers or prime ministers, people must be forced into thinking on their feet. That's where the truth lies. Prepared answers are for liars. He wanted to catch her on the hop. It was 9.30 p.m., so her children should be in bed. Hopefully she'd be alone.

His sons had installed the hands-free phone in his car; at the time he'd thought it all very unnecessary – not now. As he approached her house he dialled Diane Crowther.

'Good evening Mrs Crowther, my name's Carew. You may remember me. I represent the loss adjusters for the Manchester Victoria Insurance Company.'

There was a long pause before she replied. 'Yes, Mr Carew?'

'Sorry to ring you at this late hour, Mrs Crowther, but as I'm in the area I thought I might pop in to see you. It's with regard to your claim.'

'Is there a problem?'

'Just a few loose ends to tie up. If it's inconvenient or if you have company I'll leave it until another time. But I won't be back in Manchester for at least a week.'

'Er, well, I've just put my son to bed, so any time's convenient, Mr Carew.'

'Right, I'll be round in two minutes.'

'Two minutes? Oh, er, right.'

She welcomed him into her house, which still hadn't a single photo of Mick anywhere in sight. Plenty of her children. George

Clooney was still there, but not her dear departed Mick. She seemed over-confident and he didn't like this one bit.

For her part she hadn't heard about the man who had been attacked on the moors just outside Burnley. All she had heard was that Carew had been sorted – whatever that meant. She assumed it meant that he wouldn't give her any more trouble than the police had. This was about loose ends. She had nothing to worry about.

'You know, Mrs Crowther,' said Sam, 'my dad was killed a couple of years ago. I like to keep his memory all around me. You can't move in my place for photos of him. I'm told it's a natural reaction when you lose a loved one suddenly.'

She followed his gaze around the room. Photographs of Mick conspicuously absent. He made no further comment. Her self-confidence took a neat dive.

'You wanted to tie up a few loose ends?'

'That's correct, Mrs Crowther. I'm trying to find out why you tried to have me killed just after I came to see you last.'

He spoke just as a loss adjuster would, no emotion, just business. Her hands opened and clenched. She frowned, wondering if she'd heard him right.

'Pardon?'

'I want to know why you tried to have me killed. It's a perfectly reasonable question,

Mrs Crowther.'

'Someone tried to kill you and er, you're saying I had something to do with it?'

Sam shrugged. 'Well, yes,' he said, reasonably, 'you're not denying it, surely?'

'Of course I'm damned well denying it!'

'In that case, why did my attacker mention your name? I was lured to a meeting on the strength of your name. And at that meeting she tried to murder me. Needless to say that would have been very convenient to you.'

'She – you mean it was a woman? She'd no business mentioning my name. I had nothing to do with it.'

Sam smiled and shook his head. 'Mrs Crowther, you hired a contract killer to top your husband and when it seemed like I was causing trouble that same attacker tried to kill me. I'm not stupid, Mrs Crowther. It was you who told them I was causing trouble.'

He was pretty sure his guesswork was accurate. And conveying accurate guesswork calmly and reasonably, as though it were known fact, can be very unsettling. Diane Crowther was duly unsettled. She could see her half million slipping away, and maybe even a cell door opening. It was time to clam up. She went to the door and opened it.

'Goodnight, Mr Carew. I've got nothing to say to you.'

Sam didn't budge from the settee. 'Ah, but you haven't heard me out, Mrs Crowther.

Me being attacked is worrying the insurance company, and while they're worried they won't pay. I've put a massive doubt in their minds and only I can remove it.'

She closed the door and went back to her chair. 'What is it you want?'

'Mrs Crowther, I'm not a policeman, nor an officer of any court. I don't have the power to arrest you – but I do have the power to stop you getting half a million quid for bumping off your husband.'

Her eyes narrowed. 'Are you blackmailing me, Mr Carew?'

'Well, I suppose I am in a way. I'm here to do a deal. You tell me the name of the killer and I'll send a favourable report to the insurers.'

'I don't know the name of the killer.'

'Maybe not, but you've got half a million reasons to find out.' He got to his feet and gave her his card. 'Once they get my report you'll get the money within five working days. It's worth making a bit of an effort, Mrs Crowther.'

'This doesn't make sense,' she said. 'Even if I did know the name of the killer wouldn't it be suicide for me to tell you? If the killer didn't come for me, the police would.'

'Not if you're given immunity from prosecution.'

He was flying on a wing and a prayer now. There was no way he could ever hope to guarantee this, but it sounded OK. He elaborated on his reasoning:

'Mrs Crowther, this killer is very dangerous. She's already killed four people. There's a rumour going around that she's a serial killer, but you and I know different – don't we, Mrs Crowther?'

He studied her face. Her eyes were saying yes, but her mouth remained silent. She wasn't a bad looking woman. What had her husband done to drive her to this?

'Mr Carew, I don't know what the hell you're talking about.' She went to a drawer and took out a pencil and paper. On it she wrote. *I'm assuming you're wired.*

'You assume correctly,' Sam said. He took a pocket tape recorder from inside his coat, unplugged it from a mini-microphone wire and played back the last few seconds of their conversation. Then he flicked it open and gave her the tape. 'Here, there's nothing incriminating on it.'

'I know. I've been watching what I say.'

She lit a cigarette without offering Sam one. 'So, you're offering me immunity from prosecution and half a million pounds in exchange for me handing the hitwoman over.'

'It's a better deal than the one you've got at the moment. For a start your hitwoman knows who you are, which was a very bad move on your part.'

'I could hardly keep it a secret, with my husband being the victim.'

'You could, actually,' Sam told her. 'The first rule of putting money on the street is to make it anonymous money. I'm guessing you went through an intermediary. Did the intermediary ask who you are?'

'No,' she admitted. 'But he knew the target was my husband.'

'You shouldn't have told him. That was a mistake.'

'He already knew.'

'I don't understand.'

'No, I don't suppose you do.'

'It's a mistake you can only correct by going along with me. Oh, by the way, when you get the half million my fee is twenty-five per cent.'

She stared at him for a second and she was relieved. Relieved by the knowledge that he was genuinely bent. He wanted her to think he was bent.

'It's a fair price for the bullet I took because of you.'

'I'm sorry, I didn't know. The police came to see me and asked if I knew you. I said I did and asked them why. They just said there'd been an incident that they're investigating, but they didn't go into details.'

'And that's all?' said Sam, incredulously. 'They just asked you if you knew me. They didn't bother to mention that I'd been shot and spent hours in an operating theatre and very nearly died?'

'Pretty much, yes. A couple of hours later Mr Small rang to tell me you'd been sorted, then he put the phone down. I took it to mean you'd been warned off.'

'Mr Small's the middle man?'

'Yes. I doubt if it's his real name.'

'So do I.' Sam looked at her, trying to see truth in her eyes. He couldn't see truth, but he couldn't see deceit either.

'All I can give you,' she said, 'is his mobile phone number, but before I do that I need some guarantees.'

'I'll get right on it,' Sam promised her. 'I'll get the police to grant you immunity, then you help them track down the bitch who tried to kill me. I'll give you a clean report for the insurers and everyone's happy.'

He was amazed at how rational he made it all sound. And even more amazed that she'd fallen for it.

'How long will it all take?' she asked.

'Job number one is the police immunity,' he said. 'That might take a while. They'll have to get the CPS and maybe even a judge involved. Could be a week or two.'

'Right, so what will you do? Will you ring me?'

'As soon as it comes through, the police can get on with tracking down this bloody woman.'

'It's her you really want, isn't it?'

'Yes.' He was telling her the truth, for a change.

'You haven't asked me why I wanted him dead.'

'I assumed it was for the money.'

'Not entirely, although it is a big bonus. As a matter of fact I get the house as well, mortgage paid up and everything.'

Sam looked around and assessed the house to be worth around three hundred thousand. She'd done pretty well out of her husband's death.

'He was a complete shit,' she told him. 'To the outside world he was Mr Nice Guy, but to me he was awful – worse than awful. I grew to loathe him. I used to dread him coming home. I knew he was in the house even if I hadn't heard him come in. He gave off such an atmosphere. I can't explain it.'

'Hiring a contract killer isn't a very house-wifey thing to do. I mean, I'm an ex-cop, I move in very dodgy circles, and I wouldn't know who to go to.'

'I didn't go to anyone, they came to me.'

'I don't understand.'

'Someone rang me up out of the blue and asked me if I wanted to get rid of my husband. He couldn't have rung at a better time. I was on Valium, brandy, cannabis, you name it. The minute I agreed to have him killed the depression left me like magic.'

'Whoa, go back a few places. Someone just rang you up and asked if you wanted your husband killed? I've had people ringing me up trying to sell me Sky TV and cheaper gas but I didn't realise contract killers were into cold calling.'

'I must say,' she admitted, 'I did think about that. I tried to hide what was happening to me but I guess most of my friends knew I wasn't happy. What they didn't know, was that I was desperately miserable,' she paused for a while before adding, 'but the Samaritans knew.'

'Samaritans?'

'I rang them earlier that same day, but I blubbed so much I had to put the phone down.'

'So, they rang you back suggesting you have your husband bumped off? It all sounds very drastic.'

'I'm not saying it was the Samaritans, I'm just saying it seemed a coincidence.'

'But someone rang, right out of the blue and asked you if you wanted your husband killed?'

'Pretty much – he said it could be done with absolutely no comeback on me, for thirty thousand pounds.'

'And you said yes?'

'Well, I didn't say no. Anyway he rang me back the next day, by which time I'd had time to think about things – I'd also acquired a broken rib. Have you any idea how hard it is to breast-feed a baby when you've got a broken rib?'

'Mick gave you the broken rib?'

'What Mick did was rape me – not for the first time, either. He was a vicious bastard with a drink inside him. The broken rib was the least of my worries.'

'Oh?'

'The worst part was my son having to watch it. It happened in here and Joey came down to see what the noise was about. Mick thought it was a great laugh.'

'So, that's when you said "yes" to having him killed?'

She shrugged and nodded. 'By the way, I *did* tell them you were causing trouble, sorry, but I didn't think they'd hurt you.'

'What, you didn't think the contract killers would hurt me?'

'Like I said, when the man rang to tell me you'd been sorted I assumed you'd just been warned off. You say you were shot?'

'Almost killed, Mrs Crowther.'

She grimaced and placed a hand over her mouth. 'Oh dear, I am sorry. I thought you were looking a bit off-colour.'

Sam stared at her. She was either very naïve or very cunning. There was a sound behind him. He turned to see a small, scared-looking boy standing there, staring up at him.

'Joey, you're supposed to be in bed,' Mrs

Crowther said, gently. 'This is Mr Carew.'

'Is he a friend of daddy?'

'No, he's not, Joey.'

Joey seemed relieved. He forced his frightened features into a smile, that instantly charmed Sam. 'I thought I heard my daddy's voice,' he said, 'so I came to look.'

Sam looked, questioningly, back at the boy's mother.

'It's OK,' she said. 'Joey knows his daddy's not coming back.'

The boy had a good look around the room as if to assure himself that his daddy wasn't there. 'I don't want him to come back,' he said.

'I know you don't Joey, and he's not coming back,' said his mother.

'Promise?'

'Cross my heart and hope to die.'

Satisfied, Joey went out of the room and made his way back up the stairs, leaving behind him an awkward silence. Diane Crowther explained:

'He doesn't actually know what happened to his dad. I just told him he's not coming home, but he's finding it hard to believe. Mick scared the lad to death – just for fun, would you believe?'

'I believe there are bad men about, Mrs Crowther – and bad women.'

He left her with a promise to be in touch very soon. When he got back to his car he took out a second tape recorder and switched it on to check that everything was recorded. Always have a backup – one to show, one to go. It couldn't be used in a criminal court but it was a handy thing to have. Both Janet and Owen would realise he was right about his contract killer theory, and it would certainly make the insurers keep their hands on their money until the unlikely event of it being forced out of them by law. Somewhere down that line there was a fat commission for the Carew Investigations Bureau ... unless.

Before he played the tape to Owen and Janet he'd play it to Sally. He needed her opinion of Mrs Crowther. As he drove home he had to admit to himself that he couldn't make head nor tail of her. He had it within his power to send her down for life, and yet he wasn't sure he wanted to. He'd already done that to one man who didn't deserve it. The appearance of Joey and his appealing bloody smile hadn't made things any easier. 'Bloody kids,' he muttered to himself.

But his anger had gone.

CHAPTER TWENTY-FIVE

Sam put his feet on the desk and looked out of the office window as Sally listened to the tape with diminishing scepticism. It was Joey who clinched it.

'She's for real,' she decided, after listening to it all.

'That's what I thought,' Sam said. 'I know women can be cunning, but that kid was the genuine article. He never wants to see his dad again.'

'Puts you in a bit of a quandary, I should imagine.' Sally looked at him, suspiciously. 'Are you really going to take twenty-five per cent off her?'

'Come off it. If everything went pear-shaped I'd be in deep trouble. Theft, per-verting the course of justice, plus whatever Bowman could dream up. I'd get ten years.'

'So, you're going to give Bowman the tape?'

'I wouldn't give Bowman the time of day. To be honest I don't know what to do. If I play it to Janet and Owen it compromises them – having heard it, they'll have to act on it. I doubt if Mrs Crowther could hold out against any heavy-duty questioning.'

'Careful, it sounds like you're on her side.'

She lit a couple of cigarettes and gave him one, sitting on the edge of his desk.

'How are you feeling?' she asked.

'The night nadgers have gone. I'm sleeping better.'

'Snoring more as well.'

'I don't sn–'

'Yes, you do.'

He let her have this one. She wasn't the first woman to accuse him of snoring.

'What would you do, Sal?'

'Me? Look at it this way, Sam. Do you think she'd have been bereft if you'd died?' She threw the question in casually, as clever women do. Sam had to admit he honestly didn't know the answer.

'I think she'd have been a bit shocked – but quite relieved,' he decided.

'Sounds about right – and is that the value you put on your life? A bit of shock followed by relief?'

He shrugged. She threw him another question.

'Suppose *I'd* been the one taking the bullet?'

'I'd have shopped her, naturally.'

'I know you would – and I'd have done the same for you. She's not one of your loved ones, Sam. She's a stranger who nearly had you killed. Give the tape to Janet and Owen, let it be on their conscience. Give them the stuff on Corbally as well.'

Diane Crowther had spent that morning worrying about last night's visit. She and Sam had parted on civilised terms, with an agreement reached, but it didn't alter the fact that he'd almost been murdered because of her; *and she'd admitted hiring a contract killer*. Shit! Why did she do that? Was he to be believed when he said he wanted twenty-five per cent of her half million? Why would he say it, if he didn't mean it?

On the other hand how much would the insurance company give him if he saved them half a million? It was that disturbing thought that had her picking up the phone.

Her message arrived on Annie's phone within five minutes. Annie was at the merchant's talking to a customer about quick-drying cement. With the business being propped up by illegal money they could afford to offer great deals. Great deals meant a higher turnover, which meant more sales, more staff, respectability, and profit – legal profit. They'd acquired it purely as a way of depositing large sums of cash in the bank. At a builder's merchants this would arouse no suspicion at all from auditors. Builders, more than anyone else, paid in cash. This would be converted into regular bank drafts and either sent overseas or invested in property. A tame and well-paid accountant helped smooth the path. Tax and VAT were all paid on the nail and the company aroused no suspicion from the authorities. Both Annie and Tanya were enjoying building the business up.

Annie handed the customer over to one of the sales staff and went to Tanya's office. Her daughter looked up and frowned at the vexed expression on Annie's face.

'Trouble?'

'Yer might call it that. I've just had a call about the Manchester contract. The client's had another visit from Carew. He's hell-bent on tracking yer down. She's fobbed him off by agreeing to a deal what sounds to me as phoney as fuck.'

She told her daughter the details of Sam's deal. The part about Diane Crowther being granted immunity told Tanya just how phoney the deal was.

'I need to finish him, Ma.'

'This is a family matter, Tan. I've told Mr Small ter get rid of the phone she rings him on. He has a different phone for each client. It's the only link between her and us.'

'Ma, I don't need any help.'

'I know yer don't girl, but Carew's an ex-copper-cum-private dick so they might well treat his murder as one of their own. The papers might lean on them to do that. It has ter be done very carefully.'

'Was he well thought of in the force?'

'He had a couple of enemies, but in general they all thought the sun shone from his arse. I reckon they'll come out o' Fort Unsworth with a right fuckin' cavalry charge when we top him.'

'Hmm,' mused Tanya. 'I doubt if I'll be able to lure him out of the county again. It'll have to be done in his own backyard. The trouble is he's already seen me – although I was wearing shades and a wig. He'll know my voice – both of them, for that matter.'

'And yer don't like shooters,' added Annie.

'Ma, I don't need a gun. I just need to be careful.'

'I think it might be better for us ter put money out on the streets ourselves,' decided Annie. 'Tell yer what, get Kojak ter give some smackhead a nice lookin' pistol and the promise of twenty grams of brown when the job's done. The odds are that the smackhead'll be lifted at some point, but there'll be no connection with us.'

'If the smackhead makes a mess of it we're back to square one, with Carew watching his back,' Tanya pointed out.

'Tan, Carew'll be watching his back now. But he'll be geared up for a professional hit, not some dozy twat in a balaclava walking up behind him in a chipshop, like Wild Bill fuckin' Hickock, and blasting his head off with a Smith and Wesson.'

The image made her smile. Everyone in the shop would either drop to the floor like stones or cower with their backs to the assailant. They'd be there until the alarm was raised by a passer-by or a new customer. The killer would almost certainly get away unchallenged, but with him being a smackhead he wouldn't be able to keep his mouth shut, or his head down. He'd probably take his balaclava off in full view of a CCTV camera, or leave his fingerprints on the door. Wherever the hit took place the killer would most likely be picked up within twenty-four hours, and the case would be solved with no comeback on the family.

Tanya saw the sense in it. There was no need for her to employ her unique, professional talent on Sam. The matter was decided.

'I'll make some discreet enquiries,' said Annie. 'Oh, by the way, could yer chase up the order fer concrete blocks, we've just had a big run on 'em.'

Owen knocked, quietly, on Bowman's door, not something he did very often, but DI Seager wasn't about that day so he had no option. There was no invitation to enter but he went in, anyway. Bowman was looking at a computer screen, with his back to Owen.

'Excuse me, sir.'

The DCI swung round, as if surprised. 'I'm not keen on officers coming in my office uninvited.'

'I did knock, sir.'

'Did you really – and why are you here?'

Owen took umbrage at the fact that Bowman automatically disliked him and spoke down to him all the time. The fact that Bowman was a couple of years younger than him didn't help.

'Sam Carew's given me some interesting information, sir.'

He knew the mention of Sam's name would annoy Bowman even more. Perversely, Owen enjoyed this.

'Did DI Seager not give you my instruction not to involve Carew?'

'Mr Carew involved himself, sir. I told him you wouldn't be interested.'

'Quite right. I'm not interested.'

'Very good, sir.'

Owen turned to go, then paused. 'Mr Carew sent a copy to the Manchester Victoria Insurance Company, sir.'

'What?'

'A copy of the tape, sir. The one of his interview with Mrs Crowther.'

Bowman shook his head. 'Who's Mrs Crowther?'

'She's claiming half a million pounds in insurance after the murder of her husband.' Owen was being deliberately obtuse. He could see why Sam used to get such pleasure out of winding this man up.

'Oh, that Mrs Crowther – and Carew thinks I might be interested in some damn tape recording of him talking to this woman, does he?'

'No, sir. It's me who thought you might be interested, see. On the tape she admits to hiring someone to kill her husband, which confirms Mr Carew's theory about it not being a serial killer.'

Owen was doing his best not to smile at the ill-contained fury on Bowman's face.

'Where is this bloody tape?'

The Welshman stuck his hand in his pocket and pulled out the cassette, which had a Werther's Original wrapper stuck to it. He removed it and handed it to Bowman.

Diane Crowther was deep in thought as she pushed the baby buggie back from the nursery. Joey would be there until half past twelve and she had some decisions to make before then. She found walking the streets, pushing Rosie around, helped her think clearly. Above everything she had to protect herself and these two kids, to the exclusion of all else – even half a million pounds.

A nagging thought jumped into her mind. Carew had handed over the tape very quickly – almost as if he'd expected to have to hand it over. Supposing he'd had two tape recorders. Shit! She had to assume the worst case scenario. Assume he had a tape of their conversation. Worst case. He'd handed it over to the police. Worst case. The police came banging on her door. Worst case. She crumbled and told all. Worst case. Life sentence; kids in a home; life destroyed; all because Mick was a brute, an adulterer and a rapist.

Maybe she was being a bit greedy and uncaring herself. If she was, it was Mick who had made her like this. Normally she wouldn't hurt a fly, but to hurt someone who was hurting her and her kids – and by remote control – she could manage that. It was simply the lesser of two evils. It was the alternative she couldn't handle.

She had tried the contact, who called himself Mr Small, to find out what was happening with Carew but, instead of an instant reply, she had eventually been asked by an automatic voice to leave a message after the tone. After the fourth attempt over a period of twenty-four hours she knew she no longer had a contact.

She was on her own.

CHAPTER TWENTY-SIX

Sam was sitting in an interview room opposite Bowman and Detective Chief Inspector O'Donnell from the National Crime Squad. He'd been called in to be interviewed about the audio tape and he wasn't best pleased.

'I don't want to tell you your job, Bowman, but shouldn't you be interviewing Mrs Crowther about this?'

'She'll be dealt with in due course,' said the NCS officer, sharply. 'It might help if you treated DCI Bowman with respect.'

'Bollocks!' said Sam. 'The reason I interviewed Mrs Crowther is because it was obvious from the start that her husband was murdered by a contract killer. Christ! It's why she attacked me – and Sherlock bloody Bowman here told the Greater Manchester police not to believe me. How can I have respect for someone like that? The man's a liability. It wouldn't surprise me if he set me up for the hit!'

Sam was talking to DCI O'Donnell as if Bowman wasn't there. He was allowing a little of the *Mad* in Mad Carew to come out. He usually reserved it for times of extreme necessity but he thought it would do no harm to bring it out for Bowman's benefit. Bowman shifted in his seat, angrily. One day he would nail Carew's hide to the floor.

'You're an idiot, Carew. You're the only person in the country who thinks the murderer's a contract killer. Do you know what I think, Carew. I think Mrs Crowther saw straight through you. I think she's taking the piss out of you. I think she hates you for questioning her about her husband's death and she's

257

making you look the idiot that you are.'

'She'll probably know that an audio tape can't be used in a criminal court,' added O'Donnell, who wasn't entirely convinced by Bowman's theory.

Sam continued to direct his attention to the NCS man, completely ignoring Bowman. 'While you lot are chasing around after a serial killer, you're not pursuing the contract killing motive, which is exactly what she wants.'

'Do you have any proof of this?'

Sam put his hand in his pocket to take out a piece of paper on which he'd written the name of Corbally's benefactor and the solicitor holding the will. The sneer on Bowman's face brought to mind something Patsy Kilpatrick had said about them having *one of the coppers in their pocket*. His hand came out empty.

'The proof's out there,' he said.

Diane Crowther had prepared herself for just this moment. She had absolutely nothing to gain by telling the truth, or by helping the police in any way. DCI O'Donnell had been banking on her folding under his questioning. It began on her doorstep. He and a sergeant were holding up warrant cards for identification.

'Mrs Crowther?'

'Yes?'

'My name is Detective Chief Inspector O'Donnell from the National Crime Squad, and this is Sergeant Craven.'

She feigned bemusement by giving them a quizzical smile and a shake of her head.

'Do you want to come in or something?' She stepped back as they walked past her without a word. The DCI turned to face her. His method was instant confrontation.

'Mrs Crowther, we know you ordered the murder of your husband.'

'Oh dear,' she said, sitting down on a settee. She picked up what looked like a TV remote control which puzzled O'Donnell slightly, as he hoped she wasn't going to switch the telly on.

'I think I may have overdone things, Inspector. Won't you sit down? My name's Diane, by the way.'

The two NCS officers declined her invitation. 'Could you explain what you mean by that, er, Diane?' said O'Donnell.

'Well,' she said, 'I wasn't at all happy with the attitude of that man from the insurance company – I'm sure he's the reason you're here. I do hope I'm not going to be accused of wasting police time, Inspector.'

'Go on,' said O'Donnell.

'Well, I complained about him the first time he came and practically accused me of arranging for my husband to be killed – I complained to the insurance company. You can ask them if you like. And what do they do? They send him back late at night, just after I got my children to bed, completely unannounced. Just knocked on the door and invited himself in. Obviously I wasn't best pleased.'

'I assume you're talking about Mr Carew,' said O'Donnell, strongly suspecting he wasn't going to make an arrest that day.

'That's him. Strange chap – have you met him, Inspector?'

'I have.' He could have added that he too thought Sam Carew to be a strange chap, but he didn't.

'And I suppose he gave you a tape recording of him talking to me.'

O'Donnell made no comment so Mrs Crowther went on. 'Well,' she said, 'the first thing I noticed was a buzzing noise coming from inside his coat, then I noticed one of those tiny microphones sticking out of his lapel pocket. I thought, "he's recording every word I say." Now I know I shouldn't have, but this time I went along with his little game.'

'What little game was that, Diane?'

'Well, if you've listened to the tape you'll know he gave the impression that he was crooked and trying to blackmail me out of £125,000. I wasn't sure if he was a crook or not. Anyway, I thought I'd turn the tables on him and when he came back I'd record our conversation myself. Then I'd give my tape to the police. Only with me it would be a video tape which can be used in court. I wanted him locked up, Inspector. Losing my husband sent me a bit funny, that's the only excuse I can give you.'

'And did he come back?' O'Donnell asked.

'No, but I'm ready for him if he does.' She pointed to a wall unit on which sat a small video camera, facing the room.

'I can switch it on with this remote control,' she told them, showing it to Donnelly. 'I've actually recorded our little conversation just now. Would you like to see it?'

He shook his head.

'You think I'm a bit strange, don't you? Well, maybe I am. I really haven't got my act together since...' Her voice tailed off, as if the rest was too much to talk about.

'So,' said O'Donnell, 'you're saying that everything you said on that tape was pure fabrication. Don't you think it was a little...' he searched for an appropriate word, '...dangerous, Diane? I mean, the whole thing could have backfired on you.'

'I don't see how, Inspector. I know enough to know that a voice tape can't be used as evidence in a criminal court. If it's of any interest, everything I said on the tape about my late husband was true. He was an awful man. The only lie I told was about me arranging to have him killed – I thought that might have been obvious to you.'

'Really – is that what you thought?'

'Of course it's what I thought,' she assured him. 'I mean, ringing up the Samaritans about my abusive husband and them arranging to bump him off. Surely you didn't fall for that, Inspector. Like I said, I never actually thought Mr Carew would give the tape to the police. He's obviously more honest that I gave him credit for – or more devious. Maybe he was just hedging his bets.'

'How do you mean?'

'Maybe he was trying to squeeze more money out of the insurance company.'

O'Donnell stared at her. Her story seemed so contrived, especially the video camera set up. It was credible enough to make the CPS shake their heads, but no longer credible enough for him to be on first name terms with her.

'Mrs Crowther, we've checked your bank and credit card records and around the time of your husband's death you drew out large sums in cash – all in all around thirty thousand pounds.'

'I know, I was living in a different world, Inspector. I do hope it's not against the law, running up credit card debts like that.'

'What did you do with the money, Mrs Crowther?'

Her eyes suddenly blazed with tears, as if this was one intrusive question too many.

She screamed at him.

'You're as bad as Carew! What business is it of yours what I do with my money? Do you really want to embarrass me, Inspector? Do you really want to make my life more miserable that it already is? I was stupid, that's what I did with the money. I spent it on stupidity and if you want to know the details you'll have to go through my solicitor and even then I doubt if I can come up with an answer that makes sense.' She went to the door. 'Is that all, Inspector, or will I need to contact my solicitor?'

O'Donnell sighed. He didn't buy this manic behaviour for one second. His copper's instinct told him it was an act to cover up the truth. He'd come across it so many times before, and there wasn't a damn thing he could do about it. All they had was an audio tape which a half-decent barrister could discredit, and which was useless in a court of criminal law. He was thinking that it might be an idea to interview Carew again, to find out what he knew. This time without Bowman sticking his oar in.

'There'll be no need for that, Mrs Crowther,' he said, evenly. 'Perhaps when we catch the killer we'll find out what the motive was. Let's hope, for your sake, he doesn't implicate you.'

'Or *she*, Inspector. The papers are saying it's a woman.'

As she listened to their car drive away Diane Crowther began to sweat profusely. The adrenaline that had driven her through that interview was now driving perspiration through her pores – but she had done it. She hadn't expected to be questioned about money but she'd handled it well, she thought. Men always back away from a distressed woman – unless the man happens to be called Mick Crowther. She knew that if the insurance company refused to pay up, and they forced the matter into a civil court, she would let it drop. No way could she keep this act up throughout lengthy court proceedings.

Then she thought about O'Donnell's parting remark. Supposing the killer was caught and she was named as a client? How the hell could she get out of that? So, her whole future lay in the ability of a professional killer to carry on her work without being caught. This was not a comforting thought.

CHAPTER TWENTY-SEVEN

Sally looked at him, long and hard, wondering if she might be able to change his mind. Sam broke the silence.

'No point looking at me like that, you

won't change my mind, Sal.'

They knew each other so well. He'd explained his reasoning for planning on breaking into the solicitors' office.

'Bowman doesn't want to be proved wrong. If I give him this information he'll go about it all half-hearted, hoping nothing comes of it. You need commitment to get results. First of all he'll have to get a court order to release this will. To get a court order you have to show good reason. He might not even get that far. He'll want the judge to refuse him, to give him an excuse not to pursue that angle. No court order – no will.'

'But if you steal it, won't it be illegally obtained evidence and not permissible in court?'

'Sal, you've been watching *The Bill* too much. The police won't have obtained it illegally. An anonymous person will send it to them and they'll be obliged to look through it to find out who it belongs to. And when they make the connection with the beneficiary and the murdered man they'll be able to use the information.'

'Why don't you just give the police the name of the person who got the money from the will?' said Sally. 'Surely they can question them?'

'Because I don't know who it is.'

'Ah, right. I still don't see why you should risk your neck when there's nothing for you at the end of it.'

Sam counted the reasons on the ends of his fingers. 'First, there's a man in jail for a crime he didn't commit – and I put him there. Second, the real killer tried to kill me. Third, the police are on the wrong track. Fourth, I'm good at what I do, and fifth...' He paused with his right forefinger poised over his left thumb.

'Fifth, you get to make Bowman look an idiot – again?' suggested Sally.

'Fifth, I don't trust Bowman,' said Sam. 'Kevin Kilpatrick told his wife that they've got a copper in their pocket.'

'*They* being the people who fitted him up?'

'*They* being the people behind all this.'

'And you think it's Bowman? I thought you said that Bowman was a prat, but basically straight.'

'My judgement hasn't always been impeccable, Sal.'

Sally chose not to argue with this.

Sam had brought a tool for cutting circular holes in glass; its usual purpose was for fitting extractor fans in windows. It was one o'clock the next morning and it took him less than a minute to cut out a six inch diameter piece of glass just above the window catch. He opened the window, climbed in and pressed his foot on the carpet to find the alarm sensor pad. It screamed into action.

Sam climbed back out, closed the window and rang the firm that had fitted the alarm. They conveniently advertised their number on a box fitted to the front wall.

'There's one of your alarms going off at Bateson, Collins and Company on Blenheim Road. I live two doors away and I wish you'd get it fixed properly.' He held the phone so the man could hear the alarm. 'Would you like to sleep through that? It's always going off.'

'I'll ring the owner of the building, sir. We don't know the alarm code.'

'Quick as yer can, mate. I've got an early start tomorrow.'

He sat in his car, which he'd parked a hundred yards away, and waited for someone to arrive. The area was half business, half residential. It took half an hour, during which time the whole district would be covering their ears with pillows. This made Sam feel guilty, but only a bit.

A car pulled up, a man got out, entered the building and within seconds the alarm was silenced. To the relief of many, thought Sam.

Fifteen minutes later the man emerged and drove away. He obviously hadn't spotted the hole in the window. Five minutes later Sam got out of his car, climbed back in through the window, set the alarm off again, and rang up the alarm company.

'Someone came and switched it off, I saw him through me window, been an' gone – but the bugger's started up again. It's bloody ridiculous is this. I can't do with it.'

'All right, all right – I'll deal with it.'

Sam got back in his car. Ten minutes later the same car came back and the alarm was silenced again. Sam climbed back into the building and pressed the sensor pad for a third time. Nothing. The alarm had been switched off. The man had got fed up, as Sam had anticipated. What he hadn't anticipated was the man ringing the police to tell them what had happened, and would they keep an eye on the place because he'd had to switch the alarm off.

Using a pencil torch, Sam began to check the names on the doors until he came to the name he'd been given – Robert Bateson Snr. The door was locked, but only with old-fashioned mortice. Failing all else a good kick would have opened it. Sam took out a large bunch of keys and had the door open within two minutes. No need to leave mess behind. If the job could be done without anyone suspecting, so much the better.

The office he stepped into obviously belonged to a secretary. There was another door which probably led to the solicitor's office. Sam tried it and found it locked. He left it for the time being, remembering the only bit of advice Sally had given him.

'The file will most probably be in a secretary's office.'

All along one wall was a bank of ten filing cabinets, four drawers high and alphabetically listed. Using an electricians' screwdriver he easily sprang the lock on the one saying Br –Do.

They were three files under the name of Corbally. He took out the file of the dead benefactor and carried it to a desk. It was a good four inches thick but the Last Will and Testament of Michael Joseph Corbally was right on top.

Sam put it in a bag he had slung over his shoulder. He carefully replaced the file, locked the filing cabinet and the office door, and made his way out of the building. A police car was parked outside and one of the officers had already spotted the open window. He alerted his colleague who sent out a call for back-up.

Sam was hurrying down the stairs as one of the uniformed constables was climbing in through the window. A nearby patrol car had been diverted to give assistance. In his days as a uniformed constable it would never have occurred to Sam to ask for help, especially if he had a colleague with him.

The officer inside the building could hear Sam's quiet footsteps approaching along the corridor. He had turned off his radio, so as not to alert this intruder. His ASP was extended and he held his breath as the door opened.

In the distance Sam heard the sound of a police siren. He might not have paid it much attention, but the officer outside hadn't thought to turn his radio off. A call came through just as Sam stepped into the room. He turned to run but the officer inside made a grab for him. Sam elbowed him in the face and ran back up the stairs, with the officer eventually in pursuit, yelling to his colleague.

The jab in the face had slowed the pursuing policeman down. Sam had a ten second start but all the office doors were locked and he had no access to outside windows. He found a fire escape door up on the second floor. The sound of a police siren grew louder. Instead of climbing down the iron staircase towards certain capture, he climbed up onto the roof and waited there until the chasing officer stepped out of the open door on to the landing, shouting down at his colleague.

'I think he's gone down the fire escape!'

'No sign of him down here.'

By now Sam had scrambled up the roof and down the other side. A soil vent pipe protruded three feet above the guttering. Sam gave silent thanks that it was made of iron and not plastic as he shinned down the pipe with skill acquired as a schoolboy.

He landed in a small, enclosed yard filled

with rubbish bins. There was a gate, which was locked. The wall was a good eight feet high with broken glass set into the top. Sam wondered for a second what was so precious in this bin yard that required such protection. There were footsteps outside and someone was rattling the gate and cursing.

'Bloody thing's locked. Can we get the owner on the blower?'

Sam looked around. There was a door back into the building. He tried it, just in case. It was locked. He weighed up the pros and cons of his situation and, as usual, there weren't too many pros. If he was captured Bowman would pull out all the stops to have him jailed. Breaking and entering, theft, assaulting a police officer. He could get up to three years.

All the bins were overflowing apart from one, a brown one with a sticker on it saying recyclables only. It must have been recyclable bin day today. Sam climbed inside and closed the lid over him, just as one of the officers behind the wall had climbed on a colleague's shoulders and was shining a torch all around the yard.

'It's a bin yard,' he called down. 'No one here, unless he's buried himself among the rubbish. I'm not climbing in, I'll never get out.'

Sam heard his colleague say, 'The owner's on his way with a key, we'll check it out then.

One of us should wait out here, just in case.'

Sam cursed that officer's efficiency. He took out his mobile phone, and for the second time in a few weeks he rang for Owen's assistance.

'Owen, it's Sam. I'm in a bit of a fix.' His voice was little more than a whisper.

'Sam? You'll have to speak up, boyo, I can hardly hear you.'

'I can't speak up – I'm in a dustbin.'

'A dustbin? Of course you're in a dustbin – you're Sam Carew. Why wouldn't you be in a dustbin?' His voice was echoing.

'Owen, will you stop trying to be so cutting, and keep your voice down. I don't want the police to hear this.'

'Police? Oh, buggeration, Sam! What's this all about?'

'I'm in a bin yard at the back of number 74 Blenheim Road and I wouldn't mind a bit of help.'

He clicked off the phone before Owen could argue. He'd left his pal with a bit of a mystery and Owen couldn't resist a mystery. Even one involving Sam.

Owen arrived just before the owner of the building. He recognised one of the PCs as Johnnie Slattery. He got out of his car and called out, 'Trouble, Johnnie?'

'What? Oh, Owen – yeah, we think there's an intruder inside and we're waiting for the owner to turn up – he's here now, by the look of it.'

'Solicitors, eh? Mind if I have a scout round? This might tally with an investigation of mine.'

'Be my guest.'

Owen walked around the back of the terraced block and found himself in a cobbled alleyway. Halfway down was a young, uniformed policeman, smoking. The Constable recognised Owen and put his cigarette out. Owen tut-tutted, amiably.

'I think you'd be better employed around the front, where all the action is.'

'I'm here to stop anyone escaping from this bin yard.'

'Bin yard duty, eh? They used to stick me with that sort of job. Are there many criminals in there?'

'None that I know of.'

'Still, handy for a quiet fag,' grinned Owen. 'Tell you what, you go round the front and I'll guard the empty bin yard with my life.'

As the Constable wandered off up the alleyway Owen looked up to see Sam's head peering over the top of the wall. He was standing on a milk crate that he'd placed on top of one of the bins. Once the Constable was safely out of sight he took off his coat and placed it over the broken glass, then he kicked himself up and over the wall, knocking both the bin and the milk crate over with his foot. A window slid open above him and one of the officers searching the building called out.

'Oy! He's getting away down the back.'

Sam dropped to the ground, and pulled his coat down after him. Then he punched a perplexed Owen hard, on the nose. Owen clutched his hand to his face and looked at the blood, dark under the light of a distant lamp.

'What the bloody hell?'

'Fall to the ground,' whispered Sam.

'What?'

'Fall to the ground.'

'Oh, I see,' grumbled Owen, 'it's one of your wonderful bloody plans is it?' Nose bleeding profusely, he dropped to the ground. Ten seconds later two officers rounded the corner at speed. He got to his feet and helped them give chase, directing them the wrong way out of the alley. By the time Owen was receiving his bollocking from PC Johnnie Slattery, Sam was in his car, sedately driving away.

CHAPTER TWENTY-EIGHT

Sam caught sight of Owen's nose from afar and winced with guilt, not being absolutely certain how his pal would greet him. They had arranged to meet in the Clog and Shovel.

He'd brought Sally along as peacemaker.

'Did you do that to him?' she asked.

'He bruises easily,' said Sam, 'it won't be as bad as it looks.'

'Sam, if it's half as bad as it looks it's a wonder he's up and about.'

The Welshman's nose was massively swollen, with a wide elastoplast across the bridge where Sam's punch had broken the skin. Sam let Sally go first. Owen's gaze went straight past her to Sam, who withered under his glare.

'You are a complete bastard of the first order, Carew! Not only do I have a broken nose but I've also had a monumental bollocking from Sergeant Bassey of all people.'

'Keep your voice down, Owen,' muttered Sam. 'Look, I'm sorry – and thanks for getting me out of a fix – but I had to smack you to make the whole thing look realistic. I'd already smacked one bobby in the face so I'd hardly let you get away without a crack, would I? How is he, by the way?'

'PC Melia's got off lightly compared to me. I'm stuck with a bent hooter for the rest of my life.'

'Join the club,' grinned Sam, whose nose had been rearranged by one of his first wife's missiles.

'What the hell was it all about?'

Sam went on to tell him about the will naming the benefactor's nephew, Austin

Corbally, as beneficiary and how, because of Corbally's untimely death, another nephew, Henry Corbally, now inherited one point three million pounds. Owen nodded with vague interest, then said, 'How fascinating? But I was actually wondering why you were in a bin yard being chased by half of our constabulary.'

Sam ordered drinks for them all, then spoke in little more than a whisper, not looking at Owen as he spoke.

'I'd just picked up the will.'

'Picked up?' said Owen, into Sam's ear. 'You mean you broke into a solicitor's office and stole a legal document, assaulting a police officer into the bargain.'

'If you want to put it that way, yes. Sally went along with the idea.'

'I did not!' she protested.

'I had your tacit approval,' said Sam, 'once I'd explained things.'

Owen turned to Sally. 'What did he explain, precisely?'

The drinks arrived and they took them to a table in a quiet corner.

'I said he should hand the whole thing over to Bowman,' said Sally, 'but he doesn't trust him.'

'According to Patsy Kilpatrick,' added Sam, 'they've got a copper in their pocket.'

'*They* being the people behind the killings,' said Sally.

'Ah, the bent copper theory,' said Owen.

'Also known as the Bowman theory,' Sam pointed out, 'according to you.'

Owen fingered his tender nose, determined not to release Sam from any feeling of guilt. 'I know one thing, look you. I know I can't use any of this *will evidence* without being unmasked as your accomplice in the burglary.'

'If it comes to it, the will could be sent to Janet Seager, anonymously,' said Sam. 'Does the solicitor know what's been taken?' he asked, curiously.

'Not yet, apparently,' Owen told him, 'but it's only a question of time.'

'I left everything as I found it,' said Sam with an element of pride that irritated Owen even more. 'They'd have to look through every file in the building, and even then they might not figure out what's missing until someone actually needs it.'

'You do know that the NCS is on the case,' said Owen, scathingly. 'I'm told they're quite good at their job – I doubt if they actually need your help.'

Sam nodded. 'DCI O'Donnell's already given me a grilling; unfortunately Bowman was sitting in the other chair. I didn't find that very encouraging.'

'Look, Sam,' sighed Owen, 'To be honest this is the last straw. I, er – I did the wrong thing last night.'

'Wrong thing?' said Sam.

'I shouldn't have got involved, see. Maybe I should have let them arrest you. In the long term a sharp jolt of reality might save your life.'

'In the short term I'd have been locked up for a long term. Is that what you wanted?'

'Ah, don't lay that one on me. The real question is – is it what *you* wanted? It's you who put yourself in that ridiculous position, boyo, not me. And it's not just yourself you place in danger, it's other people as well.' He fingered his nose for effect. 'I honestly wish you'd pack all this stuff in and go back to being a full-time builder.'

There was along silence around the table that continued until Owen felt guilty about being the cause of it. He tried to justify what he'd just said.

'I mean, even if there is a bent copper involved it's highly unlikely to be an NCS man. So why couldn't you have just given your information to them? Why do you always have to do things the hard way?'

Sam tried to think of a sensible answer, Sally helped him out.

'Someone's just tried to murder him, Owen. He virtually came back from the dead – thanks to you.'

Owen corrected her. 'Thanks to you and me – I had no idea where he was.'

'All right,' she conceded, 'thanks to us. But something like that puts your mind out of kilter – I should know. If there's a chance of a bent copper being involved there's no way Sam's going to confide in the police. They did him no favours in the half-arsed way they investigated his attempted murder. They think he deserves to be treated like that because he's the most maddening person on earth, a monumental pain in the arse.'

'Hey, I'm not arguing with you, Sally,' said Owen.

'Then,' said Sally, 'miraculously, he sometimes gets things so absolutely right that he puts everyone else to shame – and he gives you a lot of the credit.'

'Thank you,' said Sam, who had been listening intently for the first sign of a compliment.

'Don't interrupt,' said Sally, without looking at him. Her attention was on Owen. 'If the police place so little value on Sam's life, why should he do them any favours? This thing started with Sam trying to put right a wrong he set in motion nine years ago when he arrested Kevin Kilpatrick. It's what Sam is. He's the Loony Lone Ranger.'

Sam looked across at her, slightly annoyed. 'Sally, I can look after myself. You understand the way I think. If Owen wants to take his bat and ball home, far be it from me to stand in his way.'

'Sam,' she said, sharply, 'just because I understand the way you think doesn't mean to say I approve of the way you behave. People like you need all the friends they can get.'

'Well,' said Owen. 'If you understand the way he thinks, you have an advantage on me.' He looked at Sam. 'You should marry this woman, see. It's just one of the many things I don't understand about you.'

'Ah, now you're taking her for granted, Owen,' cautioned Sam. 'You're assuming she'll say yes if I pop the question.'

Owen looked at Sally. 'Would you say yes?'

Sally gave him her enigmatic smile. 'Owen, do you hate me so much that you want me to marry a madman? Let me ask *you* a question.'

'What's that?'

'*Did* you do the wrong thing last night, or are you secretly proud that you did exactly the right thing, at great danger to your career?'

'I refuse to answer that question on the grounds that it might incriminate me – excuse me.' He got to his feet and headed for the Gents.

Sam looked at Sally. 'Does this mean he's back on our side?'

'He never left it,' said Sally. 'He was just making a stand.'

The young man on the stolen track-bike was doing his best to remain patient. Sam had been in the pub half an hour. The biker had been told by the bald man to walk into the pub with his crash helmet on, shoot Carew in the back of his head at point blank range, walk out calmly, and ride away. Calmly? Who did the man think he was kidding? This way was obviously a better way. The whole thing should be done at speed. Over and done with in a few seconds and him off the scene.

For the tenth time he put his hand inside his leathers and caressed the Smith and Wesson .38 he'd been provided with. He ran his fingers over the dull, black metal and felt its power. He never felt such power before. And he'd been told he could keep it, which was a bonus. That, plus a grand, plus twenty grams of smack would keep him going for a while. He looked at his watch. He could manage without a fix for a few hours yet, but he needed to get this job done round about now. If Carew didn't come out soon he'd have to do the job as per instructions. It was a question of balance. Just after a fix his judgement was always clouded. He used to get a tremendous rush of euphoria, which was why he came back for more – which was why everyone came back for more. But the rush was now one of relief rather than one of euphoria. It was a question of satisfying a desperate need. Brown heroin was meant for smoking by heating it on tinfoil – chasing the dragon – but that was too slow. Like most users he mixed it with acid and injected it straight into the vein. Mainlining. That way the fix was instant. Aids didn't scare him. He was already HIV positive. It might have been a dirty needle, it might have been his part-time job as a rent boy. What the hell did it matter? What the hell did anything matter?

In a few hours he'd become tired and distant from the world. Right now he was in the middle, like the Grand Old Duke of York's Men – neither up nor down. He often sang that song to himself when he was in this state. Heroin had taken away all the rights and wrongs. He felt OK. Nothing mattered. Life was a passing joke. If he wasn't worried about his own life he certainly wasn't worried about anyone else's.

He saw Sam come out of the pub. He checked with the photo he'd been given. Definitely his man. There was another person with him, a woman. She was walking with a stick. Might take her out as well, just for the fun of it. He kicked the bike into action and pulled out the gun.

He'd planned his escape route: second right down Mountjoy Street, then down Ackersfield steps – all sixty-four of them – then along the canal path and across Ackersfield Bridge to a part of town where there were no CCTV cameras. There he'd swap the stolen bike for his own, change into different leathers and crash hat, and home to

Castleford where the brown and the cash would be waiting for him.

The Clog and Shovel had become too crowded for confidential conversation so Sam had suggested they all go back to Carew and Son's office where they could discuss his latest idea in private.

'I'll catch you up,' said Owen, heading towards the Gents for a second time.

'He's got a bladder the size of a golf ball,' commented Sam, finishing off his pint. 'By the way, thanks for getting him back on side. If you hadn't been here I might have lost my temper with him.'

'Sam, he has good cause to be annoyed with you. He's the only copper on the force who'll go out of his way to help you – at great risk to his career.'

Sam laughed. 'Owen's a dark horse. He likes a bit of added excitement in his life. You've only got to look at his love life to see that.'

He helped her to her feet, she linked his arm and, not for the first time, she realised just how right this felt. This was her man – if only he knew it.

They stepped out on to the pavement and walked up the street towards the office. Traffic was light, which was why the high-pitched roar of the track-bike, coming from behind, was so noticeable – not to Sam and

Sally, but to Owen, who was hurrying out of the door. The biker was riding one-handed, with his left arm outstretched, holding a gun. The Welshman's deafening vocal chords came to his aid.

'Sam, down!'

Instinctively Sam threw himself to the ground, taking Sally with him. Above the snarl of the bike he heard a series of shots; a woman walking towards them fell to the ground; glass shattered in a shop window; ricochetting bullets whined across the street. The biker tried to adjust his aim whilst keeping control of his unfamiliar vehicle; the front wheel reared up and he fell off backwards, still clutching the gun – until it was kicked out of his hand by Owen. His second kick was a heavy boot to the biker's groin, putting him out of action for the time being.

Sam and Sally were kneeling over the fallen woman who was sobbing in agony with blood streaming down her thigh. Owen stood with his foot on the moaning gunman's neck, stopping traffic with one hand and phoning for assistance with the other. He had already removed the man's crash helmet and taken a snapshot of the tattooed and pierced face with his camera phone. He didn't recognise the biker as local.

Within a minute an area car screamed around the corner and pulled to a halt. PC Melia, to whom Sam had given a black eye just twelve hours earlier, got out of the passenger side. His face expressed neither surprise nor concern when he saw it was Sam.

'What happened this time?' he said.

Sam shook his head. Sometimes he didn't believe the attitude the police had towards him. 'This nice lady's been shot by that nasty man,' he said, inclining his head towards the biker.

'Ah, right, we'll need witness statements.'

'The first thing you do is call for an ambulance,' said Sam. 'You need a brain between your ears to take statements.'

'Sam, behave!' said Sally. To the PC she added, 'Owen Price saw it all – more than we did. I think he's already rung for an ambulance.'

Melia looked over at Owen with an equally unimpressed look on his face. 'Oh, him,' he muttered.

'He probably saved Sam's life,' Sally said. 'I think the shots were meant for him.'

This piece of information had the injured woman looking daggers at Sam. 'You mean this is your fault?'

Sam looked around him, wondering how this could possibly be construed as his fault. PC Melia was grinning; another police car had arrived; the crime scene was being taped off; the biker was now in handcuffs and being read his rights, and Owen was unwrapping a Mars Bar and strolling across to give his statement.

All was as it should be, it seemed, in the world of Sam Carew.

Annie Robinson strolled away, talking into her mobile. 'Silly sod's made a complete balls of it. Tried ter shoot Carew from the back of a fuckin' motor bike, would yer believe? Sets off like Evel Ker-fuckin'-ievel; bike does a wheelie, Silly Bollocks falls off the back, shootin' at whatever. I had ter duck meself at one point. It'd have been funny had it not been so serious. Give Kojak a bollockin' fer findin' such a tosser, an' tell him not ter bother droppin' the tosser's wages off. He'll be doin' time in a nuthouse fer the next ten years, if he lives that long.'

Four hours later the biker sat facing Sergeant Bassey and DC Owen Price. He was shivering, in desperate need of a fix, but with no real awareness of the desperate fix he was already in. Owen had suggested the man should see a doctor before the interview but Bassey thought it was better to interview the man at his weakest.

As the Sergeant hurled questions at him, the biker kept nodding off, then waking up with a desperate, sweating shudder. The only information he gave them was about a bald man who had approached him in the King's Head in Castleford and had given him the job and the gun. He was to be paid twenty pounds and a thousand grams of brown – or was it the other way round?

'Brown?' said Bassey.

'Type of heroin,' Owen had explained, 'comes mainly from the Indian sub-contin–'

Bassey's glare cut him off mid-sentence. The Sergeant went on to accuse the biker of lying about not knowing who set the job up.

'He said his name were Mr Small,' slurred the biker. '...a baldy blo–' He retched and vomited on his shirt and jeans. His solicitor insisted that his client answer no more questions until he'd seen a doctor. Bassey had no option but to agree. It was all they would ever get out of him because the biker was telling the truth. He would later give a description of a small, baldy bloke with a cauliflower ear – he should have been called Mr Average Scrum Half.

The papers and local television ran the story, with DC Owen Price coming out as a hero. This didn't sit well with Bowman.

Sam and Sally were interviewed at the station by Bassey, who opened with the daftest question Sam had heard in some time.

'Mr Carew, do you have any idea who might want to kill you?'

'Er, are you having a laugh?'

'I'm just following procedure.'

'Someone tried to kill me a few weeks

ago,' said Sam, 'I think there's a bit of a clue there. The woman who tried to kill Mick Crowther tried to kill me.'

'But today it was a man.'

Sam exploded. 'Bassey, are you being deliberately bloody stupid? Why isn't Bowman in on this interview? This isn't a uniform matter, it's CID.'

'It's not a formal interview. I'm just taking witness statements, as well you know. In your time you have upset many people, any one of whom might have good reason to wish you dead. It would be wrong to make assumptions at this point.'

Sam shook his head and got to his feet. Sally, equally disgusted, did likewise. 'There have been two attempts on Sam's life,' she said, evenly. 'It's clear, even to me, who's behind it and yet you deliberately turn a blind eye to the obvious, just because it would embarrass you to have to follow the correct line of enquiry after foolishly telling the papers that the murderer is a serial killer.'

Sam glanced at her, impressed. It was pretty much what he'd have said, had he not been so annoyed. 'If I get any information,' he said to Bassey, 'I'll pass it on to the news-papers. There's obviously no point cooporating with you. You've been ordered to put the block on everything I say and do. The question in my mind, is who's giving the orders?'

Bassey looked down and Sam knew he'd

hit a nerve. He pressed his point home. 'I'm told from one of my sources that there's a bent cop in this nick, working with the killers.'

'That's rubbish,' Bassey said.

'Is it?'

Sam took Sally's arm and led her out of the station. As they walked along the street to his car his spirits began to sag. His step slowed until Sally asked him if he was OK. He shook his head. His face was pale and he was sweating.

'What is it?'

'I'm scared, Sal. I need to get out of this place as quick as I can.'

'Give me your keys, Sam.'

Without questioning whether she was fit to drive yet he handed over his car keys.

CHAPTER TWENTY-NINE

Sam sat silently in the passenger seat as Sally drove his car towards the North York moors. There were people out there who wanted to kill him and he didn't know who they were. The not knowing was the worst bit. She pulled up in a parking area high on Goathland Moor from where they could see the road for miles in either direction. There was beautiful light from the early October sun, illuminating the autumn landscape and making it picture postcard pretty. It was a place of high, rolling hills, dry-stone walls, heather, gorse, many sheep, and the occasional roe-deer.

Sam looked upwards and watched a red kite gliding in a lazy circle as it waited for its next meal to make an appearance. He smiled and said, 'I want to stay out here for a while.'

'What? Do you mean just here, in this very spot?'

'I mean in a hotel somewhere near, where we can be lazy and comfortable and safe.'

'And decadent?'

'Sally Grover, you're a very racy lady at times, but if I have to put up with your decadence, I'll do my best.'

'Your best is all I ask.'

They waited there for half an hour until it became more than obvious that no one was following them, then Sally drove down into Goathland village, negotiating her way through the noisy, ill-mannered sheep that crowded the common and the main road.

The village was full of TV crew, which unnerved Sam somewhat, until he realised they were making the 1960s TV cop series – *Heartbeat*. There was an odd irony here. Sam had watched the programme and had often fancied the idea of being a country bobby back in those days. Sally was directed away from the line of the cameras by a polite young female assistant who leaned in the window and told them that had they come in an old Cortina, they'd have been given fifty quid just to drive past the cameras.

'How much is he worth?' Sally asked, inclining her head to Sam. 'He's the human equivalent of an old Cortina – he's got to be worth a tenner.'

'I think she's confusing me with a Welsh friend of ours,' said Sam. Then to Sally he added, 'That was a very novel way of handing in your notice, Miss Grover.'

The assistant grinned and directed them to a parking area. They got out and watched proceedings from a distance.

A speeding Ford Anglia police car was chasing a Triumph motor bike and sidecar along the road outside. Two cameras were recording the chase and around thirty crew and extras were watching as the vehicles were brought back, several times, to repeat the action until the director was happy. He shouted, 'Cut, that's lunch, everyone back at one thirty-five.'

As the TV people wandered off to the catering van, Sam and Sally followed suit, purely out of curiosity to see if they could spot anyone they recognised. Sam stopped to look at the menu chalked on a board.

'Pork loin with shallot ginger soy sauce,' he read, approvingly.

'Spiced chicken with tamarind sauce,' read Sally.

A heavy-looking woman approached them. She wore a fisherman's jumper, jeans and caterpillar boots. 'This is cast and crew only,' she said, irritably. 'How many times do I have to tell you bloody lot? The extras queue is the other side – and don't forget to go to wardrobe before you go on set. I don't know where casting get you lot from, I really don't.'

'Right,' said Sam, 'extras queue it is. We know our place, don't we, Sal?'

'We do indeed,' said Sally. 'It's at the end of the extras queue.'

Giggling like a couple of schoolkids they moved around the other side of the truck and went to join a queue of people dressed in 1960s clothes. An elderly man at the end of the queue smiled at them. He was dressed in cavalry twill and tweed.

'I reckon Big Lizzie's just put you in your place has she?'

'Big Li–? Oh, yeah,' grinned Sam. 'She's put us in our place all right.'

'Take no notice. Have you worked on this before?'

'No, er, not this particular one.'

'Good crowd, generally. Big Lizzie's the exception. She's third assistant – thinks she's the director. I take no notice. Come as a couple have you? Good idea. I used to bring my wife, but she can't stand the hanging about. If you don't like hanging about there's no point doing extra work. Have you done much?'

'Er, not a lot,' said Sam.

'Three rules. Don't look at the camera, don't trip over the wires and don't fart near a microphone. It's not rocket science isn't extra work. You get them what reckon it's a proper acting job. Frustrated theatricals. All am-dram and up their own arses, can't stand 'em myself. Have you been used yet?'

'Yeah, er, not yet, no,' said Sam, who didn't have a clue what the man was talking about.

'Nor me. I was here for ten hours yesterday, never got used once, still, it's their brass they're wasting.'

'We've only just got here,' said Sally. 'We haven't been to wardrobe yet.'

'I hope you have better luck than me. They've got my full details but I'm still squeezed into a thirty-six waist. I ask you, do I look a thirty-six waist? It's not like it used to be when Equity looked after us. Daren't complain nowadays. I assume you're in Equity?'

'Oh, yeah,' Sam assured him.

'Good, there's too many non-Equity doin' this job nowadays. What d'you normally do? Don't tell me, let me guess. Singing duo – am I right or am I wrong?'

'Ah, you must have seen us around the

clubs,' said Sam, now warming to the theme.

'Nay, I haven't done the clubs for ten years, lad. That game's been knackered fer years. It's all pie and peas and bloody Bingo. No, all I do is residencies. Piano and vocals. I've got two at the moment, both in York hotels, very handy. What d'you call yourselves?'

'Sam and Sally,' said Sam.

'The Soulful Serenaders,' added Sally.

The man stuck out a hand. 'Norman Fingers Cleghorn – happen you saw me on *Opportunity Knocks*. I was just beaten into second place by Freddie Starr and the Delmonts. Done well has Freddie. I don't begrudge him. No point begrudging in this business.'

'Do you know, I thought I'd seen you somewhere,' lied Sally.

Norman winked at her. 'Once seen, never forgotten, eh? Tell you what, if there's one thing about this extra work, it's the grub. First class. How they do it, I will never know. Out here in the sticks they put on a gourmet menu.'

They arrived at the serving hatch, collected their selected meals and took them to a bench on the village common, not wishing to risk further interrogation on the extras bus.

'The Soulful Serenaders?' said Sam, when they were out of everyone's earshot.

She grinned. 'Sam and Sally, the Soulful Serenaders. Great name for an act. I think we should go in for *The X-Factor* next time round.'

'Sal, I've heard you singing. It's like a lump of coal caught under a cellar door.'

'I'm better than you.'

'Excuse me, I'm a very good singer, I'll have you know – former choirboy.' He pulled a face, ''til I got kicked out.'

'Dare I ask what for?'

'Oh, the usual – acting the goat and nicking the communion wine. I don't know why, it tasted like Fenning's Fever Cure.'

'What does Fenning's Fever Cure taste like?'

'A bit like communion wine.'

Sally chewed on a forkful of illicit chicken as Sam shooed away a curious sheep. It had been a while since they'd felt so relaxed and silly.

'Sam, did you like music when you were young? There's all sorts I don't know about you. What was your favourite band?'

Sam sipped his tea and thought back. 'When I was a kid I always liked Aerosmith. I always fancied being Steven Tyler – leading the old rock 'n' rock lifestyle.'

'You pretty much do lead a rock 'n' roll lifestyle. There's plenty of rockers lead a far more sedate life than you – all of them, in fact.'

'Ah, but I always fancied the big kick you must get, performing in the stadiums. I liked Genesis, Billy Joel – and I loved all the heavy metal stuff: Metallica, Ozzie – before he became a reality TV plonker, Guns 'n' Roses, Van Halen, Judas Priest ... tell you what, this chicken's delicious.'

'So, you didn't much like chamber music, then?'

Sam shrugged. 'I probably like all kinds of music. The trouble is that marriage and the police kind of edge all that to one side. Sue's still got all my old vinyls. I must get them back. She liked Duran Duran and Spandau Ballet, although, according to the boys, she's moved on to Will Young.'

'I can see why you didn't get on.'

Norman Fingers Cleghorn's assessment of the menu proved to be no exaggeration. The fact that the food had been obtained by illicit means added to the flavour. They agreed it was the most enjoyable meal they'd ever had. Both went back for pudding and an extra cup of tea, and their presence raised just one eyebrow, that of the young assistant whom they had first encountered. Sam gave her a large wink, which she returned.

They booked into a hotel, in a room overlooking the main street, under the name of Mr and Mrs Grover. Sally went to the window and looked down at the TV set. Shooting had recommenced.

'Do you think life was ever as simple as

this?' she said. 'Even crime seems more wholesome.'

Sam joined her. 'Well, I think police work was more straightforward before drugs came on the scene,' he commented. 'And I'll guarantee that when this business unfolds, there's drugs involved somewhere.'

He put an arm around her. 'By the way, sorry for being such a wuss,' he said. 'Things have just got to me. I'll be OK.'

'I'm very happy for you to be a wuss,' smiled Sally. 'It means you have regard for your own safety, which is reassuring. You can't take on the whole world, you know. You might have to leave this one to the police.'

'Sal, I really need to know who these people are. The police could run around in circles for months chasing their serial killer – maybe years. Where the hell does that leave me? Right now I'm genuinely scared to show my face within ten miles of Unsworth.' He sat up, thinking. 'Look, I need to tell Alec what's happening. I need to tell the boys.' A dreadful thought struck him. 'Sal, what if they go for my boys?'

Sally was unable to dismiss this possibility. 'I think the least you can do is tell Sue the whole story,' she decided, after some thought. 'She's their mother. She has a right to know what's going on. Maybe Jonathan can take them all on an extended holiday until this is sorted.'

'She'll be quite annoyed,' said Sam. But Sally was right, his ex-wife had to be told the score. He took a deep breath and picked up his mobile. It rang three times before Sally heard him say, 'Sue, it's Sam... Ah, you heard... No, I'm fine, thanks, but there's er...' He was wincing now. 'There's something you probably need to know...'

That was all Sally heard before she closed the bathroom door and turned on the bathtaps.

He was standing at the window when she came out. 'Sue went ballistic,' he said, without turning round. He looked down at the TV action. 'Looks like they've captured their villain – maybe they can help me catch mine.'

Sally joined him. He was looking down at the street where a camera was tracking a uniformed policeman frogmarching a man in motor cycle leathers towards the police car. They walked past Norman Fingers Cleghorn, being used at last, just a blur in the background but earning his money for the day. Sam envied him that. Being a blur in the background right now would suit Sam down to the ground.

'I wish life were that simple.'

'What did she say?'

'Oh, many things – many unrepeatable things. Including that I could never see the boys again – ever.'

'Sam, that's just heat of the moment stuff.'

'Probably, but she has a point. I've been in one or two scrapes but I've never been targeted by a contract killer before. If these people are as ruthless as I think they are, Sue has a definite point. These people think I'm a danger to them and they'll get at me however they can. The boys are a soft target. I had to tell her that.'

'What's she going to do?'

Sam shrugged. 'She'll do whatever she thinks necessary to protect Tom and Jake. I tried to offer advice but she cut me dead.'

'I can imagine.'

'I need to sort this, Sal.'

'How?'

'Well, I've got an idea.'

'Idea? What sort of idea?'

Sam's ideas always worried her. He took a piece of paper from his wallet on which was written a phone number. He then picked up his mobile and stared into the mid-distance, his lips moving as if composing a speech in his head. Below him the TV crew were doing the fourth take of the arrest scene. Sam stabbed the number into his phone and spoke in a slightly affected voice.

'Am I speaking to Mr Henry Corbally...? Ah, Mr Corbally, we've done business recently... What business? Why business regarding your recently departed cousin, Austin Corbally. Surely it hasn't slipped your mind that my colleague arranged his departure on your behalf in order that you can take his place at the top of the list in your terminally ill uncle's will...? Why am I ringing? I'll tell you why I'm ringing, Mr Corbally. I'm ringing because, according to our figures, your account isn't fully paid up.'

There was a long pause as these words were greeted with a shocked silence, which was broken by Sam.

'Please don't mess us about Mr Corbally or we might have to arrange your very own departure... That's better, now we understand one another... Really...? And how much did you pay...? I see, well I'm afraid we charge on a percentage basis, didn't my colleague mention this...? No? How remiss of him. He should have mentioned that the thirty thousand was simply a deposit pending the money from your uncle's will being released to you. We charge ten per cent, Mr Corbally, which is £130,000. This means you still owe us one hundred thousand. You will withdraw this in cash for collection three days from today in a place I will inform you of between now and then. Please keep your phone with you, Mr Corbally. You don't want to let us down or you'll invoke our penalty clause.'

Sam clicked off his Pay-As-You-Go phone. The call would be untraceable. He turned to Sally. 'Simple as that. I get to meet a hire-and-fire man.'

'The will didn't conclusively prove it was Henry Corbally who arranged his cousin's death,' she said. 'What made you so certain?'

'I wasn't certain, but I had to sound as if I was. He might have picked up on any uncertainty.'

'You're certain now, though?'

'Dead certain.'

'Will you take the money off him?'

'Most certainly.'

CHAPTER THIRTY

Annie was looking out of her office window at the grounds of Wickham Farm. One thought crossing her mind was to pack in all the illegal stuff. They had enough money for the three of them to live out their lives in reasonable comfort. She fancied she and Tanya could successfully run the builder's merchants without propping it up with moody money. But what would Nathan do? He had a criminal outlook on life. With all the money in the world he'd still be dealing in drugs, because that was all he knew. He and Tanya were seated behind her. She turned around and sat at her desk. She put on a pair of reading glasses and opened a file

301

in front of her. It was four days after the attempt on Sam's life.

'I've had the accountant draw up a valuation of our assets,' she said. 'We each have considerable personal money, but if we add in the value of this place, the merchant's business, the properties we own and the money invested in overseas accounts it comes to a considerable sum.'

'What's a considerable sum, Ma?' asked Nathan.

'Thirty million plus – most of it in property and the business.'

Nathan whistled, Tanya nodded. It was around the figure she expected. She also anticipated what her mother was going to say next.

'I would take half, you two would share the rest.'

'That sounds fair,' said Tanya. 'So, you think we should go straight, Ma?'

'I do, Tan. This Carew business has made me think. I've got two sons buried out there and I don't want either of you two ending up there – me neither for that matter. This isn't a business that lasts forever. Eventually Carew, or someone like him, is going to bring the rest of us down.' She looked at Nathan. 'What do you think, son?'

Nathan shrugged. 'What else would I do, Ma? We have obligations to our clients, both with the girls and with the drugs. Maybe

302

you should just cut me loose and let me run them on my own.'

'Is that what you want, Nathan?'

'It's what I'm good at, Ma. You two ladies run the merchant's. I'll run everything else on my own.'

Annie stared at him, realising what a liability he threatened to be. Left to his own devices he'd soon end up inside, and he knew everything about the family business. What Nathan knew could put them all down for life without parole.

'That's what we'll do then.' Annie said. She knew he'd do it anyway, no matter what she said.

Nathan grinned and his mother saw, in his pin-prick pupils, that he was high on something. She also caught the knowing look in Tanya's eyes and the almost imperceptible shake of her head.

'We have to cover our tracks, Ma,' Tanya said. 'We still have to get rid of Carew. Word is that he's lying low.'

'There are more ways than one ter skin a cat,' said Annie, rubbing her chin. 'Carew's got an ex-wife and two boys. Get word to the mother that a contract goes out on the boys if Carew continues to come after us. He'll back off. That way we can take him out at our leisure.'

Henry Corbally knocked, tentatively, on the

door of room 425 in the Forrester Hotel, just off the A1, north of Scotch Corner. Sam called out for him to come in. Corbally entered. Sam was sitting on the bed. He beckoned for Corbally to sit in the only chair. Sam allowed himself to go into *very slightly mad* mode. It was something he was good at.

'I thought we'd meet here for your convenience, Mr Corbally, with you being a Sheffield lad.'

Corbally nodded, not knowing whether to appear grateful. He thought this man had an odd look about him. Sam inclined his head towards a small suitcase that Corbally had brought in with him.

'I trust that contains the balance of your outstanding account?'

Corbally sounded petulant. 'I've brought it – but I think yer takin' liberties. I were told the job'd cost thirty thousand. There were no mention of it bein' just a down payment.'

'You wanted us to kill your cousin so you could earn yourself one point three million pounds and all we get is thirty thousand. You omitted to tell us just how much you would benefit from this murder. You see, we take all the risks involved in murdering your cousin Austin, and you reap almost all of the benefits.'

'I'd no idea how much I'd get left – any more than I know how you found out.'

'Mr Corbally, it's our business to know everything about our clients. For a start we need to know if you can afford to pay.'

'I were just asked if I'd pay thirty thousand to have him seen to. That was the deal.'

Corbally obviously felt badly done by, which was exactly what Sam wanted. He wanted the man to put up an argument. He wanted him to discuss the matter in as much detail as possible. He scratched his head.

'*Seen to?* Let's use plain language, Mr Corbally. You mean you wanted us to murder your cousin for thirty thousand pounds – that's two point three per cent commission. We're risk-taking professionals, Mr Corbally, not estate agents.'

'He were never a proper cousin. Not related by blood ter neither me, nor me uncle. It were never right.'

'Tell me, Mr Corbally, have you any idea who you're dealing with?'

He laid enough menace into his question to affect Corbally's clear thinking. Sam was asking a question he should have known the answer to, were he who he said he was. He just wanted to be sure.

'No – 'course I don't,' muttered Corbally, scared. 'Up ter now it's just been a voice on the phone.'

'But you know enough not to upset us.'

'All right, all right, here's yer money. Yer don't need ter count it – it's all there.'

Corbally picked up the case and put it on the bed beside Sam, who held up his hands. 'I'm quite sure it is, Mr Corbally, but you're a dissatisfied customer. I don't like that. It's bad for our business.'

Corbally became wary. 'I'm sorry. It's OK. You take the money.'

Sam shook his head. 'No, no. If you're to go away from here I want you to go away happy. Remind me Mr Corbally, how did we get in touch with you? Was it our Samaritan service? I wasn't involved with your contract at that stage.'

'It were an advert in the *Daily Mail*.'

'Was that one of our Friday adverts?'

'No, it was a Monday – Monday, April the tenth. Me birthday, actually. That were the day I found out I'd been knocked back in the will. Some bloody birthday present.'

'Ah,' said Sam, 'and our advert came to the rescue. These personal columns have so many meanings, providing the wording is sufficiently ambiguous. Tell me, did you work out the hidden meaning straight away?' He was guessing, but he was fairly certain he was on solid ground.

'It sounded like something that could be handy,' said Corbally.'

Sam laughed. 'I bet you didn't realise just *how* handy.'

'No,' admitted Corbally. 'I didn't.'

'But, you went along with it just the same?

The offer to kill your cousin for thirty thousand pounds?'

'That's right, thirty thousand pounds. Yer said it yerself. Why do I have ter pay more?'

'Because we say so, Mr Corbally. And in this business we don't have to argue with anyone. Are you happy about that?'

'I suppose so.'

'We now need to break all links between you and our contact, Mr Corbally. Do you still have his personal phone number?'

'You mean the one he gave me that wasn't in the advert?'

'That's the one I mean.'

'It's on my mobile.'

'Hand it over.' Sam held out his hand. Corbally reluctantly gave him his phone. 'Under what name?' Sam asked.

'Mr Small.'

Sam tutted and shook his head. 'It's about time he started using something a bit more original. He was Mr Big for three years, now he's Mr Small.' He put the phone in his pocket and said, 'Don't even think about ringing that number again.'

'How can I? I can't remember it.'

'Right, you can go.'

Corbally got to his feet and made for the door. He paused, with his hand on the handle. 'Is that it then? Yer won't come back for more?'

'That's it,' Sam assured him. 'We have all

we require from you.'

Tanya came out into the yard from the office as Annie was signing a delivery note for a load of building sand.

'It seems that Carew's one step ahead of us. His boys have disappeared with the mother and stepfather. What's the betting they won't come back until he gets us or we get him?'

'Do we know where he is?'

'No idea.'

Annie cursed as the wagon drove away. 'The bastard's got the edge on us.'

'Only if he knows who I am.'

'Right,' said Annie, 'and no one knows.'

Tanya looked sheepish. 'Well, there might be one person–'

Annie glared at her. 'One person? What bloody person?'

'Kilpatrick.'

'How the hell will he know?'

'He, er, he knows I did the bookie's wife with a hammer, and he might put two and two together.'

'Jesus, Tan. I knew this Hammerhead thing was a bad idea.'

'I didn't ask for the label, Ma.'

'Tan, you asked for the label the minute yer smashed in yer first skull. It were fuckin' inevitable.'

Sam and Sally were still based in Goathland. They had spent their time productively as far as Sam's mental rehabilitation was concerned. Apart from his meeting with Henry Corbally he had confined himself to enjoying the countryside and Sally as much as he could. Sally joined in the fun wholeheartedly. They took a scenic trip on the North Yorkshire Moors Railway and went for long walks following gurgling streams and cascading waterfalls, through dark forests and deep valleys. Sally amazed him by identifying rare and beautiful birds such as goldcrests, greater spotted woodpeckers, wagtails, yellowthroats and jays; and trees like hazel, elm, walnut and larch. Sam amused her by accurately identifying a squirrel and a conker tree. They visited Robin Hood's Bay, Whitby and Scarborough, each night returning to their hotel in Goathland.

They had been there a week when Sam opened the copy of the *Daily Mail* dated April 10th. It had arrived in that morning's post. Sue had rung him on his mobile to say she was keeping her family away for the foreseeable future. He guessed wherever they were it was a damned sight warmer than Goathland. She didn't repeat her threat never to let him see the boys again and Sam thought it better to let sleeping dogs lie. He said he'd try and sort things out as quickly as possible and get back to her. She gave him the impression that she was enjoying wherever she was, but no way would she tell him that. Jonathan, her new husband, wasn't short of a bob or two. Sam was happy to have him lavish some of it on his boys. He found the advert in a small, discreet box on page 17:

Do you have a problem that you cannot solve because you are up against a person or people whom you cannot fight? Do you feel you have exhausted every avenue and don't know where to turn?

Are you suffering physical or sexual abuse – or have you suffered in the past and feel a need to right a wrong? Are you being blackmailed, bullied or cheated?

Maynard and Fisher may be able to help. <u>We do not judge</u> – <u>we work for you</u>. You will be stronger with us on your side, we are good at what we do and we may be able to turn the tide in your favour quite legally.

Although we are not a charitable organisation we are highly professional and our results reflect our fees.

There was a company logo depicting the scales of justice weighing in Maynard and Fisher's favour – and therefore in the clients' favour. It was a tempting ad and Sam could think of many people who might respond to it. There was a mobile number to ring. Sam tried it several times until he realised it was no longer in use. The personal number Corbally had given him was of far more value. Had he still been a copper he'd have got the newspaper to tell him who paid for the ad. It would probably have been an over-the-counter cash transaction with a false address. But, you never know. Maybe Owen could give it a try. It was time he brought Owen into the picture. He gave the ad to Sally to read.

'I think it's time we moved back to civilization,' he said.

'What? Back to Unsworth?'

'Correct. I'm sick of running from this bloody woman. It's time she started running from me.'

'Right – I assume it would be useless for me to point out the obvious danger in this bravado.'

'It's not bravado. I'm still scared but I need to get the job done and I can't do it without sticking my head above the battlements now and again. It's called a calculated risk.'

'But you will remain vigilant?'

'Sal, I'll remain vigilant to the point of looking over every shoulder available, including yours.'

'Right, where do we start?'

'I really need to see Kevin Kilpatrick – he's the only one who actually knows who's behind all this. If I can get the name off him I can give Owen the whole package – the video of Corbally in the hotel and the identity of the contract killer.'

'And how are you going to persuade him to talk to you?'

'By telling him that they're already trying to kill me. If *I'm* a danger to them, how much of a risk does he pose? I don't even know who they are. I reckon he'll have made connection between Mrs Henshawe and these hammer killings, the same as I did. He'll certainly make it if I tell him they're identical in every way. I think Kevin might want to talk to me.'

CHAPTER THIRTY-ONE

Alec came out of the cabin just as Sam drove on to the site. 'The Scarlet Pimpernel as I live and breathe.'

Sam grinned and looked over to where Mick and Curly were concreting a footing. Mick saw him and called out, 'Hello yerself.'

'Hello yerself,' returned Sam, in Mick's Mayo accent. 'How's she cuttin'?'

'She's cuttin' great, boss. Are ye back then?'

'Not yet.'

'Still chasin' dat lady wid the hammer?'

'Something like that.'

'We could do wid her here. I got some holes I need ter cut out of the wall.'

'She only does heads.'

'She'll have ter learn ter multi-skill,' said Curly, 'it's the modern way.'

Sam motioned Alec back into the hut and followed him in, otherwise he'd be tied up talking to Mick and Curly for hours. They chatted about building work for a while, then Alec nudged him onto the subject of the recent attempts on Sam's life.

'All the lads think what you're doin' is stupid.'

'I know, Alec. But I've dug myself a hole that I can't just walk away from. It needs sorting, and the police don't want to know.'

'What about Owen?'

'Owen's a small, friendly cog in a great big, unfriendly wheel. I'm up against it, Alec.'

'That serious, is it?'

'Well, it's pretty serious. Has anyone been looking for me here?'

'Well, there was one bloke nosin' around a few days ago – asked about you, which I thought was suspicious. Turns out he was from Robinson's Builders' Merchants, touting for business.'

Sam pulled a face. 'The old man never dealt with them – reckoned they were as bent as nine-bob notes. Look, I'll be keeping my head down for a while yet. Could you

313

organise the office door with some form of high security entry? You know, decent lock, CCTV camera, phone, remote opening – that sort of thing.'

'Like you have at your flat?'

'Same sort of thing.'

'No problem, and if there's anything else you need...'

'A mug of tea might go down well. I swear there's no tea on earth that tastes like building site tea. It's like camel pee but I've acquired a taste for it.'

Alec arranged a brew, then he got Sam talking about recent events. Sam told him about the naked woman who tried to kill him, and her accomplice who died and how it was obvious that she was a contract killer and how the police didn't want to believe this. When Mick arrived with two steaming mugs of tea, the site phone rang. Alec answered it as Sam took the tea.

'Blast! We need it now. I ordered it three days ago. When's the earliest you can deliver...? What? That's no good to me.' Alec put the phone down in exasperation. 'Higson's have no cement in. They reckon their suppliers have let them down.'

'Are we completely out?' Sam asked. It was a proper problem, one that seemed to have so much more value than the self-inflicted problems he'd been manufacturing these past few weeks. Alec looked at Mick.

'How many bags have we got left?'

'Enough ter last us the day, but the brickies'll be screamin' fer some in the mornin'.'

'I'll try Robinson's,' decided Alec.

'The old man'll turn over in his grave,' commented Sam.

'Beggars can't be choosers. I'll take the pickup – a ton should do us till we get Higson's delivery.'

'Just make sure it hasn't gone off,' Sam warned.

Alec resented him dropping in out of the blue and patronising him with advice he didn't need.

'I don't need telling that, Sam – and I've heard Robinson's have cleaned their act up lately. They're doin' some good deals.'

'Fair enough. I'm poking my nose in – sorry.'

Kevin read Sam's letter. It was brief enough to arouse interest:

Regarding Mrs Henshawe and more recent similar events. You need to ring me.

Sam Carew

There was a mobile phone number. At first he had no intention of ringing but, as the day wore on, he knew he wanted to know what Carew had to say. Carew. It was a name emblazoned on his memory, for all the wrong reasons. He rang Sam that same evening.

'This is Kevin Kilpatrick. I got yer letter.'

'Right. Has your wife or daughter had a word with you about me?'

'Alison has. I weren't happy.'

'No one thought you would be. Kevin, this so-called serial killer is using exactly the same method as you're supposed to have used on Mrs Henshawe.'

'Could be a copy-cat.'

'You and I know that's bollocks,' said Sam. 'The full details of the Henshawe killings were never made public.'

'What details?'

'For a start, I know it's a woman and I know she's a contract killer. She uses a heavy, ball pein hammer; single blow in exactly the same place every time, and she covers the head with a towel – apart from one time when it wasn't convenient. I also know she doesn't always work alone. There was more than one person involved in the Henshawe murders – and I don't think you were one of them. Who are these people, Kevin?'

Kevin said nothing. Sam pressed on. 'How come Alison and Patsy don't know who they are?'

'They're better off not knowing,' said Kevin, 'so are you fer that matter.'

'Hardly. They've tried to kill me twice and I don't even know who they are. My two sons have had to leave the country until it's sorted. Who's to say they won't go after your wife and daughter now I've stirred things up?'

There was a silence as Kevin pondered this. 'Yer should never have got involved,' he muttered.

'Alison got me involved. The woman who killed Mrs Henshawe's going round killing other people now. You're doing time for a murder she did and she's laughing at you because you're too scared to do anything about it.'

'There's nowt I can do. I made me decision nine years ago. No point goin' back now.'

'Kevin, you're the only one who knows who she is.'

'Yer sound very certain that she's the one who killed Mrs Henshawe.'

'I'm certain because I asked her, Kevin. She admitted it. She'd no reason not to tell me. As far as she was concerned I was a dead man. You do realise that you're more of a danger to them now than you ever were. *You* can point the police in the right direction.'

'So, why am I talkin' ter you. Why aren't the coppers talkin' ter me?'

'Because they've told the papers she's a serial killer and they're still hoping she is – otherwise they'll look idiots. You need to watch your back, Kevin. Maybe even try and get yourself ghosted somewhere miles away.'

'Ghosted?'

'Yeah, it mean–'

'I know exactly what it means, Carew. It

means the cell door opening at four in the morning and being given five minutes to dress and pack yer stuff. Then being frog-marched to a van that takes yer to another jail at the other end o' the country, but no one tells yer which one – that's fer you ter figure out when yer get there. It's the prison system's way of tellin' yer that yer no more important than the shit they scrape off their shoes. They think they can do just what they want with yer without so much as a by-your-fuckin'-leave.'

'Ah, it's happened to you,' surmised Sam.

'Once, years ago, in Strangeways. I went through a bolshie phase – ended up on the Moor. Trouble is, I were bolshie for weeks before they moved me. How do I get meself ghosted fast?'

It was a question Sam had prepared himself for. 'Tell your wing governor that you know at least three officers who are taking money on the outside to make life easy for someone inside. Tell him you've got proof and you're really pissed off about it, then wait for the early morning removal van. Prison governors don't like whistle blowers. You'll probably be whisked down to Park-hurst or somewhere, with no one knowing where you are for weeks.'

'Like I say, I do know the system.'

'Then work it to your advantage. Just keep my phone number handy.' Sam paused, then saw no reason not to ask the question again, 'Sure you don't want to give me the names right now?'

The thought had obviously been going through Kevin's mind. He paused before deciding, 'Me giving names won't get them names locked up. Me givin' names'll make it worse for Alison and Patsy.'

'I know one of them raped Alison,' said Sam, quietly, still hoping to goad him into giving the names. There was another long silence, then the phone went dead.

Kevin sat on a wall, smoking and considering his options. He'd heard nothing from the Robinsons since Nathan raped his daughter. He wept every time he thought about that. He also wondered what George would have done about it had he lived. He'd have had Nathan castrated at the very least. There was a game of football going on. He'd kicked the ball back into play a couple of times. There was a time when he'd have joined in, he could still show the young uns a thing or two about the game. But his thoughts were many miles away and many years back in time:

It was 1986. He and George Robinson were about to turn over a Bradford bookie's house. Melvin Buttercran was a course bookie who took all his takings home and stuck them in his safe, which often contained over a hundred grand. George knew the combination to this safe due to him having an affair with Buttercran's wife, who was under the deluded impression that she and George would use the money to run away together.

Mrs Buttercran had ensured that she and her husband went out that evening. She had even given George a house key. The beauty of it all was that her husband would never be able to account for having such a sum in his house in cash.

'The cops aren't going to go chasing after money the taxman dunt know about,' George had told Kevin. 'He's as bent as we are. His missis reckons that if we leave a couple of grand in the safe it'll make the coppers wonder if he's been robbed at all.'

Kevin remembered feeling good about it. It was a job that couldn't go wrong. They would wear gloves as a precaution but even that might not be necessary. It was a theft that might well not even be reported. A job with probably no comeback from the law. The perfect job.

They hadn't gone armed, George only believed in rough stuff when it was necessary to chastise fellow villains. He'd done his fair share of chastising in his time, but never to civilians. He had his standards. That's what Kevin had liked about him.

The job had gone smoothly. A hundred

and seventeen grand, not including the three grand they left in the safe, all neat and tidy. In fact, the job had gone so smoothly that they stayed longer than they should have to toast their success with Buttercran's scotch.

Then the door burst open and the bookie stood there, wild eyed, waving a twelve bore shotgun about. He and his wife had had an argument. In her cups she'd blurted out things she shouldn't, enough to send Buttercran racing back to his house, leaving his angry wife in the restaurant. He pointed the gun at George, whom he apparently knew.

'Robinson, you bastard! Not content with screwing my missis, you're stealing my brass!'

He fired, but George had seen it coming and dived to one side. The bookie was now standing over George with the gun at his neck. He was completely out of control and Kevin saw his finger tighten on the trigger. He dived at him and pushed him away. The gun clattered to the floor and Kevin picked it up. His only intention was to keep it from the bookie, who grabbed the barrel and tried to pull it off him. Kevin couldn't even remember his finger being on the trigger, but it obviously was as the blast took away most of Melvin Buttercran's face and soaked both Kevin and George in blood.

They fled the scene, with George taking the money, arranging to split it when the heat was off. But George was picked up at home within two hours.

By way of repaying Kevin for saving his life, George held his hands up to the killing, pleading self-defence in view of the fact that it was Buttercran's own gun. Unfortunately, before he was arrested, he had told Annie the true story. Afterwards he made her and the family swear an oath not to take it out on Kevin. He was found guilty of murder and sentenced to life imprisonment.

The money from the robbery was never recovered, in fact it was never mentioned in court. It was assumed that the three thousand left in the safe was what George had been after. Mrs Buttercran made no noises about it, she just hoped George wouldn't mention her part in it all, which he didn't.

It left the Robinsons with a hundred and seventeen thousand pounds with which to build up their business, and a deep grudge against Kevin Kilpatrick, who was walking around scot-free while George was in prison. When George died they felt freed from the obligation he had placed them under, and sought poetic vengeance on Kevin.

It was late afternoon. Sam and Sally were in Sam's kitchen when the phone rang. Sam picked it up. It was Alec.

'Alec, what is it?'

'Probably nothing. Janet Seager came on site looking for you. I told her where you were at home. Did I do the right thing?'

'I don't see why not, Janet's OK. Did she say she's coming here now?'

'I got that impression.'

'Cheers Alec.'

Ten minutes later DI Seager arrived with a uniformed constable. She didn't return his smile when he opened the door.

'What is it, Janet?'

'Sorry about this, Sam – Sam Carew I'm arresting you for breaking and entering with intent to commit theft. You do not have to say anything. But it may harm your defence if you do not mention when questioned something which you later rely on in court. Anything you do say may be given in evidence.'

The Constable stepped forward and slapped handcuffs on him. Sally came out into the hall. 'Janet,' she said, 'what the hell is this?'

'Yes, Janet,' echoed Sam as he was marched down the stairs. 'What the hell is this?'

Janet spoke to the Constable. 'It's OK, I can deal with him. Could you radio in that we've picked Carew up and I'm picking DC Price up next.'

'Owen?' said Sam. 'What the hell has Owen got to do with this?'

'I think you already know, Sam.'

Sam suddenly clutched his stomach. 'Look, Janet. You're going to have to let me go to the bathroom before I get into that car. I've had a stomach upset all afternoon.'

'It's true,' confirmed Sally.

'And I'll need these handcuffs taking off – unless your constable wants to be my toilet attendant.'

The Constable gave a grimace. Sam had a look of desperation on his face.

'Janet, this is a bit embarrassing, but you're going to have to take my word for it. I really do need to go to the bog – RIGHT NOW!'

'OK, take the cuffs off – Sam if this is some sort of–'

Sam was already hurrying back upstairs.

Bowman switched on the tape as Sam fidgeted in his chair. 'Stomach still giving you trouble, Carew?'

'When it does you'll be the first to know, Bowman,' replied Sam.

Bowman looked at his watch. 'Interview with Mr Sam Carew commenced at 18.37. Present is Detective Chief Inspector Bowman, and Detective Inspector Seager. Mr Carew has declined the need for legal representation.'

'Why am I being interviewed by the hierarchy?' enquired Sam. 'It's only breaking and entering, a couple of plods could do this job.'

'You're not here to ask questions, Carew. You're here to answer them.'

'It was a fair question,' retorted Sam, 'and

for the benefit of the tape, DCI Bowman doesn't seem to have an answer.'

'Could you tell me where you were at one o'clock on the morning of October 2nd?'

'You mean where was I on the night of the break-in at the solicitors in Blenheim Road?'

'Just answer the question,' snapped Bowman.

'At one o'clock I'll have been on Blenheim Road, trying to figure out why my engine had cut out.'

Janet's eyes narrowed. Bowman frowned. 'Go on,' he said.

'Well, normally,' Sam went on, 'I'd have rung the AA, but for some reason I didn't have their number in my phone.'

'You could have tried Directory Enquiries,' said Janet.

'I could,' agreed Sam. 'But I couldn't remember any of the blasted numbers they keep on advertising on the telly. When it was good old 192 you knew where you were, but nowadays there's so many numbers and I couldn't remember any of them.'

'So, what did you do?'

'I rang my pal Owen.'

'You mean Detective Constable Price?' said Janet, who was hoping that Sam's obviously manufactured story would stand up to scrutiny.

'That's right,' said Sam. 'I just wanted to get home.'

'Where had you been?'

'Well, as you know I'm a private investigator and I'd been on an investigation – a job for which I must claim confidentiality, unless it has a direct bearing on the crime for which I'm being wrongly accused.'

'We have a witness who identified you as being on the premises of Bateson, Collins and Company around that time,' said Bowman.

'Your witness is mistaken,' said Sam.

'We also have a witness who saw you drive away in your car at around one-thirty that morning,' Bowman added.

'That witness is not mistaken. I got fed up of waiting for Owen, tried the car and, would you believe it, the thing started. I rang Owen to tell him not to bother but there was no reply. I think he'd switched his phone off.'

'Did you hear the commotion at the premises of Bateson, Collins and Company?' asked Janet.

'I heard an alarm going off, then a while later a couple of police cars arrived. I learned later that Owen arrived about that time and forgot all about me when he saw there was a bit of excitement to be had.'

'DC Price told the officer at the scene that the break-in might tie in with one of his investigations and that was why he stopped.'

'Bloody Owen!' exclaimed Sam. 'He'll

make up any old tosh, just to stick his nose in.' He thought he saw a glint of admiration in Janet's eyes. She didn't want Owen getting into any trouble.

'What was stolen?' he asked.

Sam saw Janet shrug, indicating that she didn't know. Bowman glared at him. 'Like I said, I'm asking the questions.'

'Come off it,' protested Sam. 'If I'm being accused of something, I need to know how much trouble I'm in.'

'You were disturbed before you managed to steal anything,' Bowman told him.

'Now there's a comfort,' said Sam. 'At least I'm not being accused of theft, just breaking and entering – slap on the wrist from a magistrate.'

'You also assaulted a police officer, which is a custodial offence.'

'That would be PC Melia,' said Sam. 'I'm told he got a broken hooter.'

Sam guessed that their witness must be PC Melia. He was the only officer on the premises. Once the finger of suspicion had been pointed at Sam, Melia had obviously decided to seek retribution for his broken nose. Sam decided to go on the attack.

'You say you have a witness who saw me on the premises?'

'We have a solid witness,' said Bowman.

'It can only be a police officer – there were no other people – were there? Apart from the burglar, I mean.'

'It was a police officer,' confirmed Janet. Bowman glared at her for giving too much away.

'And my guess is good old PC Melia, who must really want to get back at the bloke who gave him a broken nose.' He saw Janet give a very slight, encouraging nod. 'If it was PC Melia I would want to know why he didn't identify me sooner. He saw me the following day, just after I'd been shot at. You'd have thought he'd have mentioned it to someone then.'

'PC Melia,' said Bowman, 'thought it was you straight away, but he couldn't believe you would sink so low. Your presence in the area has confirmed his suspicion and forced him to come forward, albeit very reluctantly.' He got to his feet. 'Interview suspended at 18.43.'

Janet turned the tape off. Bowman walked to the door, then half turned. 'You'll be held until we interview DC Price. We don't want you exchanging stories.'

'When will that be?' Sam asked.

'Sometime tomorrow. You'll be held in a cell until then.'

'Why can't you interview him tonight?'

'Because I choose not to,' said Bowman. 'I shouldn't worry, this will be the first of many nights' incarceration for you. You might as well get used to it.'

'You really are a bastard, Bowman.'
'I do my best, Carew.'

It was exactly twenty-four hours before he was released. Bowman had kept him for as long as he was legally allowed. He was waiting at the door as Sam went out. 'You and Price seem to be singing from the same hymn sheet. I can only assume that you had your stories worked out well in advance.'

'Owen's a much straighter copper than you are, Bowman. Oh, by the way, I was going to give you some interesting information on the contract killer, but as you don't believe she's a contract killer it'd be a waste of good information.'

'Give your information to who the hell you like, Carew. Just don't bother me with your lame-brained ideas!'

Sam smiled at O'Donnell who had appeared beside Bowman. 'You heard that from the horse's mouth, Mr O'Donnell. Bowman doesn't want my information.'

O'Donnell said nothing. Sam turned and went out of the door, wondering whether to give the DVD of his chat with Henry Corbally to the TV or to the papers. Why stint? Might as well give a copy to both.

The trouble was, how did he get around knowing all about the will? It wouldn't be long before someone from Bateson, Collins and Company made a beeline for the

Corbally file, only to find the will was missing. And tying him to the missing will was just the sort of circumstantial evidence that Bowman needed. Sam would be back in that cell with a lot of explaining to do. It wouldn't do Owen's career much good either. So, if the Henry Corbally DVD was to be of any use to him, the will had to go back where it belonged. There was no alternative. He breathed out a heavy sigh. Just another small problem that might end up with him being arrested. Why the hell didn't he just stick to laying bricks? No one came to arrest you if your brickwork wasn't straight and level; the building inspector would simply make you take it down and do it again. Police inspectors tended to lock you up for not being straight and level. On top of which there was no money to be made from this job – unless the Manchester Victoria Insurance Company paid him his 20% commission for proving Mrs Crowther's claim to be fraudulent. Revealing Mick Crowther's murderer to be a contract killer would go a long way to proving just that. It would show Bowman to be an idiot and it would possibly send a lot of money Sam's way. That thought cheered him up. He was smiling when he got into Sally's car.

'Why the big grin?' she asked.

'Well, Mr Bowman's been nasty to me and I've thought of a way of repaying him. By the way, thanks for backing me up on the stomach-ache thing – quick thinking, that.'

'Owen called round just after they took you. I gather you rang him from the bathroom. He ran through your story with me, to see what I thought.'

'And?' enquired Sam.

'And it wasn't bad for a spur of the moment effort.'

'Not bad? It was inspired.'

'I gather it did the trick. You know, Sam, considering Owen's saved your life twice in the last few weeks you take some awful liberties with him.'

'That wasn't taking liberties. That was saving his neck.'

'And yours.'

'That was just a lucky bonus,' said Sam. 'Look, if nothing else, this has made me realise that before I show this Corbally DVD to anyone I need to get the will back into its file – and before you say anything just remember whose idea it was for me to come back into private eye work.'

'It was mine, but I'd forgotten what a nightmare you are when you get going. It must have been that bullet I took. Maybe it dulled part of my memory.'

'You seem to be pretty much back to normal, Sal.'

'Apart from the stick, you mean?'

'Well, the stick will be the next thing to go.'

'It probably won't, Sam – I'll probably always need a stick. I've got a permanent weakness in the base of my spine.'

'Really?'

'Really.'

Sam went quiet. Her injury had been down to him. 'I've got Employer's Liability Insurance,' he said. 'You'd better make a claim against me. Get a solicitor to put a figure on it.'

'I can hardly claim for loss of earnings – you never stopped paying me.'

'Just see a solicitor, Sal. Get him to take me to the cleaners.' He went quiet again as his brain ticked over. 'Come to think of it,' he said, 'I know the very solicitor.'

'Now, why does that make me nervous?' said Sally.

CHAPTER THIRTY-TWO

Robert Bateson Senior took off his glasses and cleaned them with a soft cloth. Sally was sitting at the other side of his desk.

'It's impossible to put a figure on it at this point, Miss Grover, but it seems to me that there's no question that you have a valid claim against your employer. First we'll need a medical prognosis, then we can start looking at some figures. I imagine your claim will be substantial.' He was a humourless man but Sally guessed he'd be good at his job. 'I'd require you to come back with all your medical and employment details.'

'That's no problem,' she assured him. The will was in her bag, but she had no idea how to get it back into its file. She was hoping an opportunity might have presented itself. No such luck. Maybe next time. Sam wouldn't be best pleased with her failure.

'I'm a little curious about something, Miss Grover. Correct me if I'm wrong, but isn't your employer the same man who was held on suspicion of breaking into these offices?'

'He has a poor relationship with the police,' explained Sally. 'He was in the area, but he had nothing to do with the break-in – which is why he was released without charge. I suspect you've heard of him.'

'His name is not unfamiliar in legal circles,' said Bateson, sniffily. 'I gather he's a bit of a maverick.'

'That pretty much describes him.'

'So,' he pondered. 'Is it merely a coincidence that you chose this firm?'

'It was Sam's idea actually. He suggested I make this claim against him – or his insurers to be precise. I need a solicitor and, for obvious reasons, your name was at the forefront of his mind.'

'I see.'

Sally had anticipated this question and had her answer prepared. She wasn't sure if he was convinced. Bateson managed a thin smile.

'So, we must thank Mr Carew for sending business our way.' He picked up his phone. 'Carol, I'm sending Miss Grover through to you. Would you make an appointment for her to come back?'

Sally stood up and made a show of being unsteady on her feet. Bateson went to the door and opened it for her. 'Good day to you, Miss Grover, I'll set the wheels in motion.'

He closed the door behind her. Sally smiled at the secretary, then gave a sudden grimace and took a bottle of tablets from her bag.

'Are you OK, Miss Grover?'

'Just got a twinge, that's all. I'm supposed to take these pain killers, but they make me so sleepy. You couldn't get me a glass of water, could you?'

'Of course I can – I'll just be a minute.'

Sally took the will out of her bag and scanned the rows of filing cabinets, hoping they weren't locked. This was probably the only chance she'd ever get. She spotted the one saying Br-Do, just as Sam had described. Thankfully, it wasn't locked. She slid it open as quietly as she could. From the corner of her eye she saw Bateson's office door opening. She closed the drawer quickly and stuffed the will in her pocket.

'Miss Grover,' said Bateson. 'Er, what's happened to my secretary?'

'She's gone to get me a drink of water. I need to take some tablets.' She could swear she saw disbelief in his eyes.

'Really? Would you ask her to come through when she gets back?'

'Of course I will.'

He closed the door. She half expected him to be hovering behind it, planning to open it and catch her in the act. She placed a hand on the filing cabinet drawer handle, keeping her eyes on Bateson's office door. Her heart was racing. If she was caught in the act, with the will in her hand – phew! – it didn't bear thinking about. What the hell should she do? The secretary would be back any second. Bateson's door remained closed. She took a deep breath, slid open the drawer, riffled through the files until she came to the one marked Michael Joseph Corbally, and stuck the will inside. Two seconds after she closed the drawer the secretary came back with a glass of water. Sally's heart was racing. She was inwardly cursing Sam. The secretary looked concerned as she handed Sally the water.

'Are you sure you'll be OK? Can I get you anything else?'

'I'll be fine, thanks – I'll be a lot finer when I take my boss to the cleaners for doing this to me.' She said it with such vehemence that the secretary would never believe she was play-acting. Which, of course, she wasn't.

'Well, you've come to the right man for that. I pity your boss. Mr Bateson isn't a person you want to be up against.'

'Good. Oh, by the way, he'd like you to go through.'

CHAPTER THIRTY-THREE

Kevin made his complaint to the wing governor about favouritism being showed to inmates by prison officers who were having bribes sent direct to their homes.

'If I could afford it, I'd drop 'em a few quid meself, sir. But I don't think it's right.'

'Do you have any proof of this, Kilpatrick?'

'As a matter of fact I do, sir. What I do know is that some of the cons aren't happy. It's bleedin' favouritism is this, sir. It's hard ter put up with favouritism when yer doin' a long stretch an' tryin' ter keep yer nose clean.'

The senior officer stared at him, not quite knowing why he was complaining. This sort of thing went on – it was hard to stamp it out.

'In that case you'd better give me what proof you have and I'll take it from there.'

'With all due respect, sir. I think I should take my proof to the top gov'nor, sir.'

'Is that what you think? Well, perhaps I'll have a word with the governor myself. That will be all, Kilpatrick.'

'Sir.'

Kevin left the office, not at all confident that he'd done enough to get himself ghosted. Carew's phone call had unnerved him. He suddenly trusted no one. There were quite a few lifers in here who'd see him off for a few grand paid to a wife/ girlfriend/ boyfriend on the outside. There were a few nutters who'd see him off just to settle a grudge. He took Sam's letter from his pocket. Right now, Sam Carew was the only person he wanted to talk to. There was about a pound's worth of precious time left on his phone card.

'Hello Kevin,' said Sam, as the prison's number came up on the phone screen. Kevin couldn't figure out how he knew. He'd only ever phoned his wife before. Patsy didn't have this facility on her house phone.

'How did yer know it was me?'

'Technology,' said Sam. 'I don't understand it myself. What can I do for you, Kevin?'

'I've done what yer said, but I doubt if it'll do any good. Ter be honest I'm shittin' bricks in here.'

Sam felt a twinge of guilt, taking advantage of a man under such pressure. 'Maybe if you give me the name I need I can move things on from this end.'

'Or maybe yer givin' me a load of old fanny. There's word in here that they've got an Unsworth copper on wages.'

'Do you know who it is?'

'No.'

'Any idea what rank he is, or was?'

'No.'

'Who's paying this copper, Kevin?'

There was a long silence as Kevin considered his position, which wasn't great.

'I might give yer the names when I get moved.'

'So, there's more than one name?'

'Might be.'

'Kevin, without something to work with I can't help.' Deep down Sam knew he couldn't help anyway, but there was no need for Kevin to know this.

'Me givin' yer them names might make things a damn sight worse for me.'

'So, why have you rung me?'

'Because you helped put me in here, I thought yer might want to help get me out.'

An inmate, queueing behind Kevin, was bustled to one side and told to 'fuck off out of it,' in a manner that had him disappearing at speed. Three men took his place. One of them was holding a short knife.

'How can I,' said Sam, 'if you don't help me? You're not giving me anything to work on, Kevin.'

'All right, all right – I'll give yer the names, but I want yer ter promise to help me. I'm in deep shi–'

'I promise,' said Sam, with his fingers crossed. '...Kevin?' There was no reply. 'Kevin...? Bloody mobile phones!'

They'd been cut off. Sam was frustrated. He cursed his phone for letting him down at such a crucial moment. Surely Kevin would ring him back. The trouble was – and Sam knew it – phone calls weren't easy to make in prison. The odds were that there had been a queue behind Kevin when they got cut off. When he didn't ring back that day Sam thought Kevin might have changed his mind about giving him the name. He made up his mind to buy a more up-to-date phone.

CHAPTER THIRTY-FOUR

Nathan was higher than he'd ever been, but he had plenty to celebrate. Seven and a half million, plus he got to deal the gear and run the girls. He was in his apartment at Wickham Farm, sucking on his crackpipe, when Tanya knocked.

'Nathan, are you decent?'

He let her in. She blinked at the befuddling fumes that hung in the air.

'Want a puff, Tan? Be my guest. I'm happy ter be out of the old bat's clutches.'

'You're not out of them yet. Things have to be sorted out. That's why I'm here.'

'Come to sort me out, eh?' he sniggered.

She was wearing a black Moschino top with no bra underneath. Her Armani jeans were skin tight and tucked into knee-length Jimmy Choo boots. A Balenciaga handbag was slung across her shoulder. Tanya was dressed to kill.

'Fuck me, Tan – I wouldn't mind bein' sorted out like yer sort yer mugs out.'

'Behave yourself, Nathan. We're brother and sister. I'll get us a drink. I hate the stink of this stuff you're on.'

Nathan sat back in his chair and admired her. 'We're only half-brother and -sister.'

'It's plenty,' said Tanya, handing him a large glass of scotch.

'Fair enough,' said Nathan. He was leering at her through pinprick pupils. 'I'm entitled to half a show. Gimme a tit an' fanny show, Tan.'

She clinked her crystal glass to his and swallowed the contents in one go, encouraging him to do the same, which he did. 'Half a show, eh?' she said. 'What do I get for half a show? Half money? That's fifteen grand.'

'Thirty grand for the whole deal – if you're up for it,' he sniggered, hopefully.

'What? You'd pay thirty grand to shag your sister? You dirty bastard.'

'It'd be worth every penny, Tan. Come on, gimme the full works what yer give the mugs – well, minus the punch line.'

'Nathan, you are one sick bastard and no mistake.'

'What? So, you're Mother Theresa all of a sudden? I am what I am, Tan. We're all sick in this family – what's left of us.' He grinned. 'Yer want ter do it, don't yer? I can tell.'

'OK, I'll do it.' She took her top off. 'That's five grand,' she said. 'Want me to go for fifteen?'

'Wow! Them are some ... nice tits, Tan. Go as far as yer ... want ter go.'

He was slurring his words. She undressed, slowly and tantalisingly. By the time she stood in front of him, stark naked, his head was nodding forward. She lifted his chin up with her finger then, satisfied he wasn't going to wake up, she let it go.

'This is as far as I go, brother dear.'

She went into his bathroom and brought out a towel. Then she placed it over his head, took a ball pein hammer from her Balenciaga bag and ended his life with one savage blow, the way she had the others.

She addressed the spreading stain on the towel. 'Sorry Nathan,' she said, 'but my price went up to seven and a half million for a world-class tit and fanny show. You were never much of a brother.'

She was dressed by the time her mother knocked on the door. 'Come in, Ma.'

Annie walked in and looked at her son with her head, sympathetically, to one side. Nathan's head was still covered by the blood-soaked towel.

'So, it's done, then?'

'It's done – it had to be done, Ma. He wasn't to be trusted. He'd have ruined things for both of us.'

'I know, Tan. And I wish I could feel a bit of grief.' She took the towel off Nathan's head and kissed him on the cheek. 'I haven't done that since he were a baby. Jesus, he stinks!'

'He's been on the crack, Ma. At least he went out happy.'

Annie looked at her, suspiciously. 'I hope yer didn't send him out *too* happy.'

'Not that, but happy enough, Ma. He'd have liked a bit more happiness but he nodded off. I gave him a nice drink of scotch and ketamine. He was already too spaced out to taste the difference.'

'His dad were the same,' remembered Annie. 'Put me on the game ter pay for his gear, the black bastard! I soon fettled him. A month after I fell on wi' Nathan I caught him with a dirty tart, an' stuck a dagger in him.' She laughed. 'His tart screamed blue murder. I flattened her and put the dagger

342

in her hand. They locked her up for it.'

She put the towel back over her son's head and held out a hand for Tanya to shake. 'This makes us equal partners, Tan. Equal partners in a legit business. No more banditry.'

'Apart from sorting Carew,' said Tanya.

'Yeah, apart from that.'

CHAPTER THIRTY-FIVE

Sally was at her desk, doing Carew and Son's VAT. Sam looked up from his paper as Owen came into the office. The Welshman obviously had something on his mind.

'We got a call in from Wakefield prison this morning. A sort of courtesy call, with us arresting him.'

'Arresting who?' said Sam.

'Kevin Kilpatrick.'

Sam sensed a twinge of concern. 'Kevin? What about him. I was speaking to him yesterday.'

'What – on the phone, around two forty-five?'

Sam thought back. 'About that time, yeah.'

'Because that's the time he was killed, boyo. He was on the phone and someone stabbed him through the heart.'

Sam stood there in shock. 'WHAT? Jesus, Owen! I don't want to hear that.'

'I'm sorry, but it's the truth. They haven't got anyone for it, either.'

Sam sat down with his head in his hands. 'Bloody hell! They ought to call me Kiss Of Death Carew. What the hell am I doing to people?'

'It was hardly your fault, Sam.'

'Maybe not, but was I the cause?'

'I don't know the answer to that.'

'Have you told Alison and her mother?'

'Just been round to see them. They're taking it badly.'

'Did you ask them if they knew who might be responsible?' Sam looked at him, hopefully. Owen shook his head. 'I did mention it. Patsy said if she knew she'd tell us. And I believe she would.'

With shaking hands Sam took out his cigarettes, offered one to Sally. He looked at her, as if seeking permission for something. She nodded her approval.

'Owen,' he said, 'I've got a DVD that'll prove conclusively that Austin Corbally was murdered by a contract killer. Given another minute with Kevin on the phone I might have been able to give you the killer's name.'

'Has this got anything to do with stealing the will from the solicitors?'

'The theft was never discovered and it never will be.'

'Bloody hell, boyo! Don't tell me you broke in again and put it back.'

'Let's just say it's back,' said Sam, 'and no one broke in. Look, just watch this, then I need to decide how best to use it.'

Sally put on a DVD and the three of them watched as Henry Corbally completely incriminated himself from two different camera angles. It left Owen shaking his head in amazement.

'How the hell didn't he twig what you were doing to him?'

'Because,' explained Sam, 'in his mind only the contract killers could possibly have known all the details I presented him with. To him I could only have been what I said I was.'

'Someone's going to ask you how you knew all the details of the will.'

'Easy – I was given the details anony-mously in response to a newspaper advert. I don't have to say any more. If necessary, the police can get a court order for the will. The big question is, how do I handle it? By the way, our killer definitely has a mole inside Unsworth nick.'

'How on Earth do you know that?'

'Kevin told me.'

'Oh...' Sam's answer stopped Owen in his tracks.

Sam looked from Owen to Sally. 'Kevin didn't know the mole's name, but I'm guessing we've all got the same name in mind.'

'You could go public with the DVD,' Sally suggested. 'Send copies to the papers and TV companies. There's no way anyone could suppress it.'

'If I did that I doubt if we'd see our hammer killer for dust. After all she's done to me I need to catch her.'

'What you're saying,' summed up Owen, 'is that you don't want to give the tape to the police because you think one of us is in the killer's pocket and you don't want to go public for fear of scaring her off?'

'Something like that. I know I can trust you and Janet – but will Janet feel obliged to tell Bowman about the tape if I show it to her?'

'Why not show it to O'Donnell?' suggested Owen.

'Bowman, O'Donnell, same thing,' said Sam. 'The tape becomes part of the evidence file. Everyone knows about it, including the bent copper. Henry Corbally gets picked up, the contract killer gets to cover her tracks. She's been operating as a serial killer so she'll definitely change her MO. Probably pack the job in for a while until the heat dies down. Maybe altogether.'

'Which would be no bad thing,' Sally commented. 'We've no idea who she is, or any way of finding out, now that Kevin's dead.'

'What are you saying, Sal?'

'I'm saying that scaring her off might well be good for your health. Don't think I've forgotten how scared you were.'

'Scared – Carew?' said Owen, amazed. 'I hope you're not trying to tell me he's got sense enough to be scared?'

'I'm not oblivious to danger,' said Sam, defensively. 'I just have my own way of handling it.' He thought about Kevin again. 'At the moment, I'm more of a danger to others than I am to myself. Jesus! I hope it wasn't my fault that Kevin was killed.'

'It wasn't your fault,' Owen assured him. 'By the way, what are you going to do with the hundred thousand?'

'Give it to its rightful owner,' said Sam. 'I thought I'd open an investment account in young Ben Corbally's name, with the money to go to him when he's eighteen. Trouble is, I haven't got his details. Tell you what, Owen, visiting Ben could be part of your investigation. You could do it for me. Get his details, open an account, pay the money in and give the lad the bankbook. He'll be chuffed to little mint balls after the hard time he's had.'

Before Owen could protest, Sam thrust the same suitcase into his hand that had featured on the DVD. 'It's all here, I've checked. I'd do it myself but with what's going on I need to be out and about as little as possible – and this needs doing. No need to tell the lad who you are. Just tell him you're a well-wisher. He's a kid. Kids don't argue – certainly not with someone who's just given them a hundred grand.'

'Should give him a bit of kudos with the home he's in,' remarked Sally. 'It makes him a somebody – not just a waif or stray.'

Owen picked up the suitcase and shook his head, wondering what trouble this might get him into. 'I'm definitely not telling him my name,' he said. 'Might tell him your name, definitely not my name.'

'Tell him nothing,' advised Sam. 'In fact, tell him to keep quiet about it and there'll be a lot more where that came from. You can tell him who we are, then.'

'So,' said Owen, 'have you decided what you're going to do with the DVD?'

'No,' said Sam.

CHAPTER THIRTY-SIX

Annie Robinson was giving one of the yard men a severe bollocking as Alec got out of his van. Her coarse, Scouse accent reverberated off the walls of the timber shed and Alec was thinking how he wouldn't take such a dressing down from any woman, no matter how fearsome she was – and Annie Robinson was a truly fearsome woman. He went into the shop to buy some fittings the plumber was screaming for. Behind the counter, the daughter, Tanya, was talking to a young man wearing a badge that said 'Assistant Manager'.

The young man was laughing as Tanya did an impersonation of her mother. The bollocking had carried through to the shop and was the subject of conversation with many of the customers. Alec picked up the items he wanted from a rack and took them to a sales assistant.

'Do you have an account, sir?'

'No, I'll pay cash – it is trade, by the way.'

'Er, we need proof of that.'

Alec inclined his head towards the window, beyond which was his van, lettered with, Carew and Son Ltd.

'Give him full trade discount,' Tanya called out. Then to Alec she said. 'If you'd like to open an account we can offer very favourable terms, especially to a reputable firm such as yours.'

She smiled at him, and Alec smiled back, impressed by her good looks – out of place in here.

Suddenly – he couldn't quite put his finger on it – but he felt a nagging doubt about this woman. It was probably him just being stupid. 'Er, my partner does all that sort of thing.'

'Right,' said Tanya. 'I can send a rep round to your office, if you like. Will Mr Carew be in?'

'No, he's not, er, he's away at the moment.'

'Fair enough. Why don't you tell him to give me a ring when he gets back? I guarantee we'll be at least ten per cent under any of our competitors.'

'Ten per cent, really?' Alec was impressed, the doubts vanished. It'd do no harm to mention this to Sam. Ten per cent off materials wasn't to be sneezed at. 'I'll tell him.'

He was back on site when that thing which had been nagging at him returned. This time he put his finger right on it. He hated getting mixed up in Sam's detective agency business, but he couldn't let this one go. He rang Sam's mobile.

'Sam, I've just been to Robinson's.'

'Robinson's?'

'Merchants – to get some Yorkshire Fittings. Where are you?'

'I'm driving down Bostrop Road. I'm on my way to see Alison Kilpatrick and her mother.'

'Oh, is that a good idea?'

'I need to tell them he was talking to me when he was killed. It's been preying on my mind.'

'If you're seeking absolution from them Sam, maybe this isn't the right time. I should leave it a couple of weeks.'

Sam's voice crackled as he passed a heavy lorry going the other way. 'Absolution's a very big word for a joiner,' Alec heard him say. 'I hope you haven't been reading any of those grown-up books with rude bits in.'

'I was being serious, Sam. Anyway, there's something else I want to talk to you about.'

'Something else? What's that?'

'It's to do with the woman who attacked you. It could be me being paranoid but I've just met a woman who fits your description down to a T – apart from the blonde hair. Tall, really good-looking, gap in her front teeth.'

'That could be anyone, Alec.'

'I know – it was the fake Scouse accent that made me wonder. I heard her imitating her mother and she got it spot on.'

'What's her mother got to do with it?'

'Years ago they used to call her Scouse Annie – well, not to her face. On top of which, George Robinson did time for murder.'

'Alec, who's George Robinson?'

'Scouse Annie's husband. Scouse Annie and her daughter, Tanya, run Robinson's Builders' Merchants. There are three brothers in the background somewhere, supposed to be a bit moody. On the other hand, if I'm wrong, they're offering a great deal on prices.'

'My dad always reckoned Robinsons were

a bunch of chancers,' Sam said, 'anyway, it might be worth a look. Cheers, Alec.' Even as he spoke he was trying to make a connection between Kevin and the Robinsons. Was there a connection? Then it struck him. How come he didn't spot it straight away. There was certainly a connection between Bowman and Robinson's Builders' Merchants. Bloody hell!

He arrived outside Bailey Heights. An October wind was driving spiky rain straight into his face as he hurried to the entrance.

There was a message in large, red letters sprayed on the lift door, telling Muzzy to Fuck Off Back To Pakiland. This and many other obscene and offensive scrawlings had Sam wondering whether to risk the lift, as he had done last time.

Why not? His whole life was a risk at the moment. He held his breath during the malodorous ascent to the tenth floor and exhaled, triumphantly, as the lift door slid open, only to close again, immediately. He stuck out a foot to prevent it closing fully. It opened once again. This time he jumped out before it closed.

'There's a knack to it,' Patsy called out, without taking her cigarette from her mouth. She'd seen his car arrive and was waiting for him at her door. 'Come in. Have yer come about Kev?'

'I have,' confirmed Sam, accepting her

invitation and walking inside. Alison was sitting on the settee where he'd last seen her sitting naked apart from a small towel. He felt himself glancing in the direction of the bedroom where they'd made such amazing love back in July. A hell of a lot seemed to have happened since then, including two attempts on his life.

'Been keeping well?' she asked him.

Her attire wasn't quite as flimsy as last time – jeans and rugby shirt, but she still managed to look sexy. Sam remembered that night and felt pleasant stirrings.

'Mustn't grumble. How are you?'

'Fine thanks, Sam. Nice to see you again.'

'That's right – you've already met, haven't you?' said Patsy.

'We sure have,' smiled Alison. 'We had a one-on-one discussion about my problems. He didn't managed to solve everything but he went a long way.' Sam was grateful that her innuendoes seemed to go over her mother's head.

'Would yer like a drink of something?' Patsy enquired.

'No, thanks, it's a bit early for me.'

It seemed to Sam that it wasn't too early for Patsy. Her eyes were slightly unfocussed and he could smell it on her breath. Whatever it was, he didn't want any.

'I've had a couple,' she admitted. 'I need it ter keep me sanity after what's happened.

He were stabbed through his heart, the bastards. No one's been caught for it yer know. How's that? A man gets stabbed through his heart in the middle of a prison and no one sees nowt? What's all that about?'

'I don't know, Mrs Kilpatrick.'

'She's taken it bad,' Alison said, lighting a cigarette. 'We both have, but she's been bad.'

Patsy was sobbing now. 'He were me husband. How am I supposed ter take it? He were taken off us fer somethin' he didn't do, and now he's been murdered.'

If she wanted to make Sam feel guilty she was going about it the right way. Alec's advice about not mentioning that he was talking to Kevin at the time of the murder now made sense. Alec often made sense.

'What was it you wanted?' Alison asked him.

'What... Oh, I er, yes, I wondered if either of you knew anything about Robinson's Builders' Merchants. Well, specifically Tanya Robinson and her mother – and maybe her brothers.'

Alison shrugged and shook her head. 'I've heard of Scouse Annie, but that's about all. Never had any use for builders' merchants. What about you, Mam?'

Patsy was still sobbing. 'I knew George Robinson,' she said, at length. 'Well, Kev knew him from the club.'

'Bostrop Labour Club,' Alison explained.

She turned to her mother. 'What relation was George to Scouse Annie?'

'Husband and wife.'

'D'yer know, I never knew that,' remarked Alison.

'So,' said Sam, looking from mother to daughter. 'Were they good pals – Kevin and George?'

Patsy dried her eyes and snapped open one of a pack of six Carlsberg Special Brew perched on a sideboard. It fizzed out on to her face and clothes, extinguishing the cigarette dangling from her lips, but she didn't seem to notice. She took a large gulp. It seemed to inject life into her.

'I think they were just drinkin' mates. They'd known each other fer years. Blimey, it's a while ago now – must be twenty years since George got sent down. He were a bit of a jack-the-lad, were George. Got locked up fer toppin' a bookie.'

'Topping a bookie?' queried Sam, wondering if she was mixing him up with Kevin.

'Different bookie,' said Alison, reading his thoughts, '...well, obviously.'

Patsy continued with her story. 'This bookie lived in Bradford. George Robinson went to rob his safe and killed him with a shotgun – got life. He were evidently screwin' the bookie's wife and she gave him the keys an' the combination – silly cow gave the game away as well. I didn't know George all that well, but even so, I couldn't believe he'd do owt like that. Shook me, I can tell yer. Shook Kevin as well – I've never seen him so shook up. Never put a foot wrong after that, my Kevin, until this crap. George held his hands up to it, though. He was just a year off getting parole when he died of cancer.'

'Very much like Kevin, eh?' remarked Sam. 'Sort of coincidence, really.'

The Robinsons had just moved up several rungs on his suspects ladder. So had Bowman.

'It is, when yer come ter think of it,' said Patsy. 'Never thought of it like that. My Kev got put away not long after George died.'

Sam couldn't help but wonder why Patsy hadn't spotted the glaring coincidence, but it wouldn't do for everyone to have his suspicious mind.

'Patsy, you once told me that they had a copper in their pocket.'

'That's what Kev told me. He never said who it was.'

'Did you get the impression it was a ranking officer – an inspector maybe?'

She relit her cigarette as she tried to remember. 'God, it's a while ago now.' She clicked her fingers. 'Now, I do remember something. He said something like, "whoever it is knows stuff yer ordinary copper doesn't know." Yeah, I remember him sayin' that – well, somethin' like that. Mind you, he did give a load o' flannel at times.'

Sam wore three days growth of beard, a baseball cap and glasses when he strolled into Robinson's Builders' Merchants, a minute after Alec. Tanya was in the back office. Alec asked to see her about opening an account. Sam hovered behind the pvc pipe rack, pretending to check various sink-waste fittings. The very second Tanya strode out of her office and smiled at Alec he knew it was her. He recognised her voice as she asked if Mr Carew was still away and was relieved to hear Alec being so convincing.

'To be honest, love, he's taken himself off abroad, as he often does. It's very much me who runs the company but you wouldn't think it to listen to him. I spoke to him on the phone yesterday and he's approved me opening an account with you. That's big of him, isn't it?'

'Oh dear,' said Tanya. 'Sounds like there's trouble at t' mill.'

'No trouble, love, so long as he leaves me to do what I do best, running the company.'

Her proximity sent a shudder down Sam's spine as he remembered their last meeting. Alec then drew her into a discussion about facing-brick prices as Sam left. There were other people he needed to check on now, particularly the brothers.

'I've put a few feelers about, in Unsworth and in Leeds,' said Owen. 'No one's seen Lloyd Robinson for a couple of months.'

They were in the Royal Oak on the Wakefield Road. Sam had placed his usual haunts out-of-bounds. 'What about the other brothers – Nathan and Lewis?' he asked.

Owen shook his head. 'Lewis disappeared off the scene years ago and Nathan hasn't been around for a few days. It's all a bit odd, apparently. One day Lloyd was pimping in Leeds, the next day he vanishes and all the girls are freelance. Apparently Nathan took over after a while, but no one's seen Lloyd since.'

'Could have just taken his money and run,' surmised Sam. 'Was the law after him?'

'Not especially. He was known to the Leeds police but he ran a tidy organisation, so they didn't bother him much. They're taking a close look at Nathan for drug dealing, apparently. It could be that he's got wind and is lying low.'

'Maybe – I just hope the reason has got nothing to do with me. What's he like, this Nathan?'

'Well, he was a bit like this twenty years ago.' Owen took a police photograph of Nathan from his pocket and gave it to Sam. 'Very nasty piece of work, from what I hear. As a youth he's got form for violence, so has

Lloyd – nothing on Lewis or Tanya. When he was eighteen, Nathan served two and a half years out of a four stretch for almost beating a man to death in a fight. The year he got out George Robinson went down for murder. Apparently the mother's ruled the roost with a very firm hand since then. It's a possibility that the builders' merchants business is just a front for money laundering but nothing can be proved.' He suddenly fixed Sam with a meaningful stare. 'Sam, it's the same builders' merchants that I got the tip-off about.'

'I know.'

'I know you know.'

'Could be more than a coincidence.'

'Coincidence be buggered,' said Owen. 'I reckon if you're right about there being a bent cop it's got to be Bowman. Let's face it, had he been able he'd have warned his brother-in-law about the building site robbery.'

'True,' Sam agreed. 'But this is a lot more serious. It's one thing tipping the brother-in-law off to keep in the wife's good books, and another thing having a hand in mass murder. I mean, we're talking about life without parole. I don't like Bowman, but I can't see him being involved in this sort of thing.'

'Nor me, boyo, but one thing leads to another. He might have got in a bit deeper than he expected. These people might have something on him.'

Sam couldn't deny the truth of that; Bowman had used criminals for his own purposes in the past. Once, when Sam was in the force, he'd caught him at it. Bowman said the end justified the means, a philosophy Sam struggled to argue with.

'This is a massive accusation, Owen,' he said, 'and with him being a DCI it makes it awkward involving the police in this until we know the truth about him. We haven't got enough evidence to accuse him outright of being bent. There might well be an innocent explanation. We've just got to play it as though he is.'

'For once I agree with you, boyo.'

'I wish you wouldn't keep calling me boyo.'

'If it's of any interest,' said Owen, 'Annie Robinson's got a brother called Graham Erlington. I don't think he has anything to do with the Robinson family. He's a club comic – calls himself Earl Gray.'

The name going through Sam's mind was Lloyd Robinson. He'd pressed Owen to find out the exact date that Lloyd had last been seen. A couple of days later Owen told him that one of his pals in the Leeds police had questioned a prostitute who had last seen Lloyd around the time Sam had been attacked by Tanya.

'He could be the one who was killed that

night,' Sam said.

'I think it's odds on,' agreed Owen. 'But where is he? What do you do with a dead brother?'

'Well, she couldn't leave him there to be identified,' Sam said. 'It would have led the police straight to her. I'd have identified her. Bingo! Case solved.'

Owen produced an old photograph of Lloyd, but it was no help to Sam. It could have been the man he was fighting that night but he couldn't swear to it. The only clear image he had emblazoned on his mind from that night was one of Tanya. Naked.

CHAPTER THIRTY-SEVEN

The De La Salle Children's Home was not an imposing residence. It had been purpose built as a workhouse for the poor in the mid-nineteenth century and, although the cruel workhouse regime had been ended in the 1920s, it still bore an aura of oppression. It was run by a Mr and Mrs Miller, both of whom were in the office when Owen knocked on the door and poked his head round.

'Good evening, my name is DC Owen Price from Unsworth Police. I'd like to see

Benjamin Corbally.'

Mr Miller looked at him suspiciously, wondering if he was who he said he was. Owen didn't have an impressive presence.

'Do you have any er, proof of identity, DC Price?'

'Oh – yes, I have a warrant card.' He showed them his warrant card, which was subjected to close scrutiny by them both. Mrs Miller looked up at him from her desk.

'What do you wish to see Benjamin about?' Her manner was brusque, which didn't suit Owen. 'Is he in trouble?'

'Not as far as I know. I wish to see him on a police matter regarding his father's death.' His manner was equally brusque, as if her question was impertinent.

She got to her feet and went to the door. 'If you would follow me, DC Price.'

Owen followed her up a flight of stairs. It was early evening and he assumed the residents had probably just finished their evening meal. The place was brightly painted in an attempt to add to the light that the small, square, Victorian windows afforded. They passed a group of chattering children on the stairs. The chattering ceased when Mrs Miller approached. It seemed to Owen that Mr and Mrs Miller ran a tight ship.

They went into a large room containing a television, a pool table and a table tennis table. Ben was playing pool with a young man whom Owen assumed to be one of the staff. By the look of it Ben was getting the better of things. Mrs Miller called out to him.

'Ben, there's a policeman to see you.'

The other children in the room all looked round to see this policeman. Ben didn't break his concentration on potting a difficult black to win the game. He slammed the ball into a corner pocket then looked up at Owen, who gave the shot an appreciative nod.

'Hello, sir.'

The boy held out a hand, which Owen shook and asked, 'Is there somewhere private where I can talk to Ben?'

Mrs Miller clapped her hands and shouted. 'Everybody out, the policeman needs privacy.'

No one grumbled, not even the young staff member. Owen felt guilty but didn't say anything. The room quickly emptied, apart from the three of them. Owen looked at Mrs Miller, waiting for her to go as well.

'What?' she asked. 'You want me to go as well?'

Owen beamed at her. 'If you wouldn't mind, madam. This is a very confidential matter.'

'I see,' said Mrs Miller, who wished she *did* see.

With her gone Owen turned his attention to the thirteen-year-old boy who looked, to the Welshman, to be a very pleasant looking lad. 'How are you going on, Benjamin?'

'Very well, thank you.'

'My name is Owen, I'm a detective constable.'

'Have you come about what happened to my dad?'

'In a way.'

'Are you a friend of Mr Sam Carew?'

Owen was slightly taken aback. 'Well, as a matter of fact I am. How did you know?'

'I've read about him in the papers. It mentions you a lot in the stories about him. It says you're Welsh. I can tell by your accent.'

Owen sat down at a table. Ben joined him. The lad looked to have wisdom beyond his years. Maybe, Owen thought, your mother being killed in a car crash by your drunken dad, and your dad being murdered, makes you grow up quickly. But the boy didn't seem scarred by his ordeal.

'You've had a hard time, Ben.'

'Yes I have, sir.' The boy looked at him curiously. 'Does Mr Sam Carew know about me?'

Owen remembered his promise to keep Sam's name out of this. 'Yes,' he said, 'in fact this involves Sam Carew.'

Ben's eyes shone. 'Aw – wicked!'

'But you mustn't mention what we talk about here to anyone. We are investigating your father's murder, but everything is very confidential. If all goes well you should be able to leave here and go to live somewhere more...' he looked around the room, 'more suitable.'

'It's not bad here,' Ben said. 'Mrs Miller's a bit strict, but she has to be. There's some right nutters in here.'

'I imagine there are.' He paused as he wondered how Ben would take the news of his windfall. 'Look, Ben, not only has a murderer deprived you of a father, but Sam – and I – both believe you have been deprived of a lot of money. We've recovered a small portion of it and placed it in a trust account in your name.'

'I don't know what that is, sir.'

'It means it doesn't become yours until you are eighteen.'

'That's fine by me. How much is it?'

Owen took a bank book from his pocket and gave it to Ben. The boy examined it, counted the noughts, then looked at Owen. 'Does this say a hundred thousand pounds?'

'It does.'

'And this is my money?'

'It will be when you're eighteen. Until then, it'll gather interest at a good rate.'

'A hundred thousand quid! This is really wicked, mister.'

'If we can solve you father's murder there might well be a lot more to come.'

Ben studied the bank book again. 'Is this money from you or from Mr Carew?' There was a note of hero worship in the boy's voice. Owen felt there was no harm in telling him the truth.

'Sam's responsible for you getting it, but you are sworn to secrecy – for the time being at least.'

'Secrecy? Excellent! Am I allowed to know anything more, or have you told me everything I need to know?'

Owen smiled at the boy's question. 'I think I've told you everything you need to know.'

CHAPTER THIRTY-EIGHT

The bespectacled building inspector trudged back to his van as Sam looked around the completed site. 'Four weeks ahead of schedule,' he said to Alec, 'and finally approved by old Heinrich Himmler.' He was referring more to the building inspector's attitude than his appearance.

'I think I deserve a bonus,' said Alec, 'finishing ahead of schedule like this.'

'Aha,' said Sam, 'but we're not quite finished, are we?'

'Aren't we?'

'No, we mustn't forget Archie.'

'Archie...? oh, Archie. Sam we can't go round digging up skeletons at this stage.

What excuse do we give for digging a trench when the job's finished?'

'Sewer connection,' Sam reminded him. 'According to Sally, the developers want us on with the groundworks for the development in that far field, ASAP.'

'I thought that was months away.'

'It was always on the cards that they'd want us to get on with the groundworks once they got outline planning consent.'

'Sam, I've got us some indoor work for the winter. We don't want to be struggling up to our eyeballs in mud until March. It's hard to make money when you're up to your eyeballs in mud. You know that.'

Sam tapped his temple with an index finger. 'Forward planning, Alec. That's why we buried Archie where we did.'

'Did we?'

'If you look on the plan you'll see the sewer connection isn't far away from Archie. We'll have to report our find to the police – it's our duty. Job stopped while the archaeologists dig around in the mud. We come back in the spring when they've dug up all their bones and artifacts and buggered off. We're happy, the archaeologists are happy, Archie's happy – everybody's happy. I like to spread happiness.'

'What, and all that was in your mind when we dug old Archie up and wondered what to do with him?'

'Well, sort of,' admitted Sam.

Alec looked at his partner in amazement. 'Sam' he said, 'sometimes it scares me to think what goes on in that mind of yours.'

Sam, Alec, a man from the Unsworth Coroner's Office, two council officers and PC Melia looked on as a man from Leeds University climbed down a ladder into the trench. He examined the bones, which were considerably more disturbed than when they'd first been discovered. This helped to hide the fact that they'd been moved recently.

'It's a pity you disturbed them,' he called up.

'The JCB driver wasn't expecting to find bones,' replied Sam, politely. 'We were actually trying to find a 12" sewer.'

The man gave a disapproving tut, as if to say that no one should be allowed to dig beneath any ground before it had been archaeologically cleared.

'When can we get on with the job?' asked Sam.

'You can't,' said PC Melia, almost gleefully. 'This is either a site of archaeological interest or an illegal grave. Either way the job stops.'

'What?' Sam exclaimed. 'Well, I hope we get proper compensation.'

'You can always hope,' remarked Melia, happy that this seemed to be inconveniencing Sam.

'What constitutes an illegal grave?' enquired Alec, out of genuine curiosity.

'Any burials that are not officially recorded or done in properly designated ground,' said the man from the Coroner's Office. 'Some people like to plant their dear departed in the back garden without bothering to tell anyone – saves a fortune in funeral expenses. Mind you, it costs them a fortune if they're caught.'

'Very convenient though,' mused Sam, out loud, thinking about Lloyd Robinson. 'In certain circumstances – very convenient indeed.'

The Coroner's man nodded. 'The ground can cover up a lot of secrets.' He looked at Sam as if to say he knew the secret that this ground had been covering up for the past three months.

'Judging from the arrow and the belt buckle it's probably twelfth century,' called out the man from the trench. 'I'll be applying for this site to be designated a site of archaeological and historical interest.'

'An ARCHI,' commented Sam.

The man from the Coroner's office looked at him, wondering how he knew.

'It's happened to us before,' said Sam, 'in York.'

CHAPTER THIRTY-NINE

'What would they have done with Lloyd?' Sam wondered. He and Owen were driving around in Owen's car. 'He's a brother and a son. They wouldn't have just dumped him in the canal, surely?'

'Maybe they gave him a proper burial,' suggested Owen, 'they live in a house with massive grounds.'

Sam nodded his agreement. 'My thoughts exactly. I wonder if they'd mark it.'

'What, with a headstone or something? Bit risky, that, boyo.'

Sam looked at him, sharply, then asked, 'Who'd go to the burial?'

'Only those who've got a lot to lose if his grave was ever discovered,' said Owen.

'What about relatives?' wondered Sam. 'What about Scouse Annie's brother?'

Owen shook his head. 'Graham Erlington? Doubt it – but you never know. There's nowt as queer as folk, as you Yorkshire people keep saying. Annie would probably want the funeral to be as normal as possible,' he said, '–well, as normal as possible under the circumstances. I would think she'd prefer the odd relative to be there, if she could trust them.'

'Right,' said Sam. He looked at Owen who was giving a two finger salute to a hooting bus he'd just overtaken. 'Apart from this brother being a club comic what did you find out about him?'

'I found out, boyo, that he's on at Bostrop Labour Club tonight.'

The poster in the entrance lobby announced tonight's artistes as Lovely Lucinda, local vocalist, plus the comedy of Earl Gray – Everyone's Cup of Tea.

Sam and Owen sat through Graham's first set and Owen wrote down the one joke he hadn't already heard. Then the Welshman, to everyone's annoyance, sang along with Lovely Lucinda until, halfway through *Big Spender*, she switched off her backing tape and called across to the concert secretary. 'Barry, tell that twat over there ter shut it, or I'll ram this microphone up his arse, rough end first!'

This got more laughs than Earl Gray, who popped his head out of the dressing room door to see what all the merriment was about. Sam got up and went to the bar, mainly so as not to be mistaken as being that twat over there. Owen beamed munificently and called out, 'Madam, your beautiful voice mesmerised me into joining you in song. I humbly apologise.'

He sat down to laughter and a smattering of applause from customers who weren't actually being mesmerised by Lucinda's voice. The men were fascinated by her pretty face and gigantic breasts and the women were simply waiting for the bingo to start. By the time Lucinda had finished her set, Graham was at the bar. Sam and Owen joined him. Sam introduced himself.

'Sam Carew,' he said, 'and this is Owen Price. We enjoyed your act.'

'Then why didn't you laugh?'

'I did laugh,' said Sam. 'He didn't laugh because he's Welsh.'

'Ah, right,' said Graham as if this fully explained things. He looked at them and gave a half shake of his head. 'What is it you want? I know you're not members, I saw you both signing in at the door.' He looked at Sam. 'Sam Carew? Are you the Sam Carew I've heard of?'

'No idea,' said Sam. 'Which Sam Carew have you heard of?'

This drew a grin from Graham. Owen obliged him with a proper answer. 'He's that Sam Carew, all right.'

'Detective?'

'Ex-cop,' said Sam.

'Yeah, but still some sort of detective?'

'Sort of. Is there somewhere a bit more private we can talk?'

'There's the dressing room. Tracy should

be out in a minute.'

'Tracy?' enquired Owen.

'Lovely Lucinda – her real name's Tracy Ogden.'

Taking their drinks they followed him through to the unisex dressing room just as Lucinda/Tracy was coming out. She smiled at Owen and invited him to buy her a drink. The Welshman looked at Sam, like a child looking to his mother for permission to go out and play with his two favourite friends.

'Don't let him lead you astray,' Sam said to the singer. 'He's not to be trusted – and if he tells you about his fairy godmother, don't believe him.'

'Never met a feller in me life what I could trust.' She linked her arm into Owen's and led him to the bar whilst asking him about his fairy godmother.

Sam and Graham went into the dressing room, which was sparsely furnished and had a suspicious odour that had Sam wrinkling his nose. Graham opened the only window, explaining, 'Lovely Lucinda farts like a carthorse when she's had a couple of pints of Bootham's.'

Sam sat on one of the two rickety chairs in the tiny dressing room. 'Shouldn't there be separate dressing rooms for men and women?'

'We're lucky to have a dressing room at all. Half the time I have ter get changed in the bog. So, what is it you want?'

'Are you allowed to smoke in here?' Sam asked.

'Debatable – the concert room's non-smoking. It's allowed in here only if you give the comic one.'

Sam offered Graham a cigarette, which he took, grumbling. 'I never thought I'd see the day when they stop a workin' man havin' a fag in his own club. They're making criminals out of smokers when they can't even catch the proper villains. What's all that about? I'll be knackered when they ban laughing.'

Having seen Graham's act Sam felt he could give him an argument, but he chose not to. 'I assume you've heard of the Hammerhead,' he said.

'I have – they say it's a woman.'

'It is, she tried to kill me. I'm the one who got away.'

'Never heard of that.'

'It happened in Lancashire, never got in the papers over here – besides no one made any connection with the hammer killer back then. I got a good look at her – and I've seen her again, recently.'

'Right,' said Graham, 'and what's this got to do with me?'

Sam looked at him, keenly, wondering if he was completely in the dark about his niece's activities, or was he putting on an act?

'When she attacked me, she was with a man who was killed in the fight.'

'Bloody hell – killed?'

'I know he was killed because it was me he was fighting and a bullet went straight through his head, blowing his brains out, most of them over me. I was shot as well. The woman must have taken the man's body away. In fact, the police aren't even sure there was a body. I tend not to be popular with the police.'

'So I hear,' said Graham, who was remembering things he'd read about Sam. 'I still don't see what this has to do with me.'

At this point Sam could pretty much read Graham's thoughts. He was closely related to the Robinson family. Very little would surprise someone so closely related to such a family. As Sam looked at him, Graham was tying Sam's visit in with his sister and her family. Sam could see that in his face. Time to hit him with it.

'Hammerhead is Tanya Robinson, I know that for a fact.'

Graham said nothing for a while, puffing on his cigarette.

Then he shook his head. 'Nah – our Tanya, a serial killer? Never in this world. Bright lass is Tanya, went to university. She's got letters after her name.'

'She's not a serial killer,' Sam told him, 'she's a contract killer. I think the man who was killed in the fight was her brother, Lloyd. No one's seen him since that night.'

Graham stared at him, open-mouthed. 'What? Bloody hell! Our Tanya – give over.'

Sam said nothing. He sat back and smoked his cigarette as Graham ran Sam's revelation through his mind. 'Jesus Christ! Our Tanya – nah.' He shook his head. 'Don't believe it, mate.'

'When was the last time you saw Lloyd?'

'Christmas. Our Annie goes her way, I go mine. We swap presents at Christmas. I give her a box of chocolates, she gives me a two grand watch. That's the only time we see each other, nowadays.'

Sam decided to go fishing. 'Christmas and funerals, eh?' It got the reaction he wanted. It was very slight, but he'd touched a nerve. 'Did they invite you to Lloyd's funeral?'

Graham rested his elbows on the dressing table and looked at his reflection in the mirror. 'She thinks I'm a waste o' bleedin' space, yer know – our Annie. She's livin' in a mansion and here's me, scrabblin' for a few quid around the bloody clubs.'

'Comedy's a noble and honest art,' said Sam. 'You're doing a necessary job that only a few can do. You're worth fifty of your sister.'

'You know her then, do yer?'

'I know *of* her. I know her family are all criminals. So far they've managed to work under the police radar.'

'So, yer'll also know what vicious bastards they all are – I still can't believe this of our Tanya, though. She were George's favourite, yer know.' He turned to look at Sam. 'If I grassed on our Annie she'd top me as soon as look at me.'

'So, you're scared of her, are you?'

'Actually, no. Funny that, isn't it? She's me little sister – how the hell can I be scared of her? Maybe I *should* be scared, but I'm not.'

'So, did you go to Lloyd's funeral? It will have been some time in August.'

'August 17th – it were a Thursday.'

'I assume he was buried at Wickham Farm?'

Graham nodded and shaded his eyes with the palm of his hand. 'D'yer know, I've had it up to here with that lot.'

'Can you describe exactly where?' Sam asked him.

'What? Why the hell are you asking me all this? Why aren't the coppers sniffin' round?'

'The family's got a bent copper tucked away in Unsworth nick. If I don't go to the police with proper proof this could get buried deeper than Lloyd.'

'And why are *you* doing it?'

'Conscience.'

'Oh – havin' a conscience can be the death of yer. It might be the death of the two of us.'

'Does that mean you'll help me?'

'It means I'll tell yer where Lloyd's buried an' no more. And I beg of yer never ter tell our Annie I grassed her up.'

'You have my word on it.'

'Facing the house there's a big field with a pond in it, and a fountain in the pond. In the middle of the pond's one o' them pissing boy fountains. Our Annie saw the original one in Brussels an' she had to have one of her own.'

'Mannekin Pis,' said Sam, who had once built a house that required such a statue in the garden, along with many other imitation *objets d'art*.

'If yer line the pissin' kid with the left-hand edge of the house and walk backwards about 80 yards yer'll come to a rock – that's Lloyd's headstone. There's nothing on it, it's just there as a marker.' Graham blew out a long sigh that told Sam there was more to this story.

'What?' he enquired.

'Our Lewis is under there as well. I don't know the full circumstances, I were never told. He were buried there over four years ago now.' He drank his pint and put the glass down, heavily, on the dressing table. 'D'yer know,' he said. 'I'm right glad I've told someone. Never mentioned it to anyone, not even the wife. Mind you, if I told her she'd be straight down to the police, an' then where would I be?'

Sam didn't know where Graham would be had his wife told the police, but it might have been the best thing all round. It might have saved Sam having to deal with this problem.

'I've often thought of going to the police meself but our Annie'd know who shopped her. But with you bein' involved she might not even suspect me.'

'Really?' said Sam, curious.

'Aye. I remember about yer now. They say yer've got ways o' findin' stuff out that normal coppers don't know about.'

'Is that what they say?'

'Aye, so if our Annie ever says owt, I'll just say it were nowt ter do wi' me. Unless she knows yer here.'

'There's no way she can know that,' Sam assured him.

Graham was waylaid in the car park of Unsworth Working Men's Club. It was two days after he had spoken to Sam. He was blindfolded and gagged, bundled into the back of a van and taken to Wickham Farm by three men, who carried him into an outbuilding and chained him to a steel pillar where he lay blindfolded, hungry, thirsty and freezing for twenty-four hours before his sister came in to talk to him.

'Yer've been talkin' ter Carew,' she rasped.

He recognised the voice but couldn't reply

because of the gag. She ripped it off him and slapped him across his face.

'Annie,' he said. 'I thought this might be your work. Take this blindfold off, yer stupid cow!'

She did as he asked, then punched him in his face. He spat blood at her, defiantly. 'What yer gonna do, kill me like yer killed yer own kids, yer worthless piece of after-birth? Our mam allus said when you were born they threw away the wrong bit.'

He looked beyond her to see Tanya standing at the door. Hunger, thirst, and now pain was clouding his judgement. 'Hey up, Tan! Is it right you're Hammerhead?'

'Shit!' cursed Annie, 'that's all we need.'

Tanya's face tightened at the news that her cover was blown. 'What did yer tell Carew?' she asked.

'I need a drink, Tan,' pleaded Graham. 'Get me a drink, lass. I'm not a well man. I can't take all this crap.'

There was a tap on the wall, Tanya turned it on and let the water fall to the floor. Graham eyed it, longingly.

'Uncle Graham, just tell us what you told Carew, and you get a drink.'

He hadn't heard her call him Uncle Graham since she was a girl. Even under these circumstances there was something appealing about it. Blood was running down his chin from where Annie had hit him. 'Have yer still got that dolly I bought yer fer yer seventh birthday? Cost me a nice few quid, that dolly. I thought it were worth it, though. You were a nice kid. What's happened to yer, Tan? I'm yer uncle. What all this about?'

'It's about family loyalty, Uncle Graham.'

Graham's hollow laugh echoed around the empty building. 'Family loyalty? This cow's in a dirty business that kills her own son and you talk about family loyalty?' The hunger and thirst and cold was sending him delirious. He probably knew it wasn't wise to be so confrontational but he couldn't help it. This was his baby sister and his niece he was talking to. What right had they to treat him like this?

Annie kicked him in his ribs. 'Gray, just tell us what yer said ter Carew an' don't be so fuckin' stupid.'

Graham moaned with pain. 'How d'yer know I said owt to him? He came ter see me. I didn't invite him.'

'We know that,' said Tanya, 'we were told.'

'Oh, I forgot,' sneered Graham. 'Yer buy people, don't yer? That's the only way in your dogshit world. Yer buy people an' yer scare people. Yer might live in a big house, but really yer so useless that yer have ter buy people and scare people ter make money. Yer no more use ter this world than a couple o' pieces o' dogshit.'

'We run a legitimate builders' merchants

381

business.' Even under these circumstance Annie seemed to seek his approval.

'Aw, don't give me that bollocks,' muttered Graham. 'It's me yer talkin' to.'

Annie slapped him across his face. 'Yer think yer fuckin' hard, Gray. Well, I've got some people outside who'll really soften you up if you don't do yer duty by yer family.'

'Just get me a drink o' water.'

Annie signalled her daughter to comply. Tanya picked up an empty bottle and filled it. She then took it over to Graham and poured it into his mouth. He gulped at it, greedily, until the bottle was empty, Graham having drunk maybe half of it.

'I need a pee,' he said. 'I had to do it in me trousers last night. Don't leave me here in me own piss, Annie.'

'Yer'll be wallowing in yer own shit if yer don't tell us what yer said ter Carew.'

'Annie, what the hell do I know that I could tell Carew?' He looked at Tanya. 'He just came ter tell me that you were Hammerhead. I told him I didn't believe him. Come on, Annie, I really need a piss.'

'Why would he tell you that?' Tanya asked him.

'I don't know. I'm a comic not a mind reader.' He shivered and grumbled. 'Couldn't you have put me somewhere a bit warmer?'

'You were allus a fuckin' moaner, Gray,'

sneered Annie. 'Moan, moan, fuckin' moan, that's all you ever did.'

'I had a lot ter moan about with you in the house. Annie I need a piss, I'm freezin', I could eat a scabby donkey, me nose hurts like buggery and I feel really poorly. What is this all about?'

'When Carew left that club he seemed well satisfied with himself, that's what I heard,' Annie said. 'What I want yer ter tell me is, why he were so well satisfied?'

'Annie, I've told yer what happened. He talked ter me, that's all. He asked me stuff about yer, but what could I tell him? What is it I'm supposed ter know?'

'You know where the grave is,' said Tanya, watching for his reaction.

'What?' His eyes gave him away.

'I said, you know where the grave is. If he knows it's me who shot him,' she deduced, 'he'll also suspect it might have been our missing brother who was with me.' She looked at her mother as she worked out the likely scenario.

'And Carew might wonder what we did with him,' Annie added. 'He'll know we don't plant family just anywhere. Is that what yer talked about, Gray? Did yer talk about Lloyd's grave. Did yer tell him about Lewis as well?'

The water Graham had drunk forced him to empty his bladder. The sudden warmth on his legs was welcome. Annie pulled a face as she saw the spreading stain. Graham began to feel faint, his head slumped, Annie slapped him across his face. 'Did yer tell him about Lloyd's grave?'

'I don't know what I told him,' he mumbled. 'He won't go to the coppers. He reckons yer've gorra copper on wages. He won't go ter the coppers until he's got summat on yer. Nobody believes him.' His voice was barely audible, Annie had her ear to his mouth.

'Gray, what about the grave? Does he know about the grave?' But Graham had lapsed into unconsciousness.

'I think we'd better assume he knows about the grave,' decided Tanya.

'In that case we'd best get Carew's coffin ready.'

CHAPTER FORTY

Sam had decided not to tell Owen about the grave. His Welsh pal's word carried little weight down at the nick. Graham would have been questioned before any action was taken. By which time the Robinsons would have had plenty of warning, courtesy of the bent cop. All in all it was better that Owen didn't know. On top of which he wasn't absolutely certain that Graham had been telling him the truth. He waited a week before he took any action. A dark, cloudy, moonless night was needed for such work, and grave digging required strength. A bit of extra convalescing wouldn't go amiss.

He drove there at midnight. It was suitably dark. He took a pick, a shovel and two short ladders, with which to scale the eight foot wall surrounding the grounds. At 12.45 a.m. he was over the wall and in the grounds of Wickham Farm, hoping against hope that they didn't have guard dogs patrolling the place. If there were any dogs they weren't up to the job.

The only significant light came from lamp posts lighting the driveway. Light showed from behind drawn curtains of two downstairs rooms and one upstairs. Sam found the pond with no trouble. He lined up the peeing boy with the left side of the house and began to stride away from the pond, counting his steps. He had counted seventy-eight when he stumbled against a rock.

It occurred to him that Graham must have, at some time, taken care to pinpoint the exact position of the grave; just in case he ever needed to find it. The rock itself weighed a couple of hundredweight and it took Sam several minutes to lever it out of the way, using the shovel and the pick handle. The ground beneath the rock wasn't solid. It had been disturbed, and therefore made easy digging – as any grave would. His plan was to confirm that there was definitely a grave here, then to ring Owen, Janet Seager and maybe even O'Donnell, to tell them what he had found. This was as far as he could take things without police help. Even if Bowman was the bent cop he wouldn't be able to stop the ensuing investigation.

It took him half an hour to get to a depth where his pick struck wood. He was digging in almost total darkness, only the fact that his eyes had become used to the dark enabled him to see anything at all. He cleared away the earth with his shovel, took out a pencil torch and identified a coffin. He cleared away a bit more of it. There was an inscription written in what looked like marker pen. He rubbed away the earth with his hand so he could read it.

Nathan Robinson. Age 40.

'Bloody hell!' he muttered.

A voice came from above him. Startling him. He shone his torch upwards but a far more powerful beam shone back at him.

'Yer've caused us no end o' fuckin' trouble, Mr Carew.' The voice was female and thick scouse and it didn't take much to work out who it belonged to. 'Yer can just fill the grave back in. I don't know who yer think you are, comin' on people's property, digging up their loved ones.'

In the light of Annie's torch Sam caught a glimpse of a gun. He threw his pick and shovel out of the grave and climbed out after them. He knew that this was a situation that required a hell of a plan.

'Don't try the madman act, Mr Mad Carew,' warned another voice. 'First sign of madness and you're dead.'

'Tanya,' said Sam. 'How nice to meet you again.' She was silhouetted against the light from the lamp posts. 'I see you've got more clothes on, tonight.'

'Don't try and be clever,' said Annie. 'Get the grave filled in.'

Sam worked, steadily, for a full twenty minutes, during which time Annie and Tanya maintained a complete silence. His brain was racing but no ideas were forthcoming. The darkness, the bright light shining on him, his physical exhaustion, the gun pointed at him, and the fact that he was outnumbered were all working against him. OK these were women, but there were plenty of men he'd much rather come up against. The only thing he knew for certain was that they were going to kill him at the end of this.

When the grave was backfilled he looked at the rock and shook his head. There wasn't an ounce of strength left in his body.

'There's no way I can put that back,' he said.

Annie put the gun to his head and Sam gritted his teeth. There was no fight left in him, he didn't even have any last words to say. Not even a prayer. He felt tears rolling down his cheeks and he hung his head in resignation.

'Not here,' Tanya was saying, 'this is too easy.' She moved behind him and was tying his hands together behind his back. Then she prodded him with the gun. 'Move,' she ordered.

Sam walked towards a copse of trees as Tanya spoke to him from behind. 'You killed my brother, Carew, and you've destroyed a nice business. We don't know who knows what you know, so we have to leave. Our whole organisation is disbanded, many people are out of work because of you. Kevin Kilpatrick was sent down for life for doing less than you did to us.'

'What did he do?' Sam asked, amazed at his own curiosity under the circumstances, but he genuinely wanted to know. Annie told him.

'He killed a man an' my George were sent down for it. Then George died in jail, which made it a matter of honour. It were my duty ter make sure Kilpatrick suffered for making my George die in jail – stop here.' In the gloom Sam could see an open coffin. 'In there,' she ordered.

Sam hesitated. Annie stuck the gun to his

head again. 'I can do it now or later,' she told him, with unmistakeable sincerity.

Without a word, Sam lowered himself into the coffin, realising as he did, that it had ropes attached to it and was standing beside a shallow grave. He knew if he ran he would be shot dead within two paces. Never before had the old adage, *Where there's life, there's hope,* seemed so fatuous. What hope? Annie bound his ankles together as Tanya gagged him.

'If it's any comfort,' said Tanya, 'you won't have to suffer for as long as Kilpatrick. The coffin isn't quite airtight, so there'll be some air available. But you will be under the earth, which is a bit of a disadvantage. I reckon you should last about thirty minutes tops — obviously we'll be thinking about you. We'd like to make you suffer a bit more, but this is the best we can do at such short notice. Think yourself lucky our Nathan's not around to organise this. He was far more creative. Graham should be dead now. That's your fault as well — meddling in other people's family business.'

Sam heard the coffin lid being nailed into place. Then he was thrown around as the coffin was roughly dropped into the bottom of the grave. He tried to work his gag loose against the rough woodwork above him. He wanted to shout to them. He didn't know what, maybe a cry of defiance. But he was bound hand and foot and encased in this tight-fitting coffin. It wasn't the way he would have chosen to die. Apart from anything else he was dying as a loser. They'd beaten him. They were getting away with it. His death had no value whatsoever. Once again he wept tears of hopelessness. This was no way to die. He could hear the earth being shovelled on top of his coffin and he wondered what dying would be like. Would he just go to sleep or would it be painful? He tried to relax, so as to use up as little air as possible. He didn't know why.

Sally hadn't slept. She had reluctantly moved into Sam's house with him when he told her it was safer than her place. He had told her he was going out with Owen on a case and he'd be back before two. At three o'clock she rang Owen's mobile.

'Owen, it's Sally, could I speak to Sam, please?'

Had it been anyone else, Owen might have covered for his pal, but this was Sally. 'Sally, I'm at home in bed. Why would Sam be with me?'

'Because he said he was helping you with a case.'

Owen said nothing, not wanting to get involved.

'It's OK, Owen,' she sighed. 'I just wish I knew where he was. Do you have any idea?'

'None at all. If I knew, I would tell you Sal, I promise I would.'

'I don't suppose there's any point ringing the station is there?' She was grasping at straws and she knew it.

'I wouldn't have thought so, Sal.'

'No, that was a silly idea. Do you know if Sue's home yet?' She felt ashamed of the implication in the question. Why would Sam go to see his ex-wife, even if she was home?

'As a matter of fact I spoke to her today – that is, yesterday. She was ringing for a progress report. She's in Spain somewhere.'

'Right. Don't tell Sam I asked that question– Owen...'

'Yes?'

'Does he ever talk to you about Kathy?'

'Sally, I swear on the lives of my various children, he never mentions her.'

'Right – I never asked that question either.'

'No problem, Sally, and I fully understand your exasperation but I don't think Sam being out at this hour is any cause for concern.'

'Thanks, Owen.'

Their work done, Tanya and Annie walked back to the house. Burying Sam alive hadn't lifted their gloom.

'We are doin' the right thing aren't we, Tan?'

'We've got no choice, Ma. If Uncle Graham knows about me, and Carew knows about the grave, God knows who else knows. What chance do we have?'

'No chance, Tan. Stayin's too much of a risk.'

'Anyway, we're ready to go.'

'I know, girl. It kills me havin' ter leave this place behind – and the merchant's. I used ter dream about goin' legit, holdin' me head up high in the Women's fuckin' Institute.' Annie stopped by the pond so that she could have a last look at the peeing boy.

'Are we paying the wages, Ma?' Tanya asked, walking on.

Annie made to catch her daughter up. 'Bollocks to the wages! We're leaving enough behind without worryin' about wages.'

'What do you think'll happen to it all?'

'Your guess is as good as mine. We've given the accountant full power of attorney over everything. We go, we don't come back. Property apart, we've got plenty of money tucked away. The only loose end's lying under the sod back there. The bastard'll be choking his last breath before long. Give him time ter think where he's gone wrong. No one does this ter me an' gets away with it.'

'Ma, I don't think you ever really fitted in at the Women's Institute.'

Sam could really feel the cold now, and his

arms were beginning to cramp up. Lying there with his hands tied behind his back was incredibly uncomfortable, and there was no need for it. If they wanted to tie his hands together why not tie them at the front? He just wanted to break free of his bonds and move his arms about a bit, even within the limited confines of the coffin. They had nailed him inside here for God's sake, buried him in the ground. Why make things even worse? Oh Jesus! He felt a fart coming on. Must hold that in. There was little enough air in here without him polluting it. He didn't want to die breathing in his own fart. The thought amused him for a split second and he knew he must be deranged but what the hell? Sod it, let it go. It might warm the bloody place up.

That time in the derelict pub was luxury compared to this. So why had it given him nightmares? He'd had room to move about, clean air to breathe – apart from the smell of fox pee – and a mobile phone in his pocket. He probably still had his mobile on him now. Fat lot of use a mobile is in a coffin with your hands tied behind your back. What if it rings? It won't, it's switched off.

What would Sally think? Him disappearing off the face of the Earth like this. Would she think he'd deserted her for some reason? Run off with another woman. Would she find out about Alison if he was never found?

Would Alison say anything? And the boys. He didn't want to leave his boys. Tears.

Graham awoke, momentarily, as a pigeon flew into the shed in which he was imprisoned, still shackled to the steel pillar. It flapped around, trying to get out, and he tried to scream in fear, but nothing came out of his tinder dry mouth. Then the bird settled down and Graham lapsed into merciful oblivion once again. He stank of his own body waste and his breathing was slight and spasmodic. He wasn't yet dead but he was in a far worse state than Sam.

Sam could almost feel the weight of the earth on him. It was crushing his chest, making it hard to breath. How deep down was he? Not far. But he could be a thousand miles down and it wouldn't reduce his chances of survival. He wondered just how many breaths he had left. A hundred? Why not count? It's something to do. No, think about the boys and Sally. Have them on your mind at the end, not some bloody number between one and a hundred. Tom and Jake, how he loved them. How he wanted to give them one last hug. He should have married Sally. Then again, she probably deserved someone better than him. Shit! He was counting in the back of his mind without realising it. Five ... six ...

never get to a hundred. Our Father, Who art in Heaven, hallowed be Thy name...

Bowman was sitting at his desk. He was the only senior officer in the station. There was no real need for him to be doing nights, except that it was a blessed relief from having to sleep with his wife. Things weren't good between them. Him sending her brother to prison hadn't helped. Things had been improving between them before that happened.

'I can't see why you can't use your influence,' she had said. 'There's plenty of other things you influence down there, but when it comes to helping me and my family – no chance. Maybe I should go down there and tell them everything I know about you.'

What the hell did she mean by that? What the hell did she know? Had it not been for Carew he might have been able to use his influence. Bloody Carew. Bane of his life. Janet Seager popped her head around the door.

'I'm going for a coffee, anything I can get you, sir?'

'No thanks, Janet.'

She said good night and left him to it. Shame she was a dyke. He'd definitely leave his wife for a woman like Janet. Just his luck she was a dyke.

I love you, boys. I love you, Sally. I love you, Owen... Thy kingdom come. Thy will be done... Once a Catholic always a Catholic ... have I left it too late? There were noises in his head he couldn't identify. Noises that didn't belong under this ground. In this place of death. How much longer? Stop it! I want to go peacefully. It was bad enough having to breathe in my own fart, but all this noise. Louder and louder. Banging now. Cold air. Can't be Hell. Hell's hot, hot as Hell. This is cold. Cold and draughty. What the hell? Who the hell?'

'Hello, Mr Carew. My name's Ben Corbally. I came to thank you for the money.'

Sam stared upwards at the dark sky, broken by the vague outline of the boy who was untying his hands. The boy had a torch. Sam's mind began to clear. He pulled off his gag and drew in drew in deep lungfuls of air as he re-adjusted from death back to life. Not an easy adjustment to make.

'What...? Who did you say you are?'

'Ben Corbally. You sent me a lot of money. I sneaked out of the home to see you, but when I got there it was very late, and in any case I didn't know how to get into your flat.'

'Flat? The bell ... you could have rung the bell.'

'I thought of that, but ... I didn't really know what to say.'

'Shy, eh?'

'I don't know – mebbe.'

'So, you're too shy to ring my bell but not

too shy to dig me up out of this grave? It's a funny old world, Ben Corbally.'

'Right.'

'Sorry if I'm talking in riddles, Ben, but I'm still getting used to being alive.'

'I waited a bit, then I saw you driving away, so I followed you.

'Bloody hell! I can't believe I'm alive.'

'Pardon, sir?'

Such manners, thought Sam. Here at the bottom of this grave, a boy with manners. A shy boy who had saved him. Brought him fresh air, opened his coffin and said hello. Bloody hell! This was the stuff dreams are made of. Nightmares maybe, but dreams all the same. He'd take a nightmare to being dead, any day of the week.

'I'm alive.'

'I think so, Mr Carew. I came to thank you for the money. My dad always told me I should thank people in person if possible when they give you presents.'

'Did he? Well, it wasn't exactly a present. Anyway, you're more than welcome. Do you think you could sort of pull me up? I'm a bit stiff.'

'What? Oh, yeah, sorry.'

'Please don't say sorry to me, Ben Corbally. I don't want you ever to say sorry to me as long as you live.'

'Right.'

Sam talked as Ben struggled to pull him

up. 'Ben, why didn't you make yourself known to me when I was digging? I mean, it's a damned good job you didn't, but I just wondered.'

'I'm not sure – it looked very private and er, secret. I didn't think you'd like me following you. It was very exciting. I watched those two ladies bury you, but I couldn't dig you out until they went into the house. Does this sort of thing happen to you all the time?'

'Not every day, no – Ben, don't let them see the torch.'

Ben switched the torch off. 'They're in the house. I watched them go in. The curtains are drawn, they can't see us. I found the pick and the spade. They left them.'

Freed from his bonds Sam stretched his arms and winced as blood burned through his empty veins. He rubbed his wrists to get the circulation back into his hands, opening and clenching his fingers. With Ben's help he climbed out of his grave, which was no more than three feet deep. He stood upright, something he thought he'd never do again. He felt life and fresh air rushing through his brain. And quite a few questions.

'How did you know how to find me?'

'The man who came to tell me about the money told me it came from you.'

'What? Owen gave you my address?'

'Well, not your address – I found that out myself.'

'Did you now? And how di–? Sorry, I'm asking too many questions. I should be thanking you.'

'It's me who wanted to thank you.'

'So, why didn't you just write?'

'Well, I've heard about you, you've been in the papers. I thought it'd be really wicked to come and see you. I hope you don't mind.'

'Mind? No, Ben, I think I can safely say I don't mind. You've just saved my life, I assume you know that?'

'I think so.'

'I was in a tight spot there, Ben. Very tight indeed.' He took Ben's torch off him and shone it the boy. He was a pleasant looking lad, not quite as big as his sons.

'How old are you, Ben?'

'Thirteen. I'll get my money in five years.'

'You will indeed, Ben, and you'll get a lot more when I'm finished.' Questions were still flooding through his mind. 'How did you er, how did follow me?'

'I borrowed a motor bike from the home.'

'Thirteen and you can ride a motor bike?'

'My dad started taking me scrambling since I was eight. I'm a member of Unsworth Junior Scrambling Club. I got my own bike when I was nine. They took it off me when my dad was killed – said it was for my own good.'

'How thoughtful of them. Does the owner know you've borrowed his bike?'

'It's actually Mrs Miller's bike – she's the warden's wife. I'll tell her tomorrow – if I have to.'

Sam took the boy in his arms and hugged him. He hugged into Ben all the love he'd wanted to hug into his own boys, not too long ago. 'I have two sons a couple of years older than you. You'd like th–' Sam switched off the torch. 'Watch out!' he said, urgently, looking across at the house.

The two of them squatted to the ground as they watched two figures come out of the front door. All the visible house lights had been switched off.

'There go the delightful Robinson women,' murmured Sam. 'They'll assume I'm dead by now, but I reckon they're still doing a runner.'

A large car came up the driveway and stopped outside the door. A man got out and held the car door open. Sam reached into his pocket and was relieved to find his mobile had survived the ordeal. He pressed the speed dial for Owen, and spoke quietly.

'Owen, it's Sam.'

'Where the hell are you? I've just had Sal on the phone wondering where you are. She's not best pleased I c–'

'Owen, shut up and listen. I'm at Wickham Farm – the Robinson's place. I've just dug up a grave with Nathan Robinson's body in it, I think his two brothers are buried here as well. I'm watching Tanya and her mother doing a runner right at this moment. Tell Janet – she can do the rest. I wouldn't mind you coming straight out here, though. I think Graham Erlington's here somewhere. They told me he was dead but they think I'm dead as well, so what the hell do they know? Tell you what, get an ambulance, just in case. If we can't find Graham they can have me to practise on. I think I need a check-up after what I've just been through.'

'They think you're dead? Why would they thin–?'

'Owen, please.'

'Do I tell Bowman?'

'Just make sure Janet and O'Donnell know what's happening. If Bowman finds out, so be it. He won't dare stick his oar in if everybody knows. Janet might want to alert the airports.' The car set off down the driveway. 'They're going,' said Sam. 'Get here as quick as you can.'

He and Ben watched the car disappear into the trees on their left, and Sam couldn't think of what to do next. His brain kept switching from clarity to numbness, then flashes of his recent burial came back to him. He knew this night would come back to haunt him, but the nightmares would have to wait.

'Should we look for Graham?' suggested Ben.

'What?'

'I heard you talking about someone called Graham, who might not be dead.'

'That's right.'

What was it she said? *Graham should be dead by now.* What did that mean? It meant they'd left him to die, just as they had Sam. Where was he? Had they buried him as well? It was a hell of a lot of trouble for them to go to. Burying people all over the place.

He shone Ben's torch all around, looking for a mound of fresh earth. Nothing. Maybe he was buried in the same grave as Sam. He and Ben pulled out the empty coffin and prodded around underneath, then Sam sat on the ground, exhausted.

'This is useless. Look, I'm sorry to be asking so many questions, but how did you know it was me?'

'Pardon?'

'You say you saw me driving away. How did you know it was me? It could have been anyone.'

'I've seen your photo.'

'Oh, right.' Sam decided not to ask where. It was all just part of the same miracle. It seemed curmudgeonly to question it further.

'In the papers,' said Ben.

'Right – good memory for faces, then.'

'Mr Carew, who is this Graham?'

'He's the brother and uncle of the women who just tried to bury me. It's sometimes not all it's cracked up to be, family life.'

'Blimey!'

Sam was impressed at such a polite expletive from a thirteen-year-old lad. 'I'm guessing he's here somewhere and he might still be alive.'

'Do you think he'll be in the house – maybe the cellar?' suggested Ben.

'Maybe – or one of the outbuildings.'

'I think the outbuildings are favourite.'

Sam knew that, by rights, he should be sending this runaway boy back to where he came from but, right now, he needed Ben's help and energy and enthusiasm. They headed towards the house. To the right was a low building that might, in a previous life, have been stables.

'We'll try over there,' Sam said, 'bring the pick.' He found his own pencil torch and gave it to Ben, who took it without argument. Sam knew at least two boys very close to him who would have insisted that each searcher be allowed to use his own personal torch. The thought made him smile. He needed smiles right now. Then tears ran down his face and he turned away from Ben in case the boy shone his torch on him. This buried alive ordeal was going to be a right bugger to get over.

They searched every stable and found nothing. Beyond the stables was a barn, which was equally empty. Sam was exhausted once again. Sweat was pouring down his face.

'Are you OK, Mr Carew?'

'I'm fine, Ben. It's just adrenaline pumping round at top speed. It tends to do that when you've been buried alive.'

Ben grinned in the dark. He was delighted to be here with this oddball private eye. All the stories he'd heard about him were true. Sam patted his pockets. 'Damn! I left my cigs in the car. I could really do with one right now.'

'Do you smoke Craven A?'

'Right now I'd smoke an old sock.'

Ben took a packet of Craven A from his pocket and offered them to Sam, who stared at him for a second, wondering whether to chastise him for smoking at his age. But you can hardly chastise someone who's just saved your life.

'Have you got a light?'

Ben took out a lighter and lit Sam's cigarette. Sam closed his eyes and inhaled deeply, allowing the fumes to trail out of his nose and mouth. He couldn't remember a cigarette tasting sweeter. Cigarettes were meant for times such as this. He smiled at Ben.

'Aren't you having one?'

'I've been trying to give up.'

Sam felt himself chuckling. He'd just had his life saved by a motor-cycling thirteen-year-old boy who was trying to give up smoking.

'You don't drink, do you?'

'No, mug's game that. I'll never drink as long as I live.' Then Sam remembered the circumstances of Ben's mother's death and his chuckle died in his throat.

'Sorry, Ben. I'm not thinking straight.'

'It's all right, Mr Carew. I'll have a look round while you finish your cig.'

A minute later he was back. 'There's some fresh tyre tracks running past the barn into that field.' He pointed to an open gate. 'They look to be leading to that shed.'

Sam flicked his cigarette away. He grinned at the boy's eagerness and was tempted to say, *Well done, Sherlock*, but he didn't.

The tracks led straight to the shed door, which was locked with a padlock. Sam looked at Ben. 'Any good with a pick?'

Without a word Ben swung the pick down on to the lock and missed by inches, almost digging the tool into his own leg.

'Give it here,' said Sam, 'before you lame yourself.'

Sam knocked the lock off with a single, accurate blow that impressed Ben, who pushed the door open and shone his tiny torch inside.

Graham lay there, seemingly dead. Sam, groaned, 'Oh no,' and knelt down beside him. If Graham was dead it was his fault. He felt for a pulse in the comedian's neck, then listened for signs of breathing. He sat back on his haunches as Ben looked on, with a hand over his mouth and nose, to stifle the stench of Graham's body waste.

'He's alive – just,' Sam told him. He took out his mobile and rang Owen again. 'We've found Graham, he's barely alive. Where's this bloody ambulance?'

'It should be with you very shortly. We're at the gate, it was locked and we've had a job breaking through.'

'I'll send Ben down to the house to show you where he is.'

'Ben?' said Owen. 'Who's Be–'

But Sam had cut him off. He had work to do, keeping Graham alive for the next few minutes. The callous bitches had left a bottle of water just out of Graham's reach. He dripped it on to the comedian's twitching lips as the ambulance siren grew louder.

CHAPTER FORTY-ONE

'Tanya Robinson is without question the woman who attacked me in Lancashire. I have no doubt about that. I've also got no doubt that she is the hammer killer. What do you think, Detective Chief Inspector? Are you still in denial of what is patently bloody obvious – bearing in mind how Nathan

Robinson died?'

Sam's gaze was fixed on Bowman, who returned it with a bland gaze of his own. O'Donnell was there, as were Owen and Janet Seager, both brought in at Sam's request. He hadn't mentioned that he suspected Bowman to be a corrupt copper, but if he was right about that, then Bowman wouldn't be able to influence further proceedings, not with so many people in on the act. 'She worked for Henry Corbally and she worked for Mrs Crowther,' Sam added.

'They've both been interviewed and they both deny the charge,' Bowman pointed out.

'What, and you believe them?'

Bowman didn't respond. Graham Erlington was recovering, but it would be a while before he could be interviewed. Three bodies had been exhumed from Wickham farm. Ben Corbally had been interviewed and had fully corroborated Sam's version. The papers were making a meal out of the fact that Sam Carew had once again done the police's job for them. The burial story had hit the nationals and Sam was being besieged by reporters to tell the whole story.

But being buried alive wasn't a story Sam wanted to tell. It was something he wanted to forget. It was the only way he could deal with it – to put it out of his mind. The papers would just have to make up their own version of the story, as they often did anyway.

'We spoke to the boy,' Bowman said, 'and asked him why he followed you. He said it was because you'd been very good to him and he wanted to thank you.'

Sam inwardly smiled in admiration of this boy who was very good at saying and doing the right things. Ben had also been told by Sam to keep quiet, for the time being, about the money. He'd also told him not to talk to the press.

'I'm investigating his father's murder, he's very grateful.'

'He seems to be hiding something,' remarked Bowman.

'He's a boy who's been done a massive injustice,' said Sam. 'He doesn't trust everybody, and who can blame him? It's his Uncle Henry you should be talking to.'

Bowman scowled, 'It's a question of proof,' he said.

Owen looked at Sam, willing him to tell them about the DVD on which Corbally admitting hiring a contract killer. Sam was also turning the idea over in his mind. One thing he knew for sure was that as soon as the police saw that piece of evidence, questions would be asked about the money in the suitcase. This might well land Sam in trouble, and no doubt the money would be taken off Ben until the whole matter was sorted. With Bowman acting against them there was no certainty that things would go their way. Sam needed to be certain.

'If you need proof, Bowman, I suppose I'll have to do your job for you again and get it.'

'You're out of this,' said O'Donnell, sharply. 'From now on this is strictly a police matter. You so much as poke the tip of your nose in and I'll bring you in for interfering with a police investigation.'

Bowman smirked. Sam desperately wanted to wipe it off his face. Instead he got to his feet and walked out of the room.

On balance, with the Robinson women on the warpath, The Pear Tree was a lot safer than the Clog and Shovel, on top of which Sam wanted to talk to Alison. She was the main reason he'd got involved in all this and he didn't want to talk to her at her flat because he wasn't sure what it might lead to. She was behind the bar.

'I'm meeting Owen here shortly,' he said, 'I wonder if we could have a chat in the meantime?'

She glanced at the bar manager. 'Can I take a break, Jim, we're not busy?' She poured herself a drink and joined Sam at a table.

'I don't know how much you know—' Sam began.

'I know the bastard who raped me is dead.'

'Nathan?'

'It had to be him. I've done some asking

around. Big, vicious Scouse bastard – and a Robinson. It doesn't take much figuring out. My son no longer has a father, and you've no idea how much of a relief that is.'

'I can imagine,' said Sam, remembering his own dad with the usual fondness. 'A boy should have a good father. Nathan died from a hammer blow to his head, no doubt a parting gift from Tanya.'

'You mean Hammerhead?'

'Not according to the police, not yet, anyway. They're still being very reluctant to admit they got it wrong.' He placed a hand on top of hers and felt the electricity passing his way. She raised her eyebrows slightly and gave him a coquettish smile.

'Careful, Sam.'

'I know that your dad was set up, and why,' he told her.

'Oh – so he was definitely set up, then?'

'According to Annie Robinson, she told me, just before she...' he exhaled a long breath. Alison helped him out. She'd read about him in the papers.

'Laid you to rest?'

He gave a dry laugh. 'I didn't do much resting. Anyway, it seems that the murder George Robinson was sent down for was committed by er...' he gave her a meaningful look.

'What?' she asked, scanning his face for clues to what would come next.

'Your dad was with him,' Sam said.

'And ... what? You're saying that my dad did the murder?'

'According to Annie – and it's the only explanation that makes sense.'

She thought about it for a while, then nodded, slowly. 'There are things I remember from that time, that tie in with what you say. The way my dad was behaving. You're right, it's the only thing that makes sense. Jesus!'

He gave her a sympathetic nod. 'Does it trouble you?' he asked.

She gave it some more thought, then shook her head. 'Dad's life was taken away from him for committing murder. That's justice. Justice was all I wanted. I think I might even feel better about things. Does that sound awful?'

'I think it's understandable.'

'So, they did it for revenge?'

Sam nodded. 'Apparently, Kevin and George went on a job together. According to Annie it was Kevin who did the shooting, not George. George took the fall because of some weird honour among thieves thing – he'd probably have got sent down anyway. After he died in jail the Robinsons decided to punish Kevin themselves.'

'So, they set him up?'

'Yes, they did, and it wouldn't have worked if I hadn't caught him.'

'Which is why you helped me.'

'Something like that.'

'But as things turn out, dad deserved to go to jail.'

'Yes, I'm afraid he did.'

Alison sipped at her drink and pondered the situation. 'So,' she looked at him with raised eyebrows, 'in a roundabout way it sort of vindicates you.'

Sam shrugged as though it were of no consequence, but she was right. He didn't feel quite as guilty at putting Kevin away. 'The man who died,' he told her, 'was killed with his own shotgun. Owen looked the case up for me. There had been a struggle. I doubt if Kevin set out to murder anyone. Mind you, that doesn't make the victim any less dead.'

'True, but he wasn't a hard man, wasn't my dad. If he'd lived I suppose he'd have been released.'

'He'd most probably have been charged with the first murder, with time served taken into consideration. Yeah, I think they'd have let him out.'

'I'll tell Mum that. Even though dad's dead it's actually a weight off my shoulders. Everything out in the open, justice done and all that.'

'Not quite,' said Sam. 'There's still Annie and Tanya to take care of.'

'Won't you just leave that to the police?'

'You took the words right out of my mouth.'

They both looked up to see Owen standing there. 'I think you and I need to have a little talk, boyo.'

'Don't call me boyo.'

Alison got to her feet. 'I'll leave you boyos to it.' She went round the table and kissed Sam on his mouth, more than just a friendly farewell. She whispered in his ear. 'I owe you a massive thank you. Give me a ring.'

The very thought of such thanks set Sam's already confused mind spinning.

'Sweet nothings, was it?' asked Owen.

'What?'

'What she whispered in your ear. Was it sweet nothings?'

'Just get me a pint, you lecherous old sod.'

'I'm not all that old,' said Owen, cheerfully, loping off to the bar.

Sam's thoughts drifted away to Alison's bedroom and the delights it held, and did he have the willpower to resist such delights? He allowed his mind to dwell on the subject. He needed something like this to counter the dark memory of the grave. A memory that just wouldn't go away. Owen came back with drinks and got straight on to the matter in hand.

'I can't see any advantage in not telling them about the bloody DVD.'

Sam was still thinking about Alison, who was smiling at him from behind the bar. Would it do any harm to have one last fling with her? What Sal didn't know wouldn't harm her. No, he couldn't do this to Sal. Or could he?'

'Sam, are you listening to me?'

'What?'

'The DVD, you need to give it to them.'

Sam gathered his thoughts. 'Owen, I'm not throwing the DVD into the ring until I know, one way or the other, whether I can trust Bowman.'

'Sam, this is a modern police force. One man can't have all that influence.'

'Owen, that's just where you're wrong. Modern policing is about doing things by the book. There's no room for hunches, persuasive interrogation, scare tactics–'

'And lying?' added Owen.

'No, lying's still in there,' said Sam. 'Only today's lying's a lot more sneaky and a lot more dangerous. There are people very high up in the force telling very big lies to protect their own skin.'

Owen sipped at his pint with a look of bewilderment on his face. 'I don't see the connection between that and your DVD.'

Sam gave a long sigh. He was working on instinct, and the word instinct didn't figure in any police procedural handbooks. 'Owen, policing today's more about doing things by the book rather than getting results, you talk to any copper who was about in the Sixties and Seventies. Their methods were a lot

414

more direct and a lot cruder, but they had a far higher success rate than today's coppers.'

'Yes, but how often did the wrong person get locked up?'

'I know all about that, but with DNA and stuff, there's less chance of that happening nowadays. It's gone too far the other way. Today you've got DNA, brilliant forensics, computers, mobile phones, CCTV – back in the Sixties all they had was fingerprints, dodgy photofits and sniffer dogs. Nowadays you've got all the equipment for getting it right, and yet you're all bogged down with PACE, paperwork and EU Directives. Owen, I acquired that DVD by lies and trickery, what are the odds that some clever dick lawyer gets it thrown out of court for some minor loophole that you and I don't know about? Ben loses his inheritance and Uncle Henry walks free. No, the first thing I'm going to do is flush out Bowman – and you can help me.'

'How?' asked Owen, defeated by Sam's convoluted logic.

Sam gave a broad grin and began to hum, *The Entertainer*. It came from Owen's favourite film of all time, *The Sting*.

'Owen, we're going to kill two birds with one stone – two birds and a prat to be more precise.'

'And how do we do that?'

'Tell me, Owen, what do you think the

415

Robinson women are thinking right now?'

'With reference to what?'

'With reference to me – the man who destroyed their family business, then rose up from the grave they buried me in.'

'What – you think they'll come for you again?'

'Oh yes, I most certainly think they'll come for me again. They won't be able to rest while I'm still alive – which is why I don't think I'll have long to wait.'

'What a delightful thought – and how does this fit in with smoking out Bowman?'

'Ah,' said Sam, 'you'll have to help me with that.'

CHAPTER FORTY-TWO

Owen knocked, tentatively, on Bowman's office door, and waited for the command to, 'Come.'

Bowman looked up at him and then back down to illustrate that Owen was of far less interest than the scrap of paper he was reading. The Welsh detective stood there for several minutes until his boss deigned to look up.

'What is it, DC Price?'

Owen decided to get it all out in one go.

'Well, sir, I know you're not a great fan of Sam Carew, but he has placed himself in considerable danger in pursuit of Hammerhead, so much so that he's had to go into hiding. There's already been one attempt on his life and I wondered if it might be an idea to give him some sort of protection ... sir.'

'Really? And where is he living that requires our protection?'

'He's moved into his ex-wife's house, sir. She's gone abroad until Tanya Robinson, alias Hammerhead, is caught.'

'Alias Hammerhead, eh? My word you are getting ahead of yourself, Price. As far as I know, so far there's no hard evidence to link this Tanya Robinson to the serial killings. Unless you know something I don't.'

'I thought the injury to her brother was the same as those inflicted by the hammer killer, sir.'

'Is that what you thought? Well, I'll tell you what I think, shall I? I think whatever problems Carew has, he has brought upon himself. I have no intention of wasting valuable police resources on him. Is there anything else, Price?'

'No, sir.'

Annie wanted to go at night but Tanya pointed out that the house had security lights and double glazing, and it would be a noisy job breaking in, especially as neither of them were any good at burglary. She outlined her plan to her mother.

'I like it. You've a head on yer shoulders, girl. I'll do the shooting. I know what yer like with irons.'

'Ma, I can do it. Even I won't miss from where I'll be standing.' Tanya hesitated, then suggested, 'Although, this time we could get a proper contractor in to do the same job. Mr Small would be glad to organise it for us. I could return the favour some time on a quid pro quo basis.'

'This is fucking personal, Tan. That bastard has come back from the dead. I need to make him dead again by my own hand or I might start believin' in God.'

'This is not cold blood, Ma. You know yourself these things should be done in cold blood.'

'There are some things you've got ter get out of yer system, girl. And I need ter get this bastard out of me system. He has done damage to our family and what's left of our family has to do damage to him.'

'I understand, Ma.'

Sam hadn't been outside Sue's house in five days. He'd had four, very discreet, CCTV cameras fitted, to cover every angle around the house, each camera had two monitors, one in Sam's bedroom and one downstairs in the living room. Anyone coming onto the

418

property, from any angle, would trigger off an infra red, beeping alarm, switching on the DVD recorders and alerting Sam to an intruder.

Owen came to see him every three days with food. Sam had left a message on Sally's phone telling her he was going away for a few days and she knew this meant he was up to something she wouldn't approve of. She had asked herself the question, *which would she prefer:* Sam going off with another woman or Sam doing something that might get him killed? On balance she chose the other woman scenario, but only because she very much doubted if that's what he was up to. When she got no answer from Sam's phone she rang Owen.

'Where is he, Owen?'

'Oh, heck, I knew this would happen, see. You're putting me in a very awkward position, Sal. He made me promise not to tell you.'

'Why doesn't he want me to know? Is it something stupid, Owen?'

Owen couldn't think of a reply.

'It's something stupid, isn't it?'

'Well, it's not one of his brighter ideas.'

'I'll blame you if anything happens to him.'

She clicked her phone off and Owen sighed again. 'Carew, you bloody bugger. Why do you do this to me?'

Sam was beginning to think this was a very bad idea. There was nothing to stop the Robinson women leaving it several months before they came to get him. Why would they come for him now, when he was obviously on his guard? And was he right about Bowman being bent? The more he thought about that, the more he thought he was wrong.

In five days he'd had sixteen beeps, ten of them dogs, which annoyed him because the security firm had promised him that most dogs would be too small to trigger the alarm. He'd had no more than three hours unbroken sleep.

'Sam, your state of readiness is in a hell of a state,' Owen told him.

He was to await a call from Sam to tell him that the Robinson women were at his door. As a precaution he'd had to alert DI Seager to this possibility. She was told, 'with all due respect, ma'am, you mustn't tell anyone, especially DCI Bowman.'

'Why's that, Owen?'

'Because, apart from us, ma'am, DCI Bowman is the only person who knows where Sam is staying – but what he doesn't know is that Sam is in readiness for a visit from the Robinson women.'

'I see, so if the Robinson women turn up it means Sam's been given away either by you, me or DCI Bowman?'

'Precisely, ma'am.'

But Janet gave a slow nod. 'Right – you'll ring me the instant anything happens?'

'Within seconds. It would be nice if we could have people on stand-by.'

'With this being unofficial, how could that be possible? Have you any idea how Sam plans to handle it if they do turn up, which I hope they don't?'

'I doubt if Sam knows the answer to that question, ma'am.'

'That's what I was afraid of. I do wish he wouldn't do these things.'

'You and me both, ma'am.'

Sam was just coming out of the bathroom when the doorbell rang. He went into his bedroom and looked at the CCTV monitor. It was a postman carrying a parcel. When he didn't answer, the postman took a step back and looked towards the front room window, which was unusual in a postman. In their job they rang once, if no answer they stuck a note through the door telling the occupant to collect the package from the depot. The postman rang again. Sam looked at the shot from a camera positioned in a tree. This wasn't a postman, it was a post*woman*. There was another shot showing the length of the drive, where a Royal Mail van was parked. Very posh postwoman this, doing a round with her own van. There was a driver in the van. Sam pressed the zoom on the keyboard. Within seconds he was ringing Owen.

'Owen, we were right about Bowman.'

'They've turned up, have they?'

'They're outside the house, now. Tanya's in a Royal Mail van, Annie's trying to deliver me a package, only I'm not answering.'

'It's probably a 9mm package,' said Owen.

'Let's assume that,' Sam said. 'Tell Janet to get some armed people. I'll try and keep them here.'

'How?'

'I'll play it by ear.'

The door bell rang again. Sam's eyes were fixed on the monitor. Annie hesitated, then walked back to the van.

'There's someone in,' she said to Tanya. 'I heard the bog flushing when I got to the door.'

'Try round the back,' Tanya suggested. 'Find a way in. I'll stay here. If he comes out the front door, I'll take care of him. You hear a shot, you come running.' Then she added, 'Ma, any problems, we take off. This feels wrong to me.'

'I want ter get this done today, Tan.'

Sam watched Annie walk around the back of the house. She took out a silenced, automatic pistol and fired into the lock of the rear patio door. The lock held, as Sam thought it might. Locks aren't as easy to shoot off as films would have you believe.

422

They're more likely to become distorted and jam even tighter. She fired several shots at the glass, which shattered. She climbed through. Sam's heart began to race. He had two lines of defence: a substantial wardrobe he'd positioned on the half-landing and a bag of Jonathan's golf clubs. He whispered into the phone to Owen.

'Annie's in the house, downstairs, she's definitely armed. I'm upstairs. She'll struggle to get up here, I've left a wardrobe on the stairs.'

'So, that was your cunning plan, was it, boyo? The old wardrobe on the stairs trick. They should put it in every police manual.'

'What's happening at your end, Owen?'

'Troops on the way. I'm three minutes away with a car full of uniforms.'

'Any armed?'

'Not in this car. Janet's organising that. O'Donnell's been told.'

'Good. Quicker the better, mate. I'll keep this line open.'

Annie checked every room on the ground floor and was at the bottom of the stairs, cursing to herself when she saw the wardrobe. She couldn't run up, shooting. Did he have a gun? Unlikely. He apparently played by his own set of strange rules, which didn't include shooters. She took out her mobile and dialled Tanya.

'Tan, he's upstairs but he's blocked the

staircase off.'

'He's probably called the bizzies, Ma. I think we should call it off.'

Annie spat out her reaction to this. 'Fuck that!'

'Ma, if we're going to get him I reckon we've got about three minutes before the bizzies get here. I'm coming in.'

Tanya was out of the van in a flash, around the back of the house and in through the shattered patio doors. With Annie in the lead they tried to get past the wardrobe. Sam had rightly figured that squeezing up a staircase, through an impossibly small space, and accurately firing a weapon, are incompatible occupations, especially when someone's trying to hit you with a golf club.

It was a very large and heavy Victorian piece, and it had taken Sam a lot of time and effort to position it there. He had armed himself with Jonathan's driver, the longest club in the bag, with a head the size of small car. He leaned over the bannister and swung it down in a long arc, catching Annie on her shoulder. She screamed in rage and pain and fired several wild shots in his general direction. The bullets missed by a distance, some taking splinters out of the wardrobe, others going straight through the ceiling. Sam took cover behind the staircase bulkhead and awaited their next attempt. He shouted down the phone. 'Owen, they're coming for me. What the hell's keeping you?'

A car had pulled up outside. Sam darted into the bedroom and looked at the monitors. Owen, assuming the action was all upstairs, was charging towards the front door, to which he had a key. Sam was now wishing he hadn't given him one. What the hell was the Welsh idiot doing? The other officers were sensibly staying by the car. Another car arrived. This one had Janet Seager and two armed officers in it. Owen was opening the door. Sam was screaming down the phone for him not come in, but Owen's phone was in his pocket. Sam ran back to the landing, where Annie was squeezing herself past the wardrobe once again. He swung the club at her and caught her full in the face. She howled in pain, cursed at him and retreated with blood pouring from her broken nose. Sam could just see past the wardrobe. Tanya was standing on the stairs, her gun arm outstretched, as Owen pushed the door open.

'Owen, NO!'

Owen mistook his shout for, 'Owen, now,' and stepped inside. Sam got behind the wardrobe and heaved at it. Sending it toppling on top of Tanya and Annie just as Owen entered. Tanya's gun fired. She turned her face away at the last second, but she still brought Owen down. Sam scrambled over the wardrobe which had trapped her underneath, still with the gun in her hand, firing in Owen's direction. The Welshman took at least one more hit as he lay on the floor. Sam twisted the gun from her hand and took aim at Annie, who was struggling to her feet. She ran out of the front door before he could pull the trigger, her face a bloody mask of rage, screeching obscenities and shooting as she went. There was a loud burst of gunfire as the police shot back, then a very ominous silence.

Sam was sitting on top of Tanya as Owen writhed in agony just a few feet away. Tanya glared up at Sam, defiantly. He was pointing her gun at her face.

'If you struggle and this goes off it's your fault,' he said. 'Are you OK, Owen?'

'OK? I'm hurting like buggery, boyo.'

Sam returned his attention to Tanya, the woman who had tried to kill him three times; the woman responsible for his nightmares. He desperately wanted to put a bullet into her sneering face. Instead he clenched his fist and knocked her unconscious with one blow, then went to tend to Owen. It was the first time he'd ever hit a woman, but he got great satisfaction from it.

When Tanya came to she was handcuffed and staring up at DI Janet Seager. There was a bruise on her chin and blood around her mouth. She waited for her head to clear

Police were milling around. Sam was outside talking to Sergeant Bassey. Owen was on the floor being tended by two paramedics. Annie was lying on the footpath outside. Tanya asked the question with more curiosity than emotion.

'Is she dead?'

'Yes,' said Janet. She would have allowed Tanya a period of mourning appropriate for a daughter, but Tanya didn't seem to require such a courtesy.

'Madam Hammerhead, I presume?'

'Madam Headcase, more like,' muttered Tanya.

'The world is full of headcases,' said Janet, glancing in Sam's direction.

'Tell me about it,' grumbled Tanya. 'I come from a whole family of them. Why we came charging in here after that prat Carew, I'll never know. We should have contracted this out. I suggested it to Ma, but she wouldn't have it. We were too involved, which made it completely unprofessional. Carew assaulted me, by the way. I want him charged with assault. God, I hate that bloody man!'

'He does have that effect on some people,' said Janet. 'Mind you, I suppose your pal Bowman told you all about that.'

'And what the hell is that supposed to mean?'

Janet turned around to see Bowman standing in the doorway, along with DCI

O'Donnell. Janet steeled herself, but she was sure enough of her facts to make the accusation.

'Sam Carew set this up to trap both the Robinsons and you, sir. I'm sorry, sir, but you were the only person who could have possibly told the Robinsons of Sam's whereabouts.'

Owen pushed one of the medics out of the way so that he could see Bowman. 'You also knew the name of the informer who told me about the drugs deal at Robinson's Builders' Merchants, which went wrong, with the informer and his brother being murdered ... sir.'

Janet thought he did very well to get all that out whilst in such pain.

'Well, Mr Bowman, it seems they've got us both bang to rights,' said Tanya.

'What? I never did anything of the sort!' blustered Bowman. 'This is – this is just ridiculous!'

'Come on, there's no point denying it,' Tanya said. 'You take the money, you take the chance, the same as I did.'

'I didn't take any damned money!'

'I'm sorry, sir, we think you did,' said DI Janet Seager. She looked at O'Donnell, who gave her a reluctant nod before she cautioned her senior officer.

CHAPTER FORTY-THREE

'One in the arm, one in the arse,' Owen was telling Sam.

'I know, you keep telling me.'

Despite his discomfort, Owen seemed proud to have been wounded in the course of duty. 'Still, there's nothing to stop me going back to work at some stage.'

Sam glanced around the ward. 'I've been in this very same bed myself,' he commented.

'You've been in every bed on this ward at some time, Mr Carew,' said an arriving nurse. She took Owen's temperature and checked his dressings. He'd been in hospital a week. The bullet in his backside had been removed, the other one had gone clean through his upper arm, breaking a bone on the way. He was still having to lie on his side.

Sam glanced at the mountain of expensive sweets and chocolate on Owen's bedside table and decided not to hand over the packet of Riley's Chocolate Toffee Rolls he'd brought. 'You'll be pleased to know I gave O'Donnell the DVD and Henry Corbally's been picked up. His money didn't take much tracking down – it was all in his current account, earning him 1.5 per cent apparently. He's not exactly a financial whizz-kid isn't our Henry.'

'Has er, has anyone mentioned the hundred grand we put in Ben's account?' asked Owen, slightly concerned. 'It could drop me in it if the boy mentions me.'

'The boy knows not to mention you,' said Sam. 'I told O'Donnell *I* gave the money to Ben. With it being held in trust until the lad's eighteen he seems content to let it ride, being as how Ben's due to cop for the lot when it's all sorted.'

'I'm pleased for the boy, he seems a nice kid.'

'He's more than just a nice kid, Owen. Had it not been for him...' Sam's voice tailed off as his mind went back to the night he waited to die in his grave. He blew out a long breath. Like soldiers coming home from the war he had to deal with it by neither talking nor thinking about it. There was no other way.

'What about Tanya?' Owen asked.

Sam pulled a face. 'According to Janet, Tanya's completely clammed up. She's not admitting to anything – and she's hired Henry Acombe-Booker to defend her.'

'Has she now?'

Acombe-Booker had a massive reputation as an underworld defender. He rarely took on anything that would bring in less than £100,000. His fees reflected his success rate.

'Well, even he can't get her off attempting

to murder me,' said Owen.

'Nor attempting to murder me,' said Sam, 'nor Graham Erlington – who's fully recovered, by the way. Trouble is, there's not enough evidence to pin this Hammerhead label on her.'

Owen nodded. 'I feared as much, boyo. She never left a trace of herself at any of the crime scenes.'

'The police really need to track down this Mr Small bloke,' said Sam, 'and get him to cough. That way she goes down and never gets out; otherwise she gets done for three counts of attempted murder and nothing more.'

'That's still three life sentences,' Owen pointed out.

'Technically,' agreed Sam. 'But no one actually died and, with Acombe-Booker in her corner, life could mean as little as three eight-year concurrent sentences. She could be out in four. Which isn't a prospect I relish.'

'And we have no clues as to Mr Small's whereabouts,' mused Owen, 'just a smack-head's vague description – small, bald with a cauliflower ear.'

'Did anyone try and track baldy bloke down?' enquired Sam. 'Or wasn't attempting to murder me considered serious enough to merit a thorough investigation?'

'The description of him fits half the scrum halfs in the country,' Owen pointed out.

'So, that's a no, then?'

'If we found him, our motor bike assassin reckons he could pick him out of an ID parade – for some sort of a deal.'

'It'd be worth doing a deal – that smack-head's only small fry.'

'First we have to find Mr Small and stick him in the parade,' said Owen. 'That's the tricky bit – what about the Crowther woman in Manchester?'

Sam shrugged. 'If your lot can't crack Tanya she's stays in the clear. The good news is that if I get her to drop her claim against the insurance company I still qualify for my fee.'

'Will she do that?'

'I intend calling round to see her. I'm sure she'll see sense. I might threaten her with a civil action of my own if she doesn't.'

'It'll be a bugger if Tanya gets out in four years,' Owen commented. 'For you, I mean.'

'Tell me about it.'

There was a pause as they both pondered this strong possibility.

'Sue's back,' Sam said, eventually, 'playing hell about the damage to her wardrobe. Good job I got the patio door done in time.'

'Talking of wardrobes,' said Owen. 'I think you pushing the wardrobe on top of Tanya stopped her getting a decent shot at me, so I suppose I'd better say thanks.'

'I don't suppose you could mention to Sue that the wardrobe saved your life, could you? It might shut her up about it.'

'I already have, boyo. She came this morning and brought me a box of Quality Street
– which is more than some people have
brought me,' he added, pointedly, then said,
'Ah, thank you – my favourites,' as Sam took
out the bag of toffees and handed them
over.

'Unsworth are at home on Saturday,' Sam
said. 'I'm taking Tom and Jake.'

'Who are they playing?'

'Macclesfield, two above us in the league,
should be a good game.'

There was a silence as Owen waited for
Sam's real news.

'Bowman's been refused bail.'

'Ah – and what do we think about that?'

'He's in Armley, poor sod.'

'Poor sod?' exclaimed Owen. 'Carew, it's
me who's the poor sod. I'm lying here with
an extra hole in my jacksie because of him.'

'I know – it's just that, well, I've been
there. Bowman's going to spend some very
hard time inside.'

'Serves the bugger right. Still pleading
innocent is he?'

'He is – and, do you know, there's
something I don't like about all this.'

'What don't you like?'

'Well, if it had just been my say so, and
your say so, it wouldn't have been quite so
cut and dried.'

'That's sound like gibberish to me. Is there an English version?'

'If Tanya hadn't backed up what we all said, he might have talked his way out of it. He'd certainly be out on bail. Hers is the strongest evidence that he's bent.'

'So?'

'I don't know. There's something that doesn't fit. I've known him for years. He's a pillock, but I wouldn't have thought he was this bent.'

Des Broughton had served just over half his time and had been released on parole. Unlike people in other industries, he knew the building trade wouldn't hold it against him that he'd been inside. They wouldn't hold it against him because, if he stuck to sub-contract work, there was no need for them to know. He was a good joiner – the main requirement in this business. In his first week out he'd kept himself to himself, not wanting to contact his friends or family until he "got himself sorted". The shame of being jailed was hard to bear and he wanted to meet people with his head held as high as possible. He picked up some sub-contract work, first-fitting a new house in Leeds. He was taking a break when he picked up an old *Sun* and read about his brother-in-law, DCI Bowman, being arrested for being Tanya Robinson's accomplice. It was the first bit of news he'd read in weeks.

'Bloody hell!'

A smile crept across his face as he read on. He'd never liked the man. On top of which it had been Bowman who had banged him up. Then he wondered how his sister was coping. Probably even more popped up on tablets than before. No wonder, being married to that prat. He made up his mind to go round after work.

The front door was unlocked. Des hardly got more than one step inside the hallway. His sister was dangling from a piece of washing line; one end tied in a noose around her neck and the other end lashed to the landing banister rail. Her feet were no more than three inches above the hall carpet. She was wearing a nightie, her face was grey, her dead eyes were pressing out of her head like colourless marbles, her mouth lolled open, with dried blood around her lips where she'd bitten her tongue in death. Desmond threw up.

For the time being Bowman had been placed in segregation for his own safety. Jailed coppers do hard time. He had been there a week when he was called into the wing governor's office. Chief Superintendent Pickard, the Unsworth Division Commander, was standing at a window, looking out. He turned as Bowman was shown in. His face was grave.

The wing governor was sitting at his desk, waiting for the senior police officer to speak.

'Detective Chief Inspector Bowman, I have some bad news for you, concerning your wife, perhaps you'd like to sit down.'

Bowman did as the commander suggested. His face was a mask of fear and apprehension.

'What about my wife?'

Pickard looked down at the floor, then up at Bowman. 'I'm sorry,' he said, 'there's no easy way to tell you this. I'm afraid she was found dead this morning.'

Bowman slumped in his chair. The news shocked him, but it didn't tear at his heart.

'How?' He knew the answer. 'Did she take her own life?' he asked, quietly.

'I'm afraid so. She er, she hanged herself at home.'

'Hanged? Oh, no!'

The commander and the governor allowed him his silence. His shock eventually turned to anger. He glared at the floor. His head twitched, his voice was low, muttering to himself, as if unaware that they could hear him. 'You stupid, stupid, stupid ... woman! Why did you do that? Why on God's Earth did you do that? You ... there was no need for you to do that. I told you there was no need for you to do anything like that.' He looked up, in tears, and asked, 'Did she leave a note?'

'Not that we know of.'

'What? Oh, Jesus! I don't believe this. You're sure she didn't leave a note? Surely she left a note?'

'I'm sure I would have been told.'

'This is pure evil. How could she do this to me?'

'Do what to you?'

'Never mind – I want to change my statement – for what good it'll do me.'

Tanya was being held in New Hall Women's Prison near Huddersfield. Whatever sentence she received was immaterial. She had things going for her. She had guile, she had no conscience, and she had access to enough money to bribe her way out of any prison in the world. She sat in her single cell and smiled to herself at the way she'd dropped the Detective Chief Inspector in it. He'd have a far worse time than her –and he'd spend a damned sight longer in jail. Stupid bastards! Her cell door rattled open and PO Judy Beesley came in. She was a bulky woman who towered over Tanya.

'I've got a message for yer, Robinson. It seems we have a mutual friend.'

'I very much doubt that.'

'Well, he's a friend of mine – Sam Carew.'

Tanya scowled at the mention of Sam's name. 'You should choose your friends more carefully. I loathe and detest h–'

The PO interrupted her. 'He apologises

fer hitting yer. God knows why – after yer tried to kill him. Says he feels bad about hittin' a woman.'

'Does he now? Well tell him I don't accept his apology.'

'Please yerself ... he also says thanks for helping ter get DCI Bowman banged up and out of his hair.'

'Is that some sort of a joke? Why would he thank me for that?'

PO Beesley's face turned ugly. 'Joke? Do I like look like someone who jokes with murderers?'

She took Tanya by the scruff of her neck and, effortlessly, pushed her against a wall. For the first time since her arrest Tanya felt intimidated. 'I just asked a simple question,' she protested. 'No need to get ratty.'

'And I've no need ter tell yer the answer, but I will,' said Judy, 'if only ter make yer feel even more pissed off. If yer knew Sam Carew like I do yer'd know the person he hates most in the world is Bowman. There's some very bad blood between them, very bad blood indeed. They go back a long way. Bowman got him kicked out of the job – I thought yer might have known that. Carew's a lot more pleased at getting Bowman locked up than he is catching you. Apparently he couldn't have done it without your help. So he says ter say thanks. Yer must be delighted to have helped the bloke who got yer banged up.' The PO let out a raucous laugh and left the cell, locking the door on a pondering Tanya.

CHAPTER FORTY-FOUR

'Is that it, then?'

'Is what what then?'

'You know very well what.'

'Sal, I rarely know what you're talking about when you get into cryptic mode.'

'Is that it with private eye work? Have you got it all out of your system?'

It was Sunday morning, they were in bed, drinking coffee, smoking and reading the Sundays. They had made love, life was serene, and Sally wanted it to go on being serene. She had been bottling this up for quite some time. Unable to keep a cork on her emotions, she let him have it with both barrels.

'I should never have encouraged you to go back into private detective work. I nearly had a heart attack when I saw on the news what had happened at Sue's house. Honestly, Sam, I could have come round and killed you myself. It's just not worth it.'

'We're due a very nice fee from the Manchester Victoria.'

'You could have let me know what you were doing. You went out and nearly got yourself killed without so much as a by-your-leave.'

'Sal, you'd have kicked up a fuss.'

'A fuss? A bloody fuss? I'll give you a bloody fuss!'

She rolled up her Sunday supplement and proceeded to hit him with it. 'Too right I'd have kicked up a bloody fuss, Sam Carew! Prior to that you nearly died twice, as you kept reminding me in the middle of the night when you kept waking up screaming and sweating. You'd only just got over one bout of that and here we go again.'

'Hey, that hurts! Sal, will you stop hitting me? No wonder I wake up screaming. Anyway, I haven't had nightmares since we captured Tanya – which means I'm on the mend. Hey, she wants me to be charged with assault, did I tell you that? Mind you, I did hit her – knocked her out.'

'Good for you. Did it do you any good?'

'I think so, yeah. Never hit a woman before, she went out like a light. I wanted to see to Owen, so I had to immobilise her.'

'How's Owen doing, by the way?'

'Not good. Those bullets seem to have had an adverse effect on him.'

'Oh, dear,' said Sally, concerned. 'I know the feeling, is he bad?'

'Very bad. He keeps telling me he's happy to be alive. He's gone all cheerful on me. You and I went all miserable, he's gone cheerful. What's all that about?'

'Cheerful's good, isn't it?'

'I prefer him miserable,' said Sam, 'he's easier to ignore.' He put his paper down. It'd made depressing reading anyway. Macclesfield had beaten Unsworth Town 4-1. Non-League football beckoned. The scoreline flattered Unsworth, but it had been good to go with Tom and Jake. According to them, their mother had been quite concerned about him. He had to admire the way she concealed this concern when she spoke to him, playing hell about him staging what she referred to as a 'gangland shoot-out' at her home. Some of the neighbours were being openly hostile towards her, and Jonathan was livid. The boys thought it was great. Much kudos at school. Sam took Sally in his arms and kissed her.

'I must admit, nearly dying is one of the unappealing sides to the job. I hate that side of it. In fact I hate it so much I'm not going to do it again.'

'I don't believe you.'

'How do you mean, you don't believe me?'

'Because... Sam, it's not just a job with you, is it? It's a calling. I doubt if you can stop.'

'I didn't say I was going to stop doing the job, I said I was going to stop the nearly dying side of it. I've given it a lot of thought.

These situations can be avoided with a little thought. I want to die peacefully in bed with flowers and gentle music and my friends and family around me, weeping buckets and wishing they'd treated me better in life. I don't want to end up in a pathologist's fridge with a label around my big toe, waiting to be sliced open like a beef and ale pie. Anyway, for the time being I'm back on the tools. Alec needs me. We've got a rush job on that requires a good brickie.'

Sally kissed his neck and stroked his hair. 'Nothing's permanent with you, is it, Sam? You jump from one life to the other, then back again without batting an eyelid. I can't be like that. I need permanence – I'd like to think I had permanence with you.'

'Sal, I'm your boss, your lover and your carer – and I'm pretty good at all three. What more do you want from me?'

She sighed and thought, *I want you to completely forget about Kathy. She's not coming back. I'm here, in flesh and blood, and I'm the best thing you'll ever get.*

'Oh, I don't know,' was what she said, 'whatever's on offer, I suppose – talking of what's on offer, apparently I could settle for a nice lump sum from your insurers. I got a letter from Mr Bateson yesterday.'

'This means my premium will go up. I will deduct it from your commission.'

'My commission?'

'For helping to save my life, thereby ensuring we collect our fee from the Manchester Victoria. When do you get your liability insurance?'

'I can either settle in full now or I can take a smaller sum and be re-assessed in five years' time. What would you do?'

'I always take the bird in the hand, Sal. You should know that.'

A shadow fell over Sam, causing him to look up from his work. He was laying blockwork to the foundations of an industrial unit. The weather was cold, but otherwise the day was bright and all was well. He had managed to resist Alison's charms by staying clear of her. Sally was the one for him – if only she'd stop dropping hints about putting things on a more permanent footing. The only permanent footing he was interested in was the one he was working on. The shadow was Bowman's.

'Ah, DCI Bowman, they let you out, then?'

'DI Bowman to you.'

'I see. Bit rough, that. You lose your wife and they knock you down to inspector, not very compassionate employers, the West Yorkshire Police.'

'People died. I'm lucky to still be in the job.'

Sam put down his trowel and climbed out

of the trench. 'Look, I was really sorry to hear about your wife. When I heard, I put two and two together and figured she was the mole. It was the only thing that made sense to me. You're a prat but you're not a bent prat. What was it, pillow talk?'

'Something like that. She started showing an interest in my work. She hadn't talked to me much in the latter years, so I was glad to talk about anything, even confidential stuff – Annie Robinson was paying her for information.'

'Yeah, that's what I figured. How did they meet?'

'Unsworth Women's bloody Institute, would you believe.'

'No, I wouldn't actually.'

'Well, it's true. God knows what the Robinson woman was doing there – apparently she never missed a meeting. Very good at cooking, apparently.'

Sam was staring at him, wide eyed, doing his best not to laugh. 'Women's Institute? You are kidding. Does the Women's Institute know what's happened?'

'I suspect they do,' said Bowman. 'I haven't actually told anyone, and I suspect the Women's Institute hasn't either.'

'It'll be in all the papers.'

'No doubt. I'm going away for a few weeks until it all blows over.'

'Unsworth Women's Institute, eh?' Sam

whistled in amazement. 'Maybe she was just ingratiating herself into polite Unsworth society.'

Bowman gave a humourless laugh. 'Polite? Unsworth? Society? Three words you don't often find together.'

'True.'

'Prison would have killed my wife, you know. I was prepared to take the full blame rather than that happen. God knows why. She obviously thought she couldn't trust me not to turn her in. Knowing her, the anxiety would have gnawed away at her insides until she couldn't stand it any longer. She'll have been waiting for the knock at the door, and then, I suppose, she just cracked. She must have died hating me.'

'Why do you say that?'

'Because she didn't leave a note admitting what she'd been doing.'

'If her mind wasn't right–'

'Possibly, but she had a vicious side to her. She could have cleared me, but she didn't. She took her own life thinking they'd lock me up and throw the key away for what she'd done – not even you would have done that to me.' He cleared his throat, as if pre-paring himself to say something that was sticking in his craw. 'In fact, I, er, I know what you did.'

'Oh heck! What did I do now?'

'I spoke to Judy Beesley, the prison officer

from New Hall – I gather she's a friend of yours.'

'Yeah, I've known her for years. Very scary woman when she puts her mind to it.'

'She tricked Tanya Robinson into thinking that her lying about me was doing you a big favour.'

'And wasn't it?'

'Apparently she couldn't bear the thought of doing you a favour.'

'I bet you know just how she feels, Mr Bowman.'

'I'm trying to be civilised with you, Carew, and you're not making it easy!'

'Sorry.'

'I understand it was all your idea. To fool her into telling the truth.'

'My idea?'

'That's what she told me, and I believe her. Only you could have thought of such a weird way of going about things.'

Sam shrugged and grinned. 'Yeah, well – what are enemies for, eh?'

'Anyway I, er ... thank you.'

'What? You've come here to thank me? Inspector Bowman, please, you're upsetting the whole balance of nature. This isn't how things should be.'

'Don't get me wrong, Carew, I still think you're an annoying, interfering pillock who should stick to what he does best, which is laying bricks!'

He walked away. Sam scooped up a trowel full of compo, thought about what Bowman had just said, then shook his head. He and Bowman had never agreed about anything.

Tanya had been on remand in New Hall Women's Prison for the statutory 28 days and had been taken back to Unsworth Magistrates Court for a second remand hearing. Sam had gone to court more out of curiosity than anything else. Owen had gone with him, mainly to see the woman who had tried to kill him.

She was brought up into the dock knowing that she was to be remanded to Crown Court for a specific trial date. Her face was expressionless as she stared into the middle distance. The police hadn't got anything out of her. She was prepared to take whatever punishment they could make stick, and she knew it wouldn't be nearly enough to fit the crimes she had committed – Henry Acombe-Booker would see to that. One way or another she was worth thirty million pounds, which meant whatever time she was given would be comfortable time, followed by a life of great luxury. When she came out she just had one last job to take care of. She owed her mother that much.

As the officials mumbled their way through court proceedings Sam looked at her impassive face and wondered just how much of a grudge she would bear against him when she came out. Suddenly her gaze focused on him and the blankness in her eyes turned to hate. The more Sam held her gaze, the more hatred poured his way. Eventually he saw nothing to be gained from such a contest and dropped his eyes. After a minute he looked up again and was relieved to see she had lost interest in him. Her eyes were scanning the court, perhaps in search of another target for her silent venom. The expression on her face suddenly changed to one of consternation as she looked across the court to Sam's right. The look went almost as quickly as it came. Only Sam noticed it. Sam often noticed that which was imperceptible to most people – it was one of his strengths. Owen was too busy munching on a Kit-Kat. Sam retraced her gaze until his eyes settled on a man sitting near the door. A small, bald man with a cauliflower ear.